CORPSE COLD

IMMORTAL TREACHERY: BOOK 3

By Allan Batchelder

Vykers studied the giant. Even for his kind, he was immense, a mountain. And with that observation, he knew how to attack his foe.

Beesmarch swung and, to his amazement, completely missed his target. The Reaper dodged and danced away, just out of reach. "So, it's to be like that, is it?" the giant taunted.

Beesmarch unleashed a series of sweeping swings, attempting to overwhelm the Reaper with the speed and number of his attacks. None came close to the Reaper. "Stand still and fight, you little gnat!" Beesmarch roared.

Vykers did not stand still; he continued to appear where he wasn't expected and vanish before the giant could hit him, to Beesmarch's ever-growing frustration.

"This ain't a fight!" he complained. "It's a bleedin' cinque-pace! Stand still, you bastard!"

The harder Beesmarch tried to connect, the more fatigued he became, until, inevitably, he was gasping for air. In that moment, Vykers ran forward, bounded off the giant's thigh, leapt up his chest and jabbed two fingers in each of Beesmarch's eyes—not hard enough to blind him permanently, but firmly enough to disable him for the near future.

Beesmarch bellowed in pain, raising his left hand to his face and lashing out blindly with his right. The fight was over, but he could not acknowledge it. The Reaper closed in to deliver a blow of his own and the giant roared with such volume and ferocity that Vykers temporarily lost all sense of where he was and what he'd been doing. In that brief span, Beesmarch flailed blindly and just managed to clip Vykers on his right shoulder, sending him spinning through the air like a spent firework. The force of the hit and his subsequent landing in the snow cleared Vykers' mind, brought him back to the present.

"Well struck, giant!" he exclaimed.

"Enough, the Reaper wins," Igraine declared.

Acknowledgements

Gillian Avery Batchelder
Jeffrey Reid
Shay Roberts
Kim Sieminskie-Uyyek
Rodney Sherwood

And everyone who contributed to my GoFundMe campaign!

I would like to dedicate this book to my teachers—even those I hated—and to my students—even those who hated me.

ONE

Sometimes, evil is like dust in a home. This is not to trivialize evil, but instead to acknowledge and understand its ubiquity. In spite of our best efforts, it finds its way in—on the sole of a boot, on a draft; it hides and collects in the places we take for granted or seldom look. And it is impossible to eradicate or even deny.

Omeyo struggled to determine just when it was he'd let it into his own life. It wasn't a question of faulty recollection—he possessed perfect memory; his confusion was more due to the fact that he'd committed or accepted so many unforgivable acts that he wasn't sure which had been his undoing, which had been the one that tipped the scales forever against him. He sighed. It hardly mattered. Once he'd signed on with the End-of-All-Things, he'd lost all hope of redemption.

He'd been offered an unexpected second chance when Tarmun Vykers—the Reaper—slaughtered the End-of-All-Things on the battlefield. But Omeyo had become so inured to servitude that he thought only of how he might curry favor down the road and, thus, had spared not a moment's thought to his own freedom.

He regretted that now; oh, how he regretted it.

He cast a weary eye in the direction of the child he'd helped become the End's next incarnation. The boy—if one could call him that—stood just outside the cave, mumbling something brutish to his ever-present Svarren companions, the two inbred beasts Omeyo secretly thought of as "Tooth and Nail". What their actual names were, he neither knew nor cared. He wished them both dead and soon.

As if he could read the man's thoughts, the boy called out "What are you up to, old man?"

"Nothing, Master," Omeyo responded. "Is there something I can do for you?"

"Something you can do? Get off your ass and gather more firewood. There's never enough."

Omeyo got off his ass. He was well past counting the indignities he'd suffered in the child's service; they hardly registered anymore. Lugging himself off into the tree line, he stole a final glance at the boy and his bodyguards. You'd never know to look at the child that he was barely four years old. The creature that lived within him had accelerated his growth so much that he looked on the verge of his first beard, though his face, all his features, gave the impression of a waxen image set too close to a fire, so that he lacked definition or finish, as if he'd been pulled from the womb before he'd been fully developed. Grown, he was. And yet, he was little more than a toddler. And yet, again, he was impossibly ancient.

And impossibly mad.

How else to explain the boy's fitful memory of where and what he'd been? Of course, it didn't speak well of Omeyo's sanity that he'd been serving the creature all these years. And now there was no escape. When he'd rescued the End's brains and heart from the battlefield, he'd imagined the resurrected sorcerer would thank him, reward him even. What he'd gotten instead was more servitude, wretched servitude.

Gods, the trees were full of Svarren shit!

Vykers, In Lunessfor

The young woman ran with an energy, a zeal that only prey understood or possessed. She'd made the mistake of wandering into the South Shore district after dark; she'd been marked, and now was pursued by one of the district's most frightening gangs, a foul alliance of rapists, murderers and thieves. It was a mistake that would likely produce fatal results...but not for this woman, who was more than she seemed.

In his new body, Tarmun Vykers may have been

slighter-of-frame than those who followed him, but no one alive knew of more ways to kill a man. It was true that this new body could not sustain as much damage as his normal one. It was also true that if Vykers allowed this body to die, he'd probably die with it and never recover his former self.

Vykers put on a burst of speed and raced for an alley that opened up to his left. In South Shore, there was no safety to be found on the main streets at night and, thus, no point in avoiding the alleys and breezeways, either. In addition to lack of size and muscle, the Reaper suffered from a second disadvantage, in that he was relatively unfamiliar with the city of Lunessfor outside the Queen's castle (and even inside, he was mostly ignorant of the areas beyond his one-time sick-room). Vykers wasn't sure where this or any alley might take him, but he was certain those chasing him knew. Spying a pile of refuse, he quickly ducked down behind it and made himself as small as possible—a talent he'd never before possessed.

In moments, he heard his pursuers draw near. They weren't speaking to one another, but made no special effort to conceal their footsteps. Without looking, Vykers knew there were more than five of them—too many to handle in a pitched fight, in his current form. He figured his best move was to pick them off one-by-one, as he continued to lead them through the warren of South Shore. Quietly as possible, he drew the small dagger he kept at his belt. When one of the gang ventured near, Vykers lashed out with his blade, severing the tendons behind the man's right knee, and then dashed off down the alley, whilst his victim howled in agony.

One down.

But now those remaining were more committed to catching him than ever before. Once they realized what had happened and where their quarry had gone, they stormed after Vykers with renewed vigor.

"You'll bleed for that one, little bitch!" one of them yelled out.

Careening down the alley, the Reaper noticed a hole in the side of a building, too small for his pursuers, but perfect for his new, smaller physique. Without a moment to spare, he pulled himself inside, just as the gang arrived.

"Get 'er, get 'er, get 'er!" someone shouted.

Hands groped into the darkness after Vykers, but he sent them away with a solid kick. At a cry from his pursuer, another of the men suggested, "Stab 'er with your pig sticker, first. That'll slow 'er down!"

"Patience!" a new voice countered. "I ain't tupping no corpse! Let's some of us go 'round t'other side, and some wait here."

All Vykers heard was "tupping." He'd done some horrible things in his time, but never had he contemplated raping anyone; never had he been the target of such contemplation. His gorge rose at the idea, and he determined to make his pursuers' deaths all the more painful.

First, he had to get away from the sword being thrust at him from behind. Clambering farther into the building, Vykers found himself in a close, dark space—considerably darker, in fact, than it had been outside in the street, which might work to his advantage. The place reeked of rat urine, human sweat and…something else, something vaguely familiar.

It occurred to him he was probably not alone in the darkness. "Whoever you are," he whispered in his still unfamiliar new voice, "You'd best stay hidden. There's trouble comin' and soon."

"D'you need a hand?" a younger voice responded.

"How many are you?"

"Just me."

"Like I said, you'd best stay out of it. The two of us ain't enough for what's comin'."

A noise of heavy footsteps sounded somewhere in the building.

"There another way out of here?" Vykers asked his invisible companion.

"Just the door 'n the hole. What're you gonna do?"

Vykers chuckled. He'd meant to scoff at the coming threat, but it came out like nervous laughter. Damn this new body! "I guess we'll find out," he finally said.

The footsteps stopped within spitting range, and a loud thump reverberated through the little room.

"Door's locked," the hidden child said.

"I figured. Stay back."

The latch protested a moment and then, in an explosion of sound, a blast of fresher air and feeble light flooded into the space, which turned out to be a storage closet of sorts. Large, hulking shadows lurked in the doorway, the shapes of Vykers' would-be assailants, letting their eyes adjust to the gloom. It was a pause they could ill afford, as Vykers dove between their legs, slashing at their ankles and calves with his knife as he went. They bent low, either in attempt to grab him or in response to their injuries, and the Reaper had to kick his way free.

"Oooh," one of them wailed, "I'm gonna enjoy putting a blade in her!"

On his feet at last, Vykers dodged off into the darkened building, looking for suitable spots to stage an ambush or, alternatively, an exterior door or window through which to escape. Nothing presented itself. Too soon, the men at his back recovered from Vykers' attack and resumed the chase. Coming to a corner, Vykers ducked behind it and threw himself flat against the wall, hoping to stick his knife in the first neck he saw.

Instead, he heard menacing laughter. "No, you don't, little piece. One sneak attack's quite enough. Ain't it, lads?"

"Swear to Mahnus, I'll gut the bitch!" someone responded.

"When we've had our way with 'er," someone else cautioned.

"To hells with that! She makes me bleed, I make *her* bleed."

While the men argued about the order of their planned atrocities, Vykers backed away from the corner, continuing to search the gloom for any advantage or avenue of escape. He again became aware of an oddly familiar odor and suddenly understood where he was: an abandoned charnel house—a fitting place for murder, so long as he wasn't the one dyin'.

More menacing laughter. "I don't blame ye fer hidin', but it's all fer naught, ye know. My boys in the street'll 'ave come 'round by now and got ye surrounded."

Vykers risked a look over his shoulder and, indeed, heard the noise of men bungling blindly towards him in the dark. A black space in the middle of the wall, opposite, suggested a doorway. Short of other options, the Reaper ran towards it, grateful for the light-footedness of his new body, if nothing else. Before the men hunting him realized what had happened, he'd successfully escaped into a different room. Out in the hall, the gang's leader continued to cajole and reason with his prey, still unaware she'd fled.

The Reaper focused on the new room, which proved to be the darkest of any he'd visited so far. The smell of death was strongest here, too, though it was of death long past. On a hunch, Vykers got down on his hands and knees and crept forward. After a few feet, the air seemed to get thicker, heavier. Extending a hand as carefully as possible, he was not surprised when his fingers closed around an old bone—a thigh bone, he reckoned. He was momentarily transported back to his first meeting with Arune, his former Shaper. And then he was angry all over again.

In the hall, he could hear the men coming from both directions.

Exploring further, he realized he faced an enormous mountain of bones. Why hadn't they been burned like everything else? Perhaps there had been too many dead for one little oven. Or maybe those who'd worked here had succumbed to the same diseases that brought them business. These questions aside, it was clear that there'd be no back door out of this room.

"What's that, there? Another room?"

Vykers never backed down from a fight, but Vykers had never been a woman before, either. Like a rat, he scurried into and under the bones. He was sure the gang heard him, but they'd have a hard time getting their hands on him.

"She's here!"

Vykers dug for the back wall, slithering on his belly like a desperate lizard, jabbed in the ribs by ribs, smacked on the skull by skulls.

"Let's 'ave some light!" another voice declared.

Vykers heard the telltale snick of steel on flint. Soon, a flickering glow worked its way through the bones.

"Endless hells, would you look at that? There must be a thousand dead in here!"

"More!"

"It ain't the dead 'uns we's worried about. It's that girl!"

"Yes, but how do we get at 'er?"

"Well," said a voice Vykers had come to perceive as the leader's, "there's a number o' things we might try: we can wait 'er out…"

The gang voiced its disapproval of that plan.

"Or we could burn 'er out…"

That got no better response.

"We could dig 'er out…or we could herd 'er out."

"What?" one of the others asked, "Like an animal?"

"Just," the leader replied. "What we do is, we start stabbing our swords into this pile, as we work our way to the back wall. Might have to dig down a piece, but we'll get 'er. She don't wanna get skewered, she's gonna have to come out."

It wasn't the worst plan Vykers had ever heard, much to his chagrin. But if they got close enough, he'd let 'em know about it. He still had his knife and a much better view of his tormentors than they had of him. He suspected, too, that they'd find wading through the bones more challenging than they imagined.

In no time, he heard those bones crunching or clacking as they were trod upon or pushed aside. Some at the top of the pile cascaded down towards the bottom.

"Watch out you don't bury yerselves while yer at it!" the leader warned.

The man on Vykers' left was making the most progress. He pushed forward with great violence and thrust his sword into the pile at unpredictable intervals. Vykers had to take him down first, in order to slow the others' advance. Initially, he tried to move silently, but it soon became evident that he could never be heard over the noise raised by those hunting him. With stealth no longer a concern, the Reaper dragged himself to within a few feet of his target's position. The next time the man stuck a foot into the pile, Vykers would…

Something crashed past on his right. The fuckers were firing arrows into the pile! That was a problem he hadn't anticipated. He doubted they could hit him; in truth, he'd have been amazed if they could even *see* him. Still, things being as they were, he could hardly afford to get overconfident. He wriggled his way back into the depths of the mound, away from the man he'd nearly ambushed and towards, he hoped, greater cover. His central problem remained, however: he was surrounded, outnumbered and effectively cornered. The only thing keeping him alive at the moment was the dead, whose bones presented a forbidding barricade.

"Little mousie, in the brambles," the gang's leader sang out, "won't ye come out fer tea?"

The weight of the bones was beginning to wear on Vykers, another sign that his time was running out. In now-tedious routine, he wished he had his former body, his *real* body. He'd have burst from his hiding place like fury incarnate and made worms' meat of his antagonists. There wouldn't have been enough left of *their* bones to throw on the pile. But that was before Arune's treachery, before Vykers had been cast into the body of a girl. Now, he was like to die in that body.

Without thought, without reason, he decided to run for it. He'd planned to erupt from the pile, catching his foes off guard, and bolt from the room, but, again, he no longer had the strength or mass to bust through so easily. After considerable struggle, he managed to poke his head out, only to find that he was not dealing with four men, as he'd hoped, or even five, but seven. He was certain he'd taken at least one of them out. Where had the others come from? It hardly mattered. He could see well enough that he was fucked.

"There she is!" the man nearest him hollered.

In an instant, six of the seven were scrambling up and through the mound in Vykers' direction. Only the leader stood aloof, holding a torch in one hand and pointing with the other.

And then Vykers heard a crunch, and the quality and direction of light in the room changed drastically. He risked a look back at the leader and saw the man down on his knees, his right arm and shoulder gone, as black blood spewed from his torso in a geyser. The torch had fallen to the floor, where it sputtered on the edge of a growing pool of the stuff. Vykers searched out the other six men and understood that they'd seen what he'd seen, too, and had lost all confidence in their chosen course. The Reaper snapped his eyes back to the leader. In the shadows behind the doomed man, a larger figure raised a boot and kicked the leader's corpse over onto the torch, dousing the light.

Two of the men who'd but moments ago been chasing Vykers now shrieked like frightened children. The bones tumbled and rattled. A cacophony of grunts, cries and ringing steel ensued. There was a series of heavy thuds and the smell of fresh blood and bile grew heavy in the air. Vykers held his breath, straining to glean what he might from the chaos. At last, a crypt-like silence fell on the room. Still, Vykers waited. It might be a trap. Minutes passed, and a torch blossomed to life, held in the hand of a lone figure. The fellow was big—bigger than Vykers had been in his normal body—and covered in scars. Half his face was gone, as well. The brute looked down at his feet, where the bodies and body parts of the gang were now scattered, and then he looked over in Vykers' direction.

"You're safe now," he rumbled. "You can come out or stay put, as you like."

Vykers said nothing.

"Fair enough," the big man said and faded into the hallway, beyond.

Long & Company, In Camp

Crack! Yendor's head snapped back, his split lips spewing blood as he reeled from Rem's blow.

"You filthy, whoreson pustule!" the actor shouted, enraged. "I'll smash your mazard!"

Yendor spun out of the way, just in time to avoid a follow-up knee to the stomach. Snow was falling so rapidly now, it was hard to keep his lone eye open, much less track Rem's every move.

"You boil! You carbuncle!"

Give the man his due: the actor knew how to lay it on.

Without waiting another second, Yendor sprang at him, causing his old friend to stumble in the snow and fall backwards. Yendor seized his advantage and pummeled the actor about the head and shoulders.

"A carbuncle, am I? That's rich, comin' from a dandy, a fop!" Yendor roared.

Raising his hands to ward off the attack, Rem managed to poke Yendor's eye, temporarily blinding him. Short of options, the older man searched about frantically with his fingers, until they found purchase in the actor's hair. It was still short yet, but there was more than enough to pull on. With a great scream of rage, Yendor tore a prodigious clump free, eliciting a shriek from his opponent.

"Ha!" Yendor laughed. "You scream like a milk maid!"

Without warning, Rem shifted his weight and tossed Yendor to the ground, using his momentum to pull himself into the superior position. Now, it was *his* turn to rain blows and Yendor's to receive them.

The crowd of men gathered 'round to watch yelled encouragement, hurled insults and offered odds on a winner.

Yendor struggled to suppress a smile. Rem, being a professional, looked as serious as a public execution, which made Yendor want to smile all the more. With unlikely ease, he threw his tormentor and struggled to his feet. Before he could wipe the blood and snow from his beard, the actor was upon him again, howling a torrent of the most creative invective anyone listening had ever heard.

"Pull out my hair, will you, you rancid codpiece? You muffin-duster! You worthless, shiftless, faithless bastard!" On the last word, Rem ripped out a sizable section of Yendor's beard and held it aloft like a trophy, triumph evident on his face.

Until Yendor punched him in the balls. Immediately, Rem doubled over and vomited loudly into the snow. Yendor wound up to deliver the kick that would end the fight, slipped on his backswing and went down on his ass like a load of firewood. Seeing his chance, Rem spun and delivered a kick of his own. And a second. And yet a third.

Yendor turned on his side, hacked up a mouthful of blood and passed out.

The crowd grew silent, waiting for more. When it was clear the fight had ended, the onlookers expressed their approval or contempt, collected or paid off their bets and dispersed, staggering off into the storm in search of their campfires, tents or wagons.

Once everyone had gone, Yendor chuckled and rolled into a sitting position.

"You alright?" Rem asked him.

"Oh, lad, I done far worse to meself than you could ever do."

Rem stretched for a moment and then peeled his wig off. "Going to have to mend this soon. It's starting to look too patchy. How's that beard?"

Yendor, likewise, removed his beard and examined it. "Fine. Can't even see where you pulled that lot from."

Spirk and Ron, who'd been watching from a discrete distance, stepped forward timidly.

"You s'pose we fooled 'em?" Spirk asked.

"We fooled 'em!" Yendor replied confidently. "We fooled 'em. And now they know we're too batshit crazy to meddle with!"

"I hope you're right."

"Mmm," Yendor agreed. "Say, what's this 'blood' made of, anyway? Stuff tastes pretty good."

"It's got honey in it," Rem responded. "But you'll be sorry if you eat any. The red comes from teneise berries. You'll have the squirts for days."

"Too late," Yendor sighed. "Seems I never learn nothin' the easy way…"

Back at the group's campsite, Long never looked up from the fire when his friends returned, so lost in his thoughts was he. Eventually, Yendor had to give him a poke in the ribs just to get his attention.

"Oh!" Long said. "You're back, then?"

"Been back a good five minutes."

"Five?"

"Or one. Time seems to drag when you're sober. Leastways, that's how it seems to me."

"How'd the act go?" Long wanted to know.

"Excellent well," Rem replied. "I believe we came across as suitably deranged."

"We should have some peace and quiet, then."

"That's the plan," said Rem.

Long got lost in the fire again, so Rem, Spirk and Ron went about their business. Only Yendor stayed to keep the old captain company. After a goodly silence, he spoke up.

"We'll find her."

"Yes," Long answered. What he wondered but didn't say was, *Will she still be alive, though?*

Yendor seemed to read his mind. "And she'll be so happy to see you, you may never escape the next hug."

Long offered a rueful smile. "That'd be fine with me. Better 'n fine." He pulled his collar higher around his neck.

In search of his daughter and her captors, Long and his crew had wandered farther and farther north, from autumn into winter. And winter in the north pulled no punches. The first storm had nearly buried the gang alive. When the second hit, they sought refuge in a traders' camp. They'd have preferred almost any other arrangement, but the weather was relentless in its indifference to their desires. The hours stretched into days; the days became weeks.

"I'm afraid we'll lose her, sittin' idle like this," Long confessed.

"Look," said Yendor, "all we've got's the ponies 'n our packs. Them we're chasing have wagons. They won't be moving any faster through this stuff." He waved an arm through the falling snow. "I'd be surprised if they don't hunker down 'til spring."

Long shook his head, offered a crooked smile to his former drinking companion. "Seems like wishful thinkin' to me, old friend, but I'm grateful for your efforts. I know it can't be easy for you, travelin' with me."

"Are you kiddin'?" Yendor asked in mock astonishment. "Ass-deep in snow, more sober 'n the beadle's wife, and nary a wench to be found? What could be better than this?"

At last, Long smiled.

Aoife, the North

Aoife was lost in the worst of ways. As an A'Shea, she'd spent years in the service of the goddess Alheria, only to learn that goddess reigned from the throne of Lunessfor, in the person of the arrogant, imperious and always irritable Virgin Queen. Of what possible value could Aoife's endeavors be to the Queen? To make matters worse, Aoife had fallen in love with the Reaper—the worst choice a woman of peace and healing could have made. Finally, she'd done nothing to prevent what she'd known would be the inevitable ruination of the boy, Tadpole, through the Reaper's pernicious influence, making her every bit as culpable for the thing that he'd become. She might have summoned the satyr Toomt'-La for company, but even that raised dilemmas she'd rather avoid.

Thus, she languished in an abandoned woodsman's cottage, a half day's travel into a nameless forest, tormented by questions she'd no power to answer. *What am I*, she wondered, *if Alheria is not who or what I believed her to be? What is my faith? And what am I to the spirits of Nar, now that I've spawned so many forests and the End-of-All-Things is dead?*

He lives, someone countered.

Aoife's head snapped up, and she raised her hands in defense. "Who's there?"

No one answered.

The A'Shea stood, slowly turned in a circle, searching the shadows of the little cottage. She let her senses wander beyond its walls and into the woods that surrounded them.

She was alone.

And yet, someone had spoken. The voice she'd heard was as real as the timeworn floor beneath her feet.

He lives.

The End-of-All-Things, alive?

Her reaction was equal parts terror and fury. The End-of-All-Things was alive?

Arune, Searching

It was not easy being Tarmun Vykers, especially if one was merely wearing his body. Arune found it hard to go anywhere without being approached by adoring peasants, either savoring a brush with greatness or looking for the Reaper's assistance in resolving some petty dispute. What would the real Reaper have done? Arune guessed he'd have told them to sod off.

She told them to sod off.

And, really, she didn't need the distraction. With Vykers' body, she now had a singular opportunity to achieve what she'd wanted so badly for so long: Aoife's love. Yes, the Shaper was aware that Vykers and the A'Shea had parted ways, but she sensed the other woman's resolve what not as strong as she pretended. And Arune could offer something that Aoife would never expect: a penitent Reaper, a man well aware of the wrongs he'd done and determined to make amends...with the A'Shea's help, of course.

As for the true Reaper, Arune knew him to be resourceful, but stranded as he was inside the body of a girl, bereft of strength and influence, it was inconceivable that he'd ever find the Shaper, much less exact revenge upon her. And, ultimately, there was no way to punish Arune without damaging Vykers' true body. It was this conundrum, above all, that gave Arune peace of mind.

Except for the fact that she'd betrayed the Reaper. When the unexpected switch in bodies had occurred, the Shaper might have stayed by Vykers' side. That she chose to flee with his body, his *stolen* body, was something she'd have to live with for the rest of her life; she'd have to come to terms with herself as a liar, a cheat, and a thief. Still, one night with Aoife would justify everything, make everything right and whole again.

Or so she hoped.

First, she had to *find* the A'Shea, which was proving harder than she'd expected, particularly with these crazed peasants mobbing her wherever she went. It was time and past time to alter her appearance. That done, she could make whatever inquiries she needed without drawing so much attention to herself.

She briefly contemplated reaching out to Aoife's mind, as she'd done in the past, but feared she'd only make the A'Shea more wary. No, this had to be done the hard way: on foot and in person.

She only hoped the woman hadn't jumped to one of her most distant groves. Arune couldn't say why, but she felt time was of the essence.

Kittins, In Lunessfor

Kittins stood in the corner of the Shaper's study, his eyes taking everything in as he waited for Cindor to arrive. It was an odd room, not unlike the hut of the swamp witch, Croonbasket. There were strange, desiccated things hanging from the walls and ceilings; on the room's many shelves, jars and boxes fought for space with more books than the captain had ever seen in one place. Various small animals found homes in the clutter—here a bird, there a cat, across the room, a snake. In nature, they would have been at each other, but not here. Most peculiar of all was the tiny, living gargoyle, resting atop a pallid bust of Pellas, just above the chamber door.

He was considering whether to toss something at the little creature when the Shaper appeared, as he often did, seemingly out of nowhere. The enmity both men held for each other was immediately apparent.

"Your report?" Cindor sneered.

"Stopped a couple o' burglaries, saved a kid from getting raped and murdered."

"I hope you don't think this work redeems you."

It was Kittins' turn to sneer. "I'm just doing the job I was ordered to do."

Cindor fetched a small object from one of the shelves and snorted. "That, I believe." After a pause, he added, "My back is now turned, soldier. You may never get this chance again."

"I'd prefer to kill you face-to-face."

The Shaper turned, raised his eyebrows as if saying, "Well...?"

"But I'll choose the time and place. Me, not you."

"You do realize I could send you hurling into the middle of the sea, don't you? Or an active volcano?"

Kittins' grin was beyond unsettling. "But you haven't, which means, as powerful as you claim to be, you're afraid of Her Majesty...which means there's more to her than meets the eye, don't it?"

Cindor squinted at the big man. "You're smarter than I thought. I won't underestimate you again."

"That's a shame."

Ignoring the barb, the Shaper changed the subject back to the business at hand. "Try the wealthier neighborhoods tonight, near the homes of the Eight. After the recent uproar, they're likely to be prime targets for crime."

Kittins bowed his head. "As you say," he answered, with more than a hint of sarcasm in his voice.

Vykers, In Lunessfor

His new name, the one belonging to his body, was Igraine. He'd been walking through the market square when a large, gangly man yelled something at him. Not recognizing the fellow or even remembering that he no longer looked like Tarmun Vykers, he ignored the man and kept walking. Suddenly, a powerful hand grabbed him by the elbow and yanked him painfully 'round in the direction from which he'd come. The man snuffed and snorted, indignantly.

"'Ere, now, Igraine. I ain't seen you in a fortnight. You wouldn't be tryin' to run out on old Deech, would ya? After all I done for ya?"

Vykers looked down at the man's hand, still clutching the Reaper's now thin and knobby elbow. "I don't know what you're talking about, old man, but you'd best remove that hand o' yours before I lose my temper."

Deech cracked him one, right across the face, nearly knocking Vykers to the ground. Add slower reflexes to the list of things the Reaper didn't love about this new body. Still, he pretended the blow had cowed him, and when Deech stepped closer to claim his prize, Vykers hit him twice in the windpipe, and the stranger staggered backwards, struggling for breath and rapidly turning purple. Vykers shrugged as Deech collapsed. He hadn't been sure this *Igraine* was capable of defending herself. To Vykers' relief, his brains and experience were still his own, even if his body was not.

"I did warn you."

He looked around to ensure he hadn't drawn too much attention and saw only one witness…a familiar figure in shabby red wooden armor—Vykers' former slave. The knight stared back with the look of a man trying to remember where he'd left his sword. Vykers pretended not to see him, straightened his collar and walked, as blithely as possible, farther into the crowded square. After a few minutes, he spied a glassmaker's kiosk and approached, in hopes of finding a mirror or two. Despite the fact Igraine was dressed in costly and somewhat masculine clothing made especially for her by an oddly incurious tailor, the glassmaker barely gave Vykers a second glance. Fortunately, he had more than a few mirrors for sale. The Reaper picked up a handheld model.

"How much for this?" he asked, searching the crowd behind him in the glass' reflection.

"Twelve merchants!" the vendor replied curtly.

Vykers took his time. He saw no one he recognized in the mirror. "I don't know. "There's a man in South Shore sells these things for nine."

"Then go to him," the glassmaker sniped, snatching the mirror out of Vyker's grip and placing it back on the counter.

Vykers wanted to smash the man's teeth in. He glared at him, instead. "You're lucky I got other things to do just now," he growled. "You'll never know how lucky."

As he turned around, he thought he glimpsed a flash of red through the mob of buyers, sellers and gawkers. Well, he wasn't about to play at hide-and-seek with the fellow. If the knight wanted to talk, Vykers would talk. He pushed himself into a small clearing and waited. And waited. And waited some more. Evidently, the knight was not going to show himself again, and Vykers had more pressing concerns to attend to, anyway. Pushing the knight from his mind, he set off for the South Shore district, to resume the search

He had unfinished business in South Shore. When he'd gone the previous night, he'd been looking for the shop of a particular alchemist who only did business after dark and, more importantly, was reputed to despise Shapers. Word was, he'd contrived all manner of potions, talismans and charms against the Burners' prying; if it was so, Vykers thought he might have an ally in his efforts to reclaim his body from Arune. At the very least, if the man wasn't a complete fraud, he might be able to conceal Vykers' whereabouts from Arune.

But the Reaper was also curious about the nature and identity of the basher who'd saved him last night. Did the man have a name? Why had he intervened? And was he available for mercenary work? He might not have much muscle himself anymore, but Vykers certainly had the coin to *buy* muscle. If the big stranger was available, Vykers might just find a use for him. Oh, he hadn't come up with any solid plans, yet— he'd been too busy grappling with his anger and struggling to adjust to his new body—but once he did have plans, he figured there'd be some bloodshed involved.

After he got his body back. This Igraine was strong enough, he supposed, for a young woman. But her balance was all wrong and the length of her stride, too constrictive. She possessed the quickness of youth certainly, but not the lethal speed of the predator. And Vykers was nothing, if not a predator.

Well, to business.

South Shore was surprisingly orderly during the day, as if the criminals who ran the place were averse to sunlight or perhaps busy planning the coming night's escapades. Vykers had learned not to engage men when he could help it, so he asked his questions of the first woman he saw, a haggard-looking matron busily pushing an ancient wheelbarrow full of equally ancient onions.

"'Scuse me, mum. There an alchemist hereabouts?"

The woman huffed and lowered the rear end of her wheelbarrow to the cobbled street. "You with child, are you?" she snorted. "One you're not wantin'?"

Did she think Igraine a whore? Vykers supposed he should have taken offense, but couldn't muster the emotion. "No," he answered. "Just lookin' for an alchemist. One that's only open nights."

"Och! What d'you want him for?"

"Then you *do* know 'im?"

"Might be," said the woman. "What's it worth to ya?"

Vykers sighed, pulled his dagger. "I dunno. What's your life worth to ya?"

The other woman deflated. "There's no need to bring blades into it. I was havin' a bit o' fun."

Vykers extended the knife ever so slightly and stepped closer. "So, where's this alchemist, then?"

"Next street over, go to yer right, walk to the end, uh, go left. I think he's about halfway down that new street, on the left. Little shop, black triangle 'bove the door." Out of nowhere, she added, "You ain't lookin' to buy an onion or two, are ya?"

"Do I look like I can cook?" Vykers asked, lowering Igraine's weapon.

The woman smiled sheepishly. "Not so much, no."

Vykers left her to her onions and walked off in the specified direction. Not three minutes later, he found the shop...on the wrong side of the street. But there was no mistaking the black triangle above the door. Vykers looked to his left and right, saw no one, and put his hand on the handle. Instantly, he felt a painful tingling and was uncharacteristically tempted to snatch his hand back.

I hate this Mahnus-cursed body.

Despite the discomfort, he tried the handle: locked. He let go. So, the alchemist was serious about his hours of business. For a moment or two, Vykers pondered breaking in, but realized he could no longer force a door—any door, in all likelihood—and attempting to pick the lock seemed equally unwise. As sunset was still many hours away, the Reaper decided to hunt down the identity of the mysterious basher. Absent other ideas, he thought first of locating the old and disused charnel house where he'd seen him last...

Which took him over an hour, trudging up and down streets he'd never have travelled the night before had he known what they looked like in daylight. The building itself looked somehow smaller than he'd remembered. Rather than retrace his steps, Vykers found the front door, which stood wide open, and carefully poked his head inside. There was that smell, again, of cremation long completed. Overlaying it was the much more powerful scent of blood and urine. But he heard not a sound, so in Vykers went.

Eoman, On the Trail

He was sorely tempted to sleep the winter away like rest of the older giants, but feared that if he did so, he'd lose Mardine's killers forever. No, best to gut it out and remain in pursuit. But Eoman Harkin Hainin was frustrated. Large as he was, the north was larger still, and a giant could wander for ages without finding the humans he was looking for. Of course, few humans were foolhardy enough to withhold information or aid from an angry giant, so Eoman received overeager cooperation wherever he went.

He arrived on the outskirts of the little hamlet of Winthrop around sunset. The almost instantaneous barking of dogs told him he'd been seen by the animals, and their masters would shortly be on alert. Up north, things got a good deal more dangerous after dark, and a dog's warning was taken seriously every time, whether a threat eventually presented itself or not. Most of the time, the animals were right to be alarmed. It remained to be seen if that was the case this night.

By the time Eoman reached the village proper, a line of stout men with long pikes had formed across the main path. Behind them stood three or four men with bows and crossbows.

One brave fellow stepped forward unarmed, the setting sun bathing his face in yellows and oranges that made him look more like a pumpkin than a man.

"How can we help you, good giant?" the fellow called out.

Eoman hated conversing with humans. It was such labor, merely to be understood. "Those pikes don't look like help's intended," he retorted, making a special effort to raise the pitch of his voice and articulate more carefully.

"That rather depends upon what you're intendin'."

Eoman inhaled, took his time in framing an answer. While thinking on it, he looked each of the villagers in the eyes, curious to see whether they'd look away or return his gaze. None looked away. "I'm searching for a small caravan. Might be slavers, or might be only kidnappers. But they killed one of my kin, and I mean to have justice."

"And what makes you think they come this-a way?"

"It's the first town I've seen in days. Folks have to eat, no? I reckon those I'm lookin' for do, too."

One of the dogs resumed barking, until its master silenced it with a firm rebuke.

"Well," said the villager, "They ain't been through here. I promise you that."

"You object to me coming in and asking a few questions, anyway?" Eoman asked in the gathering dark.

"Don't know as that's wise. Your kind's capable of a lot of destruction."

"And your kind isn't?" Eoman shot back.

"It's a fair point," the villager allowed. "But we like it peaceful here in Winthrop."

"And it's peaceful I'll be."

"Or we'll do whatever needs doin' to put you down."

"I understand."

"'Spose you're hungry, eh?" the man asked.

"Always."

That broke the ice, and a number of fellows in the line chuckled in response.

"All right, boys, lower yer weapons," the leader called to the other men. "Let's see if we can't fill this hungry giant's belly. But look you," he said to Eoman, "No trouble!"

"None," Eoman smiled. He didn't trust these folk, but sometimes a good meal was worth the risk.

Arune, Searching

Nobody knew anything, or so they claimed. Would A'Shea lie to her? Arune didn't know, and the whole cloister was warded against scrying, so the Shaper was forced to accept what she'd been told: no one had seen Aoife in recent memory. No one had a clue where she might be found. It occurred to Arune that her current guise as a rather muscular farmer might be undermining her attempts to find Aoife, who was, after all, quite beautiful. Perhaps the other A'Shea were protecting their friend from unwanted and inappropriate advances.

If only they understood the *real* Aoife, that she felt lust, that she'd birthed countless creatures of fey origin...The sisters would doubtless have cast her out, in spite of their widely professed devotion to mercy and forgiveness.

Had they cast her out? Arune did not sense that the mention of Aoife's name invoked concern or change in demeanor in any of those she'd questioned. Indeed, the other A'Shea genuinely seemed not to have heard from their friend of late, genuinely seemed unaware of her whereabouts.

It was aggravating, but Arune had other avenues of inquiry worth considering. There was, for instance, the town from which both Aoife and the Frog had come. As Arune understood things, the A'Shea had been—what?—helping rebuild a small village destroyed by the End-of-All-Things, when she'd made the acquaintance of the boy...back when he *was* a boy. It was entirely possible Aoife had returned to said village, either to continue her mission there, or to break the bad news about the Frog. There was also something about the Fey, if only the Shaper could remember it. When she'd first heard it, she hadn't been particularly enamored of the A'Shea. Not like she was now, certainly.

Arune concluded her best course of action was to find an inn, rent a room, and send out a questing ear, for as long as it took to garner any news of such a village. Surely a woman of Aoife's qualities and nature would arouse attention and interest wherever she went.

She would not evade Arune for long.

Long, In Camp

He dreamed he was dancing with his wife—something he'd never actually done—and it was wonderful, evoking feelings of warmth, tenderness and belonging he hadn't known in some time. She held him to her chest with her massive arms, firmly but gently, and Long lost himself in the comfort they provided. He looked up at her face, to see her beaming at him, as happy as he'd ever seen her. Then it all went sideways. She made an odd mewling noise, and he fell away from her, as her arms dropped from her shoulders and crashed to the unseen floor below. A look of panic came into Mardine's eyes then, panic and crippling bewilderment. It seemed she wanted to say something, to ask why this was happening. To Long's terrible regret, he had no answers, but instead watched in horror as Mardine's head canted to one side and slid right off her neck. Still, her eyes watched him, begging for help, for salvation, as her head tumbled out of sight. Long reached out for whatever remained of his wife, only to have it drip through his hands like thick mud. A weeping assailed him then. It came from everywhere at once and was filled with such unspeakable torment and loss that Long screamed himself awake to escape it.

He sat up immediately, shivering, not from the evident cold but the terrible nature of his dream, spouting clouds of steaming breath into the freezing air of the tent that he shared with Yendor. He didn't need to look to know he'd awoken his friend.

Having been through this a number of times in the past several weeks, Yendor had run out of helpful things to say to the captain. Instead, he extended a hand, patted his old friend on the back and crawled outside to stoke the fire, or rebuild it if it had gone out.

"Think I might be able to convince one o' them traders to let go of a bit o' sausage, if you fancy a little meat for breakfast," he offered after a few minutes.

Inside the tent, Long said nothing.

"A little meat always makes a man feel...I dunno...more himself. I'll see what I can do." And with that, Yendor trudged away through the snow, the sound of his footsteps rapidly fading to nothing.

There's no meat in the wide world can make me feel better, Long thought. *I've no right or reason to feel better.* But self-pity wasn't helping anyone, either. Least of all Esmine. With a sigh that seemed to come from the soles of his feet, Long forced himself up and out of the tent.

Cold it was, to be sure. But the air was a damn sight fresher than that in his tent. Nobody bathed whilst on the road, and fewer still bathed in winter. It was a near thing whether he or Yendor smelled worse. It hardly mattered: neither was likely to be entertaining the Queen any time soon—though Long had recently been Lord of House D'Escurzy, albeit briefly.

"Just when you think it can't possibly get colder, it does. I understand it's winter, but this is unnatural."

Rem.

"Share your fire?" the actor asked.

"I'll share, but I doubt the fire will. It's a miserly thing and keeps all its warmth to itself," said Long.

"A miserly fire," Rem marveled. "You certain you're not a poet?"

"Don't remember the last time I was certain about anything."

A lengthy silence blossomed between the two men. Finally, Rem confessed, "There's a chance—a small chance—I may get called away at some point in the coming weeks."

Long looked up from the fire and shot his friend an inquisitive look.

"It's to do with Her Majesty," Rem floundered. "Believe me, the less you know, the happier you'll be."

The captain winced in response. *Happier*?

"Ah, yes…Not the best choice of words, I suppose. Forgive me."

After another silence, Rem asked, "Where's Yendor off to, then?"

"Lookin' for meat, so he says. And I hope that's all he's lookin' for."

"You're afraid he'll start drinking again?"

"Can't say I'd blame him, given the way things are," Long replied. "Still, makes life easier when he ain't drinkin'." He was about to say more when he caught sight of Spirk and his friend Ron approaching. "What news?" he asked the pair.

"None good," said Ron.

Long let loose a rueful chuckle. "No surprise, there. But let's have it: what's the problem this time?"

"Storm's got the roads closed both north and south."

"Oh, aye. I'd guessed as much."

"Won't be no travel for a least a sennight," Spirk added.

Long sank into himself upon hearing this. Rem, ever the observant one, threw an arm 'round his friend's shoulder.

"Nobody's going anywhere," he said meaningfully.

"It's what those nobodies'll do to my girl when they start to get bored that worries me."

"From a strictly business point of view," said Rem, "she'll fetch a lot less from the buyer if she's hurt in any way."

Long grimaced. "That's cold comfort."

"There's no other kind in this weather, I'm afraid."

Before the captain could get too lost in his black mood, Yendor reappeared, a handful of something bark-like in his grip.

"What have you got there?" Spirk wanted to know.

"Yes, what is that? Doesn't much look like sausage to me," Long added.

Yendor offered a sheepish smile, his one eye winking shut for the briefest of moments. "Squirrel jerky," he responded. "And it's nowhere near as foul as it sounds."

Long shook his head in disbelief. "And just what'd that set us back?"

"Nothing!" Yendor beamed. "Or as close to nothing as makes no difference."

"Uh-huh," said Rem. "And what exactly is 'close to nothing'?"

"Well, I promised ole Spirk here would stop by the fur trader's tent and do some magicking."

"What?" Spirk gasped, his voice instantly shooting up two octaves. "I can't just do whatever I want, whenever I wanna!"

Vykers, In Lunessfor

Yes, the place looked a lot smaller in the shadowy grey gloom of daylight than it had felt in the obsidian darkness of the previous night. Now that he saw the actual dimensions of the room, Vykers was astounded he'd managed to escape death. The bloodstained floor told him clearly enough that others had not. But there was one great smear that seemed to head in the wrong direction, not out of the room, but towards the very mound of bones Vykers himself had used for cover. On the heels of that revelation, he realized he could hear breathing, ragged but faint, coming from somewhere beneath those same bones.

His feet flapped almost daintily on the floor as he crossed over towards the pile. It was hardly the impression he would have chosen to make on his former assailant, but he hoped to do better in the next few minutes. Without care or concern for the wounded man's comfort, Vykers tossed bones left and right as he sought to reveal the fellow. Funny, he thought, that just a few hours earlier their positions had been reversed. A cry of agony came to his ears as he pulled a final armload of bones from the pile, revealing the bloody head and torso of a dying ruffian.

"Please," the man groaned, "an A'Shea. In Alheria's name, call an A'Shea."

"Huh," Vykers snorted. "You don't know Alheria like I do."

"A healer. Please."

"No healer."

The dying man sobbed in pain and fear.

"No healer," Vykers repeated. "But I can offer you a quick and painless death..." He let the comment sink in before continuing. "In exchange for anything you can tell me about the man who butchered your gang."

The brigand on the floor rolled a wide, feverish eye in Vykers' direction. "*Man?*" He said, his voice cracking in near hysteria. "That weren't no *man*. That 'uz the Dead 'Un."

The froth of blood and phlegm at the fellow's mouth made him difficult to understand.

"The what? The dead one?" Vykers asked.

The dying man coughed violently, whimpered in pain and then nodded his head without lifting it from the ground. "Aye. Dead. One. That 'uz him."

Vykers had fought the dead before, in the ruins beneath Morden's Cairn. "He didn't look dead to *me*," he said. After an unexpectedly long silence from the man at his feet, he added, "But you do."

The Reaper turned away and walked through the building until he found the closet he'd shared with the unseen urchin. The door was again closed and locked. Vykers put his face against it and spoke. "Hey, kid. It's the girl from last night. I was in there with you, remember?"

"So, you made it out, huh?" the kid's voice responded. "I dint think you was gonna make it."

"Yeah, well, I'm tricky that way. Listen, you don't have to open the door, but I got a few questions I wanna ask you. Might be a Merchant in it for you, if I like what I hear."

"How do I know you got a Merchant?"

"We could forget the whole thing," Vykers replied. "Then you'd never know, would ya?"

"Ask yer questions," the kid said.

Vykers did a quick visual check of the surrounding area, just to make sure no one else was listening. Damned charnel house was making him crazier'n normal. Or maybe his paranoia had something to do with Igraine, a lingering remnant of the girl's personality. "You ever hear of a big fella called the 'Dead One'?"

"'Course I have! He's been a-haunting the district for the last fortnight or so."

"Just a fortnight?"

"Mighta been a while longer. What about 'im?"

"That's what I wanna know: all about 'im: where'd he come from? Where's he go? What's he about?"

"They say he'll kill anyone does somebody else wrong. You steal, he'll kill ya. You cheat, he'll kill ya. You hurt someone, he'll chop yer head clean off."

"Huh," Vykers chuckled. "Sounds like my kinda guy."

"Not hardly. Dead 'Un's a monster—eight feet tall, an' 'is flesh is rottin' right off 'is body. He don't have no face, and what there is of it's naught but scars. And the worst part…"

"Yes?"

"He can't be hurt."

"What's that mean?" Vykers demanded.

"Means just that: you c'n stab 'im, burn 'im, hack away with yer axe. It don't bother him the least bit."

"Uh-huh," said Vykers skeptically. "And where can I find this monster?"

"Ain't nobody knows."

"Would it surprise *you* to know he was here last night? That it was him saved me?"

"Shit!" the kid spat. "I'm gonna have to find a new hole to hide in."

"Thought you said he only hurts those who hurt others."

"That's what they say, but they might be wrong! That worth a Merchant to ya?"

"No," said Vykers, "But I'll pay you anyway. Might be, we'll have other business in the future." With that, he took a coin from the pouch on his belt and forced it through a crack in the door. He thought he'd hear it hit the floor on the opposite side, but it seemed the kid caught it before it could fall.

For the rest of the day, Vykers continued his exploration of the South Shore district, as well as his search for more information about the mysterious Dead 'Un. It wasn't hard to come by, since nearly everyone he encountered was already jabbering nervously about the previous night's killings and (correctly) attributing them to the man in question. But who had discovered the bodies? Where had they gone? No one seemed to know or care; the Dead 'Un was all that mattered.

Eventually, Vykers tired of the riddle and made his way back to the alchemist's shop. As it was not quite sunset, he drew his dagger, leaned against the building, opposite, and pretended to trim his nails. Passersby—if any should happen along—would not mistake the meaning of the knife in the young woman's hand: don't fuck with me, in any sense of the word.

At last, Vykers heard the unmistakable sound of bolts being shot in the alchemist's door. He waited another minute or so and then crossed the street and tried the handle: unlocked, as he'd suspected.

It was dark beyond the door, save for a small and discrete pool of light directed onto a workbench by means of a special lantern hanging from the rafters. In the middle of this light, the alchemist's face hung like a gibbous moon, pale, pockmarked and round. His eyes lifted lazily to the door and showed no reaction to Igraine's entrance.

"Here's trouble," he said in a voice that was little more than a whisper.

"You talkin' about me?" Vykers asked.

"I don't get many women in here and none as young and lovely as you."

"Yeah, well, I ain't what I seem."

The alchemist's chuckle was like the rustling of dry leaves. "Who is, though? Who is? Yet, beautiful young things have masters, keepers and patrons, do they not?"

"This one don't."

The leaves rustled again. The alchemist's hands scuttled like spiders across the workbench, about an errand of unknown nature. "Convince me."

"I have gold," Vykers replied.

"Which makes me even more suspicious."

"There's a Shaper I want dead."

The alchemist sat up straighter, spun his face sideways like an owl, and his eyes grew larger. "Ah. Tell me."

Now, it was Vykers' turn to laugh. "I don't think so. You'll have to make do with my coin."

"Then you'll have to make do without my services. Gold is nothing. Information is the most valuable commodity in Her Majesty's realm."

Vykers sighed. What could he tell the alchemist without compromising himself? He could lie, of course, but whatever he said would have to be close enough to the truth that the alchemist couldn't tell the difference. "Very well," he said. "I work for the Reaper."

"Come closer," the alchemist urged.

Vykers stepped to within arm's reach.

The alchemist stared into his eyes, looked him up and down. "I believe you," he said finally. "I knew you had a...master. If that's what he is to you."

"And you understand why I can't share more 'n I'm allowed."

"Certainly. Still, I'd very much like to meet this Reaper."

"No, you wouldn't. He ain't a man cares for small talk and games."

"So they say," the alchemist agreed. He then settled back on his stool, slid his hands into his robe and closed his eyes. "Now, what is it you need in order to accomplish this Shaper's death?"

TWO

Omeyo and the Boy, In Camp

The Svarren's *Skargreit*, or meet, happened at intervals only the boy and the Svarren seemed to understand. It was just as well Omeyo hadn't been forewarned. He hated these occasions more than anything else in his empty, meaningless life. If two Svarren were bad, an entire camp full of them was an affront to nature itself. The loathsome brutes gathered in staggering numbers outside the boy's cave, boisterously arguing over proximity to the Master, fighting over scraps of meat, rutting furiously and indiscriminately, swallowing Skent until they were half blind, flinging their shit at each other and otherwise behaving like the accursed accidents they were. Their visit promised to be nothing more or less than a tour through the infinite hells.

Omeyo's challenge was to make himself as innocuous as possible; to be noticed by these Svarren was to become their toy, and that could never be allowed to happen.

"You stink of fear," the boy called out from the back of the cave.

Omeyo turned immediately, bowed. "Would you not have me fear you, master?"

"But it's not me you fear at the moment, is it, old man?"

"You are in the forefront of my fears, Master, but these Svarren do worry me; that is true."

The boy snorted. "You're a clever one. I suppose that is why you've survived as long as you have." After a moment's pause, he continued. "Come, dress me. If I am to be a god to these Svarren, I must look the part."

"As you say, Master," said Omeyo, making his way deeper into the cave. It was strange to hear such eloquence coming from the changeling, but the general well understood that it was no mere boy who spoke thusly.

"And while you're dressing me, you can tell me another of your stories."

"Of course, Master."

"Tell me of the Reaper," the boy said. "No, no...tell me again of my *battle* with the Reaper. I would know how he bested me, to make certain it does not happen again."

Omeyo had recounted the tale many times, but there was nothing to gain and much to lose in pointing this out. He began by rote. "Your host had engaged the Queen's army, and you had chosen to survey the scene from above, attacking with magic whenever..." He went on without needing to concentrate on doing so. His mind wandered, and his eyes followed. Outside, the great mob of Svarren continued to sully the snow with their every action. What in the endless hells were they even doing here?

"I sense you're not giving this tale your full attention," the boy interrupted, in a voice as cold as the weather outside.

There was no point in denying it. "My deepest apologies, Master," Omeyo answered in his most remorseful voice. "I haven't been sleeping well of late."

"And you think I care?"

"Of course not, Master. Nor should you. You have other, more important concerns, I am sure."

The boy pointed a taut finger in his direction, and Omeyo suddenly felt as if he were on fire. He'd seen men boiled alive in oil; now, he had some understanding of their pain. Tears gushed from his eyes, but he feared to cry out, lest he attract the Svarren's attention.

"The little you *do* know is as nothing compared to what I've forgotten. When I have fully reclaimed my memories and my powers..." With a wave of his master's hand, Omeyo's agony subsided, disappeared, as if it had never existed. The boy continued, "But that may be some time, yet. For the nonce, content yourself with the knowledge that, yes, I do have a plan—involving those same Svarren that you study with such apprehension."

"Perhaps if I knew what your plan was, I might serve you better," Omeyo ventured.

"Ha!" the boy snorted. "I doubt that. But you will have your chance, believe me. And I will have my revenge upon this Reaper, and when he's out of the way, we'll try the old Queen in her castle."

Omeyo could imagine no scenario in which his death was not a foregone conclusion. Strangely, this did not bother him as much as he might have expected.

Aoife, the North

She'd been fretting and stewing too long, agonizing over the meaning of that strange "He lives" until she'd become paralyzed with indecision. Had she imagined the message? Had it come from Alheria? Or was this another of Vykers' Shaper's sendings? No matter how she looked at the question—or how long—she was no closer to an answer.

She took an extended moment to study her breathing and release whatever tensions she held in her body. Allowing her thoughts to drift, she surveyed the small clearing around her makeshift home. Beyond her little fire, the hoarfrost occupied every inch of exposed ground, and the leaves of the nearby underbrush were rimed with delicate crystals that made them seem both precious and brittle. Aoife's breath plumed in the frigid air.

Then she heard the frost crack off to her left and her breath stopped completely. There, not twenty paces away, in the shadow of a great hemlock stood Tarmun Vykers himself.

She was euphorically angry and furiously delighted. How *dare* he? And thank the gods he had! And yet the turmoil within her told Aoife she was nowhere near ready to deal with the Reaper. Not now, and maybe not ever again.

"How did you find me?" she demanded in a voice as devoid of welcome as she could make it.

Vykers took his time in answering. "How could I not?"

A cryptic response that was too clever by half, as far as the A'Shea was concerned. She stood from the stump she'd been sitting on, stretched out her hands to the fire. "Fine, then. *Why* have you found me?"

The Reaper stayed where he was, apparently wise enough to recognize Aoife's conflicted feelings. "I owe you an apology," he said quietly. "For this and...other things."

This so astounded the A'Shea that she wondered if she wasn't hallucinating, hadn't created this vision out of her loneliness and unease. The Reaper *apologize*? When the sun travelled backwards and the rain fell upwards.

For a hundred heartbeats, the two stood staring at one another, and finally Vykers said, "I wouldn't mind sharing your fire for a minute or two. It's damned cold in these trees."

Aoife waved him on, but kept the fire between herself and her former lover. "You were saying?"

Vykers rubbed his knuckles and flexed his fingers in the fire's warmth. "Yes? Oh, yes: my apology." He took a breath, his shoulders dropped noticeably, and he somehow seemed smaller to Aoife, despite the fact he was very much the Reaper. "Of course I should have listened to you when you wanted to take the boy back to Lunessfor. I was so anxious to find the Queen that I...lost sight, I suppose, of the needs of my party."

The A'Shea could not believe what she was hearing. It was almost as if Vykers had planned and memorized these words in an appeal to the Mender's nature. But...that was as unlike Vykers as if he'd painted his face, put on a gown and danced 'round the fire singing songs about needlepoint. To apologize for anything was antithetical to the Reaper's nature.

"I see you doubt me," Vykers said softly. "And why wouldn't you, when I'm famous for letting violence speak for me?" He lowered his head, gazed into the flames. "I'll warrant you've never seen me like this, eh? I'll warrant no one has."

Aoife felt as if she were having an epiphany. Vykers was right: no one *had* ever seen him like this. That he would reveal himself to her like this suggested that, yes, perhaps he was a changed man. And perhaps she had been the agent of his change, his growth. "I imagine you're hungry, too."

Vykers laughed. "Of course. I'm like one of my old chimeras in that regard."

"Well," Aoife answered, "Let me bring you some bread and butter. I've that much to share at least."

And at that, Arune knew she had won.

Long & Company, In Camp

The snow kept falling, and Yendor noticed an odd correlation between the height of its drifts and the depth of Long's moods. Indeed, his friend hardly seemed interested in leaving their shared tent anymore, except to relieve himself. And the man needed a bath, or, at the very least, to stay outdoors long enough to air out the tent. The stink of sweat, stale breath, wood smoke and old gas combined to create a fetor so pungent that it made Yendor's lone eye burn whenever he crawled back inside.

"Gods, man!" he croaked. "Have mercy, will ya? Go and visit the fire so's I can open these flaps and let some air in here!"

Long, wrapped tightly in his blanket and facing the tent wall, only grunted in response.

"Don't make me drag you outta here, Captain. You know I will, if I have to."

Long rolled over and glared at his friend with bleary, bloodshot eyes.

"You look like shit, too!" Yendor complained. "No one should look so bad 'less he's been at the Skent, and I know you haven't done that!"

Long worked his way to a sitting position. "You planning to drive me out with all o' this chatter?"

"You do need to get up and out, Captain. Lyin' in here all day, every day ain't healthy."

"Healthy!" Long snorted. "What's that to me?"

"If you won't do it for yourself, do it for the rest of us. We ain't come so far to see you pickled to death in your own stench."

"A man scarcely ever goes out the way he plans, though, does he?"

"Still."

"Very well," Long groaned. "If it'll get you off my back."

The instant he finally emerged from his tent, the captain found himself in a new predicament.

"You the one in charge 'o these tents hard by?" a gruff voice queried.

Shielding his eyes from the snow, Long looked up into the well-weathered face of a man wrapped in heavy furs. At his side stood another who might've passed for kin.

"Might be. Who's asking?"

The gruff one hit Long right in the teeth, sending him staggering backwards, perilously close to falling onto his tent. Fortunately, Yendor had been following him outside and was thus able to catch his friend under the arms before he collapsed their shelter.

"What's this all about, then?" he bellowed.

The gruff one looked at Yendor. "You the leader o' this group?"

Before Long could interrupt, Yendor responded. "I am. Why'd you hit my man?"

Long wanted to massage is jaw, check his lips for blood, but he wouldn't give his assailant the satisfaction.

"Me n' Sutch here is Gorivar's men. We's here for the rent."

"The rent...?" Yendor echoed, confused.

"'S right, the rent. You wanna stay, you gotta pay."

"We've been here over a week. Nobody's said anything to us about rent," said Yendor.

"Yeah, well, we all just pulled in afore this storm."

Long and Yendor exchanged glances. "Is this Gorivar's camp?" Long asked.

"It is *now*," said Gruff.

"Well, maybe we're the ones chargin' your friend Gorivar rent. Ever think o' that?" Yendor asked smugly.

"Gorivar don't pay. He gets paid. *You* pay."

The "or" was implicit, but damned if Yendor didn't ask, anyway. "Or what?"

Gruff shrugged. "We kill ya."

Yendor nodded, as if this was perfectly reasonable. "And, uh, what are we getting for this rent we're paying."

"We *don't* kill ya," Gruff responded.

"So, you're highwaymen, that it?" Long couldn't help asking.

Gruff and his friend looked at one another, and then Gruff answered, "We collect what Gorivar's due fer not killin' ya."

"Which is how much?" Long demanded, rapidly losing patience.

"Two Merchants a man each week."

Yendor whistled. "Two Merchants! That's a bit steep, eh?"

"Cheaper'n bein' dead," said Gruff.

"Fine!" Long cut in. "But we'll deliver it in person. Where can we find this Gorivar?"

"He'll be in the hunter's cabin, soon as he moves the hunter out."

Long nodded brusquely. "We'll be there straightaway."

"You better be. I don't wanna hafta come back."

Gruff and his silent companion headed off into the storm, leaving Long and Yendor to fume in silence. At last, Yendor spoke.

"What're you thinkin'?"

"I'm thinkin' I don't care for bullies," Long said, belatedly rubbing at his lips and chin.

Vykers, In Lunessfor

The worst part of Vykers' day was that time when his errands were done and he had to retreat to his rented room in the back of a home for war widows. The widows and their incessant prying were bad enough, but being alone with his new body tested the limits of his patience in ways he'd never before experienced. Taking a piss, for example, was suddenly complicated. Oh, he could still stand and piss, but it was a lot messier. He understood now why women preferred to squat. But that, too, made things more difficult. After all, a man could go almost anywhere. Not so, for women. And there was the other thing, the bleeding. The cramps weren't so bad, and Vykers was used to bleeding. But never from...down there. It was a nuisance, a ludicrous inconvenience. And it annoyed him.

He consoled himself with the knowledge that the first part of his plan was complete: the alchemist had given him an elixir that, once consumed, would make him invisible to the searching magics of Shapers. The alchemist had warned Vykers of the elixir's wretched flavor and possible side effects, but the Reaper had downed it in one massive gulp. Pain, dizziness and vomiting were nothing to a man who'd once had his hands and feet chopped off.

So, Arune could not track Vykers, would not know where he was or what he might be up to—assuming the alchemist was not lying. The elixir had been obscenely expensive, but the alchemist had known it was Vykers' money he was taking from the girl. The stuff either worked, or the man had a death wish.

The next stage of his plan required Vykers to visit House Blackbyrne and have a few words with its Chief of Security. Given the lateness of the day, however, the Reaper reluctantly admitted he'd have to wait until the morrow.

Fetching his whetstone from the table near his cot, Vykers decided to sharpen his dagger again, whilst he went over everything he'd learned about the Dead 'Un: he'd only been seen at night, only went after those who'd done wrong, seemed impervious to damage, and so on. Nobody knew his real name. Nobody knew where he lived. Vykers figured him for a vigilante, but, having seen him in action, had to admit there was something uncanny about the man. Initially, he'd wanted to hire this Dead 'Un for added protection. Now, though, the Reaper felt an overpowering curiosity about the stranger and an unexpected sense of kinship. The Dead 'Un was capable of great destruction, and the Reaper was in a very destructive mood of late.

A knock at his door interrupted his musings, irritating him further. "What is it?" he called, none too gently.

"Dinner, your Ladyship," came the sarcastic reply.

That was Ethel, Vykers didn't doubt. The only woman in the whole place he found even remotely attractive. Oh, she was no Aoife, to be sure. If he still had his wedding tackle, though, he'd put it to good use. It was the A'Shea who'd ended things after all, not Vykers. He didn't owe her anything.

"Be down shortly," he said to the door.

"We can hardly wait," Ethel replied.

They weren't fond of Igraine, were the others. But they *were* fond of the young woman's money, which, Vykers supposed, explained why they allowed him/her to stay, when she so clearly was not of their ilk. If Vykers was ever able to find and hire the kind of help he was looking for, he'd have to move to larger quarters, elsewhere.

One thing at a time.

Kittins, In Lunessfor

"You seem to have cowed South Shore," the Shaper said matter-of-factly. "The Constable tells me it's gone from being one of our most dangerous, crime-ridden districts to one of our safest. Imagine that."

Kittins said nothing.

"This changes nothing between us, however. That Her Majesty was correct in this instance does not mean she'll have a long-term use for you. And when she runs out of ideas, you'll have run out of time."

This was too much. "You talk as if you know what's coming. Be damned sure about it, 'cause I won't waste time talkin' when I get my chance."

The Shaper nodded, sat down leisurely, almost theatrically, in his plush chair by the fire. "You have visions of gutting me like a pig, I'm sure. I, on the other hand, have a wide range of choices. I could drop you in the middle of the southern ocean, slowly immerse you in molten iron, have you staked to a vituvian ants' nest, inflict you with the rots...or all of the above. In truth, I'm only limited by my imagination...and I can be quite imaginative."

"You certainly love to hear yourself talk."

Cindor pulled a small, tight smirk. "Enough chatter, then. Her Majesty has another—and, I hope, *final*—chore for you."

Again, Kittins said nothing, but offered a heavy-lidded stare.

"There's an alchemist in South Shore who's gotten too powerful for the Queen's liking. His name's D'Marei. We would like him...gone."

Kittins raised an eyebrow. "We?"

"I serve Her Majesty, and she would like him gone."

"And I'm guessing this alchemist has his own private army or some such?"

Smirk. "Something like that, yes."

"So, a suicide mission," Kittins said grimly. He took a final look around the room, seeming to scrutinize everything, and then added, "I'll see you again. Soon." That said, he left.

Now, the Shaper looked about, trying to guess what Kittins had been after. The little gargoyle above the door said nothing.

Aoife, Arune, the North

Regaining Aoife's trust had required more patience than Arune could have predicted, but the Shaper felt she was getting there, day by day. Of course, it had all started with Vykers' obligatory apology. Then, Arune had bided her time, aiding the A'Shea with any number of small chores around the ramshackle cabin. A winter storm rolled in and helped immensely, as there was no question of Vykers departing in such weather, and there was little to do but talk. Aoife had not been inclined to share anything of her younger days, and though it frustrated the ever-curious Arune, it was also something of a relief, for now she no longer feared having to share Vykers' past with the A'Shea. If she'd been pressed, she would have had to fabricate the Reaper's childhood, because, despite the years she'd spent inside the man's head, he was as impenetrable as Aoife. In time, though, the A'Shea succumbed to the Reaper's presence and allowed him back into her bed.

It was the greatest period of happiness in Arune's life. She loved the A'Shea, as the saying goes, "this side idolatry," and there were many occasions when Aoife was otherwise engaged on which Arune pondered which of her lover's traits she adored most. Sometimes, the Shaper categorized these traits as either physical or spiritual in nature. Other times, she lumped them all together, unable or unwilling to separate them. Some days, she was intoxicated by Aoife's external beauty—the luster of her eyes, the soft white perfection of her skin, the luxuriance of her hair, the mysterious, somewhat fey scent of her—and other days, she spent hours pondering the woman's inner self, her soul, which seemed to Arune a thing unparalleled in all existence.

But the greatest revelation had been the sexual intimacy. She'd experienced it once as a guest in Vykers' body, and only one other time before that, with a boy in her hometown. It had been awkward and utterly unenjoyable. At the time, she'd walked away bewildered as to the reasons for its popularity. She was bewildered no more, however. Arune was not attracted to men, but to women, and not just any woman, but the most beautiful, the most breathtaking and exceptional woman in the world. In the midst of the act, the vulnerable, yearning, hungry look in Aoife's eyes provoked such rapture, such emotional ecstasy in Arune that she would happily have remained conjoined with Aoife forever. Oh, there were times the Shaper had brief bouts of insecurity, certainly. But having lived inside Vykers on the one occasion he'd made love to the A'Shea, Arune felt reasonably comfortable that Aoife could not tell the difference. And why should she? Arune had a greater passion for the A'Shea than even Vykers.

It was, all things considered, the happiest Arune had ever been.

Had she been older, possessed of more experience or not quite so smitten, the Shaper might have realized such euphoria cannot last forever. The first shadow caught her unawares.

"I believe the End-of-All-Things has returned," Aoife said one evening as she mended a hole in her cloak.

It was said so casually, so a propos of nothing, that Arune wasn't sure she'd heard correctly. "What's that?"

The A'Shea turned her gaze Vykers' way and searched his eyes. "The End. I believe he's come back."

A chasm seemed to open beneath Arune's feet, and she watched in helpless horror as bits of her world fell into it. Suddenly, the cabin felt too small. "What?" Arune repeated stupidly.

Aoife set her cloak aside and stood. "I was thinking on him a while ago and a voice came to me and declared him alive."

Arune could breathe again. "A voice? What voice? Whose voice?"

Aoife shook her head, confused. "I thought..." She reconsidered. "It can only have come from one of two sources: the Queen, Alheria, or your Shaper. I thought you would have known, if..." This last seemed to dangle into infinity before she spoke again. "So, that leaves Alheria."

"After what...what we went through in rescuing Her Majesty, do you really think she can be trusted? And then again, perhaps you imagined this voice?" Arune offered almost jokingly, in an attempt to cover up her near-gaffe.

Disappointment stole over the A'Shea's features faster than snow spread over the ground outside. She plunked herself back down in her seat, retrieved her cloak, and acted as if the subject had never come up.

Too late, Arune recognized her mistake and tried to make amends. "What I mean is, if it was Alheria, why wouldn't she provide more information? I've never known the old windbag to be so terse."

"I don't want to talk about it further."

Now Arune stood, crossed over to the A'Shea. "Look, I'm sorry. I thought you were making a joke, having a laugh at my expense..."

"A joke?" The A'Shea's voice cracked. "Do you think me a drunkard or a fool that I would make light of such a subject? Do you know me so little?"

"I misunderstood. I...don't spend a lot of time around other people. Forgive me."

But Aoife would say no more.

The Reaper—the real Reaper—would have handled things differently, Arune knew. Absent other ideas, she wrapped herself up and went out into the storm.

They slept in the same bed that night, but it would be an exaggeration to say they shared it.

In the morning, Arune woke to see Aoife packing things into a bedroll.

"It's a blizzard out there," the Shaper protested.

"I have to get to Lunessfor. I need to speak with Her Majesty," Aoife replied, frost in her voice. "And if the great Tarmun Vykers won't take me seriously, I'm fairly sure Alheria will."

Arune became angry. "Of course I take you seriously! It's just that I killed the End. He's dead and gone. If you'd met him, you'd know he's..."

The look Aoife shot back would've killed a score of lesser men. "If I'd *met* him?" The A'Shea seemed on the verge of saying more, then didn't. "Goodbye, Reaper."

With all her magic and Vykers' strength, Arune couldn't stop Aoife from leaving her. She'd betrayed her one friend in order to win the A'Shea's heart, and now she had neither.

The chasm engulfed her.

Long & Company, in Camp

The hunter's cabin was the central structure in the camp and its only permanent one. With its own fireplace and smoke room, it seemed a palace compared to the conglomeration of wagons and tents that spiraled away from it in all directions. It was, therefore, the natural place for an invading tyrant to install himself.

If Long and his crew were surprised to see a gang widening the cabin's door with axes, they were less so when they at last laid eyes on Gorivar. The man must have been born obese. That and a lifetime of filling his face during every waking moment could hardly have accounted for the ton of flesh the men saw before them. He was so large, even the huntsman's solid, four-poster bed was too small a chair for Gorivar's bulk, which was covered in moles, warts and festering bedsores. Worst of all, he gave off a stench that made Long's former aroma seem like perfume by comparison.

"What are these?" Gorivar asked in a thick lowlands accent when Long and company came into view.

Apart from the servant shoveling something from a bowl down Gorivar's throat and the men hacking away at the door, there was no one around to answer.

Long spoke up. "We were told we owe you money. I'd like to know how that's possible."

Gorivar chuffed, choked a little bit on his meal. "Would

you?" he asked enthusiastically. "Would you? 'Cuz if you don't pay up, I'll put out your friend there's other eye!" He then roared with laughter at the hilarity of his comment.

Yendor didn't find it funny.

"And how," said Rem, "do you plan to do that?"

Whereupon the actor flew up to the ceiling, dropped, rose, dropped, rose, and then dropped a final time, breathing heavily and wondering if he'd broken anything.

"You might've warned us," Long muttered to Spirk under his breath.

"'Ow was I to know?" the young man responded aloud.

"So, you're a Shaper," the captain said to the behemoth.

Gorivar grinned idiotically. "Might be. Might not. Now drop your money on the hearth, there, or I take your friend's eye."

Everyone began reaching into his pockets when Long stopped them. "I'll take care of this," he said as he walked over to the fireplace and placed the coins where he'd been directed.

Gorivar chuckled, the fat of his face wiggling like gelatin. "And remember, it's the same due every day."

"Your man said weekly," Long objected.

"Now it's daily."

The captain felt a tug on his arm and looked down to see Yendor's hand on his sleeve. "Let's go," his friend said softly.

"Yes, let's," Rem agreed.

"What in Mahnus' name do we do now?" Yendor demanded when the group got back to its own campsite. "Snow's still too deep to leave."

"And why couldn't you warn us?" Rem challenged Spirk.

Ever the loyal friend, Ron put his hand on Spirk's shoulder as a show of support.

Spirk looked about to cry. "'Cuz I'm not a Shaper?"

"Well, what *are* you, then?" Rem pressed.

"He's your friend," said Ron. "Ain't that enough?"

Long cut in, "Let's stop this squabbling, eh? Stop it. You're only helpin' that fat man by fighting each other."

"What I'd like to know," said Yendor, "is how they got 'im inside in the first place, and how 'e travels. Bastard must weigh more'n a draft horse."

"Magic?" said Spirk.

Ron hunched down and started rebuilding their communal fire. Yendor was about to tell him how pointless that was, when he realized the snowfall had let up in pace and intensity. "Might be we're through the worst o' this storm," he said, pointing his chin at the clouds.

The rest of the gang dusted off their accustomed seats and huddled around the smoking kindling. Suddenly, the wood burst into flames with an explosive whoosh, sending everyone tumbling backwards.

"Wha...?" someone asked.

"Maybe I *am* a Shaper," Spirk confessed sheepishly.

Amidst general laughter, Yendor pressed the issue. "Then why couldn't you tell us anything about that Gorivar?"

Spirk winced but held firm. "Maybe *he's* not a Shaper, like he said."

"But if he ain't a Shaper," Yendor mused, "what in the endless hells is he?"

This set off a lengthy bout of conjecture all around. Only Long remained quiet and calm—a fact no one but Rem seemed to notice. "You're not worried?"

The captain offered a rueful smile. "Friend, I got bigger worries than some bloated two-penny tyrant. And I've faced meaner bastards, if it comes to that. We just need to settle down and think this through. Could be, we'll come out on top."

Eoman, In the Woods

There are worse things in the forest at night than wolves, worse than oursine, worse than Svarren, worse than any of them. There are the dark, forsaken, hungry things, things without name or purpose but which nevertheless embody malice, things with an abiding hatred for any and all who would live beyond shadows.

These were the only things Eoman Harkin Hainan feared as he forged his way through waist-deep snow, chasing pools of moonlight across the forest. For moonlight was anathema to the creatures stalking him, a secret men had forgotten, but giantkind had not. In the moonlight, he was safe.

Normally, even a giant wouldn't take such a risk, but Eoman had heard tell of a caravan that had come through the area a few days past, rumbling northwards as if being chased, despite the inclement weather. That was mighty suspicious to the giant, and he felt that if this caravan was just two or three days ahead, he might catch it with a bit more effort.

The things in the darkness followed along and grew in numbers, chittering, hissing and calling out to him in the old languages, waiting for Eoman to make a mistake, to sink too deeply into the snow, to exhaust himself, to stumble. Eoman, in turn, rumbled an ancient charm of protection.

Tu amaii ea-ho deneska,
Di amaii lobuulo tai,
Fisk amaii denoura paa-na,
Bu amaii ea-ho dusai.

Several of the darklings exploded like chestnuts in a fire; a few others ran shrieking into the undergrowth. Many remained, too many for Eoman to handle in a pitched battle, if it came to that. Pulling his axe from his belt, the giant took a few mighty swings, hoping to intimidate those following him. It was not an especially effective gambit. He squinted up the road and estimated the things would be on him before he could reach the next patch of light. Next, he glanced at the moon, whose path did not favor him, either. Soon, she would drift off deeper into the woods, taking his little island of safety with her, and deeper into these woods was the last place Eoman wanted to go. Besides, running from light to light was the only thing keeping him close to warm. If he didn't keep moving—and at a good pace—he'd freeze to death by dawn.

Sometimes, his temper got the best of him. He hoped his reckless pursuit of Mardine's killers hadn't gotten *him* killed, as well. Nothing to be done about it now, but fight. As Eoman's pool of light continued to shift and dwindle, the darklings became daring and assayed the giant's back and flanks. He spun viciously, sweeping his weapon one way and then the next in a scything motion. Some of the creatures fell immediately, but it was not nearly enough. With each breath, each heartbeat, more coalesced out of the tenebrous trees, and Eoman soon understood that he fought some aspect of the night itself. Daggers of pain sank into one calf. Looking down, the giant spied a beastie fixed to his leg by its needlelike teeth. Passing his axe into his left hand, he grabbed the creature with his right and crushed its neck. Quick as he could, he tossed the body at some of its brothers and let out a bestial roar. There aren't many things of any disposition that will stand fast in the face of such a furor, and the darklings were no exception, falling back and regrouping amongst the shadows. They'd be at him again soon enough, Eoman knew, so he turned and sprinted for the next patch of moonlight, continuing to bellow as he went.

As expected, the creatures sprang at his back the moment he crossed into the unlit expanse between pools. Eoman tried to bat them away with his free hand, but the damnable things were too fast. Again, he roared, frightening the smaller ones into retreat whilst he pressed onwards. They swirled around him like snowflakes in a whirlwind—black snowflakes, malevolent snowflakes. Eoman kept slapping at them with one hand and cleaving with the other. To his frustration, killing them only seemed to increase their numbers. He could feel their teeth and claws digging into his flesh between the layers of leather and fur. They struggled for purchase in his beard and hair. A slow tide of panic began rising in the giant's chest. *It's only ten strides to the next bit of light!* He told himself. *Only ten!* The darklings were determined he'd never get there, and the biggest of them gathered across his intended path. Eoman was a giant, though, and *king* of the giants, at that. Gritting his teeth and hefting his axe in both hands, he charged into the mass, yelling at the top of his voice.

The axe carved up the night, slicing and crushing Eoman's path to freedom. And still the fell creatures came on. The giant wouldn't allow his thoughts to wander into the treacherous land of What If, but there was a tension in his gut, notwithstanding. And then, confusion. Tiny motes of light floated, fluttered and zipped into the melee, eliciting squeals of fear and rage from the darklings. Soon, the air about Eoman was so full of the things that it appeared to be hailing luminescence.

Will-o-wisps. He'd only ever seen them from a distance, and never in such numbers. Now, he was astonished and nearly transfixed. Yet, his work was not done. He had to finish the last of the bigger darklings on his own, or his path would never be clear.

Deep, boisterous laughter rang out from the woods on his right, and, busy as he was, Eoman glanced over to search out its source. Then he was laughing, too. His old friend Karrakan strode from the shadows, radiating a light all his own.

"Heard ye wailin' fer miles. Not very dignified behavior fer a king!"

Eoman guffawed at the comment, putting a boot on the last of the darklings. "And you took yer time gettin' here, too, I'm sure."

Karrakan pulled on his beard and japed, "From the awful sounds ye were makin', I thought sure 'twas a bear being mounted by an oursine!"

"And that were true, you'd've come faster, I've no doubt, you old lecher!"

The two comrades' laughter shook snow from the trees and banished any lingering shadows.

"But it's good to see you again, old friend," Eoman beamed, not-so-lightly cuffing Karrakan's shoulder.

"I'll bet," Karrakan replied. "Looked like you were having a time of it with those little beasties."

Eoman snorted. "Bah! I'd have ta'en 'em all down in time. But what brings you to these parts?"

"Are you daft? You won't find me in yer civilized lands! You know I'm a bleedin' shaman. And what's *your* excuse fer wanderin' so far north?"

Eoman's smile evaporated and his levity went with it. "I'm huntin' giant killers, 'Kan. *Human* giant killers."

The shaman stroked his beard, frowned. "Human giant killers," he repeated soberly. "What'd they do? Who'd they kill?"

"No one you'd know, I think. She was a child last time I saw her in the free lands." He went on to describe what he'd found in the woods so far to the south and experienced his horror and anger all over again. Soon, Karrakan shared these sensations.

"I'm a-comin' with ye," said he.

"And I'm glad of it," Eoman responded. "Might be we'll need an army of our folk when we get where we're going."

"Then it's an army we'll gather," his friend resolved.

Vykers, In Lunessfor

It was strange how events seemed to repeat themselves. He'd been walking through the market again when Vykers was accosted by a fat man. He'd intended to ignore the sot this time, when something about the man's face caught his attention and worried it like a dog with a bone. He'd seen the man before; he was sure of it. He got about ten paces farther when it came to him: this was the bastard who'd pissed on him when he'd been dumped in the forest years ago without hands or feet. A cold fury eclipsed his normally grim visage, and he turned to stare at the man.

"What's that?" the Reaper prompted.

The drunk chuckled, "I'm offerin' ta take ya fer a ride, little pony. Ride o' yer lifetime!"

Vykers gazed impassively at him. The drunk sat at the base of a wall, his legs splayed out into the street. Clearly, his fortunes had declined since Vykers had seen him last. But they were about to get a whole lot worse.

"That a fact?" Vykers asked, trying and failing to sound enticing. The mere effort almost made him puke.

"Little piece like you?" said the man. "I could diddle you 'til Winter's Wane."

"Oh," Vykers replied, "you're gonna have to prove that!"

The drunk leered. "You got someplace we can go?"

"I know a place, yeah. If you can walk that far."

"For a bit o' dimple? You'd be s'prised how far I c'n walk."

Vykers smiled. "Follow me, then."

It was a difficult task, maintaining the drunk's interest over the long walk to the charnel house. The fellow was so inebriated that the Reaper had to constantly remind him Igraine was there.

Yet, she was either more attractive than Vykers supposed, or it had been so long since the fat man had been with a woman that he was willing to put up with anything, even Vykers' rather awkward and insincere flirting. Whatever the case, they reached Vykers' destination at last.

"Wait here a moment," he instructed his companion.

Slipping into the building, Vykers headed straight for the storage closet and knocked on the door. "It's me," he said, "the girl who came in through the hole the other day."

Without pause, the door opened, and Vykers stepped into the tiny space. "I need some help," he explained. "And I'm willing to pay for it."

A short while later, Vykers was on the other side of the door when a new knock came. He went to the door and opened it a crack.

"I bought what you asked for," a child's voice announced. "Heavier 'n Mahnus' balls, though."

"Good," said Vykers. "Leave it outside the door. Now," he continued, "I need one other thing…"

"Yes?"

"I need you to leave this place and never return."

"But…" the small voice protested.

Vykers tossed a few Nobles through the door and onto the darkened floor, beyond.

"These real?" the little voice said after a few seconds.

"They're real, alright."

"Can I work for you, then?" the still-unseen child asked hopefully.

"No. Last kid I took under my wing turned into a monster. A *real* monster," Vykers clarified.

"What *should* I do, then?"

"There's enough coin there to buy your way into a boarding school. That's my suggestion, but you do what you must."

There followed an extended silence, and then the child said, "Are ya sure I…"

"Yes," came Vykers' curt reply, whereupon he slammed the door and locked it.

The fat man howled himself awake, his groin a fiery cauldron of pain. A second jolt of pain in his prick brought his attention to the young woman standing in front of him. Suddenly, fear overtook his pain, froze his bowels and stole the breath from his lungs. He remembered following the girl into the room, and then...and then...she'd struck him, hit him over the head with something heavy. His head still ached from the blow. And now, here he was. He tried to move, but found he could not. The girl had tied his hands to the dusty shelving at his back. A breeze around his legs informed him, if he had not realized it already, that his captor had stripped him of his breeches, as well.

"Here, now," he began nervously. "I like it a bit rough, meself, but this..."

The girl turned and shoved something into a small fire she had burning in the corner. "This is nothin' compared to what's comin'," she said.

"Well, I changed my mind, I have!" the man protested.

"And I ain't," she answered.

"But I never touched you, after all. No harm done, eh?"

The girl's grin was terrifying. "Not yet."

"But why?" the fat man whimpered. "Why?" he demanded a second time with greater conviction.

Again, the girl grinned. "Come now," she cooed. "I imagine a big man like you can handle just about anything. I imagine you're almost as strong as the Reaper himself."

The absurdity of the comment made the man laugh, despite his panic. "The Reaper? He ain't s' strong. Fact, I beat 'im once."

The girl nodded, went to the fire, and retrieved a dagger with a red hot blade. The blood raced from the drunk's face.

"That's what I was hopin' you'd say," the girl purred.

The fat man closed his eyes in a desperate bid to deny his predicament. It was no use. An awful, searing sensation blazed through his groin, accompanied by the sickening smell of burnt meat. Knowing it was himself he smelt, the drunk vomited, whereupon the girl struck him repeatedly across the face with an open hand, until he regained some composure.

"What...what've you done to me?" the fat man sobbed bitterly.

"Do you remember when you dumped the Reaper on the forest floor?" the girl asked unexpectedly. "They'd cut off his hands 'n feet, and he was sick as a dog and weaker 'n a newborn. You remember what you did?"

Amazed and bewildered at this seemingly trivial line of questioning, the fat man answered, "I kicked 'im, aye. What o' that?"

"You kicked 'im, true enough. And you pissed on his head, too."

"So what if I did?" the drunk asked defensively. "I never done nothin' to *you!* I never touched you. Never hurt you!"

The girl said nothing, just stared into her captive's eyes as if she would bore a hole in his skull.

"Who are you, anyway?" the man whined.

"Who am I?" the girl giggled. "I'm the last person to see you alive." She seemed to let that sink in a moment and then continued. "I've tied off your little pecker. Don't suppose you can see that over your gut, but it's true. With two leather strips I cut from your jerkin, I tied it off as tight as I could without cuttin' right through the damned thing. Then I burned the end of it, just to make sure you'll never piss again. And now..." she trailed off as she lifted a couple of enormous water skins off the floor, "now, you're gonna start drinking this water 'til you explode. You're gonna die just *wishin'* you could piss..."

A Creature, the Forest

There was pain and only pain, a pulsing, throbbing agony that defined existence, from its molten center to the very boundaries of perception. Time therefore had no meaning, until that pain was joined by a terrible cold, a grasping, invasive cold that would not be ignored. These twin horrors of pain and cold danced, fairly frolicked in their supremacy. Then darkness made itself known and, in doing so, slightly weakened the grip of pain and cold, as the entity that experienced these things began to wonder: *what is darkness? Whence comes it?* Before an answer could be found, hunger and thirst barged to the fore, demanding their own share of attention. The word 'misery' occurred to the entity. *Why am I beset?* Finally, suffocation screamed its arrival, demanding action from its bedeviled host, and the entity, the *thing*, fought to find air. After some struggle, an extremity—a hand—achieved freedom. The rest of the thing followed suit, until it dragged itself from the frozen, broken ground and rolled itself over onto the open forest floor. Suffocation fled, as if it had never existed. Darkness receded, though it would not be banished completely. Pain, cold, hunger and thirst remained to mock the creature. Exhaustion arrived, to chase them away.

The poor thing slept.

Of all its devils, cold was the one that demanded the creature awaken and act. Slowly, in fresh agony, the wretched thing complied, strove to stand. Along the way, it was startled to discover the darkness had gone: its enemies were dwindling in number, then. It could breathe and it could see; it had only to contend with pain, cold, hunger and thirst. Somewhere in the distance, it could hear the sounds of a stream rippling against an unseen shore. Thirst would shortly be vanquished, too.

Working its way towards the stream, the creature was struck by a new revelation: *I am female, I am a she.* If there was more to know about herself, it eluded her. She staggered around and past trees—*trees!*—and eventually managed to reach the stream, where memory ambushed her again. *I have been here before,* she thought. *I have...there was...*But she could not piece any more together, to her enduring frustration.

There was ice in the stream, and though its waters chased away the creature's thirst, it only magnified the cold she felt. *I can live with pain and hunger, but if I do not find warmth, I will die.* She looked down at her hands and wrists, which were covered with frightful scars and seemed horribly discolored. *I have been hurt.* She attempted to get a look at herself in the stream's calmer waters and failed, for her image would not come together. Hesitantly, she reached up and pawed through her matted hair to her ruined scalp, where great craters and gashes had crusted over. When she retracted her hand, it came away with strands of dirty red hair.

Who am I? She thought. *What am I?*

Long & Company, In Camp

Before they could formulate a plan for dealing with Gorivar, Long and his crew needed to scout the Shaper's defenses, determine the number and nature of his men and identify the likeliest avenue of escape if things went south.

Naturally, Spirk was the obvious choice for this task.

"Why me?" he whined.

"You know damned well," Long replied. "You're the only one here can walk up to that woodsman's cabin without bein' seen. That's your special talent, lad, and don't deny it!"

Spirk Nessno was not a narcissist. Neither was he given to delusions of grandeur—not since a night long ago when he'd been beaten for thinking too much of himself. But he had to allow that maybe, just maybe-kinda-perhaps, he had a gift for walking wherever he'd a mind to.

"Alright," he said. "What am I lookin' for?"

"We wanna know how many men guard the place at night. On the outside."

"And where they're located," Yendor cut in.

Long nodded. "Right. How many near the front door, how many on the sides. And if you see anything else..."

"Like what?"

"Dogs, special weapons, whatever...let us know about 'em. I don't wanna go over there and get mauled by an animal you didn't tell us about..."

"I wouldn't forget that..." the young man protested. "But when should I go?"

Long wasted no time in answering. "Nightfall. I'm sure they won't see you, but there's nothin' wrong with a little added surety."

Spirk could not disagree.

Vykers, In Lunessfor

The drunk's death left a bad taste in Igraine's mouth. Vykers was not a torturer and never had been. If he'd possessed his usual body, he'd have beaten the man to death and called it good. But Igraine would have broken her fists on the man's skull long before Vykers managed to finish him, so he'd chosen other means. It was frustrating. Maddening, even. What had seemed like justice had turned out, in reality, to be nothing more than sadism, the act of a knave…or a long-abused woman to whom unattainable vengeance had suddenly become possible. Had the Reaper acted out of some sort of reverse Brouton's Bind, some latent connection to Igraine's former self that had demanded such actions? Was the girl secretly in charge, or had Vykers' rage simply gotten the better of him? If the drunk hadn't died of an apparent heart attack, the Reaper might have been in that dark closet still. He was so furious, he could have killed the man all over again.

But it did nothing to advance his plans, nothing to bring him closer to that one act of vengeance that truly mattered: settling the score with Arune. If that were all, it would have been more than enough. But Vykers felt he owed Her Majesty a measure of punishment as well. After all, she'd been manipulating him for years, and he always turned out the worse for it. He'd saved her kingdom and wound up an invalid, confined to a sickbed for what felt like eternity. Later, he'd likely saved her life—or whatever it was Gods endured—when she'd fallen victim to one of Mahnus' traps and he'd had to free her. True, she'd cured him of the terrible, never-healing hole in his gut, but she might've done so right after he'd received it. That she had not until he forced the issue galled him still. And then to discover that the Queen had conjured four living replicas of him for the purpose of keeping him at bay?

What was Her Majesty after? Did she think these impostors could protect her from Vykers? More likely, their creation was meant to insult him in some way, perhaps even to goad him into doing something rash. Well, he wouldn't give the old bitch the satisfaction. He would ignore her little toys unless and until he found a way to use them for his own ends.

The Reaper's anger burnt away his guilt at torturing the drunk to death, incinerated even the memory of it, so that, once again, he wanted blood, was itching to mete out punishment, and consequences be damned.

It was in this mood that he arrived at the recently refurbished gates of House Blackbyrne. With Igraine's small fists and lack of mass, Vykers had trouble generating the kind of booming knock needed to grab anyone's attention beyond the wall, so he resorted to tossing stones over it.

"'Ere, you, stop that afore I put an arrow in yer gullet!" someone yelled from the gate's far side.

"I'm here to speak with your Chief o' Security, Kendell," Vykers yelled back in Igraine's voice.

"On ooze behalf?"

"On...on the Reaper's. On Tarmun Vykers' behalf."

There was a prolonged silence, during which Vykers thought the speaker must've fallen asleep. Then, a small window opened in the gate's right-hand side. The business end of a crossbow pressed up against the opening.

"You ain't but a little slip of a thing, are you?" a voice called out from behind the crossbow.

"So everyone keeps tellin' me," said Vykers.

"And you say the Reaper sent you?"

"He did."

"What proof you got?" the voice challenged.

"You get a lot o' little girls claiming to represent the Reaper coming to your door?"

"Uh, no, I don't guess we do," the man answered. "But even if the Reaper did send you, you still can't see Kendell, 'cause he's dead."

This was too much. "You don't open this door, friend," said Vykers, "And you'll be joining him in short order."

The door opened. A jowly man with sleepy eyes and a doughy complexion stood just inside, cradling the crossbow in his arms. "I s'pose you'll want to speak with Kendell's successor." Without waiting for a response, he beckoned Vykers to follow him and shuffled off into the nearest building.

There were a lot more guards around the place than Vykers remembered seeing on his previous visit. But then, that had been years ago, and clearly things had changed. To Vykers' surprise, his guide led him into an empty room, barren of furniture, artwork or ornamentation of any kind. The only features of note were the six doors ringing the room.

"I'll be right back," the jowly man said, before opening one of those doors and disappearing.

Vykers was so surprised at having been left unattended that he crossed to the same door and yanked it open, only to find a stone wall. He reached out, touched it, just to make sure it was no trick.

"Mahnus' balls!" he grumbled. "Is there no end to Shapers' deceit?"

A door on the opposite wall opened and a short, round woman stepped through. As Vykers spun to face her, the remaining doors opened in concert, each revealing a bowman, ready to fire.

Vykers looked them over and then calmly addressed the woman. "All this for one girl?"

"Better to err on the side of paranoia than be taken unawares," the woman replied. "You are familiar with the Harkness Spider, I assume?"

Vykers was. The Harkness Spider was among the deadliest known to man, and especially so because it was small and easily overlooked. The Reaper laughed, temporarily forgetting his deceptive exterior. "First time I've ever been compared to a spider."

"What was it you wanted to speak to me about?"

The Reaper let the moment hang whilst he studied the other woman. He figured her to be of middle years. Her drab brown hair was cut short, just below her ears, in a manner that seemed both hastily done and childlike, a fact that was not at all mitigated by her snub, turned-up nose and pronounced overbite. She looked by turns ridiculous and severe, and Vykers was curious to know which of the two extremes prevailed in practice.

"You're the Chief of Security?"

"None else," the woman said, "And you're wasting my time. Get to the point."

Vykers cleared his throat, spared not a glance at the bowmen. "I was sent by the Reaper to gain information from the previous Chief of Security." Now, he cast his eyes over the archers.

The other woman caught his drift immediately. "They'll abide where they are, until I've proof of your claim."

Yes, things had unquestionably changed at House Blackbyrne. Vykers sighed and launched into a lengthy recitation of the Reaper's experiences when he'd visited Kendell, including his introduction to the chimeras, the gazebo they'd met in, the lunch they'd eaten and more. "If that won't satisfy," Vykers said when he'd finished, "I'm to offer you gold."

The Chief of Security frowned. "You'd be a fool to carry around enough gold to make a difference."

"And you'd be a fool to try and take it off me without my consent," Vykers retorted, growing weary of the woman's attitude. As Igraine, he wasn't sure he could deliver on this boast, but, as Vykers, he couldn't resist making it. Enough was enough, already.

Unexpectedly, the woman smiled. "It's good to see one of our sex with a bit of swagger. Might be, I could find work for you when you're done running errands for the Reaper. If that's *all* you do for him."

Vykers brushed aside the insinuation and gestured to the bowmen, still aiming in his direction. "What I've been sent to ask you can only be shared in private. It's meant for your ears alone."

The Chief of Security nodded and waved her protectors off. Silently, they lowered their bows and closed their respective doors. "My name," she said at last, "is Cedna. And yours is...?"

"Igraine."

"Your message?"

Vykers explained that in the Reaper's first meeting with Kendell, the former Chief of Security had intimated that, because the Blackbyrnes had once been the city's foremost stonemasons, the family possessed knowledge of a secret way into the Queen's castle. If true, the Reaper was willing to pay generously for that knowledge.

Cedna listened attentively and did not respond on the instant, but took her time, composing her thoughts. At length, she said, "You know, I am sure, of the troubles the Eight have endured of late..." She trailed off, awaiting confirmation or contradiction from Igraine.

Vykers nodded. "I've heard some talk."

"Talk? If you'd been in town, you could hardly have escaped it," Cedna quipped. "At any rate, there's some thought that Her Majesty engineered the turmoil in order to weaken potential aspirants to her throne."

"But I was told Her Majesty favored House Blackbyrne."

It seemed Cedna thought nothing of Igraine's stumble, for she went on. "So we believed. Now? Everything's in question."

"And what's this got to do with a way into the castle?"

Cedna smiled a small, tight smile that made her overbite even more pronounced. "That's the point, though, isn't it? To divulge such a secret might be treason, depending upon your... master's...*intent*." Before Vykers could formulate a response, the other woman went on, "Given the Reaper's reputation for violence and destruction, the odds certainly favor treason."

That sounded like a firm 'no,' if Vykers had ever heard one.

"In which case," Cedna concluded, "we're happy to share."

Kittins, In Lunessfor

He resented these little side missions, of course, but they'd given him the time he might not otherwise have taken to study his ultimate targets and to plan. The Queen and her Shaper were not ordinary adversaries. He understood that much, at least. Unless Kittins got very lucky, they'd see his attack coming, and Kittins did not believe in luck. Oh, he'd had a number of chances to bash the Shaper's skull in or shove a blade in his gut, but the big captain had come to believe that Cindor was the key to getting at Her Majesty, that if anyone knew her vulnerabilities, it was he. So, as much as he might've enjoyed killing the Shaper immediately, he had to keep him around long enough to learn what he needed to know.

Meantime, his current assignment might prove helpful in preparing him for his eventual move on Cindor, because of the nature of his target. Better still, the alchemist was known to do business only after sundown, which saved Kittins the trouble of trying to disguise his infamous and hysteria-inducing features. Still, nothing was ever as easy as it seemed, and the big man figured the same was true of this task. He would not, he suspected, be able to walk right in and kill the man; he'd have taken precautions, laid traps and the like against such an eventuality. Therefore, Kittins would have to pose as a customer until he'd learned enough to formulate a plan and then return when he was truly prepared.

He already knew where the alchemist's shop was located; he'd passed it on any number of occasions whilst hunting the district's two-legged vermin. When he reached it this time, however, he found it on the opposite side of the street from what he'd remembered. He didn't have long to ponder this conundrum, however, before a trio of drunken bravos entered the far end of the street and began staggering in his direction, their arms intertwined like the branches of a tree in order to hold each other upright. For a moment, Kittins thought there might be trouble, but the strangers got one look at him and wisely opted to retrace their steps and find an alternate route towards their destination.

When he was alone again, Kittins approached the door and banged upon it.

"It's open," a voice yelled from within.

He turned the knob and pushed the door inwards.

And stepped from dark to darker. The interior of the shop was almost completely without light, and as soon as Kittins had come fully inside, even that disappeared. The captain put a hand on his sword.

"What in the infinite hells...?"

The shopkeeper—the alchemist, it could be none else— responded, "You're the Dead One, unless I miss my guess."

Kittins nodded, realized he could not be seen and said, "So they say. But I'm not the one afraid o' the light."

"Nor am I," said the alchemist. "But darkness does offer certain...advantages. Now, you're here to kill me, I suppose."

"I came here lookin' for a remedy for my face," Kittins lied, not in the least perturbed by the alchemist's apparent prescience.

"Just now? I don't think so."

Kittins heard a sound like sand being sprinkled on parchment, and then a lamp suspended from the ceiling cast a fixed pool of light on the alchemist's head. The captain moved to step closer to the other man, but found his feet fixed to the floor.

"Nice trick," said he.

"I've better," said the alchemist. "What I'd like to know is, which of those bastard Shapers sent you?"

"I'd heard you've no love for Burners."

"And you have? The more fool, you!"

"I got no love for 'em. Or anyone."

"Yet you're willing to do their dirty work."

"I never said that," Kittins protested.

The alchemist rolled his eyes in disgust. "Come now. D'you think I've managed to stay alive this long in a Shaper's city by swallowing every lie I hear? You've come to kill me, and I'd like to know at whose behest."

Kittins let out a long breath, resigned. "I was told Her Majesty wanted you dead."

"By her Shaper, I don't doubt."

Give the fellow his due: he was sharp. "Yes," Kittins agreed. "By Cindor."

"Yes."

The alchemist placed his forearms on the counter and leaned over onto them, deep in thought. The light from the lantern, above, barely reached the top of his head now, but Kittins could still make out the man's frown. After several minutes, the alchemist waved a hand and the lamp went out again.

"Come back tomorrow and I'll give you my corpse."

"How's that?"

"Nevermind. Just go."

Kittins went.

The Boy and Omeyo, In Camp

The boy did not know his real name. Omeyo once told him that his father had been one of the End's generals, a man named Shere. But that seemed almost incidental; the boy felt no more connection to this Shere than he did to the birth parents of Anders Cestroenyn, his previous body. The truth was that he'd been many people over the years, his essence had occupied many bodies and developed many personalities, and all of them fought, bickered and squabbled for his attention. It was maddening, in every sense of the word. Still, the boy wondered who he had been at the outset, or what accident of birth or circumstance had set him on this endless and endlessly aggravating search for...definition.

He needed a name, and if he could not recall his birth name, he would have to invent one. Again. He considered "The End-of-All-Things," but the End had been a failure, an arrogant and deluded embarrassment. In his mind, the boy heard the End's vehement denials, his impotent fury. The boy paid no heed. That which did not serve his purpose was irrelevant.

What *was* his purpose, though? He did not seek the annihilation of all life, as had his predecessor. Surely there were some creatures—like the Svarren—whose savagery had the capacity to amuse. And humans had a gift for suffering that was sublime in its constancy and diversity. The boy had seen precious few men, it was true, but he had memories. Or the ghosts of memories. There were other creatures, too, whose darker natures the boy wished to study, and yet he apprehended that before he could indulge his curiosity, he'd have to engage and subjugate these various beings, which notion thrilled him.

Omeyo reminded him often, in his fawning, sycophantic way, that any attempts at conquest would be opposed by the fabled Virgin Queen and her lapdog, Tarmun Vykers.

Suddenly, the boy knew his name.

THREE

Vykers, In Lunessfor

The Reaper was skeptical.

"We lost a lot of good people the night of those riots," Cedna explained. "And we've just about drained our treasury in repairing the damage and replacing our guards. We went from being second-lowest of the Great Eight to the verge of bankruptcy, dissolution and oblivion. It is easy to suspect the other seven houses of our undoing. Too easy. When I ask myself who profits most from the chaos sewn amongst this city's nobility, Her Majesty is the only convincing answer I can find."

Igraine nodded, as if in agreement. But the notion made no sense to Vykers. Her Majesty was a goddess and possessed the power to erase the Eight from existence if she so desired. Why bother with such petty maneuvers when…Abruptly, Vykers recalled the many games of strategy he'd played with the Queen when he'd been bed-ridden. He'd never beaten her. Where he preferred the direct approach in most cases, she exulted in doing the unexpected, the inexplicable. She lived to confound.

So: the Queen had crossed the sea in answer to an unknown summons and, in her absence, she'd set the Eight against one another to prevent them—any of them—from usurping her throne. But she did not destroy them outright, so clearly they served some purpose that Vykers was as yet unable to identify. He wondered if she'd anticipated attempts at retribution from the Eight.

"Her Majesty'll be expectin' one or more o' you houses to move against her."

Cedna shrugged. "Perhaps. But I very much doubt she'll be expecting Tarmun Vykers to show up in her bedchamber."

The Reaper hoped she was kidding. He wanted to take Alheria down a peg or two himself, but he'd no interest in sneaking up on the old hag whilst she slept. If she slept.

"It *will be* the Reaper who goes inside...?" Cedna asked rather forcefully.

"None but," said Vykers.

"Good. The dark ways are no place for a young thing like yourself."

Vykers remained unconvinced. "You've told me why you're willin' to do this, but I still don't see how it benefits your House."

The other woman chuckled softly. "I thought the Reaper wanted access to the castle. You sound like you're trying to talk me out of it."

"I wanted..."Vykers began. "I was told to ask, yes, but also to make sure I got an accurate lay o' the land."

"Here it is, then: the carrion fowl are circling House Blackbyrne. We'll gladly embrace the opportunity the Reaper offers us to direct their attentions elsewhere."

That made sense, at least as much as anything ever did in this Mahnus-cursed city.

"Do we have an agreement?" Cedna asked pointedly.

"We do," said Vykers.

"Good. I like a healthy dose of paranoia as much as the next person, but not if it stands in the way of getting things done."

After making a brief circuit of the room to ensure the two women were alone together, Cedna detailed the location and operation of the door that led into the Queen's castle. "And that," she said when she'd finished explaining, "should conclude our business."

"Not quite," Vykers replied.

Instantly, Cedna became wary. "No?" She relaxed when Igraine held forth a bank note. "What's this?"

"Ten thousand Monarchs."

The Chief of Security was agog. "But how...why?"

"Vykers sent me here to buy this secret. He's got more money than he can spend in a lifetime—ten lifetimes, if it comes to that.

So he won't miss this. And it might just save your House."

Cedna carefully took the proffered note and examined it. "Is this a loan or a gift?"

"Gift."

"Until the day the Reaper comes around looking for another favor."

Igraine frowned. "You could have worse friends."

If the Chief of Security had an answer for that, she kept her mouth shut about it.

"Pleasure doing business with you," said Vykers.

"And you," Cedna responded solemnly.

Spirk, In Camp

He'd been in scarier scrapes, he knew, but Spirk was no calmer for it. Attempting to sneak through knee-deep snow in the dark around a well-guarded cabin he'd only seen in daylight was not an especially comfortable activity. If only Ron had been allowed to come with him. Ah well, it seemed Spirk was forever destined to draw the short straw in life, no matter the situation.

To his credit, he didn't complain or seek to escape his assignment. And it was true that he'd always been able to walk in or out of wherever he'd a mind to go, without causing the slightest disturbance. In fact, he'd even walked right out of the End's camp, once upon a time. 'Course, he'd had his magic stone then. Now, he had Pellas' legacy. He hoped it was good enough—he might've used the word 'potent,' except that he suffered under the misapprehension that 'potent' meant 'penis' and visa-versa, even after he'd once been roundly derided for quaffing some ale and proclaiming, "My, but this be penis beer!"

Strong magic it was then and would have to be, if Spirk were to complete his task and return without arousing suspicion. As he plodded nearer the cabin, he chanced to look up and catch sight of the moon, playing at peek-a-boo behind diaphanous clouds that sailed in haste across the sky.

Wonder where they're goin', Spirk thought to himself. *Wish I could join 'em.*

Back down at ground level, Spirk gazed into the darkness

ahead. Long had recommended that he take "the loneliest way" to Gorivar's place and Spirk had done it. Though a number of tents and shanties pinwheeled outwards from the cabin, there was one approach from the woods that was too far from the rest of the encampment to draw anyone's interest. As much as folk disliked or distrusted one another in town, they craved proximity when camping in the wilds. Thus, they'd left one remote stretch of snowy ground unoccupied and unmolested. Spirk had the damnedest impulse to lie down and make snow ghosts, but he feared he'd be caught if he did.

He paused when he came within shouting distance of the cabin, frozen in place by the passage of two guards—the men who'd come by Long's tent earlier for the rent. One of the men stopped for a moment, as if he'd caught scent of something peculiar and only resumed his trek when his partner hissed at him. As usual, Spirk had not been seen. He thought again about making a snow ghost; again, he dismissed the idea as likely to lead to trouble.

Once the guards rounded the cabin's nearest corner, Spirk screwed up his courage and crept to the closest wall. Great icicles hung from the eaves—a sure sign of a good and constant fire roaring within. Spirk had always been fascinated by icicles and wondered, for perhaps the millionth time, if they'd make good swords. They had no cutting edge to them, of course, but the pointy end looked nasty, and maybe the cold would add something to their value as weaponry. Experimentally, Spirk reached up and yanked on the nearest one—a great spike that stretched almost from the roof to the ground—but found it would not come loose. He pulled harder with the same result. Now, it was war. No stinkin' icicle was gonna humilify Spirk! He noticed there was a corridor of sorts between the cabin wall and the frozen curtain of ice. Bracing himself against the cabin, Spirk lifted his foot to about chest-level and placed it on the back of the icicle. Taking a deep breath, he began to push. Immediately, his foot slipped, and he fell forward, smacking his forehead against the ice, in response to which he rebounded and crashed into the wall, causing both a loud thud and a small avalanche of snow from the roof. He was still trying to clear his head when he heard a shout from somewhere and the sound of men approaching his location.

"Dunno," someone yelled. "Think it came from the backside!"

"Ya," someone else said, "It's round here, I think."

Before Spirk could sort himself out, men were coming towards him from the left and right. To his astonishment, he discovered he'd succeeded in dislodging the icicle, and, not knowing what else to do, he picked it up and held it out in front of himself like the sword he wished it were.

The guards stumbled to a stop in front of him, expressions of hostility and confusion on their brutish faces, and glowered in Spirk's direction.

"What we got 'ere?" one of them asked.

"It's a prowler, innit?"

"Dunno," the first man replied. "Havin' trouble makin' him out."

"What d'yer mean? They's a man there!"

If one the guards had recognized him, Spirk reasoned, it wouldn't be long before he convinced his friend as well. Whatever spell the young Shaper had over Gorivar's men was fading rapidly. Absent other ideas, Spirk thrust the icicle at the fellow who'd seen him. A peculiar sensation of prickling, itching—*burning!*—emanated from the center of Spirk's being and radiated outwards to the very tips of his fingers and toes. In the next instant, a blue light shot from the icicle and into the first guard's chest, whereupon he yelped and stumbled backwards in the snow, only to trip and land on his ass in the knee-deep powder.

"Alheria's frozen underbrush!" the man cursed. "I'm sa cold of a sudden."

The second guard, nonplussed by this turn of events, gaped stupidly at his companion.

"Mauncy! A little help here!" the first man urged through chattering teeth.

By the time Mauncy reached his friend, however, the man was unresponsive. Mauncy let out a startled cry and yelled "Witchery! They's witchery afoot!"

The last thing Spirk wanted was another, larger rush of guards in his direction. Without thinking, he leapt out from under the eaves and bonked Mauncy on the head with the icicle. Again, Spirk was overcome with a burning sensation, and a blue light flashed from the icicle into Mauncy's mane of dark, shaggy hair. Mauncy raised his hands to the crown of his head and began to wheel around in order to get a look at his assailant... and never made it. Instead, halfway through his turn, he began to shudder violently and then, like his friend, topple over into the snow, where he lay motionless.

Spirk held his breath, listened. The expected uproar hadn't developed. He listened harder. Somewhere off in the camp, someone was sneezing uncontrollably. Spirk listened harder still and thought he heard his own heart beating. It was going frightfully fast, and he wondered if it was trying to escape him somehow.

He glanced at the men in the snow, felt a pang of conscience. The icicle in his hand was chilly, certainly, but not unbearably so. What had he done with that icicle? What had he done to those men? Carefully, he knelt down next to the closest of them and studied the man's face. Spirk saw no evidence that the guard was breathing—no telltale plumes of hot breath into the cold winter air, no movement of lips or flaring of nostrils. Worried now, he reached down and felt the skin of the guard's neck, which proved as cold as the snow on which he lay. Spirk snatched his hand back in sudden horror. He'd frozen those men! He felt an impulse to throw the icicle off into the trees, and yet...he might need its magic again before the night was over (already, he struggled to distance himself from what he'd done: these deaths were the icicle's doing, not his own). He retreated from the bodies to the safety of the shadows under the eaves, shivering from a cold within that had nothing to do with winter or magic.

"And that's when I says, 'Listen, you bitch...'"

More guards, making their rounds. Spirk wasted no time in sneaking off in the opposite direction, which was, fortuitously, the way he'd been going all along. He had no interest in encountering anyone else on this mission.

At the end of the cabin's back wall, Spirk chanced a quick peek around the corner, where he saw three figures grunting, groaning and otherwise carrying on as they engaged in what could only have been some kind of sexual activity. Time was, Spirk might've convinced himself something else was going on, something completely innocent. He knew better, now. And he felt confident that, preoccupied as these sexers were, they'd never catch sight of his always invisible self.

He was correct. He had to strike a wide arc around the threesome, because they were using the wall as leverage in their...activities. But he had no difficulty in getting past them and on to the next corner, which rounded, he knew, to the front of the huntsman's cabin. There, Long Pete had warned, Spirk was likely to find the greatest number of Gorivar's men. Stealing a quick look, he found to his surprise that Long was mistaken: there was only one man stationed at the door, albeit a big, ornery looking fellow. Spirk switched the icicle from his right to his left hand, so that he could count the number of guards he'd encountered on his fingers. There were the two he'd frozen. Two others, going the opposite way 'round the cabin, the three goin' at it. And the one in front. That didn't seem like too many to Spirk. He wondered if Long and the rest would agree.

As he had no further instructions and didn't dare try the guard in front by himself, Spirk considered his options for retreat. He knew the guards at his back would reach him soon. Unless they stopped to examine the bodies he'd left in his wake. Then they'd probably raise an alarm. Well, he couldn't go back the way he'd come, he reckoned, and forward was out of the question. Spirk took off running, or as close to it as he could manage in the snow, at an angle perpendicular to the wall. He feared discovery with every labored breath; he needn't have worried: nobody ever saw Spirk Nessno.

Nelby & Esmine, On the Road

Nelby understood suffering, none better. It was bitterly cold in the barn, and she was worried sick for Esmine. Big, the girl might be, but she was still a child. The trauma of being abducted and then seeing her mother die before her had eroded Esmine's normally buoyant spirit to the point where she seemed to have lost the will to fight. Nelby feared it wouldn't be long before the cold, malnutrition or lack of restful sleep snuffed the girl's light forever.

The slavers—for that is what Nelby supposed them to be—who had stolen the former thrall and her charge devoted just enough attention to their prisoners to keep them alive and little more, doing things like moving them into this drafty old barn, for instance, so they could stretch their legs a bit when not on the road. But they were never truly warm, never had full bellies, never got enough exercise, never had enough privacy to do their business comfortably. She would like to have hated the slavers, but that wanted more energy than she possessed. And anyway, the two she had most cause to despise were dead, or so she'd heard, killed by Esmine's mother. She only wished she could have seen it.

She pulled the one blanket her captors had given Nelby and Esmine to share tighter around herself and the girl, hoping that somehow the combined warmth of their bodies would defeat the cold's searching fingers. The girl barely responded to this momentary jostling, giving her guardian even further cause for concern.

What have I got to trade for more blankets or food? Nelby wondered. *Sex*, she thought and quickly shoved the notion aside, in an effort to convince herself such a thing wasn't necessary. *I can cook!* But these slavers didn't seem to care what they ate or how it was prepared. *I can mend things—hose, sweaters, jerkins. I can...*Nothing else came to mind, no matter how badly she wished it. She'd been a young housewife before the End. She'd learned and done everything a housewife did. Everything. She exhaled a shuddering sigh. Sex. The bitter truth was, it was better to give in trade than have it violently stolen with nothing offered in return but injury.

She looked down at Esmine again, took in the girl's hollow cheeks, faintly bluish skin.

It was time to trade.

Hanging her head in resignation and anticipatory shame,

she laid Esmine on her side in the straw, covered her in the rest of the blanket, and walked towards the barn door. She knew there was at least one man on guard on the opposite side and possibly more. She'd hope for one.

As she raised her hand to knock, she was struck by how thin her fingers had gotten, how bony her knuckles. She feared they might shatter against the stubborn wood of the door. She knocked, anyway.

"Ya?" a male voice grunted. "Wot?"

"We could use a little more food in here," Nelby said, "And blankets, too."

Coarse laughter. "Could ye, now? I reckon you'll be wantin' your jewels next, eh?"

There were sizable gaps between the planks in the door; Nelby pressed her mouth to one of them. "I'm willin' to...to trade," she breathed.

"Ha!" barked the unseen guard. "And wot 'ave you got ter trade? Nits? Amusin' stories o' life in the country?"

"You *know* what I've got to trade," Nelby hinted.

The guard cackled so hard at this that he nearly choked on his own tongue. If only, Nelby thought. "Ye think I'd go fer a pale bag o' bones like you? Might as well wait 'til yer dead, then at least I won't 'ave to listen to ye whinin'."

"Or p'raps you're the sort likes little boys," Nelby countered, letting her anger get the best of her.

"Little boys, is it?"

"Yeah, you know, them as can't fight back. Maybe you'll do like your da did to you?"

The guard angrily tore at the door's makeshift lock.

Nelby stepped backwards, but gained no advantage on the enraged guard as he stormed through the now open doorway and grabbed at her with both hands.

"I'll show you wot a real man can do!" the guard growled as he slammed Nelby down onto the frozen dirt. She was powerless to resist him, and in seconds, he had forced himself inside her. Mercifully, this "real man" didn't last more than a minute before he spent himself and then rolled onto his side, heaving like an exhausted bull.

Nelby knew there would be no trade now; not for this. As she lay on her back, contemplating whether or not she should attack the man who lay gasping beside her, he suddenly choked and began wheezing terribly. A crossbow bolt protruded from his throat, just under his jaw, and thick gouts of black blood poured down his neck. Fearing the next would land in her chest, Nelby scuttled backwards like a crab, trying to put as much distance between herself and the door as possible.

"That's a shame," an inflectionless voice called out. "I was aiming for his face."

A new man appeared in the doorway, in silhouette. There was a crossbow in his arms, but he seemed in no hurry to reload it. "What did you say to your friend there to get him so fired up?"

"I asked if I might have more food and blankets for the girl," Nelby lied, motioning towards the back of the barn with her chin.

The newcomer stepped into the barn. It was difficult to make out his features in the gloom, but he was unquestionably younger and more spry than the man he'd just killed. "Aye," said he. "I keep tellin' 'em your girl won't fetch as good a price if she's doin' poorly. Do they listen? Nah. Things'd be different an' I was in charge." With that, the stranger made his way to the still-twitching body on the ground and, loading a new bolt into his crossbow, ensured the guard's death. "Understand, I'm gonna hafta tell the others this 'un tried to defile the girl. If I tell 'em I killed Warny fer goin' after *you*, well, it'll go hard fer me. Most of 'em don't give two shits fer you, beggin' yer pardon."

Nelby nodded, feeling some sort of response was warranted and unable to think of anything better.

"Truth to tell, I been lookin' fer a reason to fix this one fer some time," the young man went on, as he pointed to the corpse with his crossbow.

"Why?" Nelby asked, her voice almost a whisper.

"Why? I didn't like his teeth. Great, big grey slabs they was. His mouth looked like a graveyard full 'o tombstones whenever he smiled. And his breath? Gods!"

Nelby couldn't decide was which worse, her savior's attitude, or his description of the dead man's teeth.

"But now I figure, you done me a favor and I done you a favor. We're bound-like. In a blood pact."

That said, he took another step closer to Nelby, into a spot where the light was somewhat better. He was the handsomest man she'd ever seen, despite the utter lack of compassion in his expression.

Vykers, In Lunessfor

Vykers hoped the woman had been joking. The passage, she'd said, lay underneath the executioner's block in Judgment Square, a place the common folk referred to as Camis' Yard. Once Vykers found the place, he was dismayed at the size of the challenge before him. For one thing, the block itself was gigantic, with enough space across its top for five condemned men to lay their heads side-by-side. The Reaper wondered what sort of an axe could behead five men at a time, or whether the condemned were sent to it one at a time, in full view of their equally doomed neighbors. The other major difficulty was that the yard was surrounded by tall, many-windowed buildings. Even if the block could be moved, he wasn't at all certain it could be accomplished without witnesses. Assuming those miracles had been achieved and Vykers slipped down the hole, the block then had to be returned to its original position, so as not to attract attention.

He'd once been led out of the castle by means of another secret passage, but upon searching for it, discovered the building which contained it had been reduced to a mountain of rubble. Weighing his choices, the Reaper fumed.

But not for long, as he suddenly recalled a ruse he'd been involved in as a younger man, something to do with his old sergeant, Hobnail. Worried he'd lose the thread of this memory, he stopped where he was and leaned against a wall until it came back to him in full force. Yes, he had an idea how he might solve this puzzle, and it was a good thing he had so much gold stashed away, because this plan was likely to prove costly. That bothered him less than the amount of time it would take to execute.

Execute. Executioner's block. Arune would've had something witty to say about that.

So: Vykers needed to hire carpenters, several stone masons, blacksmiths or equally burly types, and a fireworks expert. Fortunately, tradesmen were not hard to locate. Oh, a Shaper could've solved Vykers' problem in seconds, but since he was planning to kill one soon, he didn't think it wise to alert them to his existence. As far as anyone knew, Tarmun Vykers had gone off somewhere (wherever Arune had taken him), and Igraine was just another winsome waif.

The rest of the day flew by whilst Vykers sought out and hired those necessary for the implementation of his plan. In the afternoon, though, he was reminded that his exterior attracted attention in ways and under circumstances altogether different from those that affected the Reaper.

He was walking down a side-street near the barbican in the day's waning light, searching for a brothel he'd heard about as part of the next stage in his plan, when he became aware of the shuffling of numerous feet behind him. Turning about, he saw four men walking directly towards him. Why not? It seemed Igraine could not go anywhere in Lunessfor without provoking some sort of aggressive reaction. Well, Vykers was tired of running. Drawing his dagger from its sheath, he assumed a defensive stance and called out, "You've never seen a young woman before?"

"Not one spends as freely as you do," the foremost of the men replied, as he continued to approach.

"And here I thought it was my good looks," Vykers cracked.

"Oh, aye," another of the men said, "There's that, too."

"Well," the Reaper said, "unless one o' you is fixin' to propose, you'd better back the fuck off, 'cause I ain't in the mood for dancin'."

All four men pulled to a stop, shared a look, and grinned at one another.

"T'aint dancin' we got in mind," a third man offered. "You don't wanna get hurt, you'll do as we say."

As the man spoke, Vykers examined his stance, as well as that of his comrades. The Reaper noted which hands held weapons and the type and length of each. He observed other weapons in belts, or partially hidden under jerkins or heavy fleece vests. He studied the conditions of his would-be muggers' boots, and he spied frost in the shadows at the base of the walls on either side of the street. Finally, he sized up and understood the space available for movement between and around his foes. All this, in seconds. Even without his original body, he felt more than ready for violence.

The men likewise sized up Igraine and couldn't imagine why this sweet little slip of a thing hadn't turned tail and run off yet.

"Come on, then!" the girl spat in challenge.

They came.

The man in front lunged at Igraine, flailing at her knife with his heavily gloved left hand whilst his right groped for her hair. The men behind him spread out, hoping to prevent the girl from slipping past on either side.

Vykers had no trouble ducking under the first man's arms and spinning into his gut, where he planted Igraine's blade halfway to its hilt. *Halfway?* Vykers thought in angry disappointment. *Hate being this weak!* Meanwhile, the target of Vykers' wrath groaned in pain and doubly so when Igraine yanked her blade back out and whirled on to the next victim.

The next man was smarter, holding his short sword at arm's length, trying to keep Igraine from doing to him what she'd done to his friend. A third man grabbed the first and lugged him over to a wall, where he collapsed and lay mewling pitifully. *And these are men?* Vykers sneered. The fourth man moved as carefully as possible to get behind Igraine. Vykers let him. Baiting the fellow into charging, Igraine stepped aside at the last possible moment and smirked as his momentum carried him right into the path of his sneaky companion, resulting in a brief but not-quite-brief-enough tangle of arms, legs and weapons. In the moment of their confusion, Igraine again swooped in and slashed at the backs of legs, gashing through tendons in knees and ankles. Both men went down, howling.

The remaining man, having forsaken his wounded friend, turned towards the uproar and immediately assumed a defensive posture. He was a lean, bandy-legged fellow with a riot of freckles and a wild mop of brown hair. To Vykers' surprise, he was smiling. "Well, that was a right tits-up, eh?" he said merrily. "For us, I mean. Not you."

Vykers was less inclined to kill a man with a sense of humor, though he couldn't have said why under torture.

"I'm of a mind," the smiling man continued, "to mosey back the way I come and forget these last few moments ever 'appened."

Igraine rose to her full height, lowered her blade just the tiniest bit. "Another day, I'd've never let you. But today..." The Reaper was not inclined to be merciful, but he had other, more pressing business on his mind.

Smiles nodded, slowly pulled a pipe from his pocket, slid it between his teeth and sheathed his weapon. "Think I'll go and find a light," he said amiably. "You have a good 'un."

Vykers waited until the man had gone before he turned his attention to the wounded. The man with the belly wound was likely doomed, unless an A'Shea came by unexpectedly. The other two idiots would live, but they'd never be able to run again. The Reaper didn't care. They'd been more than happy, the four of them, to attack a lone girl. Lame as they now were, it was entirely possible these predators would soon become prey. The thought of it made Vykers grin.

After his brief but eventful delay, the Reaper resumed his journey. Upon reaching the end of the street, however, two new figures rounded the corner on his right. Both were familiar. The shabby red knight locked eyes with Igraine and mumbled something to his companion, a towering Ntambi warrior. They stopped in their tracks and watched as Igraine moved past. Once she'd turned the corner herself, Vykers picked up the pace in order to put as much distance between himself and his former trophies as possible. Perhaps a minute later, he heard boots slapping the cobblestones behind him, as both men endeavored to catch up. They'd seen the damage he'd done to the gang up the street and—what?—wanted to question him? Why? Vykers simply did not have the time or the patience for such games. He put on another burst of speed and disappeared into the warren of streets beyond the next intersection. He would find the brothel later; for now, he needed only to remain free of his former slaves.

Kittins, In Lunessfor

At sunset, Kittins returned to the alchemist's shop, only to find it again on the wrong side of the street. He was dead certain it had been on his right the previous evening, and now it was on his left. What kind of fresh fuckery was this? He stood, watching the sun's last light disappear on the west end of the street. Satisfied, he turned and pounded a heavy fist on the alchemist's door, which creaked open at the blow. Kittins' sword was out of its scabbard faster 'n a bat swoops down on a moth. He used the point to push the door open wider. As expected, the shop's interior was dark. An equal absence of sound greeted the big man's ears, no matter how long he held his breath and listened. He stepped in through the door and felt gooseflesh come to his arms and legs. Something...Once his eyes adjusted to the darkness, he saw a pair of legs on the floor, jutting out from behind the counter. The alchemist, he recalled, had promised to produce his own corpse...was this the result? Proceeding around the counter, the rest of the body and the answer to Kittins' question revealed themselves: the alchemist was dead.

Or was he?

Kittins himself was evidence of the uncanny. Why should he suppose otherwise from a man who dealt in it by profession? Bending down, he discovered the alchemist's head had been separated from his neck, though little blood had spilled forth onto his clothing or the floor beneath him. Suspicious, Kittins dragged both body and head out onto the doorstep, where the light was better. That there might be witnesses to his actions bothered him not at all, and he wanted to make sure the head's half of the neck and the body's half were of a piece. He was soon satisfied that they were, which begged the question: why separate them? There were easier ways to kill a man than lopping his head off—a quick thrust to the heart, for example, would serve just as well. And surely the alchemist hadn't beheaded himself...? He must've hired someone. That made no sense, either, since the previous night, Kittins had come for the very same purpose. Why not let Kittins do it, after all?

A voice from inside the shop called out, "Take my head and go. We'll speak again one day."

What in the infinite hells? Kittins turned from the body, stood, and the door slammed shut. As taken aback as he was by this strange turn of events, he knew better than to try the door. It would be locked and warded against any attempt at entry.

He bent down again and grasped the head by an ear, pulling it up into the crook of his right arm. He let loose with a dry, ironic laugh. The people of Lunessfor were in for a treat tonight if they chanced to catch sight of the Dead One stalking by with a severed head in one arm. There'd be many a wench huddling closer to her man this night, and no mistake.

It was Cindor's reaction, however, that most interested Kittins. The Queen's Shaper had sent him on what might as well have been a suicide mission and yet the captain would return victorious, without having sustained any injuries or exerting himself in the least. If that didn't stick in Cindor's craw, he had even colder blood than Kittins imagined.

On that thought, it started to snow. Kittins pressed on, hoping to get back into the castle before too much accumulated. In the first days of his new service to Her Majesty, he'd been forced to go through the castle's main gates. Eventually, the Queen and her Shaper realized that Kittins' activities required greater discretion, so he was directed to an out-of-the-way but still heavily guarded entrance where his comings and goings were far less likely to arouse interest. Fortuitously, this entrance was a good deal closer to Kittins' current position than the main gate, and he expected to be indoors shortly. If there was one kind of weather the big man couldn't abide, it was snow. Fucking snow. Drown him in a pouring rain, roast him in the desert, but keep him out of the fucking snow. Somewhere off in the night, a loud, low boom sounded. Kittins didn't even flinch. Whatever it was, someone else could worry about it. Kittins had a Shaper to antagonize.

The castle guards were well-chosen and well-trained. If they felt any shock or surprise at seeing the captain approach with a head under one arm, they gave not the least sign of it. They knew damned well who the Dead 'Un was, yet they remained as taciturn as mummified corpses. Kittins waved the head at them by way of identification, and they turned slightly to let him pass.

Once inside the castle, Kittins trudged down its long, poorly lit hallways on his way to the Shaper's wing. He couldn't wait to see the look on that bastard's face when he sauntered in and tossed the alchemist's head at him.

But he would have to: the Shaper's door was locked and, Kittins surmised, probably warded as well. He considered leaving the head on the floor outside Cindor's rooms, but he knew that, as his only proof of success in his assignment, the thing was too valuable. It would be just like the duplicitous Shaper to take it and pretend he'd never seen it.

Kittins hoisted the head to eye level, gave it a good once over. He supposed he'd have to keep it in his rooms until the Shaper summoned him. There were a couple of things he didn't like about this arrangement, but he'd have to live with them. He'd been through worse. And the unexpected free time would give him the chance to think more on Cindor's demise. Resigned, Kittins stomped off to his own chambers. One way or another, he'd bring his days as the Shaper's lackey to an end.

The Boy & Omeyo, In Camp

He was asleep, and then he was awake. Confused, Omeyo sat up, looked about himself. The boy stood not three paces distant, watching him with avid interest.

"How do you feel?" he asked.

Omeyo dared not take another moment to assess. "Awake, Master. Wide awake."

"Good," the boy responded. "I might've tried the trusted boot-to-the-backside, but as I need to keep working on my Shaping, magic seemed a better choice."

"I am grateful."

"I am sure you are. It was not done with your comfort in mind, however."

Of that, Omeyo was likewise sure.

"Now tell me, old man, what you observe about your surroundings?"

Omeyo saw the change in an instant. "The Svarren are gone," Omeyo almost sobbed in relief. "Excepting...your sergeants," he said. He almost called them "Tooth and Nail." But he knew the boy would not be amused, and he seemed in a good mood. Best to keep him so.

"And do you know why?"

This one was trickier. Answer poorly and things could get ugly quickly. "You've made a decision about...the Reaper."

The boy nodded, pleased. Beaming, in fact. "No wonder I've kept you alive so long," he said. "I have indeed reached a decision: we are going to war."

Omeyo was surely wide awake now. He'd always known this was coming, but he didn't much understand it.

"I can see you're at a loss. It has to do with my new name, you see."

The old general recognized his cue when he heard it. "Your new name?" he asked like a dutiful sycophant. "And how shall we address you henceforth?"

"Call me 'The Reaper'," the boy commanded, an unmistakable glint of pride in his eyes.

"The Reaper? But won't..."

"Precisely!" the boy roared, his voice a mixture of triumph and rage. "When Tarmun Vykers hears of the atrocities committed in his name, he will, of course, be compelled to come defend that name and stop those crimes. And we shall be waiting for him."

Omeyo felt his bowels turn to ice. If the Reaper had not killed him the first time they'd clashed in battle, he assuredly would this time—especially now that there were two Reapers.

The boy laughed. It was a hard, crackling sound devoid of joy. "Your expressions run the gamut from uneasy to terrified. Do you know no other emotions? Do you not look forward to crushing Tarmun Vykers once and for all?"

"Forgive me, Master, I..."

"Reaper. I am the Reaper," the boy reminded Omeyo, his

voice echoing throughout the cave.

"Yes, Reaper," Omeyo fawned. "I only...where is your host?"

The boy sat down on a pile of pelts, his makeshift throne. "That's the beauty of it! The Svarren have a grudge against Tarmun Vykers. They feel they've been ill-used by him. They tell me they were sucked into a couple of his conflicts, without warning or reason. Their shamans feel the Reaper used magic to cozen them into servitude and pointless death. And now it seems they want revenge!" The boy let this sink in for a few seconds and then concluded, "I shall give it to them. This latest Skargreit was my successful attempt to unite the countless Svarren tribes. Soon, the Reaper and his Svarren companions shall sweep down on the villages of men and our savage friends shall glut and gorge themselves on human flesh. Tarmun Vykers cannot help but respond."

There was nothing else to be said, but "It is an excellent plan...Reaper."

The boy nodded his agreement. "Gather your things, Omeyo. You shall soon be a general again."

Aoife, On the Road

The farther she got from Vykers, the more convinced she became that he'd changed in some fundamental way, that he'd undergone some strange metamorphosis and instead of emerging as a brighter, sharper version of himself, he'd turned into a slug, a dull, shapeless thing of slime. Aoife told herself this feeling was an overreaction on her part, that she'd merely been disappointed, after all they'd been through together, in the Reaper's lack of respect for her. In many ways, he *seemed* a better man, *seemed* more patient, *seemed* more humble. And that was the problem: Tarmun Vykers—the real Tarmun Vykers—was a wildfire, and wildfires are neither patient nor humble, but exist only to destroy.

The A'Shea felt a twinge of self-loathing that she'd ever found such a creature attractive. It went against everything she believed and everything she yet aspired to be or achieve. Thus, she wanted, needed to get as far from Vykers' pernicious influence as possible until she was safe within the walls of Her Majesty's castle in Lunessfor. To accomplish this, she had to reach one of her groves and make use of the Here-There. Strong and resourceful Vykers might be, but he and his Shaper could never follow Aoife through the Here-There. It was a magic only she and the fey were privy to.

And so she forged onwards, pressing ever south and east. It was bitter cold in the forest, both night and day, but the A'Shea didn't care. She'd become almost a thing of the woods, herself, and even in the open fields or on the moors, she was able to make herself comfortable in ways that defied the skills of her sisters.

Comfortable, aye, but driven. For apart from her misgivings about the Reaper, there was also the constant, gnawing worry that her brother had somehow returned. Rather than let this fear feed upon her, however, Aoife resolved to feed upon it instead, to let it fuel her push for Lunessfor, imbue her with the strength of conviction she'd need to convince Her Majesty to act. The truth of it, she felt, was plain: the world could not endure another End-of-All-Things.

Aoife reckoned she could reach the Queen in a week—six days if luck was with her, eight or nine if the weather proved uncooperative. Nine days seemed like eternity.

Spirk, Long & Company, In Camp

"You what, now?" Yendor demanded incredulously. "You say you killed the guards?"

"Not all of 'em," Spirk snapped defensively. "Just a couple or so."

It's amazing, really, how much skepticism a person can convey with only one eye. Yendor, for example, was emoting as if born to the stage, much to Rem's chagrin. "Or so?" Yendor boomed. "Now, what's that mean?"

Spirk quailed at the older man's outburst. "Well," he stammered, "it means I'm not s' sure if I killed a full two or not."

"Explain," Long commanded.

Spirk explained.

When he'd finished explaining an hour later, the group was as confused as they'd been at the start.

"You say you froze these men with a magic icicle?" Rem asked.

Spirk nodded.

"If he says that's what 'e done, that's what 'e done," Ron insisted. "None o' you seen 'im at House D'Escurzy."

It was meant to bolster his friend's spirits, but Spirk turned pale at the reminder.

"But if he killed them," Rem went on, "then Gorivar and the rest of his men will be looking for trouble."

"Not necessarily," Long cut in. "What's suspicious about a couple o' drunken guards freezing to death in a snow storm?"

Eyebrows shot up all around the group, as if directed by magic.

"It's a fair point," Yendor conceded.

Long noticed that Spirk did not seem mollified by this possibility, but he didn't have time or the interest to coddle the young man any further. "Let's talk about how we're gonna handle this Gorivar," he said.

After much discussion, the group decided to kill or disable as many of Gorivar's men as possible. Once they'd dealt with those outside the cabin, they hoped to lure more out into the night. If they got lucky, there'd be no one left inside to defend Gorivar, but the bastard himself. If, on the other hand, Gorivar and his last few men barricaded themselves within, Long felt confident he and his crew would emerge as victors in the resultant siege. A thing like Gorivar couldn't last long without constant feeding: either he'd starve, he'd eat his men, or they'd eat him. Surprisingly, none of those prospects bothered Long in the least.

It was well past midnight when they set out for Gorivar's cabin. As expected, they put Spirk in the lead to scout the way ahead. Rather than split up, they figured their best chance of success lay in attacking whomever they encountered as a solid five. Long was comfortable with five on two, three or even four. If it came down to one man apiece, though...Best not to think about it.

Along the way, Long passed the time in second-guessing himself, which seemed as familiar a practice to him as eating, sleeping or breaking wind. Still, he'd rather be second-guessing himself on tactics and strategy than on the life choices he'd made over the years, particularly with regard to his wife and daughter. He understood that there had to be better ways to resolve his differences with this Gorivar creature, but a large part of him was done with being pushed around by other people and forces; a large part wanted to hurt someone beyond the point of treatment. To his way of thinking, this Gorivar was in the wrong place at the wrong time, trying to shake down the wrong son-of-a-bitch.

Gorivar had extorted the last shim he'd ever see.

There was a brief commotion up ahead. For a moment, Long thought they'd frightened a deer out of the underbrush, but it turned out to be Spirk, panting furiously and white as the snow at his feet.

"What is it?" Long asked impatiently.

"Golibar's got all 'is men outside!" Spirk breathed. "Lined up around the cabin!"

"Mahnus' balls!" Yendor muttered. "Now what?"

Sometimes, timeliness of inspiration is the only difference between a leader and a follower. As it happened, Long suddenly got an idea. "Let's go into the camp and stir up some trouble."

His companions looked at him quizzically, and then Yendor said "I think I've got wind o' ya."

"Sorry," Long replied. "That was last night's dinner."

Long instructed his crew to remain silent until they reached the camp's central bonfire, at which point he'd begin spinning a lie with Rem and Yendor's assistance. He was adamant that Spirk and his friend Ron stay out of it, no matter how badly they might wish to participate. "This has to be done just so," Long cautioned. "One wrong word and we may as well throw ourselves in the fire." Judging by the grave expressions on the two younger men's faces, Long's words had hit their mark.

The bonfire burned day and night and attracted a crowd at all hours, largely because it provided better warmth and light than any of the camp's private fires, but also because, snowed in as they were, the camp's denizens had little else to do. They were not the reading sort, for the most part, and those few who *could* read had long since finished, traded or sold whatever materials they'd brought with them. Card games were a popular pastime, but required a goodly amount of consistent light, whereas dice required a hard surface, and the snow was uncooperative. Wagon beds were best for dicing, but, again, only if there was sufficient light. Absent these options, those around the fire resorted to boasting, singing, drinking or brawling. It was the brawling Long hoped to encourage and to fan, like the fire before him, into a roaring, ravenous conflagration.

He began by stumbling into the back of the biggest body he could find within the bonfire's radius.

"How?" a bearlike voice grunted in irritation. The face from which that voice came was equally bearlike, and before Long could lose his nerve, he launched into his lie.

"Sorry, my friend. Deeply sorry. It's just that I've been runnin' from Gorivar's men…"

"Ha!" the Bear Man barked. "Forgit t'pay yer rent, did ye?"

"Could be," Long replied. "But then, I go up to the fella's cabin, and what do I see?"

Bear Man looked from Long's face to Yendor's and Rem's. Finding no answers there, he asked, "What *do* ye see?"

"He's got his whole gang lined up outside his cabin, like he's fixin' to attack the camp!"

"I heard one o' his men boastin' o' the lootin' he planned to do down here!" Yendor added.

By now, Long's lie had attracted the attention of the men on either side of the Bear Man, and more were getting drawn in with every passing second.

"I heard tell o' rapes they're plannin'," said Rem, assuming a dialect his audience could trust.

"Rapes?" cried the man to the Bear Man's left. "And what's to rape down 'ere but us?"

"I ain't gettin' raped!" yelled a man on Bear Man's right. "I'll *do* the rapin' afore I *get* raped!"

"Stow that!" the Bear Man growled before turning his full attention on Long, Yendor and Rem. Squinting his eyes, he then noticed Spirk and Ron, just at the edge of the fire's light. "Who's them with ye?"

"Those boys? Just stable boys. I'm s'posed to be teachin' 'em a trade, but they're duller 'n whorehouse bathwater."

The Bear Man let loose a tremendous laugh in response and then slapped Long on the shoulder. "You certain they comin' fer us?"

"Can't think of another reason a man 'ud have his private army assembling so late at night..."

Bear Man's eyes took on a dark, steely aspect that spoke of violence brewing. "Murfin, Deaks, you two go and check out my friend's tale. If he's right, you run back here as fast as you can. We won't have much time to git ready."

The men on Bear Man's left and right groused and griped but followed his orders nonetheless. In seconds, they vanished into the darkness. "Now, you boys," Bear Man said, throwing his arms over Long and Yendor's shoulders, "had best sit with me 'til my men return."

Long offered an awkward smile and motioned for the rest of his crew to join the throng 'round the fire. Worst came to worst, his five would have to battle with Bear Man and his two friends. Long imagined that might get the whole camp involved, and the subsequent chaos could somehow be turned against Gorivar. But his primary hope still rested in getting the mob at the fire to act *with* him.

A large bottle of...*something*...was making its way around the fire, and Long kept a close eye on his friend, Yendor, for he knew too well the dark, seductive allure that liquor held for such men. He'd been one himself once upon a time, or as near as makes no difference. Just as the bottle was about to be passed into Yendor's hands, Long reached across the Bear Man's chest and flicked his friend's ear, eliciting a yelp of pain and surprise from the other man.

"I'll have your share!" the captain stated.

Bear Man guffawed at this and said "And I'll take both o' yourn," which was secretly more than fine with Long. Bear Man quickly snapped up the bottle and took a mighty swig, followed by a second and, at last, a third. He then wiped his bearded face with his forearm and let out a lusty belch. "An excellent stout!" he declared. "By Frumda, a most excellent stout!"

Yendor licked his lips, and his lone eye took on the shrewd and shifty quality of a man calculating risks and rewards. Again, Long reached across Bear Man and flicked his friend's ear.

"Ow!" Yendor wailed. "Will ya stop that, Long? I've done nothin' wrong!"

"'T'ain't what you've done, but what you're thinkin' o' doin' worries me."

"And what's 'e thinkin' o' doin'?" Bear Man intruded.

"Stealin' your drink is what!" Long replied. It may or may not have been the truth, but the captain wasn't about to let his friend sink back into an endless stupor if he could help it.

"I didn't...I wasn't..." Yendor protested.

Until Bear Man thumped him on top of the head with the bottle and Yendor fell over backwards into the snow.

Long leapt to his feet and scurried around Bear Man, fervently praying that his friend hadn't been killed by the big stranger's surprising move. Why did every little choice so quickly degenerate into pandemonium? Why did every little action so reliably lead to disaster? Falling to his knees, Long reached down and cradled Yendor's head in his lap. There didn't seem to be any blood anywhere, but that didn't mean...

Yendor groaned. Without opening his eye, he cracked, "Doubt I'da felt worse if I'da drunk that whole bottle, Long." He opened his eye and sought out the captain's face. "In tryin' to save me a deadly headache tomorrow, you've given me a worse one tonight."

"My apologies, old friend," Long chuckled. "Let's pack some o' this snow on top o' your head and see if we can't keep the swellin' down."

Behind him, Bear Man said "I didn't mean to hit 'im s' hard. Guess I..."

"The whole cabin's surrounded by armed men!" came a voice from the shadows beyond the fire's reach.

"That you, Deaks?" Bear Man asked. "Where's Murfin?"

"Comin'," answered a voice clearly gasping for breath.

"We run all the way back, once we seen 'em," Deaks said, drawing nearer the fire. "Big crowd of 'em, all carrying swords 'n axes 'n whatnot."

"Strange thing to be doin' after midnight, no?" Murfin added, finally staggering into the light.

Bear Man looked sternly at Long, Yendor and the others. "Seems you was right. "Can't see no other reason that Gorivar'd 'ave 'is men out like that." So saying, he put his head down for a moment, nodded, and then announced in a booming voice, "There's gonna be a fight. Question is: do we wanna be gettin', or givin'?"

There were twenty or thirty immediate answers to that query, and though they were all different, their meaning was the same: it was better to give than to receive.

Long's eyes sparkled with anticipation.

The Creature, In the Forest

She was drawn from the forest by the odor of wood smoke, a sensation she recognized but could not name. In the distance, black against the snow, stood a small cluster of buildings, a farmstead. The creature, the Wretch, made her way from the shelter of trees out into the open, where only the darkness offered protection. The scent of that smoke pulled at her, though, promising things—nameless, mysterious, wonderful things—and she could not resist.

Her progress towards the farmstead was slow and always painful, made all the more so by her fear of discovery and further hurt. If she could only make the nearest building, she—

Sharp noises assaulted her, made her pull back. Something was lurking in the shadows of that building, something growling and...and barking. The Wretch was frustrated. She knew what the barking thing was. She knew what it meant, but somehow could not put her thoughts together in any useful way. As the thing—the animal—continued to bark at her, she grew frightened, panicked. If she could not make the animal stop barking at her, eventually *they* would come. Who they were, what they wanted was of no interest to her. They were bad. They had caused her great pain, and she wanted nothing to do with them. But...

The wood smoke continued to promise comfort and well-being.

The Wretch rushed at the animal, which snarled and barked more frantically than ever. When she was within reach, it snapped at her, struggling against the rope that restrained it. It barked a final time and then sank its teeth into her arm. The pain was significant, but having suffered much, much worse, she was not distracted by it. With her free hand, she gripped the beast's head, still fastened on her flesh, and began to squeeze. Within seconds the animal whined and let loose of her. In the next moment, she felt its bones crunching in her hand and the warm, wet sponginess of its brain as it oozed through the fissures in the creature's head.

A voice called out into the darkened yard, and the Wretch, still holding the animal's corpse, vanished into the shadow of the nearest building. Then someone tugged on the other end of the rope. The Wretch tore it free from the animal's neck and watched as it seemed to crawl away, around the corner of the building. After several heartbeats, she heard the same voice cursing loudly, in words she was tantalizingly close to understanding. One thing she did comprehend: the owner of that voice was angry. She was afraid of that anger and wanted someplace to hide.

She looked down at the tracks she'd left in the snow. They'd be a problem when the sun came up. For now, she crept back along the wall, away from the voice, and around the building's far side. It was only when she'd reached the opposite side that she realized she still held the animal's—the *dog's*—body. *Can I eat this dog?* She wondered. It did not look like something she'd eat, but then she was terribly hungry. As she hadn't heard the angry voice in a while, she dared a quick peek around the nearest corner.

Across the snow-covered yard stood a small cottage. Yes, that was the word: *cottage*. The cottage was the source of the wood smoke that had beckoned her from the safety of the trees. She breathed in deeply through her nose. She stood, hungry, naked, and cold in the darkness, and still the wood smoke seduced her with its vague promises. She leaned her head—her aching, throbbing head—against the weathered planks of the barn—it was a barn!—and struggled against the temptation to steal or take by force what the wood smoke offered. That path was certain to bring more pain and suffering.

But this time, the suffering would not be hers.

Arune, In Teshton

Arune could not find Aoife. The Shaper had taken too long in deciding to follow the A'Shea, and now the woman might be anywhere. Of course, her stated objective was Lunessfor, but Arune wanted, needed, to intercept her before then. She couldn't risk the possibility—no matter how remote—that Aoife might run into Vykers, or, more likely, that he'd see and make himself known to her. In a city the size of the capital, such a thing seemed implausible, but Arune couldn't afford to be careless. Not where Vykers was concerned. There were forces at work whose desires were as enigmatic as they were ambiguous. That fact alone gave the Shaper pause.

Reviewing everything she knew about Aoife's Here-There, Arune decided the A'Shea would end up on foot well before reaching Lunessfor and probably even its outer villages. Using her Shaper's Jump, Arune could leap into one of these—say, the drab little hamlet of Teshton—and await any news of Aoife's approach. Convinced that further planning was less effective than action, the Shaper willed herself across the leagues in an instant.

And was surprised at how much had changed in Teshton. In such villages, decades and on rare occasions even centuries could pass without the apparent disturbance of a single leaf. The streams ran where they always had, the cows lay in the same shade, the old barn cats chased the same mice. Farmer So-and-So was replaced by Goody What's-Her-Name, and everything ran its usual course...forever.

Except this time. Granted, it was still hours before sunrise, but the place seemed smaller, dingier, sadder somehow.

Walking around in her mercenary guise, Arune noticed the town's three inns had become two, neither of which was open for business—a strange state of affairs in and of itself. But the third inn, which had always been Arune's favorite, was undergoing extensive renovations. The old inn's sign had been taken down and replaced by a new, crudely painted one that read Tharn's Knackery. The Shaper couldn't conceive of a worse fate for the old building and wondered what had befallen the innkeeper and his family.

With little else to do until the town woke up, Arune walked to the bridge, leaned against the rail, and sent out a Questing Ear. If Aoife were nearby, Arune would hear of it.

Kittins, In Lunessfor

A light blazed in the darkness. "What sort of man sleeps in his clothing?" a voice sneered.

Kittins sat up in bed, squinting the sleep from his eyes and working the kinks from his neck and shoulders. He didn't bother to look over at the Shaper when he replied, "Kind o' man who's got Shapers poppin' into his bedchamber without leave and wakin' him the fuck up." He jumped to his feet, a mean-looking knife already in hand.

Glancing at the blade, Cindor remarked, "That's quite a trick...for a brute. You came by my rooms, so I assume you've got something for me?"

Kittins laughed, a cold, ugly sound. "Oh, aye, I've got *something* for ya."

Cindor laughed in return, a sound no less appalling. "Alas, the Queen's already got a fool, though truth be told, neither of you is very amusing. I was referring, of course, to proof of completion of the task you were given."

Kittins' eyes flitted to a small cupboard in the corner, from which a trace amount of blood had leaked.

"Crude," Cindor observed, "but effective. Tell me that's his head and not some other, less useful piece of his anatomy."

"I think he found them all useful. But, yeah, that's his head."

The Shaper waved a hand and the cupboard opened. The alchemist's eyes seemed to be staring at the mage. Cindor shrugged this off. "You might've made a living dressing store windows, if you hadn't become...whatever it is you are." Without pausing to give Kittins room to respond, Cindor went on, "I'm guessing that explosion in South Shore was your clumsy attempt at destroying the evidence of this murder?"

"First of all," said Kittins, "as you commanded me to do this, it was an assassination, not a murder. Blood's on both our hands. Second, what explosion are you talkin' about?"

Cindor offered a sarcastic smile. "Oh, come now. You, with your penchant for setting things on fire? You ask what explosion?"

The captain had heard something on his journey back to the castle, but it was none of his doing. "Yes. I'm askin'."

Now, the Shaper's smile was the widest and most malevolent Kittins had ever seen it, which told him his nemesis was about to strike.

"Let us see how much you love fire!" he said, whereupon flames leapt from Kittins' head, shoulders and torso. In a heartbeat, he was enveloped in a vast robe of fire, trailing off his fingertips, running up and down his legs, sprouting from the tops of his feet. And the pain! The pain was incredible.

Kittins dropped his knife and staggered backwards. Eventually, he fell to his knees. Though his eyes were closed, he could hear the Shaper stepping closer, hoping to get that last, biting jibe in before the captain was completely incinerated.

Like a serpent, he suddenly snapped to his full height, startling Cindor, and latched his hands around the Shaper's neck. Now, Cindor was burning as well.

Then, a whirl of lights and sound, and both men were in a different setting. Smiling now was agony, but Kittins did so, anyway: the Shaper had tried to magic himself out of the captain's grip and failed.

Again the setting changed. Kittins held fast. A tremendous force buffeted against the captain, and still he would not let go of the Shaper's throat. Now, Cindor howled and beat Kittins about the head and shoulders in a panic.

Abruptly, the fire went out, and Kittins discovered that neither he nor his severely damaged adversary could move. Darkness took both men.

FOUR

The Alchemist, In the Castle

The eyes of the head in the cupboard scanned the ceiling as if listening for footsteps on the floor above. From there, they moved to the door and from thence to a spot in the center of the room. The mouth pulled into a smug little grin. Shortly, a whirling speck of blackness appeared in the air above that spot and started to grow. In no time, it was the size of a window, large enough for a man to pass through. And so a man passed through, or most of one, anyway. A headless body clad in dark robes stepped clumsily through the blackness and into the room, whereupon the mysterious portal dissipated completely. The body straightened and turned about several times, like a lost traveler attempting to get his bearings. The head whistled noiselessly through pursed lips and the body, hearing the uncanny, silent trill, spun and ambled towards it, whereupon both parts were reunited. The hands set the head back in its place atop the neck with a wet slurp and made final adjustments to its attitude.

The alchemist was whole again. And inside the castle.

He smiled and then began to fade, becoming a feeble shadow, a paucity of light.

Long & Company, In Camp

The camp had been going stir-crazy. All Long and his boys had to do was give it a little nudge and the resultant hurly-burly took on a life of its own. Bear Man's friends slogged through the snow to rouse as many of their fellow campers as possible, and the ever-growing rumors and conjectures about the pending attack by Gorivar's men enflamed the righteous indignation of any and all who might otherwise have contemplated neutrality.

In a mad rush, the boisterous throng of campers set off up the hill in the direction of Gorivar's cabin, brandishing burning limbs from the bonfire, hammers, pikes, drover's whips or whatever else came to hand in addition to the usual assortment of weapons. The campers made no effort at stealth, but roared and bellowed, cursed and howled their way to the cabin.

The men on guard had been put there in response to the baffling deaths of two of their number and not, as Long had claimed, as prelude to an attack on the camp; however, they were the sort of mercenaries who were well used to arousing the ire of those they oppressed, and so were not especially surprised when the Bear Man's mob came raging towards them out of the frozen night. Or, if they *were* surprised, it was pleasantly so, as they were also the kind of men for whom inactivity was agony and a good fight was better than sex. In their eagerness to engage their attackers, the guards failed to alert their master, charging, instead, headlong into the approaching wave of enemies.

Long was amazed at the clarity with which he perceived all of this as well as the ease with which he had engineered it. He had not, of late, been much used to success and had become wary of anything that smelled remotely like it. Somehow, he feared, this little raid to unseat Gorivar would be Long's undoing. Somehow, it would explode all over him, like something out the back of a dyspeptic cow. Everything in life seemed to do that nowadays.

The majority of the campers were drunk (else they might not have undertaken such a foolhardy task), and Gorivar's guards were not. Most of the campers were not particularly skilled with weapons, and Gorivar's men had years of experience. In their favor, though, the men of the camp had superior numbers and were more rested than their opponents.

In the area around the cabin, the conflict looked like a war of shadows, between shadows. It was difficult to tell friend from foe, except that the Bear Man's crew continued to holler, grunt and boast, whilst Gorivar's guards fought mostly in silence.

It was this difference that allowed Ron to choose targets for his bow and arrows. Yes, he'd famously shot himself in the foot once, but he'd no interest in getting close enough for sword work.

Spirk, too, stayed towards the back of the assault, trying to determine how best to contribute.

Yendor fought to keep up with Long and privately worried about the lack of light. Having only one eye, his depth perception suffered mightily in the dark. He had little confidence in his ability to parry an incoming blow, should the need present itself.

Rem pushed his worries aside. There was no profit in second-guessing himself now. All that mattered was surviving the present, and seeing that his friends did, too.

Long Pete was everywhere, hacking, stabbing and slashing like a man possessed. For weeks—months?—he'd been swallowing his emotions, his despair, his rage, and now that he had occasion to vent, to exorcise the demons that tormented him, he swept through the fracas like a butcher's mechanical meat grinder. He took injuries, of course, but those he meted out were far greater in number and severity. The silhouettes of nameless guards became the embodiment of everything that had hurt Long over the years, and he punished them accordingly. He was no master swordsman, but in the darkness and chaos of combat, he might just as well have been. Fleetingly, he marveled at this strange transformation that had turned him from a soft and middling officer into an avatar of destruction. What in the infinite hells was happening to him?

During a brief lull in which he'd been unable to find an adversary, Long saw that the dead were piling up on both sides. Through a small stand of trees, he caught a glimpse of Bear Man, pounding someone's skull to paste. In the other direction, a camper and guard rolled on the ground, grappling for any advantage that might end that one exchange and free the victor for the next challenger. Most surprising, to Long's eye, was that the path to the cabin's front door was free and clear. *It might be a trap,* the captain warned himself. And then: *fuck it. Might Be's never been a friend to me!* The captain put two fingers to his lips and whistled in Yendor and Rem's direction

They stumbled to his side. He simply pointed at the unobstructed front door.

"Where's Spirk and that other fella?" Yendor gasped.

"Right here!" Spirk protested, thumping himself a little too hard on the chest and gesticulating at Ron. "And don't start tellin' me you didn't see me. That's only for enemies!"

"Well," Yendor answered, "in fairness…" He pointed to his eye patch.

"What's the plan?" Rem asked, cutting through the banter.

"We rush the place and focus our attacks on the monster."

"Monster?" cried Spirk, alarmed.

"Gorivar," Yendor clarified.

"Right," said Long. "We kill him, his men should lose their *enthusiasm* for the job."

The captain made a special point of looking everyone in the eye. He wanted everyone in agreement, everyone in unison. They were a terribly small force, and if even one of them wandered off on his own…It didn't bear thinking on. "Let's go," he said.

As hoped, they had no trouble reaching the entrance with everything else going on. Long swept aside the curtain of skins that served as a door in the newly remodeled opening and led his crew inside.

Gorivar lay sprawled on an enormous pile of furs atop the former occupant's bed, wearing an expression of irritation but not anger. "I mighta guessed," he drawled, and before Long or any of his companions could so much as lift a finger, they rushed towards the ceiling and crashed into it with great force. Everyone except Spirk, that is. Then, following the pattern they'd all seen before, they fell to the floor with an equally great crash.

"You stop that right now!" Spirk yelled at the gelatinous tyrant on the bed.

The group smashed into the ceiling again, with a chorus of grunts and cries.

"Do something, boy!" Long yelled from the rafters.

Long and company fell again. Spirk noticed, to his horror, that Yendor was bleeding from a split lip and Rem seemed unable to open his left eye.

"Stop doin' that!" Spirk screamed at Gorivar, who laughed heartily in response, so that his whole body giggled like pudding.

"Or what?" the fat man gloated.

Whereupon he, too, shot to the ceiling. Because of his mass, however, he crashed right through the roof and disappeared into the night. Snowflakes and splinters were all that returned though the ragged hole he'd made.

Long looked up from the floor and saw that Spirk's face had turned an unhealthy shade of crimson, and his mouth had pulled into a small, tight line. With some effort, the captain got to his feet and staggered into a position just shy of the hole. He stared at it. "Shouldn't he be coming back this way?" he wondered aloud.

A very loud, very wet thud sounded outside the entrance. Everyone turned in that direction, consumed with the same question: was that…?

Ron ran to the door, slipped past the skins, and was gone. "It's him!" his voice called from outside. "Gods, what a mess!"

The group felt powerfully tempted to stare at its erstwhile Shaper, but no one dared. He seemed in a fragile mood, to say nothing of the fact he'd just thrown a thousand pound man through a ceiling and into the sky beyond. Long rather conspicuously pondered his own feet, whilst simultaneously marveling at the change in his young friend. Time was, the boy couldn't have counted to two without getting lost on the way to one. Now? He'd become every bit as strange as the monster he'd just killed. He'd become someone capable of turning enemies to crystal, or ice, or, as the current case seemed to suggest, jelly.

"One o' you boys did that?" the Bear Man called from the doorway.

Not wanting to tip his hand, Long simply nodded.

"I never seen the like of it," the other man said, shaking his head in disbelief. "Whoreson brute went crashin' right through the roof an' up into the sky. Right through the roof, I say, like sparks up a chimney, and then down into the snow. Never heard a sound like that, neither."

Long moved closer, placing himself between the Bear Man and the young Shaper. "He's dead, though, and that's all that matters."

"What o' the rest of 'em?"

The captain slid past the larger man and peered out into the night. There were few men on either side left alive, but the guards that remained quickly appraised their chances of survival and concluded, predictably, that they needed to demonstrate that they held no lingering allegiance to the dead tyrant, and so turned on each other. Safety lay with whoever had killed Gorivar, and loyalty be damned.

Long, Bear Man, and the rest of the campers let the guards go at it. Eventually, only two remained. They dropped their weapons and stood where they were, hoping that somehow their actions had earned them another sunrise.

Bear Man turned back to Long and his crew, an eager glint in his eye. "And the spoils?"

"You and your friends can have the lot, whatever you find."

Bear Man couldn't believe what he'd just heard. "The lot? Mahnus' balls, man, that's the cabin, everything *in* the cabin, everything on these dead, and everything our dead mates've left back at camp."

"The lot," Long confirmed. "My boys and me are leavin' soon as the skies clear and the snow abates." Having nothing more to say, he nodded at his comrades and turned back toward his own campsite.

The bloodstained snow he traversed along the way reminded him too well of another, larger and more desperate battle he'd once fought in snow. Try as he might, he could not avoid thinking about his old friend Janks, how Long had killed him, and how Janks had somehow risen from the grave. Bad as that was, the man had lost all memory of his previous life. He was alive now, yes, but the friendship, the history, the bond between the two men had disappeared like an ill-remembered dream, something that had only seemed real in the moment, but which faded with the rising sun. And so, Long had abandoned the new

Janks to his fortune in the capital, but not before Long offered the same good wishes he'd have extended to any stranger.

But why had Janks come back in the first place? How was it possible? When Long needed escape from the guilt and grief that tormented him over Mardine's death and his daughter's abduction, his mind invariably sought out what he thought of as the 'Janks Conundrum.' But although he'd spent countless hours going over and over these questions, he never got any closer to understanding. He wondered if he was cursed, in some way, to spend the rest of his life approaching but never arriving, gaining on, but never grasping.

If that proved the case with Esmine...

Kittins, In Lunessfor

Kittins had never imagined that opening one's eyes could be so painful. His charred lids creaked and crackled just wide enough to allow him to acknowledge Her Majesty's jibe, and then he closed them again.

"Yes," the old bitch sniped, "I get more thoughtful service out of my livestock."

"I'd heal faster. If I had. A little peace. And quiet," Kittins rasped.

"You'll find no shortage of either in the grave," Her Majesty quipped. "Which is where you seem bent on going, in spite of that amulet you wore."

Wore? That got Kittins' attention. Once again, he forced his eyes open, only to see the Queen grinning at him.

"I haven't taken it, if that's what you're thinking." She paused for dramatic effect. "No. It seems to have sunken into your chest, strangely. If you could move your hands, you'd feel it right under that bacon you call skin." Again, Her Majesty paused, thinking. "It's a curiously powerful object, that amulet. Well beyond the abilities of a mere swamp witch, and I wonder: why give it to *you*?"

"Is there. Any. Water?" Kittins asked.

A pair of hands appeared on the left side of his head. A ladle made its presence known against his lips—or whatever was left of them. Much of the water trickled through his teeth and down his chin.

"The A'Shea have been attending you constantly. You might thank them, when you have a moment," the Queen said archly. "Now, what was I...? Ah, yes: you and my Shaper are done fighting. Am I understood? Nobody cares which of you can piss the farthest."

"Then he's. Still alive," Kittins managed.

"Of course he's alive, you big oaf! I go to great pains to protect my assets—which include you, by the way—and I won't have you doing any more damage to one another. There are bigger things at stake here than your laughable need to be cock-of-the-walk!"

If she said more, Kittins missed it, lapsing into unconsciousness before he was even aware it was happening.

There was less pain the next time he awoke, but his eyelids still creaked when he opened them, a sound reminiscent of a man shifting in the saddle.

"Drink," a voice said softly, and the ladle reappeared near his mouth.

This time, Kittins caught a glimpse of his Mender and offered his thanks. She said not a word in response, but nodded in acknowledgement.

Beyond her, Kittins saw another body in a second bed. Cindor. Her Majesty had put them in the same room! In a castle the size of a small city, with hundreds and hundreds of rooms, she'd put the two men in the same bloody room. Of course she had!

As if he'd been following Kittins' thoughts, the Shaper turned his head—with some difficulty, Kittins was pleased to note—and glared at him. The hatred was still there, burning as brightly as ever, if the actual flames that had scarred both men were not. Kittins glared right back at his nemesis and saw great bruises along the man's neck. On either side of these were gruesome burns that spread either up or down for a good ten to twelve inches. The Shaper's face was burned to his nose, making him look as if he were wearing a mask of some sort. His lips were swollen and misshapen, but in better shape than Kittins' nonetheless.

"Cat. Got. Your tongue?" Kittins croaked.

In lieu of a response, Cindor continued to stare.

"Fuckin' Shapers," Kittins muttered. "No sense. Of humor."

Later, Kittins woke in excruciating pain. Someone was shredding his skin to...An A'Shea was gently cleaning his burns with a wet cloth, but each stroke felt, to the captain, as if he were being flayed alive.

"Stop!" he barked.

An aged and familiar hand came into view from his right side and touched Kittins on the chest, whereupon the pain disappeared immediately.

"You will be nice," the Queen commanded, her voice level and calm, "or the pain you've felt will seem pleasant in comparison to what's coming." She lifted her hand, and proved her point: Kittins screamed in agony. Her Majesty's hand returned to his chest: the pain vanished. She raised her hand again: the pain returned. She restored her hand a final time.

Gasping for breath, Kittins squawked, "You're an A'Shea?"

A faint upturn at the corner of the Queen's mouth was the only evidence of her amusement. "You could say that. And so I don't take kindly to anyone abusing my staff, especially when they've devoted untold hours making you comfortable."

Kittins shot a glance over at Cindor, who appeared to have been smirking throughout this exchange. Returning his attention to Her Majesty, Kittins asked, "How bad is it?"

"I was under the impression you didn't care about such things." The Queen waited for Kittins to confirm or deny her assessment, but he said nothing. Eventually, she went on. "You won't die, if that's what you're worrying about. In fact, you're healing better and faster than expected, and you already know why. But I very much doubt you'll ever reclaim your boyish good looks. There's only so much your little amulet can accomplish."

"So I'll be even. Uglier than before."

"Vanity, Captain? You surprise me."

"Used to dream of. Having a son or five."

"And now you're afraid the ladies will run in terror at your visage?"

Kittins would have laughed if he'd been able. "They've been doing that. Since the End. But now..."

"You're a monster, yes. No face to speak of, the rest of you an horrendous mass of scars..."

The sound of wheezing in the far bed let Kittins know that his suffering was Cindor's delight. Her Majesty gestured at the Shaper, and he went silent.

"What's the point in this?" Kittins demanded, nodding in Cindor's direction.

"I should have thought it obvious," Her Majesty responded. "It's a test. And the mere fact you're asking doesn't bode well."

But Kittins had lost interest at the word "test." He'd lost all patience with others' plans for him, too. Sooner or later, he had to escape Her Majesty's influence. Only then could he resume his quest for vengeance.

The False Reaper, On the Attack

They came out of the hills just before dawn, silent as snowfall—a challenge for Svarren, but one whose rewards promised to exceed all precedent, if the Master could be believed. And because of their silence, they managed to reach the first homes before the town's dogs caught wind of them and set to baying their primordial alarm.

The little town's militia scarcely had time to arm itself ere the savages were through the outer circle of homes and into the more populous center. Before many of the townsfolk even had the opportunity to rub the sleep from their eyes, they were granted permanent sleep.

The Svarren burnt, smashed, devoured and ravaged, all whilst repeating the name of Tarmun Vykers over and over in odd, reverential tones. It was not long 'til they'd butchered everyone in town, save for a single family. As the sun rose, a father, mother and two daughters found themselves in the snow-covered fields behind their cottage, completely surrounded by a sea of Svarren. The little family pulled together as tightly as possible. The mother and her eldest daughter closed their eyes, not wanting to see their deaths approaching. The father and his youngest daughter, however, kept their eyes wide—he, in order to fend off the first attacker, at least, and she, in simple defiance. A voice at the back of the Svarren spoke a single word and the creatures parted, allowing the speaker passage to the doomed family.

A figure in crude armor appeared, strolling almost casually into the center of gathering.

"Who are you?" the father demanded with a slight quaver in his voice.

"Ah!" the armored figure replied, "There are four of you. Excellent."

"Who are you?" the youngest daughter repeated boldly. She would not live to see her next meal, perhaps, but she'd done her father proud.

The stranger advanced and put out a hand, as if to touch the girl's hair, and she batted it away. Her father gasped. The mass of Svarren fell silent, and this time, the stranger's hand moved so fast it was barely visible. He grabbed the girl by her hair and pulled her close to his faceplate. "There are worse things than death, girl." He manipulated her head so that she could see the Svarren surrounding her.

"Please don't," the girl's father said as forcibly as he dared.

"Or perhaps I should give the other two to my Svarren and make the little one watch..." the stranger mused aloud.

"I'd rather you killed us all," the mother said at last.

"You'd rather?" the stranger laughed. "You'd *rather*, would you?" He turned to the Svarren, now practically drooling upon the little family. "Our captives would prefer we killed them! Isn't that wonderful?"

If there's any sound more frightening than the bloodthirsty howling of Svarren, it has to be their laughter. The family seemed to shrink under the weight of it, as if they would melt into the snow beneath their feet.

"Your desires," the stranger snapped, "are of no interest to me." He waved his hand, and the Svarren ceased laughing. "You asked who I am," he said to the father. "I am the Reaper." He was gratified to see confusion and yet more fear on the man's face. "Your little girl, here, will travel south and tell anyone she finds that I have mustered an army and intend to claim my kingdom at long last. Your other daughter, the coward, will go north with the same message. Their dam shall go west with the same, and you, east. You'll likely never meet again, but with any luck, one or more of you may survive." So saying, he turned back to his Svarren and said "Give me four teams of five, to ensure these good folks do as I've commanded. Run them until they drop."

In no time, the little family, each of its members weeping, was ushered out of the False Reaper's sight, though not out of his awareness. "Let us make camp here whilst we scout our next target. Your brethren," he announced to the Svarren, "need to know where to find us. They'll have an easier time of it if we if we're not spread all over the countryside."

Tooth and Nail nodded their agreement.

Omeyo, however, bit his tongue. It seemed he was destined to keep making the same mistakes over and over, landing himself in the same predicaments. Again, he was part of a gathering hoard, led by a monster that meant to take on the greatest warrior the world had ever known. Omeyo anticipated a similar result, though he very much doubted he'd survive this second go-round.

Vykers, In Lunessfor

With the sunrise, construction began in Camis' yard, and Vykers' latest plan was in motion at last. He was pleased with the efficiency of those he'd hired, for although the prospect of wasted money bothered him not at all, he was positively itching to get inside the castle, and wasted time would have been unendurable.

In less than an hour, the solid framework of a gazebo-like structure rose around the execution block. Shortly thereafter, walls of thick canvas enclosed the space, making the whole thing look like a multi-tiered cake. By noon, artists had arrived and begun painting the canvas. Curious locals wandered by occasionally and were told the structure was meant in celebration of winter and that there would be dancing girls and fireworks after the sun went down. An officious looking fellow came by and demanded to see building permits. Fortunately, Vykers had anticipated such an occurrence and hired a big bruiser to handle both intimidation and bribes. The official went away with a handful of Merchants and his dignity in tatters.

By late afternoon, the structure was complete. The bruiser stood guard while Vykers awaited his "dancing girls," some additional muscle, and the fireworks master. A sizable crowd had gathered along the yard's periphery, but the Reaper was not concerned. By and large, people were fools for spectacle.

Just as the first flakes of snow began to fall, the dancers arrived—a mob of scantily clad whores whose only nod to the weather was a bit of fur here and there. Behind them came five large, burly fellows that Vykers had hired away from their regular jobs as blacksmiths, stone masons, and the like. Bringing up the rear, as if they'd all travelled together, was the fireworks master. Being something of a celebrity, his appearance set off a round of cheers amongst the spectators that quelled the catcalls offered the whores. As planned, the Bruiser lifted a flap on the structure's exterior and the fireworks master and the whores crept inside. Nobody seemed to notice that Igraine had joined in with the women. Moments later, the girls reappeared on the structure's topside, on the first and second levels. Then the fireworks master opened a hatch on the third level and climbed into view, setting his large case of surprises by his side. Finally, the muscle went through the flap, which was then closed and guarded by the Bruiser. At the edges of the crowd, previously unnoticed musicians began to play a boisterous tune, which set the girls to dancing, much to the crowd's delight. Atop the structure, the fireworks master set off his first explosion.

Vykers didn't see it, though, because he'd remained inside, on the ground level, directing the muscle into position to slide the executioner's block aside. He'd intended to wait until the fireworks had reached their loudest point, but the crowd made so much noise that waiting wasn't necessary. With a gesture, he set the men in motion, grasping and heaving the big block inch-by-inch to one side. It seemed to take an eternity, during which time, the interior of Vykers' structure was intermittently bathed in weird shadows, cast by the fireworks exploding beyond the dancers, just overhead. The Reaper worried that the fireworks master would run out of supplies before the secret entrance to the castle was exposed, but he needn't have. A cool draft wafted up from below, carrying with it an odor of dust.

If the muscle were surprised at this turn of events, they kept their thoughts to themselves. They'd been hired to move something heavy...and shut up about it. Igraine had threated Vykers' ire if they disobeyed this order. That was usually enough to guarantee silence.

"Pull this stone back into place once I've gone down," Vykers instructed. "The man who showed you in has your pay and further instructions." Vykers pulled a torch from a bundle he'd laid by earlier, sparked it to flame and took the rest under Igraine's arm. He made a final survey of the men he'd hired, looking each in the eye, and then cautiously stepped to the edge of the hole. A well-fashioned if dusty stairway descended into blackness. "Now, that's my kind of hole!" Vykers breathed, thinking of his experience in the tunnels of Morden's Cairn.

About ten steps down, he heard the stone begin to slide back to its former position. He felt no need to look up and confirm this, since the stairwell grew darker by the second and the occasional flashes of fireworks completely disappeared. Up top, he knew the show would go on for another quarter hour or so, after which his builders would disassemble everything and keep the materials as part of their payment. Only the muscle he'd hired knew of the structure's true purpose, and they'd never defy the Reaper.

Vykers moved down the passageway, all of his senses on alert for anything unexpected—sounds, odors, flashes of movement. The dust beneath his feet—his ridiculous, tiny feet—was undisturbed as far as the light from his torch revealed it. No one had come this way in ages. Consequently, Vykers relaxed, confident that he was unlikely to encounter anyone. Although he usually wielded a sword in battle, he'd always been something of a blunt instrument himself. Now, his success and continued survival depended on stealth and guile, two qualities he'd never tried overmuch to cultivate. Almost, he laughed. It was never too late to learn, it seemed.

Hundreds of steps later, he came to a crossroads of sorts, a square-ish chamber from which other passages led off in unknown directions. Vykers cursed. Which should he take? He moved to the middle of the chamber and considered the entrance of each tunnel. A few looked as if they'd never been used. An equal number appeared quite popular. One, however, stood out as the path most likely to lead into the castle, by virtue of the myriad scuff and scrape marks along its floor and the relative lack of debris. Of all the options, this passage had clearly seen the most use, which meant that it came from or went to the most important destination. With a satisfied smirk, Vykers entered.

After an hour's walk, though, the Reaper's confidence in his choice began to wane.

Why am I always choosin' the wrong fuckin' tunnel? He asked of the Shaper who was no longer around to hear his complaints. "And the wrong fuckin' friends," he said to himself.

Abruptly, he came to a tee in the passage. "Dammit." He'd chosen left when he should have gone right in Morden's Cairn. He chose left again. Ten minutes down this latest passage, he came across footprints.

They weren't human.

The Giantess, On a Farmstead

There was no point in delaying any further.

She rushed at the house and smashed through the door like a boulder thrown from a catapult. In the moment it took her to come to a stop and gain her bearings, she discovered she'd trampled one of the cottage's occupants into the floor. If he was not yet dead, he was well on his way.

Someone—a man—screamed from across the room, and she looked over just in time to see a sword swooping towards her face. She flung her left arm at it, in hopes of batting it away, but the weapon dug into her flesh, halfway between wrist and elbow. Jerking her arm away, she pulled the sword from her assailant's hands and made ready to bash the man's face in with her right fist.

And then she spotted the girl.

Tiny, she was—wouldn't have come up to the giant's knees. The child stood in the corner, still clutching her bedclothes, eyes as wide as full moons. There was such fear in those eyes that the giantess felt a pang of...*something*. Shame? Memory? Whatever it was, it stole her breath, burned worse than the sword still lodged in her arm. With a roar of confusion and frustration, the Wretch yanked the sword free and tossed it aside.

Her attacker retreated a couple of steps and cast about for something else with which to continue his assault.

The giant used the opportunity to storm back through the hole she'd created and dash off into the brightening dawn. At her back, she heard voices—the dying man and the child had not been alone in their home. The giantess continued to run, racing past the barn and making for the woods as fast as her legs would carry her. She felt a sharp blow to her shoulder and without knowing why, understood she'd been hit by an arrow. Unless she eluded pursuit, there would be more and more, until she fell.

Twigs and branches snapped endlessly under her feet; trees flashed by like memories. The sounds of pursuit grew fainter, but the giantess knew she was running from more than corporal jeopardy: the sight of that little girl had awakened something in her mind that threatened far worse than physical harm, that promised more-lasting damage.

The giantess pushed it aside, focusing only on her next step. Arrows continued to fly around and past her. Another one slammed into her lower back. The unseen archer, it seemed, was not to be shaken as easily as his companions. The giantess risked a glance over her shoulder...and tumbled headlong down a steep, almost cliff-like incline, smashing into trees, bushes and boulders as she fell. Finally, the hillside disappeared altogether, leaving her in panicked freefall towards the forest floor far below. She had a moment to wonder how much the impact would hurt, and then she found out.

She was warm. A soft, amber-colored light crept through her cracked eyelids, and the scent of food both tantalized and tortured her nose. If she'd harbored any illusions that things could not get more bewildering, they were quickly dispelled when she opened her eyes all the way.

She lay in a bed, an enormous bed that was nearly giant-sized, with several blankets spread over her aching body. A wondrous pillow supported her head. On a small table to her left sat a pitcher, accompanied by a mug. The light came from an ornate oil lamp on another table to her right. There were windows farther to her right, but they were shuttered against the night.

Was it night already?

The walls of the room were decorated with an intricate woodland mural that stretched from floor to ceiling. Will-o-wisps and faeries danced amongst the mural's trees and undergrowth. The foot of the bed faced the room's only door, which was slightly ajar.

The giantess considered calling out, but wasn't prepared to encounter anyone or anything else at the moment. Her head hurt like the infinite hells—and wasn't *that* a curious phrase? Where had it come from, and what did it mean? Her joints throbbed, her left leg was a blaze of agony, and her ribs complained with every breath. But the arrows she'd been stuck with had been removed, so the news was not all bad.

The giantess dozed off, only to be awakened by the sound of the bedroom door creaking open. Apprehensively, she gazed over her blankets to learn the identity of her savior and wondered if she wasn't in fact still dreaming.

At the foot of her bed stood a matronly, well-groomed and fashionably dressed Svarren woman.

Aoife, On the Road

The last few days of travel would have to be done on foot, or, if she was lucky, on a pony or atop someone's wagon, because Aoife's Here-There could only carry her from grove to grove. And then, only those she'd birthed. Lunessfor and its environs were beyond her magic.

But walking gave her time to think, or, more accurately, to dwell upon the questions that had been plaguing her for leagues. Chief among them was: who had spoken to her of the

End's survival? The voice had been brief, "He lives." She'd barely had time to register the message, much less note its character. Had it been Vykers' Shaper? Was it impossible that it might have been Alheria? And could the A'Shea completely rule out hallucination? As much as that prospect disturbed her, it was nothing compared to the thought that the voice had come from Anders, himself.

No matter. Her sisters, the other A'Shea, would help her sort this mess out. Oh, they were wary of her, and some held barely veiled resentment towards her, but when it came to the End-of-All-Things, everyone in the kingdom was on the same side—or had been.

As much as Aoife wanted to share her fears with the Queen, she was also looking forward to a long, hot bath. She'd become impressively self-sufficient over the last few years and could spend months on her own in the deepest wilderness without the least discomfort. But a hot bath was one of life's great indulgences, and she yearned for one the way a drunk years for his next drink.

Ah, but the Queen. What if Her Majesty refused to see Aoife? Or saw her, but dismissed her concerns? No one alive knew Anders like Aoife, just as no one alive knew they were siblings. That secret might be her trump card, if the A'Shea played it correctly; it might also be her doom if anyone supposed that she and the End shared more than blood. Or they might simply convict her of guilt by association. But of course she hadn't *associated* with him since she was a girl, and he…well, he'd been different, then.

Shadows stole across Aoife's path. Somehow, dusk had snuck up on the A'Shea, catching her all but unawares. *I've got to pay more attention to the world outside my head*, she scolded herself. The cry of a lone wolf somewhere off to her left seemed to underscore the point. *And I've got to make camp.* She was not afraid of the wolf, or even a pack of them. She was as much a thing of the forest now as they were. For all that, she hoped to pass the night without incident.

She was not like the Reaper, ever invigorated by the prospect of battle. She was, as she'd once tried to tell him, the very antithesis of Tarmun Vykers.

And yet, she could not chase him from her thoughts.

Action, perhaps, was the best tonic, and so Aoife strode

from the path and into the trees. After a hundred strides or so, she found a spot to her liking and reached into the earth with her thoughts. In no time, vines broke through the crust of old snow and sprouted into the air, curling and weaving around one another. Aoife stood at their center, and, within minutes, was completely surrounded by a thorny, impenetrable barrier that reached well over her head. The snow and ice melted into the soil, and a rich carpet of moss rapidly took their place. Next, a small clump of mushrooms burst into view, glowing with faerie fire, offering the A'Shea light, warmth, and a source of food.

These were not powers enjoyed or practiced by anyone in the Sisterhood. But to the Sister-Mother of Nar, they were as natural and as easy as breathing.

Inside her fey shelter, Aoife was safer and more comfortable than most of the people in Her Majesty's realm.

Nelby & Esmine, On the Road

Her handsome savior's name was Innoman. Whether that was his first name or his last, Nelby hadn't the courage to ask. The young man seemed nice enough, but there was something about him too eager to please. And who was Nelby, that he should worry what she thought? She played along, of course, out of concern for Esmine, humored Innoman's moods, nodded after his every suggestion, and in all other ways did her utmost to convince him of her loyalty to him. Trust him, though? Not in the least. The former thrall had learned through painful experience that people were very seldom what they seemed, with the possible exception of Mardine, Esmine's mother.

But Mardine was dead.

And why did it always seem that the good paid, whilst the bad stayed?

"Hungry," Esmine said, from the pile of blankets Nelby had won for her.

"I know, love. He'll be by soon, I'm sure." At least she *hoped* Innoman would be by soon.

She looked through the bars of the cage she shared with Esmine. It was bad enough on its own, but fixed atop one of the caravan's flatbed wagons, it offered no shelter from the cold, no protection from sudden, bone-jarring jolts caused by unseen or unavoidable potholes. The girls' captives claimed they wanted Esmine in good condition when they passed her along to her new owners, but they surely didn't behave like it.

Except for Innoman, whom Nelby didn't quite trust.

Now that the storm had abated, the caravan had resumed its journey north. Desperate as she was, Nelby wondered for the thousandth time if escape might be possible. With snow on the ground, she and Esmine were bound to leave obvious tracks wherever they went. Too, food would be virtually impossible to find. Finally, without shelter and fire, an icy death was a foregone conclusion.

But was it worse than whatever awaited at the journey's end? Might it not be better to die cold and hungry but free than live warm and well-fed but a slave?

I hate being a coward! Nelby admonished herself.

"What's that faraway look portend, eh?"

Innoman appeared out of nowhere, riding beside the girls' wagon. Again, Nelby was struck by his looks.

"Nothing. Just missing home."

Innoman chuckled. "You'll 'ave t'get used to that, love. You're not like to see it again."

"True enough." What else could she say?

"I've got somethin' for ya," said Innoman slyly.

"'Ave you?"

"Nice little bit o' rabbit." He looked around first before handing it over, which told Nelby this kindness was a risk on Innoman's part. And when men took risks for women, well, they usually expected something in return.

"Thanks," she said, avoiding eye contact as she reached for the meat.

"Just tryin' to make sure you two stay strong," Innoman smiled.

"And we're grateful. We know you been good to us."

"Aye," said Innoman, before putting his heels to his horse and riding away.

"Aye," said Nelby to herself, still worried what the future

cost of such kindness might be. She, too, looked around to ensure no one had seen her receive the rabbit's leg, and then, comfortable it had gone unnoticed, she examined her prize. It was a pitiful thing. Hardly enough meat on it for one person, let alone two. Well, she'd give it all to Esmine. Maybe the girl would leave a small bone or two for Nelby to chew on. There might even be a bit of marrow, if she was lucky.

Gently, she leaned into the child and held the rabbit under her nose. It took a moment, but eventually Esmine's eyes cracked open and she squinted at the gift. "Rabbit?" she whispered weakly.

"Aye."

"All for me?"

"Aye. All for you, sweetheart."

Against Nelby's expectations, Esmine did not wolf the meat down, but gently, almost tentatively, pulled it apart, putting only the tiniest of slivers into her mouth.

"Taste alright?" Nelby asked.

"Mmm," was all Esmine said in reply.

While her charge ate, Nelby sat back and considered their cage again. There were bars on three sides, with a solid back wall where it met the wagon. Sometimes, the girls' captors threw an old tarp over the cage to keep out the sun, wind or rain. Other times, they didn't seem to give a shit. Near the back wall, was a bucket for waste, a prisoner's chamber pot. At the front, a large wooden cup lay on its side in the filthy straw the girls used for bedding. Often, the only drink the girls received was snow they'd melted in that cup. Once in a while though, they were given hot broth—not very hearty, but the warmth meant almost more than any nourishment it might offer. Nelby had survived worse, but the child?

Once more, the former thrall's thoughts drifted to escape. With every sunset, the caravan came a day closer to its destination—whatever that might be—and the captives, a day closer to their undoubtedly unpleasant fates. For weeks, Nelby had sought comfort in the belief that she and Esmine would be sold as a pair. Now, she had lost all confidence in the possibility. Now, she feared the caravan's arrival would result in a final parting. She felt she'd failed Mardine; she couldn't bear the thought of failing Long Pete and especially Esmine. She couldn't bear the thought of leaving the child alone to her fate.

It was time to escape, whatever the risks.

The Giants, In the Forest

Eoman and Karrakan stood side-by-side, pondering the snow at their feet.

"More blighted Svarren."

"All headed the same direction, too."

"You know what that means."

"One o' their cursed meet-ups, at the very least."

"Or war, in the worst case."

"Should we follow 'em?"

Eoman pulled at his beard, torn. "I don't want to lose Mardine's killers…"

"But?"

"You know as well as I: when Svarren gather, it bodes ill for the rest of us."

Karrakan nodded. "What to do, what to do?"

Eoman exhaled vigorously, as if he'd come to a decision.

Karrakan raised an eyebrow at him. "Well?"

"Spoor's fresh. I reckon if we hurry, we can catch a straggler or two. Find out what they're after."

"I was hoping you'd say that."

The king of the giants shrugged. "But let's mark this place, so we know where we were when we left off."

Karrakan waved his right hand over his head and said "Done!"

It was Eoman's turn to raise an eyebrow. "How so?"

"Trust me, old friend. I'll know the place," Karrakan laughed.

His king grumbled. "Let's just find these Svarren bastards and get it over with. I'll not have Mardine's spirit haunting me for failing to avenge her death."

Just as the two giants veered off their previous path and onto the Svarren trail, the snow began falling again.

"Going to be an especially cold winter, this."

Eoman was silent. He'd seen so many winters, one was the same as another in his mind. It was a harsh time of year, if occasionally beautiful. This winter, however, would not be beautiful if Eoman had his way.

As they trudged along, Karrakan sent his will-o-wisps out into trees a good fifty strides on either side of the Svarren track. "How many Long Teeth in this pack, you reckon?"

Eoman stopped, stretched his back for a moment. "How many? Too many and not enough."

It was an old giant saying used only against enemies. It meant too many for one giant to handle and not enough to keep him employed in the happy business of killing them.

"Too many and not enough," Karrakan agreed.

"When's the last time you saw Beesmarch?" Eoman asked unexpectedly.

"Hmmm," Karrakan replied. "Can't say, really. A ten-year, perhaps? You thinking of inviting him along?"

"Aye," said Eoman. "If I can find him. Can't have enough strong hands if it comes to fighting."

"The Svarren?"

"Or the humans."

Karrakan shook his head. "Still...*Beesmarch*? He's a right grumpy old bastard."

"I'm not looking for charming."

The two giants continued in silence a while, and then Karrakan said "Have you thought about what happens if our actions touch off a war with men?"

"It's always been a war," Eoman responded. "We'd just bring it into the open."

"But suppose, while we're at it, the Svarren come after our goodwives?"

Eoman stopped in his tracks and fixed his friend with his most gruff expression. "I'm killing the scum that butchered Mardine, and that's as far as I'm willing to think about it."

Karrakan shrugged. The future had a funny way of playing out differently than anyone planned or foresaw.

Vykers, Under the Castle

Vykers stared at the footprints. He recognized them…and he didn't. Why this was so bothered him more than the footprints themselves. In the past year, he'd been having more and more experiences like this. He wondered if he wasn't going mad. Then he figured it didn't matter. A mad Vykers wouldn't behave much differently from a sane.

He'd had a particular goal in sneaking into Her Majesty's castle, but his curiosity got the better of him, and he decided to follow the strange prints. Best to find out who or what else was lurking in these tunnels. And the Reaper was always looking for an excuse for violence.

He trudged up a new tunnel, not caring overmuch if anyone heard him. As it turned out, he was the one who heard things. The passageway was alive with whispers, punctuated every so often by music, by banging, or by laughter or tears. Little gusts of air from his left or right told him there were cracks in the walls on either side, through which sound, scents and perhaps even light might issue from the rooms beyond. Despite the darkness, Vykers was able to find one of the cracks with relative ease—and discovered it was not a crack, but a carefully carved depression, specifically designed to accommodate an ear or eye. Not wanting to expose his own eye to potential injury, he thrust a finger into the space and felt a small hole at its center, which immediately stopped the flow of air into his face. He lifted his finger, and the air resumed. As no light came through the hole with it, Vykers concluded the room or hallway beyond was as dark as the tunnel in which he stood. He wondered how many other such holes he might find and whether the great Alheria knew of their existence. It was hard to imagine she did not.

Vykers moved on. In time, he came to another junction that offered several more tunnels. He chose one at random and continued his journey, fascinated by the complexity of this heretofore unseen world. Forget the holes, was Alheria aware of these *tunnels*? As a goddess, how could she not be? But then, why did she allow them to exist? How did they serve her ends?

The bitch is too crafty to let something like this escape her attention, Vykers thought.

As he continued onwards, he gradually became aware of a mewling sound somewhere in the darkness before him. Naturally, he drew his knife. The path ahead took an unexpected turn to the Reaper's right, and he sensed that the source of the mewling was just around the corner. Another man—*man?*— might have exercised more caution, but Vykers slid to the far corner and held his knife before him, ready to defend himself or attack as the occasion demanded. Worldly as he was, he was unprepared for what he found.

Despite the tunnel's near-obsidian gloom, the Reaper made out a small, misshapen mass huddled against the closer wall, its face against the stones. Evidently, it hadn't heard Igraine's movements over its own weeping, for it continued unabated.

"Hold," Igraine said quietly but firmly.

The thing looked up and froze, petrified by the unforeseen intrusion.

Goblin, Vykers thought. And then, *Mahnus' balls! How do I know that?*

"Please, mistress, do not kill me!" the creature wailed.

Mistress? Ah. Of course. "How is it you speak the Queen's tongue?" Igraine demanded.

The goblin glanced behind Igraine and then back behind itself as if to make certain no one else was coming. "I live with it, day and night, night and day." It had even acquired the Queen's accent.

Suddenly, Vykers understood the origin of the tunnel's peep holes. "So, you spy on these castle folk, do you?"

"Castle folk?" the goblin echoed, tilting his head in bemusement. "Are my people not castle folk? Do we not live in the castle?"

Out of habit, Vykers reached up to scratch his beard and felt only soft, smooth skin. He grunted in irritation. "Why's Her Majesty allow goblins to live in her walls?"

"An...*arrangement*...was reached long ago, before I was born."

Igraine stepped closer and the goblin flinched.

"Please don't kill me!"

It was almost funny how many times the Reaper had heard those words throughout his life. The goblin's pleas meant nothing to him. Still, why hadn't the little fellow tried to hail his own kind or attempted to run away? And why had he been weeping? "What are you doin' here, anyway?" Igraine asked.

The goblin wiped his nose with a forearm. "As I said, mistress, I live here." He then moaned miserably before adding, "For now."

Vykers ignored that last part. "Where's this tunnel go?"

"The answer's rather involved, I'm afraid," the goblin giggled nervously. Seeing that Igraine did not share his mirth, he quickly continued, "Many places, many junctions, many more tunnels."

"And how many more o' your kind are in here with us?"

The goblin hemmed and hawed, until Igraine pointed her dagger directly at the creature's eye.

"Five thousand—four thousand, nine hundred and ninety-nine." That was an oddly precise answer, and Vykers' confusion must have shown on Igraine's face, for the goblin went on, "It *would* be five thousand, but, as you can see, one of us—me, actually—is with you."

"Why five thousand?" Igraine asked. Before the goblin could even begin to respond, she cut him off. "Never mind: I don't care. Why aren't you tryin' to escape from me?"

The creature's face pulled into a frown, and his eyes seemed to tear up again. He looked down in the darkness at his feet. "Because I am lame," he confessed. "How far would I get? Not very, I'll wager."

"But you were cryin' *before* I came upon you," Igraine pointed out.

"Again, because I am lame. My kin ridicule me mercilessly for it, and I have had enough. They act as if mobility is all that matters, as if my brain is of no value to the clan."

Vykers could see the goblin was intelligent, no question. In fact, he was rather stunned by this revelation. Perhaps, he could make use of the creature. "You got a name?" Igraine asked.

"Trrlkktkk."

"Turr..."

"Trrlkktkk."

"I'm gonna call you 'Turley'."

"I would rather that you..."

"So, Turley, you and me are gonna be workin' together for a while. You try anything, you won't have to worry about bein' lame anymore. Understood?"

Turley stepped away from the wall, into the middle of the corridor, and spread his hands wide. "Understood. And what may I call you, mistress?"

Suddenly, Vykers couldn't remember his new name and, not wanting to look a fool, he simply sputtered, "Mistress'll be fine."

"Mistress," Turley repeated. "And what, mistress, will we be doing?"

"An alchemist told me there's a man in the castle keeps the keys to all Her Majesty's warehouses. I wanna get my hands on those keys."

"Can't you just break in to her warehouses?"

Igraine sneered at her new companion. "Anything worth stealin's guarded by magic wards. I need a key that cuts through all of that."

"May I ask...?"

"No," Igraine answered sharply. "Now, do you know where this fella can be found or don't you?"

Turley stared back, a pained expression on his face.

The False Reaper & Omeyo, In Camp

The Pretender, as Omeyo had come to think of his master—the man who would usurp Tarmun Vykers' name—was strangely subdued. He'd left the celebrations at his army's communal fire and gone off to his tent, taking his general with him. Once inside, he'd retreated to his chair, where he sat, brooding, as he stared into a candle flame.

"May I be of service in some way, Master?" Omeyo asked. Better to act before being acted upon.

"How many villages have we sacked thus far?" the Pretender asked without looking away from his candle.

Of course he knew the answer. What could Omeyo possibly add? Almost, he said "Just three," but he knew that 'just' would see him whipped. Under the Pretender's rule, as under the End's, any news had to be couched in the most glowing of terms. If His Magnificence took a shit, it was incumbent upon all and sundry to ooh-and-ah, as if that shit were a gift from the gods, a work of unsurpassed beauty and genius. "Three!" Omeyo offered, doing his best to sound impressed by the accomplishment.

"Three," the Pretender confirmed. "And yet, no word from the Reaper or the Queen. Do they think me of so little consequence? Do they truly dare ignore me?"

"They cannot, Master. I wonder if perhaps they're beset by other problems, distracted."

The Pretender stood. "Then we shall give them something they cannot ignore. Fetch my Svarren!"

They were *all* his Svarren, Omeyo thought. But the Pretender was referring specifically to Tooth and Nail. He clearly derived great pleasure from watching his human servant squirm whenever his Svarren bodyguard came near.

"As you say, Master," Omeyo gulped. There was no point in delaying, much as he wanted to. The Pretender's commands were to be obeyed on the instant, or misery would follow.

Omeyo left his master's tent and worked his way through the camp towards the communal fire. It was the last place he'd seen Tooth and Nail, and they tended to stay put once they'd settled in for an evening. As he navigated his way through the camp, Omeyo kept his eyes down and took shallow breaths through his mouth. Snow and stench were not two things that most folks associated with one another, but most folks had never been in the midst of a horde of Svarren, either. The pungent reek of sweat, urine, feces and other unspeakable substances mingled with wood smoke nearly made the general sick to his stomach. The disturbing cacophony of noises that came from the assembled Svarren was no better. If Omeyo had thought he would never experience worse than he had in the End's horde, the Pretender's army disabused him of that notion both quickly and constantly. Surely, there was no more foul company in all the world. Even the blanket of night did little to conceal the loathsome nature of

Omeyo's predicament. Indeed, what his eyes could not verify, his imagination embroidered, to the point where the general feared he'd go mad if he spent another sunrise in his master's service. And then he *hoped* he'd go mad; what sweet release that would be!

He looked up and found he'd arrived at the bonfire; his feet had taken him where his mind was reluctant to go. A sea of savage, stupid faces glanced over at him as he stepped into the light, and he noticed a sly look pass between Tooth and Nail when they caught sight of him.

"Tarmun Vykers requests your company," Omeyo said to his nemeses with as much authority as he could muster. He felt ridiculous referring to the Pretender as Tarmun Vykers and even more ridiculous delivering his message to such thick-witted monsters, but he dared not let it show on his face, in his posture, or in his voice. He could not give these Svarren any excuse to turn on him.

With Tooth and Nail now trailing behind him, time seemed to slow to a standstill. Every step was an eternity in which either beast might lunge at the general's back, and he'd never see it coming. As a soldier, he'd often wondered what it must feel like to be impaled on someone's sword, to have an arm shorn from its shoulder, or his head split in two, and he found none of those possibilities frightened him half so much as the thought of being disemboweled, ripped to pieces by the filthy claws and slavering jaws of the Svarren. And then to be eaten—*eaten!*—before he'd completely lost consciousness. Mahnus forbid!

And yet, why should Mahnus care what happened to a fool who'd placed himself on the wrong side of every war?

Before Omeyo could explore this new worry much further, he arrived at the Pretender's tent. Stepping aside at the last moment, he ushered the two Svarren inside ahead of him.

The Pretender sat in his chair, wrapped in furs, with his right hand over his eyes, as if attempting to remember something elusive. Long minutes passed while Omeyo and Tooth and Nail stood in pregnant silence. Out of the corner of his eye, the general caught the Svarren leering at him.

They'd never dare! Omeyo assured himself. *Not in the Pretender's presence.*

The Master spoke, breaking that tension and commencing a new one. "Can all your women stitch?"

At first, Omeyo thought the question was directed at him, but it was so detached from anything that had gone before it that the general could make no sense of it. Yet, the penalty for failing to answer in a timely manner was usually severe. Omeyo opened his mouth, hoping something useful would tumble out, when Tooth unexpectedly came to his rescue.

"Yes," he grunted.

Just 'Yes'? No honorifics? None of the fawning required of Omeyo? If he'd had any doubts about the hierarchy in the Pretender's chain of command, that simple 'Yes' destroyed them: he was last, the lowest of the Master's servants. He alone had been responsible for the Master's continued existence, but it availed him nothing. Omeyo seethed.

"I have a task for your women," the Pretender smiled.

Despite his anger, Omeyo was intrigued.

The Giantess, In the Cottage

Under the care of the mysterious Svarren woman, the Wretch was no longer wretched. Indeed, she now understood herself to be a giantess, though her given name continued to escape her, along with other details of her current plight. Why, for instance, had she been lying in the frozen earth? Why had she been naked and so terribly scarred?

Her external scars were rapidly fading; the ones inside, however, stubbornly persisted, and she feared to learn what lay beneath them. Fortunately, her Svarren savior entered the room and chased those thoughts away.

"More stew, dearie? You've a giant's appetite, and that's certain!"

"Yes, please," the giantess replied rather timidly.

"You may call me 'Tinalia'," the woman instructed.

"Thank you, Tin...Tinalia. How long...?"

"How long have you been here?" Tinalia cut in. "Ooh, a week, I should think. But it's no matter to us; you can stay as long as you've a mind."

The giantess sat up, propping herself up on a large pile of pillows. "Have I...have I taken your bed?"

Tinalia waved her off lightheartedly. "It's nothing. We've an extra room since Leris...since my youngest son left. I sleep in there. But you, now," the Svarren woman said, "you must have a name, no?"

The giantess frowned. "I must. It's muh...muh...een." She fell silent, frustrated.

"Mureen?" Tinalia asked. As her guest did not immediately object, she went on, "Mureen it is, then. For the time being. And now, Mureen, we must talk about some exercise! Much as I like you, I can't be cleaning your night waste forever."

Mureen was mortified. "I didn't know..."

"It's nothing," said Tinalia. "Nothing at all. Only, can you stand, do you think? Take my hand, and let's try."

Mureen took the woman's hand and worked her way to her feet. She felt a little unsteady, having been in bed for a week, but was pleased, as well, to sense her strength returning.

"Good, good!" Tinalia cooed. "And now, let us see if you can walk a bit. Would you like to see the rest of the cottage?"

Would she? She'd been staring at the same mural for a week! Lovely as it was, she was terribly curious about the other rooms. She nodded enthusiastically.

Tinalia led her through the doorway into a large common room, adorned in the style of a hunting lodge. There were animal heads mounted on the walls, alongside various weapons, and even a few farming and woodworking tools. The furniture was fashioned of small logs, sufficient to support large Svarren men and even, perhaps, Mureen herself. There was a huge fireplace in the far wall, in which a healthy, hearty fire blazed. Mureen noted three doorways on the room's other walls, one of which, she imagined, was the door leading outside. But why should she care for that? This place, this home, was the only comfort she'd known since...she couldn't say when. She shoved that mystery aside. Tinalia was saying something.

"And Baris will be home soon, with something for dinner, no doubt. We'll have a spot of work to do then, to get whatever it is cleaned and ready for roasting. Oh, but I promised you some stew, didn't I?" The Svarren woman walked over to the fire and poked into a pot that hung over the flames. "It's a hunter's stew," said she, with her back to the giantess, "but it's a fair sight better than pottage. He's not the most refined lad you'll ever meet, but my Baris can surely hunt." With that, she turned and presented Mureen with a large bowl of steaming stew and a spoon.

The giantess felt a moment's trepidation as she considered the bowl, worried, vaguely, about Mahnus knew what. Then her stomach got the better of her and she dug in, much to Tinalia's delight. The stuff was surprisingly delicious, full of venison, as it turned out, and onions and numerous root vegetables. She wasn't sure what she'd been expecting; she'd eaten some earlier without qualm. But Mureen—the name still didn't feel quite right—had never known anyone who'd tasted Svarren cooking, and while she felt certain this wonderful stew wasn't typical, its mere existence was a revelation.

Without a word, Tinalia urged Mureen to sit on a big bench by the fire. It was a cozy enough circumstance that the giantess wished fleetingly that she could stay forever. There was something she needed to do, however...if only she could recall what it was.

Fully awake and alert for the first time in days, Mureen took advantage of the opportunity to get better acquainted with her unusual host. First, she stole fleeting glances at Tinalia while she ate. Despite her growing familiarity with the Svarren woman, Mureen continued to feel disoriented by Tinalia's appearance. Mureen, of course, had suffered some great trauma and had lost most of her memory. Still, she was aware that Svarren typically did not care much for clothing, especially fine, custom-made clothing, and yet Tinalia was attired as if she were attending an event at the Queen's court. In addition, she'd painted and powdered her face a stark white. On top of this, she'd rouged her cheeks, lined her eyes and even decorated the mole on her left cheek. Most disconcerting of all, however, were her blood red lips, framing a mouthful of crooked yellow and grey teeth. Her smile was apt to curdle milk, for it certainly made the giantess lose interest in her stew of a sudden. Gods, that smile!

The Queen & Cindor, Outside of Lunessfor

The object appeared just before sunrise, sitting in a field a thousand strides from the city's main gate. It was a gigantic head, three and a half to four times the height of a man and half as wide, a nightmare of mottled whites, reds, purples and rust colors sculpted in the likeness of an angry man. It was a hideous, uncanny thing that exuded an aura of agony and fear.

"What do you make of it?" the Queen asked her Shaper.

Another test, always another test. "It appears to be a gift from the Reaper."

"Appears?"

"Yes, well it's a little too ghastly to be well-intentioned, so it can't be a gift. And it seems out of character for Tarmun Vykers."

"It's *entirely* out of character," Her Majesty nodded. "If Vykers had something to say, he'd say it in person, most likely with an army at his back."

"Then who...?"

"I know who," the Queen said dismissively, suddenly fascinated by the condition of her fingernails. "The real question is: what does it *mean*?"

"It is either a provocation or a threat."

Her Majesty dropped her hands and walked to within ten paces of the head, far closer than anyone else had dared. It was stitched together of human faces, a rare few of which were still attached to their owners. "Both!" she declared.

"Please," one of the faces moaned.

The Queen waved a hand and the whole thing caught fire. There was a brief howling from the head's inhabitants, and then there was nothing but heat, light, and the stench of burning flesh. Her Majesty watched for a while, lost in thought, before making her way back to Cindor's side.

"And the author of this atrocity is...?"

"Who do you think? It's the imbecile who called himself The End-of-All-Things. Of course now, he's calling himself Tarmun Vykers."

Cindor was quiet for a long time after hearing this. Finally, he said, "So, he means to try us, to relitigate his last battle."

"Or," said the Queen, "he wants us to engage the Reaper, hoping we'll weaken one another enough that he can sweep down and annihilate us both."

"My Queen," the Shaper said carefully, "you have a longer, deeper history with this End-of-All-Things than I believed."

"By design," Her Majesty snapped. "I need you focused on other issues, as you know."

The Shaper reached up, ran his fingers over the scars on his neck and lower jaw. "This Captain Kittins hardly helps my focus."

"That is a problem of your own devising."

It was the answer he'd been expecting, and Cindor hardly knew why he'd mentioned it. Quickly, he changed the subject, gesturing towards the sickening fire. "And these unfortunates?"

"Shall be avenged in time, as you know. But the fool is baiting us, and I refuse to play by someone else's rules."

A snowflake landed on the end of Cindor's nose and remained frozen, as if the man's body had no heat of its own.

"Winter!" the Queen exclaimed. "Why must we always fight in the snow?" Then, after a pause: "It seems there are some rules even I must obey. For the time being."

Back in her throne room, Her Majesty summoned the aforementioned Kittins, whilst a disapproving Cindor looked on. The ghoulish Captain arrived in his own time, unconcerned with incurring Her Majesty's wrath.

"You took your time in getting here!" the goddess barked at him.

"I was primping in front of a mirror," Kittins cracked.

Somewhere off to the Shaper's left, one of the guards struggled to suppress a snicker.

Cindor glanced at the Queen, hoping she'd decide to punish the fellow once and for all.

But she did not.

Instead, she pursed her lips and regarded the big man in silence for a span of heartbeats. "We hear rumors that the Reaper has attacked a number of villages in the North. I am sending you to investigate the truth of it."

Incredibly (to Cindor's mind), Kittins asked, "Why me?"

Her Majesty glared at him. "Because your other choice is a slow, painful death."

Kittins appeared to think about it for several seconds. "If you insist."

"I'm finding it rather hard to believe you're not mocking me, somehow."

The captain would have blown out his lips in exasperation, if he'd had any. Instead, he simply released a gush of air through his teeth. "You think I'd dare mock anyone, with a face like this?"

Her Majesty ignored the remark. "Cindor here will see you supplied for your journey. And mind you," she warned both men, "your mutual hatred is of no interest to the rest of the kingdom. Comport yourselves as I expect or suffer the consequences."

"As you say," Cindor and Kittins responded in unison, further aggravating them both.

The Shaper stalked imperiously from the room, and the captain lurched into step at his heels.

"May this journey result in your death," Cindor snarled quietly.

"Wouldn't that be nice?" Kittins answered.

Aoife, On the Road

Winter howled outside Aoife's verdant cocoon like an angry suitor who'd had the door slammed in his face; inside, the A'Shea was so comfortable, she might've hibernated if she'd been able.

But the voice of an old friend woke her.

"The goddess of men is already aware of the news you would bring her."

Aoife sat up from her bed of moss, rubbed her eyes, and looked about. "Toomt'-La?"

The satyr seemed to have grown from the very walls of the A'Shea's shelter, as much a thing of vines as the vines themselves. "The same."

Aoife hurried to embrace him, as difficult as that was.

"You look well," he smiled.

"And you," the A'Shea countered, "look like a thicket!"

The satyr laughed. "You do me too much honor!"

"It wasn't meant as a compliment."

"I'll take it so, nonetheless."

He ran a hand over the A'Shea's head, feeling her hair, and assessed her features like a midwife examining a newborn.

"You were saying something about Alheria?" Aoife prompted.

Toomt'-La put a hand on both of her shoulders, fixed her with his timeless gaze. "I was. The goddess knows what you would tell her. How could she not, being a goddess?"

Aoife stared at her friend, bemused. "Then...what?"

"Why journey south? Your battle's to the north."

"How can you know that?" Aoife demanded.

The satyr's eyes grew wide and black as infinity. "I am the voice of the ancient ones, some of those killed in the Forest of Nar. You know this. What you do not yet seem to grasp is that you are our body. Yours is the life and the strength of the woodland world."

"As sister-mother?"

"As our priestess. No longer are you Alheria's conduit."

Aoife sat, uncertain how to feel.

"Does this displease you?" the satyr asked, concern evident in his voice.

The A'Shea shook her head. "No, no. I was unprepared for the news; that is all. An A'Shea is all I've ever been..."

"Not all, surely."

"I don't care to dwell upon my time before I joined the sisterhood. But now...how will I invoke? To whom shall I direct my prayers?"

Toomt'-La chuckled. It was a warm, familiar sound. "You will find your magics much more intuitive now. The Green will always recognize your need."

"And what shall I call myself, old friend? I've been an A'Shea so long..."

Again, the chuckle. "You've been a Mender. Now, become a *Tender*. Protect the Green. You are *Umaena*."

"Umaena..." Aoife echoed experimentally.

"There! You see? You speak it without accent!"

"But are there others? More Umaeni?"

"You are the only human."

"And how shall I protect the Green?"

Toomt'-La began to fade into the foliage of Aoife's cocoon even as he spoke. "Go north!" he urged. "Go north."

"But..."

He was gone.

North?

It was the second time in her life that Aoife had been heading to Lunessfor with a purpose, only to be turned aside by the spirits of Nar. Last time, she'd become their sister-mother and this time, their priestess? Without conscious effort, she parted the walls of her sanctuary and peered into the icy morning. She wondered if the countless leagues between herself and the thing that was once her brother would allow enough time to learn the powers of her new office.

FIVE

Long & Company, On the Road

Yendor awoke to the cock's crow of panic. The lashes on his one eye had frozen together, and the old campaigner thrashed about in mounting hysteria, completely blind and afraid the condition was permanent. Whether it was the clouds of hot breath that escaped from the man or the warm tears that gushed from his eye, his lashes eventually parted, and his vision returned. Thankfully, it revealed nothing untoward, no audience of smirking companions, giggling at Yendor's misfortune. He'd no doubt, however, that they lurked just outside the tent, waiting to ambush him as soon as he emerged. Ah well, better to be assaulted with the jibes of friends than the knives of enemies. Putting himself in order as best he could, Yendor stepped through the tent flap and into the frigid dawn.

Not ten paces away, the rest of the crew sat 'round the fire, slurping something hot out of mugs.

Rem caught his eye and looked about to say something when Long silenced him with a subtle nod of the head. *Very well*, Rem's expression seemed to say, *I can get him later.*

Not if Yendor could preempt him. "I froze my fuckin' eyelids together. Got a glimpse o' what real blindness is like."

"You got a glimpse of blindness?" Rem repeated smugly, as Yendor stepped up to the fire. "This was sometime a paradox, but now the time gives it proof."

Yendor stared at the actor a moment and changed the subject. "What's in them mugs? I'm assumin' it ain't mulled wine, 'cause old Grammy Long Pete, here, won't let me near no spirits."

"Not liquid ones, anyway," Long chipped in.

"It's just boiled oats 'n a drop o' honey," said Spirk. "Ain't that right, Ron?"

Ron, the least gregarious of the group, merely bobbed his head in agreement.

"Oats?"

"Just the leftover feed for Gorivar's mounts. But we call it oats. Leastways, I think there's some oats in there. And with that honey, it don't taste half bad," Long offered.

"Well," said Yendor, "You all look to be in fine fiddle this mornin', whatever you're eatin'."

"I think the captain's just happy to get back on the trail," Rem opined.

"Aye," Long agreed. "That's so. Searchin' ain't findin' o' course, but it's a damned sight better'n sittin' on yer ass in a snow drift."

"We'll find 'er," Yendor assured his friend for what seemed the thousandth time. "Whoever's got her has to stop now and again for supplies, and your Esmine's a rare one. Someone's got to have seen 'er!"

This was greeted with general agreement all around, and even Ron expressed his confidence in the truth of it.

"Say, Remuel," said Yendor, "I wonder...could you pass me a mug or bowl o' them oats?"

But as the actor filled a bowl and began to pass it along, he suddenly disappeared altogether, leaving only a faint crackling sound in the air where he'd been standing.

"Magic!" Spirk confirmed, a little too loudly.

"Damn," said Long softly.

Yendor turned to his friend. "What's this about?"

The captain pulled his collar closed and huddled closer to the fire. "He warned me he might have to leave abruptly—for a time. I was just hopin'..."

"And you didn't tell us earlier, because...?"

"Rem's comin' and goin's beyond our control. So's the weather, for that matter, and every other part o' this blasted chase. Only thing we can control is our own determination."

"And that's all that matters," Spirk concluded.

Long smiled at the young man, grateful for his unending support. "Bless you for sayin' so, Spirk. Makes this wind a bit more tolerable, anyways."

The little group finished the last of the oats in silence. As Spirk and Ron rose to begin breaking down their tent, Yendor leaned in to the captain. "I'm hearing you mighty well these days."

"And?"

"I'm *hearing* you, Long. Your voice is all but mended."

It had happened so slowly, so gradually, that no one but Yendor had noticed. "I don't...know what to say," Long replied.

"Point is, you *can* say. You can talk all you want, now. The End-of-All-Things musta lied to you, eh?"

It was a mystery, and Long had more important things on his mind. "Time to get going," said he. "Onward."

"Onward," Yendor agreed.

Nelby & Esmine, On the Road

There was no way to get the cage open that didn't involve one of the girls' captors, and all of the options that did seemed far too obvious to Nelby. She could attempt to seduce one of the guards, but that hadn't gone well last the time she'd tried it. She could ask Esmine to feign some dire illness, and when the guards came to investigate...well, that's where the plan fell apart. Nelby knew she could not overpower a single man, much less two or more. But if such an opportunity presented itself... what would she use for a weapon? She looked at her nails: gone, chewed to the quick. She didn't feel any pain, though, which worried her. Perhaps her fingers were in the early stages of frostbite. Alheria knew she couldn't feel her toes. She searched for a bit of bone from any of the scraps of meat they'd been tossed: nothing. The bucket they used for a latrine was made of wood that had started to rot. It wouldn't survive a single blow. How in Alheria's name were she and the child to escape? She'd convinced herself that the caravan's destination was within a few days' travel, and her desperation seemed to grow worse each time she thought on it.

Yet, she would not allow herself to give up. On some level, failing to escape seemed the same as doing nothing, making no attempt whatsoever. And Nelby knew Mardine would at least want her to *try*.

She rededicated herself to the problem. She still had her teeth. That, at least, was something. If nothing else, she could bite into a guard's neck and refuse to let go until Esmine had run off into the woods. Even without nails, she could gouge a man's eyes, or perhaps rip an ear off—anything to cause a momentary panic in which Esmine might run free.

Steeling her nerves, she crawled over to where the girl lay huddled under a pile of blankets and rags. Time to have that talk.

"Sweetie," she said, reaching a hand under the pile to touch Esmine's head. "Sweetie, I need to tell you something."

Esmine moaned, rolled over and pulled the blankets tighter around herself. Anymore, she didn't like to come out into the air. Too cold, perhaps.

"Sweetie, this is important, now. They've got bad things in store fer us, and we can't let that happen."

This got Esmine's attention, and she poked her head out of her makeshift nest. She said nothing, but the expression on her face was clear enough: *save me*.

It had been some time since Nelby had really looked at Esmine, and she was shocked at what she saw: the girl's cheeks were so hollow, the bones stuck out like armored plates. Her eyes appeared to have dwindled almost to nothing in their now-cavernous sockets. Her skin's formerly pinkish hue had grown waxy and pale. *And no wonder,* Nelby thought. *We're starving, the two of us.*

"Next time a guard comes by, I'm goin' to jump 'im. While I'm at it, you have to bolt for freedom."

Esmine looked unconvinced. Smart girl.

"I'm serious, now. I'll catch whoever it is by surprise and be right behind you. They won't chase us in the dark and the cold."

"But…"

"And you gotta take all o' our blankets and such. We hafta stay warm 'til we find shelter, you know."

Esmine remained unconvinced, forcing Nelby to play her last card. "Look, sweetie, it's run or die. Maybe it's run *and* die, but at least we'd be together. At least we'd know freedom for a time." Nelby stared into the child's now-watery brown eyes. "They're never gonna take you away from me, nor me away from you. I won't let that happen."

The child turned away briefly and when she turned back, she was holding a large wooden splinter in her hand. "You want?" she asked.

It was about seven inches long, three at its widest point and maybe a half inch thick near its base. A splinter like that was better than nails on all ten fingers. "Thank you," Nelby said softly, tucking the splinter under her shirt. "It's the very thing we needed."

Esmine's face lit up at this news, and the appearance of hope in her features was almost more than Nelby could bear. "First guard comes our way after dark is the last guard we ever have to see," she said, more to bolster her own nerves than to calm the child's.

Esmine smiled weakly and crawled back under her mound of cloth.

"The last guard we'll ever have to see," Nelby repeated to herself.

It was dark and bitterly cold—corpse cold—when Nelby heard someone wrestling with the cage's lock. Quickly, she pulled Esmine's head closer and spoke into her ear.

"It's now or never. I attack, you run past us and don't look back. I'll be right behind you."

She heard Esmine whimper as she pulled away, but she forced herself to ignore the girl's fear; she had enough and too much for both of them. The sound of the cage's door creaking open was Nelby's clarion call. She looked over and saw that one of the caravan's women had come to deliver some hot slop. There was no advantage in the guard's being female, though. Nelby knew these slaver bitches were every bit as fierce as their men, if not more so. Nelby just had to be worse.

"'Ere's ya dinna," the slaver wench drawled.

Nelby descended upon her like a winter storm, upending the hot slop onto the woman's chest with her left hand, while her right hand brought the splinter crashing down towards her left eye. The woman might have blocked the blow, but her shock at the hot swill splashed upon her distracted her just long enough for Nelby to strike home. It was a mixed victory, however, as the splinter tore down the side of the woman's face, pierced her cheek and staked her tongue to the bottom of her mouth. It did not, unfortunately, prevent her from screaming. When the first shriek rang out, Nelby kicked the woman in the throat as hard as she could, over and over, until the guard sank out of sight.

Angry that Esmine had not followed her directions, Nelby turned to look at the girl and discovered her weeping. "We've no time for this, girl. It's run or die, now. And you know what death looks like."

Esmine clutched her blankets and dashed from the cage, landing on the guardswoman's body before she rolled onto the snowy ground. Nelby grabbed the last of the rags and bolted after her. The guard was still alive, struggling to breathe, but Nelby's anger and courage had been spent. She slunk off after Esmine, wishing she'd been able to put the other woman out of her misery.

There were no trees nearby, but it was dark, and there were bushes, so Nelby and Esmine were able to dodge from clump to clump, but it would amount to nothing, they knew, if their footprints gave them away.

After a time, a faint yell sounded out of the darkness. The girls' escape had been discovered, and now the chase would begin in earnest. Nelby would like to have carried Esmine to speed up their pace, but the child was much larger and sturdier than the typical human toddler. Nothing for it now but a headlong dash into the night.

And if they managed to escape their pursuit, they still had hunger and the cold to deal with.

Vykers & Turley, Under the Castle

Turley was far too talkative, and there were countless occasions when Vykers nearly put his knife in the goblin's throat just to shut him up. Still, the little monster knew these passageways much better than the Reaper did or ever would. Annoying as he was, Vykers needed him.

"And down this way," Turley said, pointing to a side passage, "is Servant Speak, the best place to listen in on the castle's help."

"Why would I wanna do that?" Vykers demanded, disgusted.

This gave the little goblin pause. "Why? Well, er…"

"Forget it. How long 'til we get where we're going?"

"To the Warden's chambers? As I said earlier, he lives a few floors up, on the other side of the castle and, unlike the humans who live here, we goblins can't take the most direct…"

"How long?"

Turley flinched. "Add in the fact that I need to keep you hidden from the rest of my clan, I'd say 'til the evening bell at the soonest."

"You don't have to keep me hidden," Igraine snarled. "I'm not afraid o' your kin."

"No," Turley grimaced, "I can see that."

"Then let's be on with it."

The complexity of the goblin warrens was astonishing, considering that they existed only behind, between and sometimes beneath walls. Every so often, Vykers made out the voices of other goblins in the murky distance, but Turley was careful to ensure they never crossed his path. At regular intervals, the goblin risked Vykers' wrath by stopping to rest his misshapen leg and foot. He did so in as unassuming a manner as possible, but Vykers could tell it was hurting him.

"What's the story with that leg?"

"One of our tunnels collapsed on me when I was younger." Turley replied with a shrug. "It happens."

"I've heard o' different tribes that set their weak or injured out to die in the wilderness."

Turley shot back a look that suggested he feared Igraine's words might come true. "It is not so different with my people. To be weak is to be a liability to the clan."

"A what?"

"A burden, if you will."

"But they don't leave you alone in the forest."

Turley sighed. "In some ways, that would be better. One of the things my people do is to make you feel so unwelcome that you eventually take your own life."

Igraine must have been gawking in disbelief, for the goblin continued, "No, it's true. I've known two others to go to it in my lifetime, and, of course, there are tales of many more."

"So, your fellows have been torturing you in hopes you'd kill yourself." Igraine shook her head in disbelief. "Seems to me it's the arm wields the sword, not the leg." Vykers wasn't familiar with the landscape of goblin faces, but it appeared the little creature smiled at this. "It also seems to me you wouldn't care if I killed one or two o' the bastards." Turley's smile faded.

"That would be tantamount to declaring war on my kin."

Vykers had no idea what 'tantamount' meant, but suddenly the goblin looked very sad.

"I'd never be able to come home again," the creature sighed.

"Why in Mahnus' name would you *want* to?"

"You don't understand."

"No shit," Igraine sniped. "That leg recovered enough to get us goin' again?"

Turley bobbed his head in response, straightened up, and proceeded down the corridor.

Now and again, the goblin pulled up and peered through a spy hole.

"How much farther?" Igraine demanded.

"We are about halfway there."

The Reaper was stunned. The place was fucking huge.

In time, they came upon a large room with stone benches set into the walls. The light of hundreds of spy holes illuminated the chamber enough that Vykers got his first good look at his guide. Turley stood about three and a half to four feet tall— it was hard to be certain with his constant stoop—and wore a dull, knee-length tunic over his purplish-grey skin. His four-toed feet were unshod, making it all the easier to see the twisted malformation of his left foot, ankle and shin. A short cloak hung from Turley's shoulders, meant, Vykers supposed, to provide a little extra warmth in the constant cool of the tunnels. And the goblin's face? It was not a thing of beauty, but neither was it especially gruesome or frightening. Of course, nothing frightened the Reaper, but he very much doubted that even a child would scream at the first sight of Turley's visage. In fact, the creature's ridiculously long, pointy and erect ears gave him a doglike appearance that made him seem somehow more trustworthy than threatening.

The goblin noticed Igraine's attention and asked "You've never seen any of my kind before?"

"I might have," Igraine allowed. "I don't remember."

"And yet you seem surprised."

"I was expectin' you to be green."

Turley chuckled. "Green? Why *green*?"

"Your kind is always green in the children's stories."

"You tell your children stories about us?" Turley was amazed.

"I ain't got any children," Igraine responded gruffly. "Let's find this warden." The Reaper wondered at the change in himself that would tolerate such banter. What was this little goblin to him? In days gone by, he'd have killed it on sight and enjoyed the doing of it. Was it the influence of his host body? Again, he wondered if Igraine somehow held sway over his actions and emotions.

And who had she *been*, really? Somebody's slave or concubine, it seemed. But what else? Vykers felt a flash of anger. Such thoughts were an unwelcome distraction from his current purpose, to find the man with the keys as quickly as possible and get on with the next phase of his plan, for rather than fading with time, his hunger for vengeance against Arune seemed to grow with each sunrise, until he felt certain it would soon consume his sanity.

"No. Not this way."

Those four little words pulled Vykers up short. The goblin, in front, had also stopped and was slowly backing towards him.

"What?"

"Shhh shhh shhh," the goblin whispered. "Back the way we came and quickly."

Vykers reached out a hand—Igraine's hand—and pushed

Turley to one side, so he could see for himself what the problem was. The goblin stumbled and slid down the wall, struggling as he went to make as little noise as possible. Up ahead, a large group of goblins blocked the passageway. The only mercy was that they were facing away from Turley and Igraine. For the moment.

The Reaper was always itching for a fight, but he let Turley gently pull him away anyhow. There were too many unknowns, after all. How many goblins had there been up ahead? What had they been looking at? What lay beyond them?

"I know another way," the goblin breathed once he'd led Igraine safely away.

"You'd better," said Igraine.

Turley winced at the anger in Igraine's voice, but bowed his head and resumed limping along.

"What was going on back there, anyway?"

Turley seemed to sink into himself just the slightest bit as he mumbled, "Moorsit."

"What?"

"Moorsit," Turley echoed. "They gather to expel weak ones. Or one."

"You mean you."

"Yes."

This last was said so softly, so quietly, that Vykers might have imagined it, had he not also seen the defeated slump to his companion's shoulders. "So, they're tired of waiting for you to kill yourself. What now?" he asked the little goblin.

A shrug. "I die, I suppose."

"Oh no," Igraine objected. "If anyone's gonna kill you, it's me."

Turley cast an odd, sideways glance at Igraine. "That is a comfort, mistress."

"None o' your bastard kin are gonna kill you, is what I mean."

Turley offered a rueful little laugh. "I don't see how you can stop them."

Again, Vykers lost his patience and shoved the goblin into the wall, turning his face around until he and Igraine were nearly nose-to-nose. "You got no idea who I am, Turley. And you don't wanna know, either."

The goblin withered under the malice in Igraine's eyes and turned his own towards the floor. "As you say, mistress."

Even the word 'mistress' grated on Vykers' nerves, but there was nothing he could do about it. "Let's find that other route you mentioned," Igraine said at last. "I'm tired of all o' this chit chat."

They walked for a while, and then Turley slowed to another stop. "The path ahead is...challenging," he warned.

Vykers adjusted Igraine's stance. "What's that mean?"

"First, we go past Her Majesty's throne room. Her powerful magics seep through our spy holes into the passageway. It's possible the Queen will discover your presence."

Igraine smirked. "No, she won't. I've taken steps to prevent that. And if even she does, I'd like to see her catch me!"

"I see," the goblin said dubiously.

"But you said 'first.' What else we gotta worry about?"

A look of profound anxiety came to Turley's face. "There is a dark, an evil thing in the wall beyond the throne room. Something Her Majesty has stashed for safekeeping. Most find the tunnel too painful to approach."

Immediately, the dark, evil thing was all Vykers cared about. "What is this thing?"

"None of us knows. None of us would dare get close enough to find out."

"You said the tunnel's painful...?"

"As if the very air were poisoned."

"Show me."

Rem, Inside the Castle

It was just like the Queen's Shaper to keep Rem waiting. Cindor had yanked him away from his friends, deposited him in his chambers, and left him to rot from just after sun up to well after sundown. Mahnus knew what the rush was all about, if the Shaper couldn't even be bothered to greet him when he arrived. Rem would like to have taken a nap—the Shaper's chair looked comfortable enough, if the actor could work up the courage to sit in it. But the rest of the room's contents were too odd to be ignored for the length of time sleep demanded. No, Rem would no more shut his eyes to the Shaper's weird menagerie of critters and trinkets than drink from a tavern's jakes. And so he paced, stood, leaned, and even found the courage to sit upon the floor. Just when he got more or less comfortable, the Shaper materialized behind him, nearly frightening the actor to death.

"What are you doing down there?" Cindor demanded.

"Waiting for you."

"Is that so? I would have thought the chair a more suitable place for that, but I'm glad you avoided it. I understand you actors have the most regrettable hygiene. "

Rem stood up, dusted the seat of his trousers off. "You were misinformed, milord. A duchess could eat off my naked bum. In fact, one has. But you were saying?"

Cindor stepped out of the shadows, and Rem noticed his new scars for the first time.

"Have you always been so cavalier, I wonder? And will you continue to be through what's coming?"

Rem swallowed, as subtly as possible. "Why? What's coming?"

The Shaper snapped his fingers and a small flame burst into existence beneath a tea kettle across the room. Cindor brushed past without responding immediately, almost as if he hadn't heard Rem's question. Rem would be damned, though, before he'd give in to the wizard's gamesmanship. He watched without further comment as Cindor brewed himself (but not Rem) a cup of tea and then ensconced himself in his chair.

"Excellent," he sighed. "No trace of actor musk."

It almost seemed as if the Shaper liked him on some level. Almost. Still, Rem refused to take the bait. "You mentioned something coming."

Cindor looked startled to find Rem still standing nearby. "Ah! Yes, what's coming is...*you're going.*"

Rem was not amused. "You brought me all the way here from the north to tell me I'm going."

"Yes. To the north."

Rem cackled, incredulous. "You brought me from the north to send me to the north." Oh, the things he would *like* to have said.

The Shaper blew softly upon the surface of his tea. "If that is how you choose to perceive it. The fact is, Her Majesty has dispatched your old comrade-in-arms, Captain Kittins, to investigate some rumors about the Reaper's activities up north."

Rem threw wide his arms. "So? What's that to do with me?"

Cindor spoke a single syllable and Rem became paralyzed. *"Listen,* and I'll tell you," he said sternly. "You know more of this Kittins than I. The Queen may trust him, but I do not. I would like you to follow him. Act as my eyes and ears on this journey. If anything untoward occurs, I can be there in an instant."

Oh, yes, there was a lot Rem would like to have said, but he was reduced to glaring at the magician.

"Hmmm," the Shaper intoned. "I think I almost like you like this. Silent, I mean. You should consider having your tongue removed."

Rem glared.

"In any event, where was I? Ah yes, you're following the captain. It shouldn't be difficult, as big and ugly as he is—and he's gotten a good deal uglier since you saw him last, I'll wager. He'll be headed northeast, and I'm certain he'll leave many jaws agape as he passes. Should you have any trouble in finding him, however, remember this: he's chasing rumors of the Reaper. Find the source of those rumors, and you'll find the captain." The Shaper concluded by tossing a small purse on a workbench nearby and removing whatever hex he'd put upon the actor. "That's for provisions, and there," Cindor pointed, "is the door."

The Giants, In the Forest

The captive Svarra hissed and spat like a cat. Or maybe a snake. Or perhaps some damnable combination of cat and snake. Eoman kept his big right foot planted squarely on the beast's chest, whilst he held his axe under its chin. The warning was clear enough: move, and you're dead. The creature looked up at both giants with strange, filmy eyes. Eoman would've thought it blind, but it gave every sign of seeing him quite clearly.

"You speak the old tongue?" Eoman demanded.

The Svarra hissed.

The king of giants turned to his companion. "Just our luck we'd catch an especially stupid one."

"Maybe that's why we caught him," Karrakan suggested.

Eoman scowled. "I'm for tearin' his head off and making a fetish out of it."

"Get off!" the Svarra shouted.

The giants exchanged looks.

"Queen's tongue?" Karrakan asked, arching an eyebrow in surprise.

"Figures, really," Eoman replied, disgusted. Switching over to the human's language, he readdressed the Svarra. "What are you doing out here?"

If the creature was caught off guard by his captors' sudden change of language, he didn't show it. "Hunting."

Eoman leaned on his right leg, putting still more pressure onto the Svarra's chest. "Hunting? This wood is fouled with the tracks of your kind. You're not hunting."

The Svarra snarled and howled, but said nothing worthwhile.

The king of giants nodded at his companion. "Give him something to howl about."

A spark shot from Karrakan's staff and into the Svarra's jaw, causing the creature to twitch and writhe as if it were being eaten alive by ants. And, yes, it howled in earnest now.

"You're not worried the noise will attract its fellows?" Karrakan asked.

"I'll be disappointed if it doesn't," Eoman grinned.

The two giants spent another half hour interrogating their prisoner, and, finally, Eoman stomped down with his full weight, collapsing the Svarra's chest and sending a cascade of blood out of its mouth and nose.

"That was messy," Karrakan sighed unhappily.

"What? You think he deserved better?"

"No. I just think it's going to get a lot messier before we're done."

"I'm only sorry none of his mates showed up. We didn't learn much from this one."

Karrakan looked down at the corpse. "Might be that tells us more than you think."

Eoman looked askance at his friend. "Oh?"

"Either his secret's worth dying to protect...or there *is* no secret."

"Svarren don't migrate in such big numbers unless they're about something," Eoman insisted.

"Then their secret is worth dying to protect."

"Let's see how many of 'em feel that way..."

A half day's hike brought them within sight of a large group of Svarren, forging across a half-frozen river in the waning light of afternoon.

"Damned fool time o' day to be fording a river."

"Well, that's Long Teeth for you."

"How many, you reckon?"

Karrakan squinted into the distance. "Forty, fifty."

"Can you and your little...*sparkles*...do anything to slow their crossing?" Eoman asked, gesturing towards the river.

Karrakan beamed in reply. Then he whirled his staff 'round and 'round over his head before finally flicking the end towards the river. An improbable wave of will-o-wisps spewed from the staff and streaked at the Svarren, who bellowed and roared in surprise. That surprise rapidly became fear, however, when the ice around their legs began to thicken and spread. In no time, several Svarren became trapped, frozen in place from the waist down. Seeing this, a few of their comrades tried in vain to pull them free, only managing to ensnare themselves as well. Others made a break for the far shore, or attempted to retrace their steps and regain the near. It mattered little, though, as the ice had plans of its own and clutched at the savages with a will that would not be denied.

Eoman's smile was wider than Karrakan had seen it since they'd reunited. "Can you freeze the whole river enough to support our weight? I'd like to go out there and break some heads."

It was a cruel request, Karrakan knew, but he'd never known the Svarren who was worthy of mercy. "No trouble at all!" he boasted and made it so.

The king of giants trod almost gleefully onto the ice, hefted his axe, and limbered up his arms. "Now," he yelled in the Queen's tongue, "which one o' you ugly bastards wants to tell me what you're up to?"

Even immobilized and helpless, the Svarren were not prone to cooperate.

"I was hopin' you'd feel that way," Eoman grinned. Then he swung his axe.

The False Reaper, In Camp

The False Reaper lay on his back on a bearskin rug in the middle of his tent. His eyes were closed, and though there was no one else nearby, he was not alone, for he was haunted, tormented by the spirits of those he'd been in previous lives. In his mind, he stood amongst them in a darkened space. A room? A tent? A cave? Hard to say and unimportant in the grand scheme of things. What mattered was the never ending contest of wills the boy endured.

For a moment, he shut out his companions' voices and studied their faces. In the foreground, the End-of-All-Things stood shrieking at him in his typically self-centered manner. His pale hair and paler eyes somehow blazed in the darkness with a fire that burned cold instead of hot. Across from him, to the boy's left, a more intriguing being murmured ominous somethings in the young man's ear. This creature had a face better suited to a tortoise than a man. Only holes existed where ears and nose should have been. For eyes, the creature had drops of pitch so black that not even light reflected off them. Beyond the tortoise-man, loomed a woman so short, she would barely have reached the boy's chest, had she been closer. Shaggy hair cascaded over a heavy brow, giving the woman a primitive aspect. There were others: a dark-skinned man with white hair, a tall, gaunt woman. Farther into the gloom, more figures paced or wandered in and out of view as they felt the need to make their views known. In all, the boy counted nine other iterations of himself. Or perhaps he and eight of the others were iterations of the first being, whichever one that had been. It mattered little to the false Reaper. It was his turn to rule.

"You had your chances, and look where you've ended up!" the boy admonished. "Why should I pay the least attention to your thoughts on anything?"

"Because," the End sneered, "you would not exist but for us!"

The boy laughed at this. "And if I did not, I'd never know or care."

"Still," the Tortoise whispered, "you risk joining us sooner than you'd like if you ignore us altogether."

"Failure for you is failure for all of us," the little rough-featured woman added.

"And success?"

"The same."

"I think not," the boy replied. "I am not such a fool as to face the combined forces of Alheria and the Reaper. And I will not face them on a field of their choosing! When we engage, it shall be upon *my* terms."

The End cackled. "Oh, bravely spoken, little one! Bravely spoken! And yet, what have you accomplished thus far that I have not made possible?"

"And I!" the tortoise intoned.

"And all of us," the small woman concluded. "And this is why we must act together."

The boy resisted. "Must?"

"You think you understand our previous failings?" the white-haired man challenged. "Each of us failed because we insisted on doing things our own way, making our own stamp upon the world. Had we consulted our...*forebears*..."

"So, it's all down to hubris, is it? Too much pride. Is that it?" the boy cut in, irritated.

The faces of the other nine stared back at him, momentarily nonplussed by the vehemence in the boy's voice.

"Understand something," the white-haired man said at last. "There is no guarantee of reincarnation. Despite your immediate predecessor's claims, we might have been lost forever had not your servant, Omeyo, decided to salvage the End-of-All-Things' brains and heart. We might have seeped right into the soil."

"But I planned..." the End objected.

"Shut up!" the white-haired man roared. "As the boy says, you've had your turn, Anders, and you squandered it!" The man then turned his full attention back on the boy. "All that matters now is that you understand the precariousness of your—or *our*—position. Take care, be mindful, leave nothing to chance."

That, at least, seemed like sound advice to the boy.

He forced himself awake, temporarily silencing the voices of his other iterations, and considered what he'd learned. At least one of his former selves was no fool, might in fact even be useful as a sort of advisor.

The false Reaper sat up.

The next time he fought Tarmun Vykers, the outcome would be much, much different.

Arune, In Teshton

She must have made some kind of mistake. She'd known where Aoife had started her journey, as well as where she'd been going. Arune assumed—quite naturally—that the A'Shea would pass through any town between those two points. She'd been wrong. She'd waited in Teshton. And waited. And waited. Finally, she rented a better, more secure room and sent out Questing Eyes and Ears.

But she'd found nothing.

And this made the Shaper paranoid. How could anyone with as powerful a presence as the A'Shea simply disappear? Was Aoife intentionally hiding her actions from Vykers, or had she been waylaid by an unknown party?

A disturbing possibility presented itself: what if Vykers-the-girl had somehow run into Aoife by accident and decided to reveal herself as the real Tarmun Vykers? It seemed unlikely, far-fetched, even. Nonetheless, Arune could not shake the feeling that this was exactly what had transpired.

Again, she sent out Questing Eyes and Ears. This time, however, she searched for any sign or mention of a young woman with violent tendencies, animosity towards the Reaper, or professed hatred for an absent Shaper named Arune. It wasn't like Vykers to lie down and accept the lot he'd been given. No; small as he was now, weak as he was, he'd fight to get his life back. And, barring that, he'd fight for revenge. He would never give up until he had it.

Arune slumped back onto the bed in her rented room and stared up at the ceiling. Suddenly, she felt claustrophobic; the room seemed too warm and too small. *I have Vykers' body*, she told herself. *I'm the strong one. I have a Shaper's magic. I'm the powerful one.* For all that, she was afraid, and it took hours to calm herself enough to begin her Questing.

By dawn, she had learned nothing, which terrified her even more. It was as if Vykers, like Aoife, had completely vanished, winked out of existence. And this only seemed to confirm Arune's fears that Vykers and the A'Shea had found one another.

The Shaper had no idea what to do or how to proceed and so sank into herself in a kind of paralysis. After a time, she realized she was hungry and wondered how long it had been since she'd eaten. A quick glance towards her window revealed the lengthening shadows of evening, which told her she'd lost an entire day to her doubts and suspicions. *And that is all they are*, she told herself, *suspicions*. The only way to allay her fears, however, was to hunt down Vykers and see for herself what he'd been up to in her absence, to ensure he hadn't reunited with Aoife.

Of course, Arune could not risk being recognized. She'd have to further alter her appearance, but, given her skills, that wasn't an especially daunting challenge. No, what worried Arune was the Reaper's indomitable will, that the connection between his body and soul that appeared severed might prove otherwise. She feared he would recognize his own body no matter what she did to disguise it.

And if the Reaper identified Arune...

She couldn't answer that question. He could hardly kill her, could he? That would condemn him to spending the rest of his days in the girl's body.

A chill breeze carried snowflakes into Arune's room, so she got up, crossed the room, and closed the shutters.

Vykers could not afford to kill her.

With that thought, she packed her few meager belongings and made ready to depart for Lunessfor in the morning.

Vykers & Turley, Under the Castle

"Her Majesty's throne room is on our left. You may view it through Pinda."

The look on Igraine's face must have been quite sour, because Turley wasted no time in clarifying. "Some of our spyholes, as you call them, are rather special. We give them their own names, so that everyone will understand when we speak of them."

"Everyone?" Vykers echoed irritably.

"Everyone in my clan."

Vykers stared at the hole-pitted wall. "Seems like any o' these should work."

"But they don't," Turley cautioned. "Some are too low, others are cut at odd angles. Only Pinda offers the perfect view."

He was about to ask how the goblins had arrived at the name Pinda, but decided he didn't care. Another long-winded story, he didn't doubt. Without another word, the stepped over to the wall, braced his hands on either side of Pinda, and peeked through the hole.

The light in the throne room stayed at a constant level, through the use of wall sconces, candelabras and arcane means, so Vykers wasn't able to determine the time of day. However, Her Majesty reclined in a little chair at the foot of the enormous dais upon which her actual throne sat. Her mage, Cindor, lurked in the shadows at her left, just as he had the last two times Vykers had visited the throne room. As the Reaper watched, four guards detached themselves from those surrounding the chamber and approached the Queen.

The four Vykers! And be damned if the lead man wasn't wearing the Reaper's supposedly destroyed sword! Ah, that Alheria was a deceitful bitch—a conniving, manipulative, deceitful bitch. Vykers pulled away from the wall and nearly spit on the tunnel floor to rid himself of the rage, the bile that had risen in Igraine's throat. Must he always be two moves behind Her Majesty?

He wanted to hole up somewhere, to think and brood on what he'd seen. But he returned to Pinda and took another look. This time, the four Vykers were no longer visible, and Alheria was conferring with her Shaper.

The injuries she'd done to the Reaper over the years were many, and every gift she'd bestowed upon him always came with an unexpected cost. He'd long thought of toppling her from power, of usurping her throne—not out of any particular animus against her, but because he was the Reaper, and such actions were as much a part of his nature as violence was to a boar. But now—now!—he had reason, and reason upon reason to kill Her Majesty.

But first, he needed to retrieve his own body.

"How much farther to the warden's chambers?" he demanded of Turley.

"Not much, mistress. But we must pass the bad thing, first."

Vykers laughed without the slightest trace of merriment. "You're *looking* at the bad thing."

He hadn't had time to digest his anger when Turley pulled to a stop in front of him and shivered visibly.

"What?"

"It is just ahead, trapped in the wall on our left."

Same side as the Queen's throne room.

"Show me," Vykers said.

"I'd rather you went first."

No surprise there. Igraine shouldered past and took several steps. Suddenly, Vykers felt it in his bones, and he smiled. "I know this bad thing," he proclaimed. "None better." He looked back at Turley who was now clearly uncomfortable.

"You…you *know* it?"

As low as he'd been mere moments before, Vykers was exultant now. Triumph surged through his veins and set giddy fire to all his extremities. "Steal my sword, will you?" he chuckled, much to Turley's bemusement.

Igraine took a further two steps and laid a hand on the wall. The look on her face was of near euphoria. "So, it's inside the wall, is it? In some kind of vault, I'm guessing. Probably spell-protected on the other side, but this side?" Again, Igraine laughed, which sounded more like a giggle to Vykers' ears, making him laugh all the harder at the absurdity it. He caught a glimpse of Turley watching him, goggle-eyed, and redoubled his laughter. "Turley!" he called out.

"Yes, mistress?" the little goblin replied nervously.

"You little fellers are tunnellers, diggers..."

"Yes?"

"You got any tools hereabouts or nearby?"

"Tools?"

"Tools! Hammers, chisels. Tools!"

"There's always a small supply at every junction. I thought you would have noticed..."

"Go fetch me some and hurry back!"

If Vykers was worried Turley might run off and never return, it wasn't evident in Igraine's face. The little goblin turned away and scuttled off down the corridor.

In his absence, Vykers set to work on the wall with Igraine's dagger. If the Reaper was correct about what lay behind the stones, he'd have no further need of the girl's weapon. With this thought in mind, he attacked the mortar between those stones with gusto, scoring, pitting and digging at it until he had outlined a good-sized block of granite. In time, Turley returned with the promised collection of tools, which included a small pick, a hammer and three different chisels.

"Ah!" Vykers called out, "Give me that hammer and one o' those chisels."

But the goblin hesitated.

"Hand it over!" Vykers insisted.

"I'm just worried the noise may attract my brethren."

Vykers stopped. "It might?" He turned back to the wall and began pounding. "Because I would *love* to kill something right about now."

Turley scampered over to Igraine's side and planted his back against the wall. If anything was headed his way, he wanted to see it or them before it or they saw him. The trouble was, he couldn't hear over the sound of Igraine's hammering, and the longer it went on, the more anxious he became.

"I think I got it," Vykers announced at last. But, of course, he didn't have it. Vykers could have lifted the block from its hole and tossed it aside; Igraine could not. She hadn't the strength, and it galled the Reaper that he continually forgot that and was continually reminded. "Maybe I don't," he said.

"Can you pull one end out and reach behind?" Turley inquired helpfully.

Vykers wasn't sure what the little creature was saying at first, but he eventually got the idea. "Give me that pick."

Turley passed it to Igraine, but his head whipped back the other way when he thought he heard footsteps approaching.

"What is it?"

"I am...uncertain. Is this thing you're after a weapon?"

Igraine only winked in response. Winked!

"Well," Turley fretted, "I hope you secure it soon!"

"Workin' on it."

Too soon, Turley became aware of footsteps in both directions—large numbers of footsteps.

Igraine had the stone turned and reached gingerly into the hole. From the goblin's perspective, she appeared fearful of spiders or some such. But he was mistaken, for Vykers knew well the sting of the thing he sought and had no interest in suffering even the tiniest scratch. Some torments, you need only suffer once. To Vykers' relief, Igraine's fingers lightly swept across something scabbard-shaped.

"Mistress!" Turley interrupted in a tone of rising alarm. "Forgive the intrusion, but..."

Twin mobs of heavily armed goblins advanced from the left and right. Turley dropped to the floor at Igraine's feet in a panic and curled into a ball. Igraine yanked the blade from its hiding place, whipped it out of its sheath, and passed it in a broad arc in front of her chest.

Both packs of goblins lurched to a stop and stared from Igraine to Turley and back. Slowly, their eyes gravitated towards Igraine's forward hand, which appeared to hold... nothing. The foremost goblins leered at the girl.

"I know you fuckers speak the Queen's tongue. You take one more step—any o' you—and pain's the last thing you'll ever know," Igraine said.

An especially large goblin pushed his way through his fellows and advanced on Igraine. Though not as quick as Vykers, she flicked out her arm, just as he intended, and sliced the creature's nose right off his face. And that was just the beginning of his troubles. In moments, his face caved in on itself and left his body twitching and convulsing on the floor. Seeing this, his shocked comrades fell back in terror and disbelief.

"That's right, fuckers. You come near, you die in agony."

Both mobs backed away, to the edge of vision.

"Hey, Turley," Igraine said. "Your friends got any arrows or spears or other distance weapons?"

Turley peeked out from behind his arms. "Those are not much use down here, with so many twists and turns."

"That's a relief," Igraine said.

"Of course, there are always the poisoned blow darts..."

"Shit!" Igraine tucked the still empty scabbard into her belt, reached down, grabbed the goblin's arm, and heaved him to his feet. "We'll have to run over or through 'em. Can't stay here and let 'em shoot at us."

Turley was heavier than he looked, and his mass slowed Igraine's charge enough that Vykers figured they'd never bust through on momentum alone. Again, Igraine extended her new weapon. "Who else wants a taste 'o my blade?" she yelled.

Just ahead, several of the goblins had decided they could achieve in a group what their fallen leader had failed to do by himself. Many of them brandished their hatchets, their picks, their hammers and knives in Igraine's direction. But Vykers' growing confidence in his new body's abilities, along with those of the nasty weapon in his hand, made the Reaper eager to brawl with Turley's former kin. Igraine let out a roar and ran into their midst, her hand flashing about like a hummingbird. Everywhere it went, a new cry of agony followed. In the fray, Igraine dropped her hold on Turley, and he sank to the tunnel floor again, covering his eyes and ears with his overlarge hands and muttering constantly. It might have been a prayer of some sort or a recipe for pottage, for all Vykers knew. He was too enthralled with his new dagger to pay any attention to the little goblin's predicament. Once he'd killed or frightened off all the others, however, he was again able to focus on Turley.

"They're all gone, now. These ones, anyway." Igraine looked back down the tunnel, but was unable to determine what had become of the second mob.

"They'll be back," Turley gasped. "And in greater numbers."

There was a strange gleam in Igraine's eyes that frightened the goblin. "Then I'll kill them in greater numbers."

Turley could hardly speak. "Yes," he whispered. "That's what I'm afraid of."

Igraine radiated aggression from every pore; her sweat stank of it. "And what do you care? Those bastards all want you dead, too."

The little goblin was smart enough to know when to cut his losses. There was no point in trying to explain goblin ways and beliefs to a human, especially one as hostile as his companion. Besides, this human now held the bad thing—whatever it was. Turley could not see anything in the girl's hand, but he'd seen death flowing out of it, spectacular, greedy death.

Igraine pulled him forward until they reached another junction. It was time to make for the Warden's chambers.

Nelby & Esmine, On the Run

It was not merely cold or even terribly cold; it was the-gods-hate-us cold. Nelby had known it would be, of course, but that foreknowledge had availed her nothing. She confirmed the beginnings of frostbite in her toes and imagined it wouldn't be long before it appeared in her fingers, nose and ears as well. She was more concerned for Esmine, but, so far, the child showed no signs of the affliction. Perhaps Alheria had not forsaken the two girls after all. Or maybe the constant running had kept the child just warm enough to avert disaster. Whatever the case, they ran—and would continue to run—until they lost the men on their trail or died trying. A small part of Nelby hoped for the second result. It was better to die free than endure another moment in the slavers' caravan. Surely the cold wouldn't take long in killing them both, if they chose to stop fighting it.

So, yes, it was cold, it was dark, and the fugitives were

starving and exhausted. Nelby was seconds from deciding to end it when a distant shout got her moving again. *Why?* She wondered. *Why am I runnin'? Where am I leadin' this lost little one?* But no answer presented itself; she knew only that she had to keep them both on their feet and moving forward. She gave Esmine's hand a reassuring squeeze and was unnerved to receive no reaction from the girl.

Still, they ran, stumbled, shuffled, plodded. Their pursuers were not far behind, but mercifully never seemed to get any closer, either. If only the countryside offered some hiding place—a cave, an old cabin, a sheltering deadfall, anything.

At times, Nelby slipped on icy snow or tripped over an exposed root she hadn't seen and went down on all fours. Gods, it was hard getting back to her feet and seemed to take longer and longer each time. Esmine, by contrast, appeared to possess some inner reserve, some hidden source of strength that defied understanding. *How does she do it?* Nelby wondered. *Poor girl watched her mum die in front of her, and she's not seen her da in ages. What keeps her goin'?*

The bedraggled brush gradually gave way to taller trees and then forest, and Nelby's mood improved with it. There were places to hide in a forest—or ought to be, anyway. But there were also new dangers. Nelby decided she'd rather take her chances with wolves than with those following her. Wolves killed out of need, but slavers? Alheria knew what they might do if they caught up with the girls.

"There!" a voice yelled from the darkness.

And Nelby pushed harder, fairly dragging Esmine behind her. The thrall woman didn't know how much strength she had left—a few more minutes, perhaps. If an escape didn't present itself soon...She was unable or unwilling to complete the thought.

The woods were lovely, dark, and deep, or would have been under other circumstances. Now, they were an unhelpful maze that favored neither pursued nor pursuers. Nelby could no longer feel her feet and suspected her life was a handful of heartbeats from ending. Beside her, Esmine continued to trudge along without emotion. She'd feel something, surely, if she found herself alone in the next few minutes…

A gigantic paw swept out of the darkness and sent Nelby tumbling through the air and into the bole of a great fir. She hit it spine-first and abruptly lost consciousness from the trauma and pain.

But something was tugging, dragging her through the snow. She wanted to drift off into oblivion, but this rough handling kept jostling her awake. Or semi-awake. Try as she might, she could not regain full command of her senses. The forest was swirling around her and fading in and out. A better-fed person might have been sick, but Nelby's stomach was emptier than a dead man's purse. Unable to focus on everything and unwilling to trust her eyes, she decided to put all of her strength into listening. Had she run into a bear? What had befallen Esmine? And what of the slavers who'd been chasing her?

The dragging stopped, and Nelby heard feet crunching in the snow. Something was thrown over her, and then another something. The cold, though still present, abated slightly. In spite of her best intentions, Nelby sank back into nothingness.

Long & Company, In the Forest

The weather had been brutal, *was* brutal, as if the sky had challenged itself to produce more snow than had ever been seen and then dump it upon any souls unlucky enough to pass beneath. Long Pete clung to the leeward side of his half-frozen pony and hoped their combined body heat was enough to keep them both alive. He'd been forced to dismount hours earlier and now put all of his energy into steering the poor beast to shelter—wherever and whatever that turned out to be. His comrades, he saw, had followed his lead, and each also struggled to lead his suffering mount. Earlier, there had been the suggestion of a road. Then it was only a path. Now they plowed a channel through drifts that rose to chest-height on the horses. If it reached the withers, they were all dead, sure.

A sound like thunder frightened the ponies and their masters, despite their exhaustion. Long had never heard of thunder happening in a blizzard, but up in the Mahnus-cursed north, anything was possible, he supposed. The ground beneath the group's feet shook under a second deep, rolling rumble. Earthquake? A loud, jarring crack shocked everyone to a stand-still, and then the whole party was toppling, tumbling downward, into a blackness that hadn't been there moments before. The horses screamed in terror, even as their riders clung to their sides like drowning sailors, grasping at pieces of floating wreckage. Down, down they rolled and slid on an ever-steepening slope, out of the white and into the black. Long caught a glimpse of his pony's eye, wide with fear, and for an instant they saw one another. Then there was not enough light left to see anything. Still, snow pounded down from above like an avalanche, offering no quarter and driving the beset travelers deeper into the abyss. Against all odds, Long managed to stay atop his mount's heaving ribs, until a sudden and final bone-rattling thump launched him off the poor beast and into a deep mound of snow some yards distant, where he lay shivering, from cold and fear alike.

It was some time before he could catch his breath and still his trembling arms and legs enough to extricate himself from his icy tomb. Somewhere off in the shadows, he heard the eerie screams of someone's pony in mortal agony. If he could find it, he'd have to put it down. "Yendor?" he called out. "Spirk? Ron?"

"Here," a voice groaned, not far to Long's left. "Leg's broke, I think. Arm, too." A breathy, laboring cackle. "If I lose anything else, you'll have naught left but my pecker!"

"The gods forfend!" Long joked, working his way towards Yendor's voice.

"The fuck we fall into?" Yendor asked.

"Can't say. We'll find out soon enough, though. Hold up your good arm and let me see if I can find you."

But it was the toe of Long's boot that found Yendor's ribs first.

"Aaaagh! Alheria's a bitch!" Yendor yelled. "Those are my ribs, not my arm!"

"Apologies," Long muttered. "I'm as blind as you, down here."

It was hard going, but in time they both managed to get Yendor to his feet, leaning rather heavily on Long's shoulder.

"Gotta find those boys, now," said Long. "Don't know if we can get out of this place without 'em."

"We're here," Ron said, catching the captain by surprise.

Yendor spoke through gritted teeth. "You don't sound the worse for wear."

"Well," Spirk admitted, "once we started fallin', I kinda floated us down, like."

"Floated?" Yendor bellowed. "Why the fuck couldn't ya float *us* down, too?"

"I lost sight o' you almost from the get-go," Spirk replied defensively.

"Easy now," Long said. "The boys ain't to blame for this latest disaster."

"Bleedin' miracle any of us survived."

"The horses didn't," Long answered. In the distance, one of them continued to scream. "We'll have to put that one down. Don't want her dyin' to bring anything after us."

This comment so alarmed Spirk that he nearly started to weep. "What'd come after us?"

"Nothing, lad," Long replied. "Just bein' safe."

Snow continued to pour on them in rivers from the surface, which was so far above and behind them, the sky was no longer visible.

"How far you figure we've fallen?" Yendor asked his captain.

Long shrugged. "Farther 'n the tallest tower in Moon's Crossing."

"And where 'ave we ended up?" Ron wondered.

But no one had an answer or even a guess.

Long wasted no time in determining the horse could not be saved and put his sword through its heart.

"Hate to do that," he muttered. Then, more loudly, "Maybe we should huddle around this old girl while she's still got some warmth in her. Take some time to figure out what we're gonna do next."

Yendor slid down the horse's belly into a seated position. "I guess this is where I bravely tell you all to leave me," he said.

"Where I say I can't let myself become a burden to ya...only, I ain't saying it. I can see that I'm fucked. I can bloody well see that. But I don't wanna die alone."

His eyes had adjusted to the darkness just enough to let Long see the sad, deflated shape of his old friend against the darker, larger bulk of the dead horse. "No more talk o' dyin'!" he commanded. "That isn't helpin' anyone. Let's just...let's just set a spell, like I said, and try to figure what's next."

"We need to bind Yendor's breaks," Spirk offered. "Somehow. And maybe I can dull his pain somewhat. Maybe."

"You do that, lad, and I'll never tease you again," Yendor promised.

"First, I gotta..." Small flames appeared at Spirk's fingertips. When he pulled them together, the flames joined to form a decidedly larger one. "We got anything to burn?" he asked. "I need both hands to help Yendor."

"Guess we can use some of this pony's mane. Don't suppose she'll be missin' it," said Long, as he sheared away a good handful. "Only, how will you keep it from burning up too fast?"

Spirk reached out and touched the hair, transferring the flames from his hand. "It won't. I don't know why, exactly, but it just kinda holds the fire in place."

And so it did. The fire behaved like a normal flame in every regard, except that it didn't consume the horse's mane. Long swept it to his left and right, casting the light into areas he hadn't seen before. It appeared tons of snow and rocky debris had come down into the hole with him and his companions. But where it hadn't fallen, patches of stone flooring were visible.

"Can you make us a proper fire with that?" Yendor grunted, pointing his nose at Long's makeshift torch.

"Prob'ly," said Spirk.

Once Yendor's 'proper' fire was burning at the group's feet, Spirk set about tending to the older man's injuries.

"I can help bind him," Long offered, handing his torch to Ron. "I've done it often enough on the battlefield."

It was a difficult task, but they got it done to Yendor's satisfaction. Or what passed for it. "'S good," he groaned. "Might need a little sleep," and "Wish I had me some Skent," he whispered as he drifted into unconsciousness.

"What do you think?" Long asked Spirk.

"I'm kinda hungry."

Long sighed. Despite the young man's new abilities, he remained a boy inside. "I was talkin' about Yendor. What do you make of his chances?"

"Oh! Uh…I think he's gonna be okay?" Spirk responded, as if hoping he'd given the right answer this time.

"But if we try to move him too soon…well, one thing at a time. Let's make camp here. Ron and I can explore this hole a bit while you keep a watch on Yendor."

In truth, the most important part of said exploration was finding the other horses, salvaging supplies, and determining whether or not there were any immediate threats nearby. Holding his horse hair torch, Long beckoned Ron to follow him into the shadows.

Spirk, of course, was unhappy to see his leader and his best friend depart—especially in such a lightless, eerie place—abandoning him with no one for company but the unconscious Yendor. Seconds passed like hours. Minutes felt like days. And all the while it was cold—teeth chattering, limb-shivering cold. In spite of his anxieties and his physical discomfort, Spirk fell asleep.

Such is the power of magic.

SIX

Mureen, In the Cottage

If Mureen found Tinalia's appearance unsettling, the Svarra's eldest son was positively horrifying. It was true that some Svarren had one eye, and others had three, but Baris had multiple eyes all over his head. No wonder he was such a talented hunter! Unfortunately, once he'd entered the room, Mureen never felt free of his gaze, as if a part of him was staring at her at all times. Worse still, it quickly became apparent that Tinalia harbored a not-so-secret desire to make a match between her guest and her son.

As the three worked to skin, clean and butcher the boar Baris had brought home, Mureen could not escape the feeling that she was the one being readied for consumption.

"And isn't my Baris a strong one!" Tinalia remarked. "How many other hunters can bring down a boar single-handed?"

"And it *was* single-handed, you know, mum. I hit him a good one right between his ears, and the fight went out of him!" Baris winked at Mureen, and a more disturbing sight she'd never witnessed.

"What do you say, eh, Mureen? Isn't my boy a marvel?"

"Yes," the giantess was quick to reply. "Certainly, certainly." It wasn't much, but it was all she could think to say, her mind now being so occupied with nightmarish visions of conjugal relations with the Svarren male. Shaken, she rededicated herself to the chore she'd been given: collecting the various cuts of boar and placing them on the counter. Baris had already bled the beast, so it wasn't as messy a job as it might have been.

Still, there was something about the dismembered boar that bothered Mureen.

When the task was complete, Baris excused himself in order to clean up and change into fresh clothing. Mureen had never known or even heard of a Svarra who cared for cleanliness, but then Tinalia and Baris were not normal Svarren. How they had come to be as they were was a question that vexed the giantess. She had little opportunity to dwell upon it, though, because Tinalia never stopped talking, even as she selected a good-sized piece of loin and prepared it for the fire.

"Baris, you know, is nearly your size. Quite large for one of our people. You'd make a good match for one another, if you learned to fancy my boy."

"Yes, mum."

"You couldn't ask for a better provider or more stalwart companion."

Mureen let the comment hang in the air. She could think of no suitable response and hoped that a lengthy silence might communicate what her words had not. But no such luck.

"After all, dearie," Tinalia crooned, "It's the least you could do to repay us for all the trouble we've gone to on your behalf. It isn't easy feeding and caring for a woman of your size. And, as I say, my Baris is quite the prize!"

Tinalia gestured for Mureen to follow, and the women went back into the sitting room, where the Svarren woman placed the meat and some root vegetables on the fire. "I should do this in the kitchen, but I just adore the aroma of roast meat wafting about the cottage!"

Baris entered the room, accompanied by a cloud of some powerfully scented perfume. His clothes, like those of his mother, were rich in fabric, cut and design, but seemed somehow out of date and at least one size too small. He actually bowed slightly whilst entering and proceeded to set a table for dinner.

"And his manners!" Tinalia sang out. "You'll hardly find better in Lunsford!"

If Mureen was expecting a bashful Baris to silence his mother, she was sorely disappointed. Instead, he poured something dark from a decanter into three goblets and offered the first to the giantess.

"It's only wine," he smiled, his myriad eyes twinkling at her.

"Only? That's Her Majesty's favorite red or I'm one of the fey!" Tinalia put in.

Whether it was or wasn't, Mureen waited until both her hosts had taken a sip before she did the same. The gratitude, the trust she'd felt in Tinalia was slowly metastasizing into virulent paranoia, and throughout dinner, it only got worse. At one point, a now tipsy Tinalia leaned in to whisper in Mureen's ear. "He's a bull 'twixt the sheets, I can tell you that. But I need a little relief now and then!"

Mureen put her goblet down. "You've both been awfully kind, but I'm afraid I'm still too weak for wine just yet. I wonder if I might lie down for a spell?"

The rapidity with which the levity fled from Tinalia's eyes was astounding. "Lie down?" she asked. "Already?"

Mureen nodded.

"Well, if you must. But be ready to contribute more generously to your new family when you awaken."

"Of course!" Mureen replied with feigned enthusiasm. *New family?* How had everything gone so wrong, so quickly? As she walked away from the table, she couldn't escape the feeling that her hosts were staring at her back, plotting. When she stepped into her room and turned to close the door, she discovered they were, indeed, watching her every move.

"Good night!" she said, as sweetly as possible.

Tinalia waved dismissively and returned her attention to her meal. Baris, on the other hand, maintained eye contact until Mureen had closed the door. Just as the giantess was preparing to climb into bed, she heard the telltale signs of something heavy—the hutch, say—being moved in front of her door. It was nothing Mureen couldn't work her way past, but it sent a very clear message: *you are not leaving any time soon.*

Kittins, On the Road

It was as biting, as miserable a winter as Kittins could remember, and he'd been commanded to slog through it in order to accomplish a task that could have been done by magic with much less time and effort. Thus, he could only assume the real goal in sending him forth had been banishment. And if he died in the effort? Well, no one in Lunessfor would mind, that was certain.

And why was he again letting Her Majesty dictate what he would do or not do? Hadn't he sworn revenge upon her for what he'd been forced to do under Lord Gault, for what he'd become in Gault's service?

His mind unaccountably went to thoughts of Tarmun Vykers, the Reaper, the man Kittins was supposed to locate and spy upon. Now there was a fellow who knew how to obtain vengeance, if the stories were true. Vykers burned for vengeance with the heat of a blast furnace.

Kittins, though, was cold, colder than the ice crusting on his cloak, colder than the snow blowing in his face. In that regard he supposed he was in his element, that he'd found a kindred spirit in this worst of all winters. There was nothing the weather could do to his soul that he hadn't already done to himself. Freeze to death? Not bloody likely.

His horse, however, was a different matter. The Queen's stable master had given him one of those northern ponies—not large, but stout and with a good, thick coat. Hard to believe the beast was in any way related to the proud stallions of the Queen's Swords. The pony was used to snow, but *this* snow? *This* cold? Kittins reckoned he'd be eating the animal before the week was out.

A bigger problem was the tedium he'd be facing throughout the trek north. In the army, he'd made longer journeys, but he'd had company, been *part* of a company. He didn't need companionship, but he worried how he'd respond to endless solitude. He feared going mad, like the End-of-All-Things, and deciding the world would be better off if everything in it died.

He scanned the road ahead: nothing but grays and whites.

Thinking of the End brought his mind back to the Reaper. Kittins wondered what it would be like to fight him. The Reaper was faster—faster than anyone, it was said. And he might be stronger. Kittins would give him that. But could Vykers take as much damage as the enspelled captain? It would be interesting to find out.

An especially powerful gust of wind forced Kittins to rewrap the scarf around his face and pull down on the flaps of his hat.

Gods, it was going to be a long trek.

Rem, In Pursuit

Not far behind him, Remuel Wratch likewise battled his way through the snow, wishing himself anywhere else in the world. The captain, it seemed, was immune to the cold. That might have been due to his military discipline, or he might simply have taken too many blows to the head. Whatever the case, he plowed forward without the slightest change in pace or direction. Rem, though, felt bullied aside by every clod or clump of ice in his path. For a man who'd made his living on his imagination, he was hard pressed to envision himself surviving this journey. The very idea was laughable, really.

The Queen's Mage had conscripted Rem into this spying business, and Rem, ever the narcissist, had fancied himself well-suited to the job, had even supposed it might be fun. *Fun!* What an idiot he'd been, what a clodpoll! The last time he'd indulged in this sort of work, the Lord and Lady Hawsey had killed one another. And who knew how many others had suffered because of Rem's clumsy espionage?

Maybe his current assignment was payment for deeds—or misdeeds—done. There must have been faster, more efficient ways to dispatch an unwanted servant. But sending Rem off on a hopeless task whilst he slowly froze to death? That Cindor had a disturbing sense of humor.

Other men might plot revenge in such circumstances; Rem thought only of how to survive the next mile.

Vykers & Turley, In the Castle

Vykers pressed his injured guide forward without compunction. Yes, it was possible Turley's leg might not withstand such stress and strain, but time was growing short. Ever since the encounter with Turley's kin, Vykers worried that one or more of them might run off to warn Her Majesty of Irgaine's presence, perhaps even of her theft of the End's dagger.

For that is what the 'bad thing' had been, and now Vykers possessed it. Whether he used it for its intended purpose or as a bargaining chip to force concessions from the Queen, the Reaper finally had an advantage that Her Majesty had not already anticipated and countered. He hadn't felt this confident since he'd been in his own body. And the beauty of the situation was that Her Majesty would assume someone had broken in to steal the dagger. She might even assume it was Vykers, and that he'd make his escape as quickly as possible. She was far less likely to imagine that he'd continue working his way further into the castle—unless it was to assassinate her—and she'd never guess his actual destination.

Vykers just needed to get out of these rat tunnels and into the castle proper.

"How much farther?" Igraine demanded.

"Not. Much," Turley panted.

"Good. You get me there, I may let you live."

Turley didn't reply. He wasn't sure that was a blessing.

Vykers listened during their flight, paradoxically dreading and hoping to hear the sounds of bodies approaching. Having whetted his appetite for carnage with the unfortunate goblins, the Reaper began to hunger for a greater challenge and more bloodshed. In a moment of rare clarity, he wondered if this was due to his own nature or the dagger's malevolent influence. He knew from experience that such weapons had a will of their own. The only question was: did they share the same goals? Seeing as the dagger had nearly killed him, Vykers was more than a little skeptical.

Suddenly, he and his guide arrived at a crossroads.

"The passage to the left opens behind an arras in the corridor you're wanting," the goblin wheezed.

"Well," Igraine said, "You can show me. I'm not leavin' you here with those bastard kin o' yours."

Turley shook his head, sadly. "But they are my kin, as I am theirs. Outside these tunnels…"

Igraine yanked him forward. "Not interested. You're coming with me."

If Vykers was expecting a door of cunning design, he was sorely disappointed. The actual door was just a door, painted on the far side to look more or less like the rest of the hallway.

"What's to keep castle folk from wandering into your tunnels?"

"You'd have to ask them," said Turley, sulking.

"Uh-huh. Which way?"

"I believe your warden can be found to the right."

Turley was quite dramatic about his distaste for the enhanced lighting of the hallway, flinching and mewling as if he was in pain. Vykers ignored him.

"What will you do if we encounter any of the castle folk?"

Igraine shrugged. "Prob'ly kill 'em. I ain't got time for chit chat," she explained.

They only encountered three people, and all were avoided with minimal effort. When they reached the appropriate corridor, Turley had a final surprise for Vykers.

"Now which one o' these doors is it?" the Reaper demanded.

"I've no idea," Turley answered, keeping his voice low.

"I thought you knew where to find the Warden's chambers."

Turley shrank into the wall at his back. "Generally, yes."

Igraine let out a growl of frustration and turned to the first door. Without knocking, she tried the handle and found it locked. "Nothing's ever gotta be easy, does it?" She was about to try to kick it open when Turley stopped her.

"In this case, there might be an easier way," he said. He slipped his fingers into a pouch at his belt and produced three or four oddly-shaped wires.

"Why didn't you say you could pick the lock?" Vykers asked, accusingly.

"That has yet to be determined."

Igraine stepped back and let the little creature work. Just when Vykers was about to give up and resume his attempt to break the door down, he heard a faint click, and Turley gently turned the handle. Without thanking the goblin, Igraine pushed past him and into the room beyond. To Vykers' surprise, Turley followed.

"What are you doin'?" Igraine whispered.

"Do you think I'd be safer in the hallway than inside with you?"

Lippy little bastard. "Fine: follow, but don't make any more noise."

The room was unoccupied.

"It's not all bad. We'll use this as our base," Igraine explained. "We run into trouble or need to hide, we'll come back here."

"Or I could just wait here for you until..."

"No, no. I might need you to pick some more locks."

Turley sighed and shook his head. "Yes, mistress."

The next room turned out to be vacant also, but only newly so. Someone had just eaten a hot meal and departed before the remains had gone cold. Vykers and Turley were delighted to finish the leftovers.

"What do you call this?" Turley asked, holding a chicken wing by its pointed end.

"You never had chicken?"

"I didn't say I've never had it. I just don't know your word for it."

Vykers was not a clown like Her Majesty's fool. He opted for the truth. "That's a chicken wing."

"Chicken wing," Turley repeated. "They're very tasty like this."

"Like how?"

"On this bread, heated. We usually pull things like this out of the garbage chutes. Cold, congealed. Not nearly as flavorful."

Igraine dropped the thigh she'd been chewing on. "I'll bet."

"Aren't you worried that our mystery diner will return?"

"No," Igraine scowled. "He's no threat."

The little goblin's mouth gaped. "How do you know he's male?"

Igraine chuckled. "Spying on us all this time, and you still don't know us. Well, for starters, those are men's boots by the wall over there. But the leather's soft and they're small. Our man's not a big one. And he walks with a cane. That explains those scuff marks on the floor." Igraine pointed them out. "Reason he didn't finish this bird is his teeth are bad. See how 'e ate up those boiled carrots and custard? He's hungry, all right. He just can't chew."

"But where did he go?"

"To the jakes, I imagine. These older fellas are always runnin' off to the jakes. I could probably tell you more about 'im, but I want to move on. He ain't the Warden."

Turley cast a wistful eye behind him as he followed Igraine out the door.

The two rooms across the hall were locked but unoccupied. When Igraine and Turley turned back to the third door on the wall they'd started on, they both reacted in surprise.

"Shoulda just walked the hallway before startin', I guess."

Turley nodded.

This new door had the most complex lock they'd seen so far.

"Shall I open it?" the goblin inquired.

"No. Duck outta sight. I'm knockin' on this one." The goblin must have appeared concerned, because Igraine barked, "I said hide!" Without waiting to see if the order had been followed, she pounded on the door.

An eyehole that Vykers had not noticed opened on a spot just over Igraine's head—another unforeseen consequence of living inside the young woman. In his normal body, he'd have seen the eyehole at chin-height. Evidently, Igraine's appearance appealed to the room's occupant, because Vykers suddenly heard a variety of latches being thrown, locks being turned and the like. The door swung wide to reveal a man of middle age with an absurdly styled beard, ridiculously parted hair that hung just below his ears, and an outlandishly decorative robe that lay open at his chest, exposing a forest of curly chest hair. He leered when he set eyes on Igraine, but stopped when she punched him in the throat. In fact, he toppled over, curled up into a ball, and struggled to breathe.

Igraine bent over, grabbed the man's ankles, and dragged him through the door. Turley slipped in behind her, just before Igraine shoved it closed again. "Watch him," she told the goblin. "I need to make sure he's alone."

Aoife, the North

The Here-There was now much easier than it had ever been. In the past, Aoife could only move between groves she herself had birthed. Now, though, from anything green to anything green, from thicket to copse, from scrub brush to mighty forest, she could make vast leaps with a thought, even to places she'd never visited before. Thus, she was able to reach the outskirts of her brother's new horde in little time—before, in fact, she realized that she had no idea what to do once she arrived.

About her feet was a small, sad little clump of stunted evergreen bushes, wind-blasted and cold-bitten, forcing its way through a frozen crust of snow. The newly ordained Umaena worked to fortify them, for their own sake, but also her use. In minutes, she'd turned the pitiful plants into a towering hedge, bristling with thorns. Aware that her creation's sudden appearance might attract undue attention, Aoife reshaped its bulk, sculpted the whole of it into something shorter but deeper, something that could be gazed over, but never hurdled— anything attempting to do so would land in the thick of this verdant barrier and be torn to shreds by its countless thorns.

The sun peeked through the clouds, but affected the temperature not one bit. What it did do was allow Aoife a better view of her distant enemy, which hunkered down into smaller camps, gathered, presumably, around a central army—and in the middle of all that, her brother. Or so Aoife believed. The Svarren were too far away to be seen clearly, but she knew the reverse was true as well: she was beyond their surveillance, and so safe, for the time being.

Aoife continued to shape her hedge until it formed a large circle around her. She then set about summoning a few of the fey who might serve as her sentinels and protectors. Even Umaeni need sleep, after all. She decided against the taller folk, like trolls, because they'd be too visible from a distance, and even mistaken for trees, they would have appeared to have come from nowhere. And so she called gnomes, a sprite or two, a talking hedgehog, and a will-o'-wisp. Toomt'-La, she did not summon, for she feared he would not approve of her plans. Invited or not, though, she suspected he would appear if things went awry.

She spent the rest of the day acquainting herself with her new guardians and her fortress, making sure that everything was as it should be. In the evening, when her fey companions brought her honey, fruit and vegetables, Aoife spied the light of fires in the Svarren encampments. She knew that Long Teeth were more active at night, and her experience watching the End's previous host told her that patrols would soon be sweeping the area around his camp in wider and wider circles, looking for threats, plunder or food.

They would find Aoife's hedge, if not her redoubt, and then the trouble would begin. But Aoife held an advantage she'd not enjoyed in her previous clash with her brother. If she managed things correctly, she could nip at the End's heels forever and he'd never catch her. Last time, Toomt'-La's influence had held her in abeyance. This time, Aoife would act when and how she wanted.

The light fled from the sky, as if unwilling to witness what was to come, and the sounds of the Svarren rousing themselves reverberated across the distance between their camp and Aoife's fortress. Soon, soon they would stumble upon her, and the war between the Umaena and her former sibling would be rejoined.

The Giants, In the Forest

Eoman and Karrakan sat by the roaring campfire they'd built, vigorously scrubbing the Svarren blood from their skin and personal effects with rags fashioned from Svarren clothing.

"How do those fell things prosper with such ichor in their veins?" Karrakan wondered aloud.

"How do rats, dampworms and ticks prosper? Is it the will o' the gods, or of something infernal from the endless hells?"

"Speaking of the infernal," said Karrakan, "Are you set on Beesmarch?"

"Him and any others we can find and rally to the cause."

Karrakan looked unconvinced. "But the cause," he said, "seems to have split in two..."

Eoman stood, stretched, threw his bloody rag into the fire. "I made a vow, and I mean to keep it. Those who killed Mardine will die equally violent deaths. As for the coming war," Eoman sighed, "it won't be fought or won in a fortnight or even a season, in this weather. We'll join once we've finished our other business and at a time of our choosing. Like to have as many of our kin assembled as possible if we do jump in."

The king of the giants bent low, chose another rag, filled it with snow, and set it upon a rock near the flames.

"Have you any idea why they'd want to butcher this Mardine as they did?"

"I've been askin' myself that for weeks now. But, you know, humans have a strange sense o' what's right an' what's wrong, what's good an' what's evil."

"Aye," Karrakan agreed, staring into the fire, "that they do."

"Like snakes, they are, bending back and forth, every which-a-way, and whatever serves their turn."

"But there are some more good than bad."

"Some," Eoman admitted grudgingly. "Is some enough, though?"

Karrakan had no answer and so did not reply.

It was hard work, cleaning the Svarren filth from their bodies, but Eoman had few complaints. There was no better way to get dirty than killing such creatures, and the exercise was always welcome. When he and his companion had finished their work, Eoman laid out his bedroll and stretched out by the fire. Karrakan and his will-o'-wisps would take the first watch, whilst the King slept, and then they'd switch positions.

That was the plan, anyway.

Karrakan nudged his king awake with the end of his staff, but said nothing. Eoman immediately sensed multiple beings in the dark, surrounding them.

"We came by to thank you for the fresh meat."

Oursine. Their voices had a peculiar, gravelly quality that made them easily recognizable in any circumstance. They must have been referring to the Svarren dead, which the giants had left miles behind them.

"Not even maggots will eat Svarren. Are you so desperate?" Eoman asked, attempting to locate and count as many of the beasts as he could.

"We eat what winter offers, giant. If you're smart, you'll do the same."

Grasping his axe, Eoman stood. "Never been known for my brains."

"There's no need for weapons, here," the unseen animal insisted. "We came in thanks and offer a gift of gratitude."

A gift? From oursine? Eoman was about to rush towards the voice when a small body came tumbling into the firelight.

"What's this?"

"As I said: a gift. Too skinny for us lot to eat and unnecessary, after all the meat you provided."

Karrakan strode towards the unconscious figure and knelt to examine it. Eoman watched him for a moment, and when he looked back into the trees, he knew the oursine had gone.

"I wonder what all that was about."

"Hard to say," said Karrakan, distracted.

"Never trust those bastard beasties. What 'ave we got there?"

Karrakan was now fully seated by the body, gently running a massive hand over its head. "Human woman."

"Dead, eh?"

"No," Karrakan replied. "Not yet."

"Perhaps we should leave her to it."

Karrakan regarded his friend with a scolding look. "That is not in my nature."

"Huh. What then? Can you save her?"

"She's frostbitten, starved and injured from a blow to the head. We'll see."

Eoman didn't care for this turn of events, not one bit. He had one goal and one only. Rescuing some half-dead human lass didn't come into it. Frustrated at his companion's choice, he tossed another log on the fire and sat on his bedroll.

"You save her, she's your responsibility," Eoman groused. "I'll 'ave nothin' to do with 'er."

"Mardine?" the figure moaned.

The King of the giants tripped over himself, scrambling to reach to the woman's side.

Vykers & Turley, Inside the Castle

The Warden slumped in the chair, barely conscious, with a large goose egg on his forehead, just above his right eyebrow.

"Find something to tie him up with, or tear his sheets into strips," Igraine commanded.

"Your will, mistress."

Was the goblin mocking Igraine? Vykers wasn't sure and didn't care. If he didn't like how things were going, he was more than welcome to return to his bloodthirsty kin. Not that there was anything wrong with being bloodthirsty.

Turley returned sooner than Vykers had expected. "Will these work?" he asked, holding a pair of manacles above his head.

So, the Warden liked it rough. Vykers was more than happy to oblige. "Let's just make sure there's no secret catch that opens 'em," Igraine answered. She grabbed the manacles away from the goblin and tugged on them, good and hard. Then she scrutinized every inch of their surface and connecting chain. "Looks good." She slapped them onto the Warden's wrists just as he was coming 'round and followed up with a vicious head butt on the same goose egg. The Warden didn't even have time to yell out in pain.

"Do you plan to beat him to death?" Turley inquired.

"And what if I do?" Igraine retorted. "You friends with this fella?"

"No," said Turley, perplexed by the question.

"Good, 'cause I will have to kill him. Eventually."

"But why?"

Igraine shot Turley a look that would have frozen fire. "Can't have him tellin' anyone what happened here, what we were after."

"Do I...have to watch?"

Igraine appeared to think about it for a moment and then responded, "Yes." After a brief silence, she continued. "Way I see it, you've got two choices: stick with me, or get killed by your brothers."

"That's not much of a choice," Turley grumbled.

Igraine laughed. "That it ain't. 'Specially since folks who run with me usually end up dead anyway." The pained expression on the goblin's face made Igraine laugh all the harder, once again rousing the Warden from his stupor.

"Who are you?" he challenged. "Why have you done this?"

He was a pitiful sight, with his robe hanging open, his carefully coifed hair now splayed across his face, the blackening bump on his brow, and a thin trail of snot dripping from his nose.

"Tie his feet to the chair and then get his waist," Igraine said to Turley. To the Warden, she said, "Who am I? You wouldn't believe me if I told you. Now, I want the key to Her Majesty's salt stores."

"The...? Her salt? But why?"

"Just give me the key."

Of course, of course, the Warden tried, belatedly, to uphold the standards of his office. "I can't help you. I won't."

Igraine nodded. She stepped back and admired Turley's knots, and then pushed heaved the chair over backwards, so that it crashed to the floor with a resounding thump. The Warden let out a brief yelp of panic and began to sob.

"As luck would have it, I've had my fill o' torture this week. I think I'll just..." Igraine said, before straightening up and looking about the room. "Wait a minute. You got any wine?" she asked the Warden.

"Wine?" he echoed feebly.

"Yes, wine!" Igraine shouted. "Wine. For drinking."

"Through the door on the left," the Warden answered, gesturing with his head. "Next to the bath." He had no idea where his young captor was going with this, but it didn't sound much like torture.

To Turley, Igraine said "Go get it. As much as you can find."

The goblin trundled off and came back with three bottles. "There's a good deal more..." he said, hoping his new mistress would be satisfied.

"Bring it," she replied, curtly.

No sooner had Turley set his three bottles down, than Igraine opened the first and held it near the Warden's quivering mouth "You're gonna drink this down, mate, or I shove the whole lot up yer ass."

"I'll drink!" the Warden said hastily. "I'll drink!"

But an entire bottle in one attempt is challenging for anyone, and the Warden sputtered, coughed and gagged like a drowning man. Once he got the last of it down, Igraine stepped back and said, "Let's take a little break. Perhaps I'll have some, too." Without waiting for the Warden's response, Igraine, took the top off a second bottle and took a healthy swig. "Not bad," she said. "Little fruity for my taste, but I've had worse." With that, she began a slow circuit of the man's chambers—a series of rooms, as it turned out—poking into everything she saw. Turley continued piling bottles near the Warden's chair, until Igraine caught sight of him and said, "I think that'll be enough."

She returned to the Warden's side and noted the color had returned to the man's cheeks, and he was visibly inebriated.

"So," she said, "where's the key?"

"But I don't understand," the man slurred. "Salt? I s'pose you could sell it, but..."

Igraine jammed the bottle in the Warden's mouth and forced him to swallow more. When she was satisfied, she took the bottle away. "You know what happens if you drink too much o' this?"

The man nodded, or tried to. "You broke one of my teeth n' I swallowed it!"

"Friend," said Igraine, "that's the least of your worries."

Igraine came out of the bath holding the Warden's keys. "It's done," she told Turley. "Whoever finds him will think he drank too much, slipped on the wet floor, and broke his head. And why not? Man looks like he spent half his time drinkin' and assaultin' the ladies."

"Still," Turley interjected, "it's a shame he had to die."

"Of course he had to die. We all have to die sooner or later."

"That's not what I meant."

"I know what you meant," Igraine countered. "Now, let's get the key we need off this ring and put the rest back. Then I need something from you."

This caught Turley off-guard. "Oh? And that is?"

"A way outta this castle."

Turley was disappointed, and it shone like a beacon on his homely face.

"What? You didn't think I was stayin' here, did you?"

"No," the goblin said softly.

"And you'll have to come with me."

"But it's too bright outside! I'll be blind."

Igraine scowled. "We'll…figure something out. Point is, you can't stay here, can you?" With a smile, Igraine held the key aloft and examined it in the light. "Got it!" She tossed the ring to Turley who just managed to catch it before it hit the floor. "Now, put the rest of those back."

While Turley was occupied with the dead warden's keys, Igraine ransacked the man's wardrobe, eventually settling on a large, billowy shirt and a wide-brimmed hat.

"I daresay those won't fit you," the goblin said as he emerged from the next room.

"They ain't for me," Igraine replied, holding them out in Turley's direction. "Put 'em on, and show me a way out o' this castle."

The sour expression on Turley's face was quickly obscured by his new hat.

Long & Company, Underground

Spirk was awakened by a loud crackling noise, followed by a burst of miniature stars and smoke and a high, shrill shriek that faded into nothingness. The flash of light blinded him, made the darkness so much worse than before.

"Yendor!" he called. "Yendor!"

But Yendor did not respond.

Spirk rubbed at his eyes with the fingers and thumb of his right hand, while holding his left in front of his chest, as if to ward off an attack. In truth, he had already done so, and when his vision returned, he was shocked at what he saw. Spread across the ground in front of him were the charred bodies of... something. One of the creatures survived, floating in the air over Yendor without any apparent effort to do so. Spirk struggled to understand what he was seeing. The thing looked like a giant mosquito—about the size of a large dog—made entirely of cobwebs, bracken and mucus. He thrust his hand violently in the creature's direction and, before it could escape, it, too, exploded in a hail of sparks. Spirk spun left and right, cast a panicked glance in the air above: nothing. Having dispatched the immediate threat, the young mage ran to his comrade's side and found him still unconscious, though now also bleeding profusely from a hole in his chest. He was no A'Shea, not even a proper Shaper, but he knew that in the absence of a needle and thread such wounds could be cauterized. He tore open Yendor's shirt, put a hand to the still-gushing wound, and thought *burn!* There was a sudden stench of burnt flesh, and Yendor groaned in his sleep, but the wound stopped bleeding. Again, Spirk looked around, this time hoping to see the approach of his friends, Long Pete and Ron. The dark, cavernous space was all that stared back at him.

After checking to make sure Yendor still breathed, Spirk stoked the fire and then turned his attention to the carcasses of the creatures he'd killed. Closer examination brought him no better understanding, though he did notice they had long, ropy snouts, the ends of which all oozed blood. Was that Yendor's blood? Spirk saw, too, that the horse's body had collapsed in upon itself, 'til the poor beast was little more than a husk. Holes like the one in Yendor's chest dotted the horse's remains, and, as much as he wished in that moment to be the clueless dunce so many thought him to be, Spirk finally understood what had transpired while he slept. It even seemed possible that one or more of the creatures had attempted to attack *him* as well, and he'd somehow defeated them in his sleep. That would explain the explosive lights and noise that awoke him.

Not bad, for a dunce.

But now he was worried: how long had he been asleep? How

long had the Captain and Ron been gone, and had they fallen prey to more of the creatures? His fire was almost lost in the sepulchral space, the broken ceiling so high above that it was all but invisible. Despite his ever growing—and ever amazing—abilities, Spirk had rarely felt so small. What if Yendor and he were all alone now? And what if Yendor got worse?

Tortured by these thoughts, Spirk sat next to Yendor, where he could watch the man breathing, and hugged his own knees to his chest, resting his chin on their knobby tops.

Improbably, he must have fallen asleep again, for a hand on his shoulder startled him. He cried out in alarm and was further frightened by the sound of his voice echoing off the unseen walls.

"Easy, easy," Long Pete cut in. "Don't wanna go disturbin' anything doesn't need disturbin'." Before Spirk could sort that out, Long continued. "Speakin' of which, what happened here?"

Spirk followed his gaze to the burned cadavers of the bloodsuckers. "Uh," he began, "well...these things attacked us, I guess, and..."

"You guess?"

"I was sorta sleepin' at the time, and..."

Ron walked up to Long's side. "Well, at least you weren't hurt. Were you?"

Spirk shook his head. "No. But look what they did to the horse. And they bit Yendor, too."

Long knelt down and bent over Yendor's chest, probing. "You did this?" he asked Spirk when he found the cauterized wound. The young man's nod did nothing to improve the captain's mood. "Poor son of a bitch," he muttered. "He's short one eye, to begin with, and now he's broken some bones and lost a lot of blood from the look of things. I...don't know what to do for him."

Sometimes, dwelling on a problem makes it feel worse. Spirk decided to change the subject. "What'd you find out about this place?"

"We didn't go too far," said Ron. "We just wanted to find the other horses, gather any supplies that survived the fall."

"Yeah?"

"We did okay. Found my bow and some arrows."

"And one sword and a wood axe," Long pitched in. "One tent, a couple of packs. A little food and a canteen. Not enough. I left the other horses where they lay 'cause I didn't want to butcher 'em so far from the fire and have to carry the meat all the way back here. But seein' what's happened to this one..." He looked at the shriveled pony. "Guess I figured wrong."

A funereal silence descended upon the little group, and no one seemed willing or able to break it. From time to time, Long checked on Yendor's breathing, made his old friend as comfortable as possible, whilst Spirk or Ron fiddled with the fire. At some point, Spirk discovered his friends had joined Yendor in sleep, leaving him alone in the oppressive silence and blackness.

The bloodsuckers did not come back, but the young Shaper had no doubt they were out there, somewhere, massing for another attack. He wondered what Pellas would do in such a situation, and he wished—not for the first time—that he still had his magic stone. He thought briefly of his family and realized he was having difficulty recalling their faces. But he'd had an old cat, an old, beat up tom...

"Feel like a prize-winning cow sat on my chest and broke wind," Yendor said.

"You're awake!" said Spirk.

"Awake, is it? Then why's it so damned dark? And where's all the naked, dancin' girls?"

"They took one look at you and humped it on back to Ternsmallow," Long croaked, roused by his friends' conversation.

Yendor coughed—a wet, crackly sound. "Did you show 'em the right end o' me? Hate to think they went away with the wrong impression."

Long pulled himself into a sitting position next to Yendor. "We've been through some shit together," he said seriously.

"Ain't we just?" Yendor's one eye travelled desperately from the captain to Spirk and back again, looking for any evidence of hope.

"The thing is," Long sighed heavily, "I don't know how to help you, old friend. You're broken."

"I prefer 'smashed'," Yendor quipped through gritted teeth. "Anyway, if you're goin' where I think you're goin', forget it. I told you I'm not doin' the noble thing here, so you can stop hintin' at it. You're takin' me wherever you go."

"Yes, but *how?*" Long asked, exasperated.

"Make a litter?"

"Out of *what?*"

"Well," said Yendor, "I s'pose you could make it out of this pony, here. Out of her skin and bones."

"Forget it!" Long snapped. "Too messy and it'd take too long."

"Why don't we unroll the tent, put him on it, and just drag him?" Ron asked.

Long considered the suggestion a moment and saw that the other three men were willing, however much he hated the idea. "Fine," he said. "But you two boys can drag him."

Long was angry; that was the truth of it. Oh, it wasn't Yendor's fault they'd all fallen into this Mahnus-cursed place and lost their horses and most of their supplies. It wasn't his fault that he'd broken an arm and a leg on the way down, either. But the man couldn't even walk now, probably couldn't hold his own pecker when pissing! That was another task Long would pass on to the younger men. And all the while, Long imagined his daughter getting farther and farther away, slowly but inexorably inching beyond his grasp forever. Part of him wanted to abandon his mates and pull himself out of this hole by his fingernails; the other part, the bigger part perhaps, suspected they'd die without him. Of course, it was possible they'd die *with* him, too.

He wanted to find and rescue his daughter; he *had* to rescue his friends.

"Should we wait 'til the sun comes up?" Ron wanted to know.

"What's the point?" Long replied. "Don't think we'll see much of it down here, anyway."

He stood and watched as Spirk and Ron fashioned the litter and then rolled the loudly complaining Yendor atop it. "Startin' to think the gods have it in for me," Long muttered under his breath.

The False Reaper & Omeyo, In Camp

Omeyo watched the last of the light fade from the sky with something approaching dread. For all their inanity during the day, the Svarren were downright vicious at night. It was almost as if they blossomed in the absence of sunlight, or metamorphosed into something infinitely more malignant. The fact that Omeyo could not see well in the dark made him even more distrustful of the creatures, if such a thing was possible.

"I require your council," the False Reaper said at Omeyo's back, almost causing him to jump out of his boots. It seemed so petty, really, this constant frightening of his servant, but the general knew better than to complain. He turned and bowed in one motion. His master liked to feel superior at all times.

"How may I help?"

The boy, changeling, Pretender, False Reaper, Master looked at him for a time before answering. There was none of the insanity in those eyes that Omeyo had seen in the End's, but he knew the boy was just as crazy for all that. And potentially even more dangerous.

"I would like your thoughts on Her Majesty's failure to respond to our...gift."

Omeyo chose his words carefully. It was how he'd managed to last as long as he had. "It seems to me, Master, that there are many kinds of responses, many ways in which a person might respond to such an invitation."

"Meaning?"

"She's a sneaky one, Master. Deceitful and cunning."

"Thus, her response—or responses—will be neither direct nor obvious."

"That would be my guess, Master. But only a guess."

The Pretender nodded, apparently satisfied. Then, "The Svarren are particularly aroused tonight, are they not?"

Omeyo felt a chill at the back of his neck and shivered. "Indeed they are, Master."

The boy clasped his hands behind his back, smiled.

"They've sniffed something out, I shouldn't wonder. I find when they're like this, it's best to let the dogs hunt."

Woe to whomever or whatever it was they were hunting, Omeyo thought.

"So," said the boy, "it is your opinion I should look for a response from the Queen in directions I might not otherwise suspect?"

This sudden shift back to the initial topic of conversation caught the general off guard and rattled his nerves, as the False Reaper intended, no doubt. Was Omeyo under suspicion himself?

"I seem to recall some difficulty with one of my other generals, Deda-something or something-Deda."

Omeyo remembered the incident. Hard to forget, really, when a man explodes for no reason. But was the Pretender implying that Omeyo was somehow an agent of the Queen?

"Why don't you accompany the Svarren on their patrols tonight?" the boy suggested. Only Omeyo knew it was no mere suggestion. "Do you good to get out into the air and get some exercise." When the boy—and the End before him—behaved in a solicitous manner, trouble was coming. And anyway, the boy knew of Omeyo's discomfort around the savages. The coming patrol was not about fresh air and exercise; it was instead a test of how deeply into the shit the general was willing to go to prove his loyalty.

"Thank you, Master," Omeyo said, bowing. "Excellent advice, as always. I shall find a patrol and leave at the first opportunity."

The boy nodded, his expression a model of smugness and self-satisfaction. "Very good, then. You may go."

The only thing worse than the False Reaper's company, however, was being outside of it for very long. Around the boy, Omeyo had only to worry about being set afire or frozen solid. The Svarren, however, practiced baser and more vicious methods of punishment. The general harbored visions of being urinated upon, having an arm ripped off and being forced to eat it, or being made into the creatures' sexual play thing. Mahnus knew, they'd screw anything that moved. Well, if he dwelt upon the possibilities for much longer, he'd become too terrified to leave the boy's presence. Damned if you do, damned if you don't.

Omeyo tightened his cloak around his shoulders, adjusted his boots, and went off to retrieve his horse.

She was the one good thing to enter his life in ages, and he supposed she must have meant just as much to the now-dead farmer to whom she'd once belonged. The increase in raids had resulted in better food and equipment for the boy's inner circle, and Omeyo had almost wept when he'd been given the horse, wept for his own unworthiness, wept for the comfort and companionship she'd offer, wept for the knowledge he had nothing to give her in return, wept for the certainty that her end, whenever it came, would not be pleasant. But Omeyo had learned long ago not to dwell on the future, which was, after all, nothing more than a vapor of dreams and misgivings that had little relevance in the present.

A human slave had been put in charge of the False Reaper's horses—a fact for which Omeyo was especially grateful—and so the general found his horse in good shape and ready to ride. She was a strong and graceful filly, with a brown coat and a mane and tail of deeper brown. If she'd remained on the farm, she might have had another twenty years in her. As a soldier's mount, however…

Omeyo forced his thoughts back to the present. He checked his saddle and climbed onto the filly's back. One of the many things he loved about her was that she gave him a stature and mass that even Svarren had to respect. On foot, they could jostle, bully and trample him into the snow. Not so, on horseback.

With a gentle tug on the reins, the general turned her around and went looking for a smallish pack of Svarren to accompany on their nightly patrol. The boy hadn't specified the size of the group Omeyo was to join, and he was not fool enough to think he would earn anyone's esteem by attaching himself to a larger group. No, the fewer Svarren, the more safe he was like to be.

Vykers & Turley, Inside the Castle

The new tunnel was also concealed behind an arras.

"Can't believe anybody's fooled by this!" Igraine cracked.

"I believe it's more the case that the castle folk would rather not know."

"Are you shittin' me? No curious youngsters lookin' for something new to explore? No lovers lookin' for a place to…"

"People have been known to disappear in these tunnels. I think Her Majesty has cultivated some healthy superstition amongst her guests," Turley cut in. "And then, of course, my people play a role."

Igraine sneered. "Only, they're not your people anymore."

Turley fell silent, and Vykers could see he'd hurt the goblin. *So much the better,* he thought. *If you're gonna survive in this world, you've gotta get used to pain and lots of it.*

The passage leading out of the castle was much more direct than that those he'd taken coming in, and Vykers wished he'd known of it earlier, especially when he learned where this one led.

"It's a…what is your word for it? A bawdery?"

"A what?"

"A harloteria?"

"Huh?"

"Brothel?"

"Ah!" Igraine smiled. "A whorehouse. That makes sense. Those fancy folks in the castle have their needs…" He was just getting warmed up to the subject when he remembered Igraine. "The hells," he muttered. "Looks like I won't be partakin'…"

The corridor cut sharply to the right and came to an abrupt end at a wooden panel. At its base, a thin line of light seeped through from the room beyond, carrying with it a thousand aromas, a soup of perfumes, expensive wines, sweat and burning candle wax.

"How do we open this thing?" Igraine asked, nodding at the panel.

Turley's eyes grew wide, as if the need to open it had never occurred to him. "I have no idea. I've never used it."

Wasting no time, Igraine threw herself into the panel. Vykers would have gone straight through; Igraine bounced off, stumbled backwards and collided with the corridor's far wall, where she chose to rest for a moment. She caught Turley staring at her and quipped "Used to work...in the old days."

Before Vykers could formulate an alternate plan, the panel creaked open, revealing an extremely tall and equally unattractive woman in silhouette.

"You couldn't just knock?" she demanded, in a deep, husky baritone.

Igraine pushed forward, snagging Turley by the front of his new shirt, and propelled herself and the goblin past the stranger and into the new space. It was, as Vykers had suspected, the sitting room of a brothel, perhaps one of many such rooms. Behind him, he heard the panel scraping shut and turned to see the tall woman swinging an armoire back into position against the wall. Looking more carefully at his host, Vykers realized she was a he, a man dressed in woman's clothing. The Reaper was not unaware of the irony.

"You've got the stink of a fugitive about you," the man said.

"And you?" Igraine asked. "What do you stink of?"

"Charming!" the man said. "And what in Alheria's name is *that* thing?"

Igraine glanced over at Turley, who had collapsed onto a nearby couch, swimming in his enormous shirt and with his hat pulled down so far his face was invisible. "That is...that's my little brother, Turley. He was born with the cord wrapped around his neck and, well, never grew quite right after that."

"I see," the man responded, barely hiding his distaste. "But you...you don't look so bad."

"So I been told."

"I'm not surprised," the man cooed. "In fact, we're a bit short on fresh young faces around here. If you're not in any trouble, do you fancy a bit of night work? Pays well!"

Igraine shook her head. "Sorry. I got all the work I can handle."

"I bet you do!"

Igraine ignored the comment. "What's the fastest way out o' here?"

"There's a stairway through those doors," the man pointed. "But you don't..."

Vykers didn't wait around to hear the rest. Igraine grabbed Turley's arm and rushed through the doors...and into the middle of an orgy. From the look of things, the participants were in some type of drug or alcohol-induced stupor, which explained the absence of the usual grunting and groaning that might have served to warn the Reaper. In his haste to escape the whorehouse, Vykers ignored the proceedings. Turley, however, stood slack-jawed and goggle-eyed, seemingly unable to move.

"Move it, or you're gonna find yourself livin' here."

Turley moved it.

There were other doors, other possible exits, but the pair bolted up the stairs, down a short hallway, and out through a door of very sturdy design. Dawn was approaching.

"Still dark enough to smuggle you into my quarters. We'll have to find new ones soon, though. The widows are a nosy bunch, and I won't be able to keep 'em off you for long."

Turley had never been outdoors, had never seen the castle from the outside, had never smelled so much raw humanity. Again, he was nearly transfixed by the excess of sensory stimuli. Finally, Igraine took ahold of his collar and dragged him along behind her, like a farm girl leading a cow to slaughter.

"Actually, we gotta make one visit first."

The visit turned out to be a stop at Igraine's tailor, an open-minded but tight-lipped fellow who'd had no qualms or questions about making masculine clothing for the young woman some weeks earlier and who, Vykers was certain, could again be trusted in clothing Turley.

"I've got a problem," Igraine said, as she barged into the tailor's shop right at closing.

The tailor swept over her with his eyes. "You're looking a little more muscular. Can I let something out for you?" he asked.

"No. It's not me." In the interest of saving time, Vykers decided to come clean. "I've got a goblin friend just outside the door who needs to look more human."

The Reaper was surprised at the tailor's lack of surprise.

"Bring him in," the man said, adjusting his spectacles.

In seconds, Turley stood forlornly in the middle of the shop, whilst Igraine locked the door behind him.

"Interesting," said the tailor. "Can't really fit him in a boy's kit; his arms are too long and his legs, too short."

Vykers watched with interest as the fellow circled the goblin, looking him up and down and tallying something up on his fingers.

"Could put him in a robe, though. That'd hide the real length of his arms and legs. Might pass for a dwarf. Head's a bit small, but a good hood'll hide that, too." He turned to Igraine. "You good with a dwarf?"

Igraine nodded. "Anything's better than a goblin."

"Dwarf it is, then. Let's take him in back and see what fits."

If Vykers was impressed with the tailor's demeanor, he was even more impressed with the man's skill. In no time, Turley was transformed from a freakish oddity into something passably normal. If he was rather mysterious, at least he was no longer an obvious monstrosity. Even Turley, standing in front of a full-length mirror, was amazed by his new disguise.

"You'd never think, to look at me now, that I'm just a castle goblin," he mused.

Igraine laughed. "We're none of us what we seem. None of us. Now, let's go get a few hours' shut-eye."

Kittins, On the Road

Someone was following him, unbelievable as it seemed. Despite the weather and the endless, empty miles, someone was on his trail and had been for some time. Who, though? Who in the wide world would choose to follow the Dead One, especially once his journey led him out of the city and into the wild? While it was true that he'd done much wrong to many, Kittins had only one enemy that he knew of, and that was Cindor. But the Shaper possessed the ability to spy on him at any time. Why send an actual person into such hardship and peril? Perhaps Kittins' confusion was reason enough? That would be just like the Shaper.

If memory served, there was a town of good size just a half day's travel ahead of him, Barnaby or Birnaby or some such. There, the captain would find a dry bed, a warm fire, and a hot meal. And a tankard of ale or two. If this spy wanted to watch Kittins up close, the Dead One would give him every opportunity. And besides, his horse needed some care as well if it was going to survive the long trek north.

Imagining that hot meal did wonders for Kittins' morale and endurance. The miles evaporated, and he found himself at the gates of Qirnby much sooner than he'd expected. It was less than half the size of Lunessfor, but it was still large enough for Kittins' purposes. It boasted a number of inns, a larger number of brothels, and even a theater—not that Kittins gave a damn for such foppery. Point was, a man, even an ugly man, could get his needs met in Qirnby.

Or not.

His old face had been bad enough, but his new one flat out terrified everyone he encountered, including the guards at the town gates. After much debate and not a little intimidation from Kittins, they finally agreed to let him enter Qirnby, but only with the understanding that he would be followed and watched, wherever he went. *Great*, he thought, *I'm at the head of a parade. So much for stealth.*

In larger cities, everyone was a stranger and few noticed newcomers. In Qirnby, Kittins was as conspicuous as a dog with wings and considerably less charming. Thus, he had a difficult time finding welcome anywhere, and there were even establishments that refused him entry. He might've made an issue of it, but guessed his not-so-secret escort would attempt to intervene, and, after all, he hadn't come to town to start a brawl. No, he wanted only to refresh himself and his mount and perhaps get a glimpse of the person who'd followed him out of Lunessfor.

Just when he was about to abandon hope of meeting these needs, he stumbled across a tavern called *The Last Place*, and, indeed, it was both the last place he checked and the last place he *would* have checked. Painted a blinding white with unspeakable pink shutters, *The Last Place* did not, on its surface, appear to be the ideal spot for a hard man to get drunk in private. The tavern's inside told a different story, though. It was just as gloomy, smoky and fragrant as Kittins would have hoped. And as crowded.

And while each and every one of the tavern's patrons gave the captain a good once-over, none seemed overly concerned about his intentions. He got the distinct impression they were leery of him, but unafraid. He could make them afraid, of course. For the time being, he chose to sit back and savor the sensation of normality.

He made his way towards the fireplace, where he found all the seating was occupied. He was about to look elsewhere when a whole table of patrons got up and moved into a darker corner. Interesting: even when he meant no harm, his visage, his overall aspect told folks otherwise. *Just as well*, he thought.

No sooner had he found a seat to his liking, than the barkeep appeared as his side, an awkward, gangly sort who looked like he'd been broken and put back together incorrectly—not that Kittins had any room to make such judgments.

"What can I do fer ya?" the man asked in an accent Kittins had never heard before.

"Something hot, something cold and maybe a bed?"

The barkeep studied Kittins for several heartbeats before he replied, "Yah. I can do that. Cost you a Merchant, though."

Which was fine with the captain. "I got a horse, too. Anyplace nearby I can stable him?"

The other man nodded. "'Nother Merchant, and I'll take care of it meself."

Kittins considered arguing that a Merchant was too high for one night's stabling, but decided against it. He had the money, and it wasn't as if he was saving up for his wedding. "Done," he said at last. "Pony's out front. Only one out front."

The barman nodded again and headed off about Kittins' business. The captain leaned back, put his feet up and settled in for what he anticipated might be a long wait.

Rem, In Pursuit

Kittins had decided to pull off the main road and enter Qirnby, to Rem's profound relief. Another mile, another hundred paces, and the actor might have frozen to his mount, requiring a joint burial. Or an especially large funeral pyre. Frankly, the notion of being set afire wasn't half as unpleasant as it ought to have been.

Rem had followed the big man for days, always keeping him on the very edge of vision. Sometimes, the weather was so bad, this meant trailing Kittins at a stone's throw. Other times, when the storm let up and the snow stopped falling, Rem let his quarry dwindle in the distance until he was little more than a speck on the horizon. If Kittins pulled into a roadside inn, Rem found another, farther along. If the big man made camp amongst some trees, Rem backtracked until he found a suitable spot to do likewise. But it wasn't easy. The captain seemed impervious to the cold and immune to fatigue. A harder man, Rem could not imagine, unless it was perhaps the Reaper.

Unlike Kittins, Rem had no trouble entering Qirnby, although he waited a good half hour after the captain passed through the gates before following him. By that time, it was getting dark, and Rem could think only of a hot bath. He figured Kittins would find his way into a tavern somewhere, and a man of Kittins' description wouldn't be difficult to locate, so Rem could catch up with him later.

That was his plan, anyway, until he saw the billboard: "Wratch & Company Present *Rampage of the Reaper*."

His astonishment could not have been greater if Mahnus himself had come dancing down the street at the head of an army of milkmaids. In the first place, *he was Wratch*, and Wratch was supposed to be dead. In the second, Wratch & Company had allegedly disbanded. Third, there was no such play as *Rampage of the Reaper*. The effrontery of these people—who and whatever they were—defied belief.

Rem stopped the first person who passed and asked him, "Where is this performance being held?"

"At the Black Stag, off Market Square."

"And which way is that?"

The man pointed, obligingly.

Rem spurred his tired pony in the designated direction. After a few false turns, he found the place he was looking for, a long, low building with a riot of signs and billboards out front, an indoor theater, of course. They were not as spectacular as the outdoor variety, but were growing in popularity nonetheless. A fad, Rem thought them. It just wasn't right to see or perform in a play with a roof overhead. As he was in something of a hurry, Rem paid the overly expensive stable boy at the theater's front door, bought himself a ticket and went inside.

The Black Stag must have borrowed or stolen every candle in town in order to light the place, and still the shadows lingered. On stage, a number of glowing spheres of magical origin improved matters, and Rem had to admit he was both impressed by and jealous of the troupe's ingenuity. In time, a small group of musicians appeared to the left of the stage and began playing an old air with which Rem was very familiar. He became so lost in thought and reminiscence that he scarcely noticed when the play began. When next he looked, his old friend Keez had come onstage and begun to perform one of Rem's most famous monologues in the person of Tarmun Vykers.

Rem's heart sank. It was obvious what his former fellows had done: Keez had assumed Rem's name and position, and the company had continued on its tour unabated. They'd even changed the name of Rem's greatest play to something more... *pedestrian* and, if he was honest, accessible.

Rem watched in horror as Keez gave a brilliant performance and received a hero's applause. As for the rest of Wratch & Company? They seemed as happy and hearty as Rem had ever seen them, and he was torn: a part of him felt betrayed, as if something of inestimable value had been stolen from him. And yet another part of him understood how difficult it was to find work as an actor, and he couldn't begrudge his old friends their apparent success. He felt resentment...and pride, envy and relief. In the end, as the crowd chanted his name—his very own name!—he stood and slunk out of the theater, allowing his counterfeit to bask in adulation.

Somehow, he ended up drunk in the middle of the street, well past midnight. He couldn't recall how he'd gotten there, much less what he'd done with his horse and gear. All he knew was that he was still conscious, and he wanted to change that. A block away, the sounds of raucous merriment erupted from a hideous white building with pink shutters. It seemed like just the place.

He bumbled up the steps, and tumbled through the door. The interior swam before his eyes. He wasn't sure he could make it all the way to the bar, so he threw himself into the closest chair, not caring one whit that it was already occupied.

"'Ere! What's the meanin' 'o this?" the seat cushion shouted.

"Watch yerself!" yelled the table.

"Hello!" said the floor.

It was filthy and stinking, was the floor. But it possessed one fine quality, in that it halted Rem's downward motion. Just when he began to feel settled, he flew upwards and threw upwards, dangling at the end of somebody's arm.

Captain Kittins.

"'Ello, Captain," Rem offered, wiping his mouth with the back of his hand. If Kittins said anything by way of response, the actor missed it, falling rapidly into unconsciousness.

"So, you're the spy," Kittins rumbled.

At first, Rem couldn't guess what the man was talking about, largely because he wasn't sure he hadn't died the previous night. "Where am I?" he slurred.

"In a bed," the captain answered. And then, "Your own. Mine's on the other side of the room."

Rem rolled over to get a better look at his host and almost threw up again. He found none of the humor in the situation that his old friend Yendor so often did.

"What happened to you?" said Kittins.

"Lot of stuff, most of it bad. And the worst of it is, the world's kept on turning without me." Having finally gotten a good look at the newly remodeled captain, he asked, "What happened to *you*?"

"Shaper's fire."

"If you're still here to talk of it, I'm guessing the Shaper didn't come away unscathed." Suddenly, Rem made the connection: "Cindor!" he said.

Kittins stood up, began to pace. "Aye, Cindor. And the fact his name comes so easily to your tongue tells *me* something, too."

Rem didn't have the energy to hold up his end of the

conversation. Besides, it was better if the captain guessed at his mission than confessing it of his own volition.

"You're the spy, and Cindor sent you. Question is, why you?" Kittins sneered at the actor, or it might have been a smile. With that face, it was hard to tell. "You're hardly a match for me in combat, are you? How are you supposed to deal with me if things go south?"

Rem grunted. So much for staying silent. "Cindor says he'll be checking in on me from time to time. You probably shouldn't spend too much time in my presence."

Kittins laughed. "On the contrary. Might be you're just the cheese I need to catch a rat."

SEVEN

The Giants & Nelby, In the Forest

"Can you save her?"

"I think *we* can, my little friends and me."

Eoman watched the will-o-wisps circling the woman's head. Occasionally, one or two would break off and hover over her chest or loop down around her legs. It made no sense to the king of the giants, but he was afraid to say so aloud, lest he anger the very creatures he now depended upon.

"Well, how does she look to you? Improving?"

Karrakan flexed his hands and cracked his knuckles. "I can see now why you've got no lady wife: all this questioning's enough to drive anyone mad."

"But you heard her, 'Kan. She said Mardine's name."

"Could be. Maybe."

Eoman was adamant. "No maybe about it. She said 'Mardine'."

"Good and fine. But if she comes 'round, she'll still be starving half to death. We'd best rekindle that fire and fix her a bowl of something hot," Karrakan said. "And, as it happens, I have just the thing." He reached into his shoulder bag, rummaged around briefly, and came out with a handful of dried herbs and a small brownish lump of something possessed of a wonderful, meaty aroma. "Have you got your boilin' bag on you?"

"I do," Eoman answered sheepishly. "Been using it to pad my britches o' nights."

"I bet that'll prove right flavorful," Karrakan cracked. "Now, fill it with snow and put it on those hot rocks there."

The king lifted several layers of animal hide and cloth and pulled the bag from the back of his pants. It was made of a curious material whose origins had been lost to time, but which, when filled with liquid, could be set on a fire to boil without burning through. In little time, Karrakan had a wonderful broth simmering, while Eoman turned his attention to the human woman. He felt her forehead, tapped ever so lightly on her cheeks, and fussed over her every breath. Eventually, Karrakan's broth was ready. He produced a heel of bread from somewhere, dipped the end in the hot liquid, and carried it to the woman's side.

"How do you expect her to chew if she's not conscious?"

"I don't," said Karrakan. "I'm going to drip some of this broth into her mouth." He knelt down in the snow and touched the bread to his patient's lips, and she responded almost immediately, mouthing the crust as if she would eat.

"Easy now," the giant urged. "There's no hurry."

Finally, the woman's eyes opened.

Eoman could not restrain himself. "You said a name: 'Mardine.' What do you know of her?"

"Easy now. There's no hurry," Karrakan repeated in Eoman's direction. "I meant it for her, but I see it's needful you both hear me. Nobody's going anywhere tonight, so let's allow the girl to get some strength back."

The king plunked himself down beside his friend and chewed on his upper lip. It was as close to a pout as he dared go without risking the loss of all dignity. As Karrakan continued to minister to his patient, Eoman grabbed a stick from the kindling pile and proceeded to break it into smaller and smaller sections, until there wasn't a piece left that was large enough for picking teeth. Karrakan inwardly chuckled at his friend's nervous energy: same old Eoman.

Now, the young woman was slurping the broth out of a bowl Karrakan had found amongst the king's possessions. Eoman wanted to complain, but...his friend's magic was clearly working. At last, Eoman deemed that he'd waited long enough and spoke to the woman again. As he did, she seemed to see him for the first time, and her expression became a lamentable mixture of fear, hope, and awe. And then she began to cry.

"I did suggest waiting..." Karrakan began.

"And I'm ignoring you," his king replied. "Now, woman, you spoke the name of one of my people. Tell me why."

The woman struggled to sit up, until Karrakan gave her a hand, gently moving her closer to the fire and wrapping a fur around her shoulders. "What are you called?" he asked the woman.

"Nelby, and it please you."

"Nelby," said Karrakan pensively, as if he were trying to remember the lyrics to an epic ballad.

"Nelby," Eoman cut in. "Tell me about Mardine."

Again, Nelby exploded into tears.

Eoman threw his chin at the sky and exhaled loudly in frustration. Seeing that nothing coherent was going to come from the woman in the near future, the king of the giants turned and stalked off into the trees to collect more firewood. When he returned, he found Nelby sitting in Karrakan's lap like a child, dazzled by the shaman's will-'o-wisps. This time, Eoman simply sat nearby and waited. To his surprise, Nelby began to talk, although her eyes were now focused on the fire.

"I was her nanny," she began. "Not Mardine's, but her daughter's. Esmine's. We...we lived on an apple farm. It was just the three of us, since Mardine's man was away on business. Royal business, as I understood." She fell silent for a while, gathering her resolve, and then continued, "This fellow came around. I thought maybe...maybe he fancied me. Stupid, I know. So terribly, terribly stupid. Anyway, one day, he catches me off guard and threatens to kill me and Esmine if we don't cooperate. I didn't want...I couldn't...well, he makes me help him poison Mardine, and when she passes out, he and his bitch bundle us out the door and off into the forest." Nelby took such a lengthy pause that Eoman thought she'd finished.

"That doesn't explain how I found Mardine," he challenged gruffly.

Nelby resumed crying, but continued her tale as well. "This fellow I mentioned? He wanted to get his hands on Esmine, on account of her bein' half giant..."

Eoman started. "Half?"

"Well...her da, Long Pete, he's just a man."

The king leapt to his feet, too agitated to remain seated. "A man? A *man*? How is that possible?"

Karrakan raised his hands, as if to say "Don't ask me!" Even his will-'o-wisps appeared confused, but their presence gave Eoman an idea.

"Magic," said he. "It can only be magic." Then, to Nelby, "Continue."

"Mardine followed us, came lookin' for her daughter. The kidnappers figured she might and set a trap for her. They hurt her and captured her. When she broke free and tried to rescue her babe, they killed her." Nelby drew a long, shuddering breath, as folks will do after a good cry. "Not much to tell after that. Esmine and me, we were locked in a cage atop a wagon, where we froze and starved and knew never a moment's peace nor comfort. We busted out, made a run for it, and then...and then...that's all I know."

"I don't believe those oursine would have offered this girl to us if they'd taken the child. They can be ornery brutes, but they're not stupid," Karrakan said.

Eoman grimaced. "Then she's still out there, somewhere. You willing to carry this woman a while?"

"Do you mean to resume the hunt this moment?"

"I do."

As gently as possible, Karrakan scooped Nelby into his arms. "Douse that fire, pick up your boiling bag, and let's go." He looked down into the human woman's face and thought he spied hope. He wished he shared the feeling.

Innoman & Esmine, In the Forest

The pile of boulders might have been enormous blocks of ice for all the warmth they provided. They did keep the oursine at bay, though, and that was good enough for Innoman. The creatures could neither move the massive stones nor squeeze their bodies between them to reach him and his captive. Eventually, they lost interest and wandered off in search of easier prey.

Innoman hunkered down onto his haunches and glared at Esmine in her meager bundle of blankets and rags. If he was expecting her to look away, he was sorely disappointed, for the child met his gaze as if she were studying an ant crawling along her arm.

"Tough one, are you?" Innoman prodded. "Well, you'll have to be. Your friend's thrown us right in the shit—lost, no food, no fire and no help. And where is she now? Probably in some oursa's belly."

Esmine blinked, pulled her blankets tighter.

"You've survived this long; I guess the cold don't get to you, eh?" Innoman stood. "But I've gotta find a way to make fire, or you'll be alone before too long." The slaver surveyed the walls of his stone sanctuary. It was almost a cave, really, with just a bit of sky visible through a gap in the boulders. "A man could get by in here, if he had a bit of food, water and warmth. Place isn't so bad. Anyways, I've seen worse."

Esmine yawned and rolled onto her side, clearly seconds from falling asleep.

Innoman became frustrated. "Are you unaware," he snapped, "that we might not live to see the morning?" To his continued annoyance, Esmine said nothing. "Well, damned if I'm gonna freeze to death on your account, girl. Push over and share some o' those rags with me. We're not leaving 'til I'm certain those beasts are gone."

Now, Esmine was wide awake. She didn't like this strange man, this enemy, pressing himself against her. He would forever be part of the group that killed her mother and, for all Esmine knew, her nanny as well. What if he meant to kill her next? No, the cold did not bother her as much as it did others, but she began shivering nonetheless, shivering with fear. The mere touch of the man's skin against hers made Esmine want to vomit.

An eternity later, she heard him snoring into her neck, his drool running down her shoulder. She could hardly contain her revulsion. Yet, the man was asleep, and he couldn't hurt her as long as he slept. Esmine wondered if she could make him sleep forever.

Long & Company, Underground

Whatever it was they'd tumbled into, it was undeniably vast, and its countless passageways or streets crawled off into a darkness so complete that it seemed possible they'd reached the very borders of the world. Were it not for the sorcerous light Spirk had conjured on the end of an arrow, Long and his fellows might have lacked the courage to leave their fire. As it was, each feared to break the oppressive silence with speech. Who knew what lurked in the shadows, ready to pounce at the first disturbance?

In some places, it was hard to determine if the walls *were* walls, or instead the sides of buildings. Broad archways periodically opened on either side, but Long seemed content to keep the group on its initial path, and no one was inclined to argue. The ceiling, if there was a ceiling, was so far overhead that Long despaired of ever finding a way out in that direction.

Spirits sagging, they trudged onward, dragging Yendor's litter behind them. In time, they came to an immense open space, octagonal in shape, which seemed to have once been a hub of activity. The rectangular ghosts of kiosks marked or marred the carefully tiled floor, such that every man in the group recognized straight away where they were.

"It's a market!" Spirk exclaimed.

"Was," said Long.

The kiosks had long since been removed or disintegrated into dust.

Yendor endeavored to sit up and groaned terribly. When he was himself again—or as close as a one-eyed cripple could be— he said, "If this was a market, there's bound to be storage nearby. Might be there's somethin' left somewheres."

Long frowned. "That's what worries me." He scanned the plaza and kept a hand on the hilt of his sword. "Something or someone." Seeing he'd put a good and necessary scare into the younger men, he continued. "Let's scout the perimeter o' this place. Find out what we're dealin' with. But...uh...keep an arrow nocked, eh, Ron? And Spirk, be ready to do whatever it is you do."

"How are they gonna do that if they're dragging me about?" Yendor complained.

"A good question," Long responded. "An excellent question."

Yendor must've heard something in his old friend's voice, because he instantly objected. "Oh, no!" said he. "You're not leavin' me alone whilst you go gallivantin' about in the dark."

The captain shook his head, ran a hand through his thinning hair. "Well, dammit it all, Yendor. What would you have me do?"

"The two of us can scout it," Ron offered, referring to himself and Spirk.

Yendor looked hopefully at his captain.

"Fine," said Long, resentment clear in his voice. "But you scamper back here at the first sign o' trouble. And can you put some light on something for us, too?"

Spirk appeared baffled by the request, but he obligingly touched the point of his glowing arrow to the hilt of Long's sword and the weapon began glowing with a warm, yellow-orange radiance.

"How do you do that?" Long asked, amazed.

"Beats me."

The young men shuffled off into the space, the light from Spirk's arrow getting smaller and smaller as they receded into the darkness. The echoing of their footsteps unexpectedly took on the quality of a heavy rain or the bubbling of a brook, and then that, too, grew softer and softer until it was no longer audible.

Long hunkered down beside his friend and placed the sword between them. "I never would've figured Spirk for a Shaper."

"Funny old world."

"How are you holdin' up?"

"I'd laugh, but it might kill me."

"I'm tempted to start tellin' jokes."

Yendor did laugh then, before gritting his teeth and whimpering in pain. "Fucker," said he.

"That's me," said Long sadly.

"Who d'you think that is?" Ron wondered aloud.

"Um...Alheria?"

The young men stood at the base of a gigantic head, a sculpture of a woman that rose from the flagstones to several times the height of a man. Her open mouth formed a doorway, which was reached by steps climbing from the floor, up her chin and over her lower lip.

"Should we see if that door's unlocked?"

"Not by ourselves," said Ron. "Best to bring Long and Yendor back here."

Spirk envied his friend's common sense. It was, to him, as elusive and mysterious as his own magic was to others. "I s'pose yer right," he agreed.

"Not so cold down here as it is up top," Long said, making conversation to keep his worries at bay.

"Cold enough."

"Aye." Pause. "But what about that young Shaper, now? He seems to be growin' stronger every day."

"'Magine what 'e could do with some trainin'," Yendor grunted.

"If he's right about this Pellas thing, this legacy, might be he won't need training. Might be it's instinctive." Just as Long finished that thought, the Shaper in question reappeared, with his friend in tow. "You finish your scoutin' already?"

"Nah," Spirk called out, "we just found something you hafta see."

Yendor rolled his lone eye at Long. "Oh, I can't wait."

"Alright," Long told Spirk. "But you and Ron'll have to drag this surly bastard along. I'm not touchin' him."

That they obeyed the captain without qualm or hesitation continued to astound and humble him. What had he done that they should trust him? Why would *anyone* trust him? Hadn't he, in fact, about ruined the lives of everyone who dared to associate with him? Long ground his teeth. Was he doomed to bully and abuse himself forever?

He needed to get himself and his crew out of this hole and resume his hunt for Esmine.

Before he realized it, he and his fellows had reached their destination, the huge stone head Spirk and Ron had found earlier. The first sight of it gave Long a strange, visceral thrill he couldn't identify. Had he seen this thing or some variation of it before? He looked over at his companions and saw they were all watching him, awaiting his impressions. He held his still-glowing sword at arm's length over his head, hoping to catch a glimpse of the sculpture's entirety, but the top of its head, like everything else in the Mahnus-cursed place, stretched up into the gloom.

"Well?" Yendor asked impatiently.

"Well what?" Long retorted. "It's big."

"Even a one-eyed man can see that!"

"Is it Alheria?" said Spirk.

No, kid, Long thought. *This ain't Alheria.* But how could he know that? Why did he feel so certain? "I don't know," he said finally. "Could be."

"Should we try the door?" Spirk, again.

Long shook his head no. "I'll do it."

"But if you get hurt…"

"I said I'll do it!" the captain snapped a little too harshly. The looks on his friends' faces told him he'd gone too far. "Look," he said, "I can't be always puttin' others in harm's way. You boys have been through the shit on my behalf. Least I can do is step up once in a while. You wouldn't be where you are if it weren't for me."

"I wouldn't be *who* I am, either," Spirk reminded him. "I think I've gotten better since I met you."

Long knew that was soulfully meant, but he couldn't help feeling worse for it. "Still, let me…let me do this on my own. I'll be fine."

There was just something about a glowing sword that gave a man courage. Long held his out and calmly climbed the steps leading into the statue's mouth, noting the heavy wear that had polished the stones where feet had run like a river in either direction for untold years. Whatever lay beyond that door, it was unquestionably important to those who had once lived here. As Long extended a hand to try the door, he felt his courage abandoning him. "Spirk," he called, "I think I'll need your help after all."

Of course, the young Shaper was only too happy to oblige.

In his haste, he tripped coming up the stairs, and arrived at his captain's side a bit more disheveled than he'd planned.

Long knew better than to mention it. Instead, he said, "You sense any magic in this door? I don't want to grasp the handle and burst into flames."

Spirk screwed up his features like a man fighting constipation and at last proclaimed, "Nothin' like that. It's more of a keepin'-us-out-and-them-in sorta feel."

...Which answer was, perhaps, more alarming than the prospect of catching fire. "What's that mean? Can you tell me more?"

"I just feel like we gotta, I dunno, break the door down or something. Like this." Spirk thrust his hands towards the door, and there was a stupendous crash, accompanied by an equally powerful gust of wind. The door blasted inwards, whilst Spirk and Long were propelled backwards and down the steps in a tumbling mass of shrieks and grunts. Somewhere along the way, Long lost his grip on his sword, and it clanged off into the plaza, where it continued to glow in a rather forlorn manner.

Spirk, being younger, got to his feet first. Achieving a sitting position was enough of a challenge for Long.

"Shit," he said.

"You alright, Captain?" Spirk asked sheepishly.

"I think I heard something crack in my shoulder. Like we can afford another broken bone in this company."

Ron and Spirk crossed over to the captain and gently helped him to his feet.

Not one to miss out on the festivities, Yendor said, "Well, you're not sharing my litter, that's for damned sure!"

Long Pete ignored him and focused on working the aches and stiffness out of his shoulder. "Least it's not my sword shoulder. That coulda been disaster." He looked out into the plaza where his sword had landed and was astonished at how far away it seemed. "Say, Ron...walk me over to my sword? I don't think anyone should go anywhere by himself in this place."

When he reached his sword, however, he looked back to see Yendor alone at the bottom of the steps, Spirk's arrow clasped firmly in his hands. Where in the countless hells had the Shaper gone? As if reading his thoughts, Ron nudged him on his uninjured shoulder and pointed at the statue's mouth. Suddenly afraid he might lose another friend, Long rushed back the way he'd come, and made his way up the stairs. Spirk stood in the open door, unmoving, transfixed by whatever he saw in the room beyond.

"They're children," he cried. "At least, they was."

Mureen, In the Cottage

Mureen hadn't slept for as much as five minutes the whole night. She was troubled by the uncomfortable energy and expectations Tinalia's son had brought with him into the cottage, troubled by the fact they'd seen fit to bar her door and prevent her from leaving of her own accord, which meant she was not a guest, but a prisoner. And prisoners lived behind bars. And bars filled her with an equal mixture of fury and dread, though why this should be so she couldn't guess. There was something...no, there was *someone*...But the answer eluded her. All that really mattered was what she was going to do once her bedroom door opened. Could she talk her way out of the house, or would she have to resort to violence?

She was still trying to make up her mind when she heard the hutch moving away from the door. She stepped backwards, bracing herself for unpleasantries, but none appeared. The door creaked open a few inches and stopped.

"Well," Tinalia's voice called from beyond. "Are you going to lie in bed all day, or will you come in here, have a little breakfast, and help me peel these potatoes?"

It felt like a trap. Every fiber of the giant's being urged caution. Still, she couldn't spend the rest of her days in the bedroom. Her eyes swept the room, looking for anything that might serve as a weapon, but nothing presented itself. In the other room, however, she'd seen an old two-man tree saw over the fireplace, an awkward weapon for a human or Svarra, but potentially lethal in Mureen's hands. If she could just reach it in time.

"Mureen?" Tinalia called, a bit more stridently.

The giant took a deep breath and pulled the door wide.

Tinalia sat in her chair by the fire, a large tub of potatoes at her feet. When she saw Mureen, she pointed to the bench the giant had used the night before. A platter full of food had been set there.

"I tell myself it's all the excitement of finally meeting Baris. That must be it, am I right?" Tinalia smiled. "Well, just calm yourself down and have a bit to eat. Baris has gone out for a while, but he'll be back shortly."

Mureen caught herself, a large slab of bread halfway to her mouth. Again, she thought of poison. It seemed ridiculous after all the meals she'd safely eaten in this cottage, but she couldn't chase her suspicions from her mind. Clearing her throat, she set the bread back on the platter.

The Svarren woman made no effort to hide her displeasure. "No appetite, dearie? I find that hard to believe."

"Oh, it's not that," Mureen answered. "It's...well, I was wondering..."

"Yes?" Tinalia demanded impatiently. Where had all of the woman's charm gone? She'd never had much of a surplus, but now she was openly irritable.

"Who...who painted that mural in the bedroom?" It was a foolish question, certainly no reason to delay her breakfast, but it was the only thing Mureen could think to say.

Tinalia looked quite mystified by the question. "The what? The mural? Oh!" she brightened. "Yes, well, you've been looking at that for days and days, haven't you? I imagine you would be curious about it." But she did not answer the question. Instead, she resumed peeling her potatoes. "Have a bite to eat, dearie. You'll need your strength for Baris."

Mureen didn't trust anyone who couldn't answer a simple question directly. Or, at least, she believed that was her policy. Much was still lost to her. What she did know was that the longer she sat on this bench and engaged in this conversation, the fewer and fewer her options became. She was not going to eat this meal, and Tinalia would become angry. Sooner or later—sooner, if Mureen had to guess—Baris would be home, too, and the giant would be outnumbered.

She picked up a bowl of stew as if she were ready to eat and abruptly flung it in Tinalia's face. Whilst the Svarren woman screamed in shock and pain and endeavored to clear her vision, Mureen raced to the fire and ripped the saw from the stonework. The wires that held it in place bit into the giant's fingers and hands, but that was the least of her worries. Tinalia had risen from her chair, potato knife in hand. Somehow, it seemed much larger than it had mere seconds ago. Mureen whipped the blade around with all her strength and took the top of Tinalia's head right off. For a moment, the Svarren woman looked almost pleasantly surprised, and then she toppled over onto the floor, her brains spilling out onto the rug and her body twitching.

Mureen turned her attention to the room's various doors, but none opened. The cottage had fallen silent.

Had she been wrong about Tinalia's intent? Well, it didn't matter now. The woman was dead, and if Mureen didn't encounter Tinalia's son soon, she certainly would later. Baris would make sure of it.

Knowing the younger Svarren might appear at any moment, Mureen grabbed the blanket off her bed, spread it on the table, and wrapped as much food in it as she could find. In, too, went three bottles of wine and Tinalia's paring knife. In went tinder and flint she'd found on the hearth. In went rope. The two-man saw was a fearsome weapon, but not especially practical. This, Mureen replaced with a small sickle that had been nailed to one of the room's other walls. Feeling as prepared as she was ever likely to be, Mureen pulled the front door open...

...And was hit in the face by a bitter blast of wind. Some things hadn't improved over the last several days (or weeks?). Mureen looked left and right and then left and right again. Baris was nowhere in sight, so the giantess raced from the cottage into the snow. She got about fifty strides into the adjacent woods and came across an old smoking shed, half hidden in drift. As there were no fresh footprints in the snow, she hazarded a peek inside and immediately wished she'd left well enough alone.

Hanging from beams across the ceiling were venison haunches and half a boar. Those, she'd expected. But there were also the well-dried and thoroughly smoked limbs of humans, one of which still had toes.

Mureen did not run away in terror or even grow sick to her stomach. It was more or less what she'd feared since she'd first awoken in Tinalia's presence. Here, Mureen thought, were the original owners of the cottage, here, the painters of the bedroom's lovely mural. If she'd had any misgivings about killing the Svarren woman, they were gone now. Tinalia and her son were murderers and might well have killed her as well, had she failed to satisfy Baris.

But then Mureen remembered the farmhouse she'd stormed a while back, in a desperate bid for food and warmth. Hadn't she, too, killed someone recently? She readied herself for the anticipated wave of guilt, but felt nothing. Less than nothing. Killing seemed as natural, as commonplace as, say, pissing.

Had she been an assassin in her younger days?

It was time to get moving again. Mureen pushed the door open, stepped into the air, and caught sight of a huge knife streaking towards her in her peripheral vision. At the last second, she flinched backwards, and the knife buried itself in her left shoulder.

Baris had found her.

He'd made a mistake, though. Mureen noticed he wasn't wielding a second knife, so that his only weapon was temporarily unavailable. Mureen rolled away, along the shed's outer wall, until she was able to stumble into open space beyond the small building. She reached up to pull Baris' knife, and the Svarra bull-rushed her onto her back. The next several seconds were a blur of thrashing about, grunting, and struggling for control. The Svarra was strong and furious, but Mureen outweighed him significantly and was probably stronger, too.

"If I can't get some sons on you," Baris growled, "Be assured I'll have my fun with your corpse before eatin' ya!"

He was on top of her, battling her right arm for possession of the blade still lodged in her shoulder. With her left arm, she tried to put enough pressure on his throat to force a retreat. It wasn't working. He glowered at her with all his eyes, like some hellish insect advancing upon its prey. If only Mureen had thought to draw that sickle from the cord around her waist.

Somehow, Baris finally got ahold of the knife and, instead of yanking it free, gave it a good twist, eliciting a scream of pain from Mureen. That she'd felt far worse in her day was perhaps one secret advantage she held over the Svarren brute. She let him continue to twist, while she reached up and popped one of his eyes like a grape with her thumb. Now, it was his turn to yowl.

And yet he did not. What was one eye when he had so many? Mureen knew she had to burst a good deal more before Baris would even begin to consider protecting himself. And so she did. Squish! Two. Pop! Three. The Svarra got the message and attempted to grab the giant's arms.

Mureen caught his nose in her teeth and bit down with all her considerable might, and Baris made the mistake of pulling away. Blood gushed from a newly made hole in the center of his face, as well as the slightly older holes where eyes had been.

"Bitch!" he yelled and began buffeting Mureen's head and shoulders with a torrent of blows.

Strangely, they didn't hurt much.

In one motion, Mureen pulled the knife from her shoulder and swept it across Baris' throat.

He was still throwing punches when he realized he was dead. He put both hands to his neck and fell over onto his side.

Mureen stomped on his head twice to make sure the Svarra died. When he stopped moving, she searched through his clothing for anything that might be of value. She found a few coins and a smaller, collapsible knife.

And then she left him in a fast-freezing pool of his own blood.

The False Reaper & Omeyo, the North

The Svarren attacked Aoife's fortress as she had known they would, because it hadn't been there the day before. Its appearance, therefore, was a provocation, a challenge to their domination of the local environs. But it was an attack that was doomed to fail, because they did not understand their foe.

Initially, a few Svarren scouts attempted to investigate the great hedge. When they didn't return, a larger party was sent to locate and retrieve them. That party walked into an ambush, the like of which none of the Svarren had ever witnessed or experienced. Tremendous vines snaked out of the wall of greenery like thorny tentacles and crushed or choked their prey. Deep pits opened beneath Svarren feet, swallowing the savages in twos and threes. Noxious gasses and gouts of faerie fire erupted without warning. Dart-like needles laden with paralyzing poison exploded from plant stalks. In the end, it was an utter rout, an affair so disastrous that Omeyo was afraid to relay its outcome to his master.

"Show me," was all that the Pretender said in response.

But Omeyo could not. The hedge had disappeared, taking the dead with it and leaving only a few small piles of dirt or puddles of blood on the filthy snow.

"And do you expect me to believe this hedge simply ran away?" the boy asked, his voice a deadly calm.

"I would never lie to you, Master. I know the price could well be death."

The boy knelt, scooped up some of the frozen dirt and sifted it through his gloved fingers. "As it happens, I believe I know what occurred here: it can only be Anders' sister, the End's sister. I should have predicted this." The Pretender returned to his horse and climbed into the saddle.

"Your will, Master?" Omeyo asked.

The boy shrugged as if the answer was obvious. "Return to camp. Attend me. There's nothing we can do about this woman until she returns, but when she returns—and she will—we must have a better response."

The False Reaper was unaccountably tired, which worried him. Sleep had never been important to him before, but now it pulled at him constantly. And why? What had changed of late? Was it prelude to a hoped-for transcendence, or was he ill, as he feared? Surely a brief nap couldn't hurt, and a survey of his condition afterwards might prove informative. Before he knew it, he was stretched out on his bearskin rug on the floor, rapidly descending into unconsciousness...

WherehefoundhimselfintheclutchesoftheEnd-of-All-Things.

"Miss me?" the fiend shrieked.

The boy tried to shove him away to no avail; Anders' grip was unbreakable. "Where are the others?" the boy asked, endeavoring to sound less concerned than he felt.

"The others?" the End giggled maniacally. "Why, I've consumed them, of course."

"Of course," the boy replied, with a bravado he did not feel. "It's just as well. Makes for less noise when I'm trying to concentrate."

The End's face bobbed in the darkness before him like a dandelion seed on the breeze.

"What is it you want, anyway?" the boy asked.

Again, the End cackled. "But you already know that: you must give yourself over to me. You will, in time."

At last, the False Reaper was able to break free of the End's grasp. "No. You were a failure. I will not have that stench lingering about me and my efforts."

"You have no choice! I am stronger than you, and I continue to grow in strength with each passing hour."

The boy thought to wake himself, to escape the End's presence, but could not.

"Do you see?" Anders cooed. "For all your hubris, you are still a child! Soon, I'll take your place, and you'll be trapped in here. Soon, I'll…"

One of his Svarren jostled him awake. Normally, the False Reaper would have been enraged at the creature's presumption. Not this time. The Svarren had saved him from dissolution.

"What is it?" he said to the Svarra at his side.

"You crying out."

"A bit of indigestion," said the boy. "No cause for concern."

If the Svarra was unconvinced, he had the brains to keep it to himself.

"Omeyo!" the boy called out.

The general appeared in a trice. "Your will?"

On his feet now, the boy straightened his clothing. "Do not let me sleep anymore."

"Your pardon, Master, but…"

"I'll sleep no more, and that is final. Do not fail me."

This last was said with such passion, such force, that Omeyo could only bow and digest his thoughts in silence.

Vykers & Turley, In Lunessfor

Being a goddess, the Queen would figure out that the dagger had been stolen, if the resident goblins didn't tell her first. She would also discover her warden had been killed and his keys taken. Vykers had a hard time imagining her connecting those two events in any meaningful way, goddess or not. She might conclude that an especially gifted thief was responsible, but the Reaper? It seemed beyond unlikely.

Now, it was time for the next phase of Vykers' plan. The trouble was, he couldn't quite figure out how to make it work. He had Igraine pacing back and forth in frustration, whilst Turley watched her in abject silence. After several hours of this, Vykers finally gave up.

"It's like this," Igraine told Turley, "I need to lure someone into a trap, but I don't know where this person is, or even if she's...*he's* still in the city. And I can't move on 'til I've taken care of this...issue."

"And who and what is this person to you?"

"It's Tarmun Vykers." Igraine could see by the alarm on the goblin's face that he recognized the name. "As for what he is to me, well, you'd never believe me if I told you. Can you help me?"

Turley closed his eyes, seemed to think about the problem for a while, and eventually said, "Why don't you post bills, advertising that the Reaper will be at a certain location on a certain date. People will talk, rumors will spread. The Reaper will be dying to know why this promise has been made and who, if anyone, shows up in his name. Thus, his curiosity will compel him to attend, allowing you to...to...spring your trap?"

Vykers was stunned. "That is fuckin' brilliant," Igraine smiled. "I'd no idea you were such a sneaky little bastard."

"Thank you?" said Turley, unsure if he was being insulted or complimented.

"Now, I've just got to find a scribe."

"Actually," the goblin said, "I'm a fair hand at the Queen's script."

Igraine was agog. "Of course you are."

"But I'll need supplies."

"Perfect. We need a new place to live, anyway. I'm tired of these crazy old women pryin' into my affairs."

The new place turned out to be an apartment upstairs of a vintner who was down on his luck. He owned the whole building, ramshackle as it was, and was desperate to rent the space and offset his losses. Vykers was only too happy to pay for two months, though, in truth, he could just as easily have purchased the building. Previous experience, however, had warned him against being too free with his money—especially whilst living in Igraine's body. And if the vintner had any curiosity about the young woman occupying his apartment, he showed no sign of it.

Once Igraine and Turley had settled in, Igraine went off in search of ink, quills, and parchment. Along the way, she bought a week's worth of breads, dried meats, cheeses and other foodstuffs to sustain herself and the goblin while they worked and waited.

By morning, Turley had crafted several dozen posters announcing Vykers' appearance at a blacksmith's shop in the warehouse district a week hence, though the goblin had been rather reluctant to oblige once he learned of Igraine's intended target.

"Gotta say, Turley," Igraine announced when perusing the goblin's work, "you surprise me at every turn. I figured if I ever saw any goblins, they'd be like rats, like mindless vermin."

Turley pursed his lips. "You'd be even more surprised at what my people think of humans."

Igraine scoffed. "You don't need to tell me. We're worse than mindless vermin."

Patience had never been the Reaper's strong suit, and the next week felt more like a month. He used that time, as Igraine, to spread the news of Vykers' impending visit. She gossiped in every tavern, brothel and market stall she encountered. Igraine also made an effort to learn about her goblin companion, and to fill Turley in on the finer points of the plan. When and if they caught sight of Vykers, the goblin would have a role to play, too.

Turley was frustrated, though. He understood the details of Igraine's plan, but not the reasons for or behind it. Why do these things? Igraine hadn't explained that part, and it didn't look like she was in any hurry to do so. Too, Turley worried about his own future. Igraine might well have saved him from death in the goblin warrens, but how long could he survive outside, in the humans' world? Somehow, his calm, settled existence had been thrown completely out of order, and he now lived moment-to-moment, at the mercy of a woman who was generous with *things* but not with her innermost thoughts. In short, Turley had no idea where any of this was going.

The big day arrived, as all days do, regardless of Igraine and Turley's readiness. Igraine had chosen a blacksmith's shop near the warehouse district. The weather had warmed a bit, turning the accumulated snow to slush, and the air was smokier than usual; too many fires in too many stoves and hearths, and not enough breeze. If the problem grew much worse, Shapers from all over Lunessfor would convene and summon a storm to scrub the sky over the capital. As it was, the weather seemed to emphasize Vykers' mood: it was a dark, dreary day, a day for vengeance.

Arune, In Lunessfor

There was a mob in the blacksmith's street, with the greatest concentration located just outside the man's shop. Although Arune was baffled by this event, it wasn't until she spied the young woman at the mouth of an alley across the street that the Shaper knew she'd been drawn here on purpose. But what *was* that purpose? Arune didn't sense Aoife's presence anywhere in the city, so the Shaper's worst fears hadn't yet come to fruition. There didn't appear to be any other magicians of any sort in the vicinity, either. If this was a trap, Arune couldn't for the life of her imagine how Vykers might spring it.

As she pondered the question, the girl happened to make eye contact, and she recognized Arune, disguise notwithstanding. The girl then turned away down the alley. The Shaper set off in pursuit, at what she gauged to be a safe distance. Arune used all her arcane gifts to look for Vykers' hidden accomplices, but she found none, no assassins hiding on rooftops, no ruffians lurking just beyond the next corner. And Vykers' young woman gave every indication of trying to escape any encounter with the Shaper.

The alley opened into a broad industrial street, fronted by a row of large warehouses. From Arune's perspective, Vykers' girl appeared to be looking for a place to hide. The first two warehouses were guarded and, the Shaper presumed, locked. When the girl reached the third warehouse, however, she found it abandoned and unlocked. Once the girl went inside, Arune crossed the street and followed, scanning the building for signs of magic or hidden henchmen. Strangely, she found no sign of life, despite having just witnessed Vykers' girl run in. Arune was aware there were magics that made a person invisible to Shapers, A'Shea and others. Somehow, Vykers must have gotten a hold of such magic and used it to hide from Arune. But if anyone should have been hiding, it was Arune, from Vykers.

Then, there was the mystery of the front door. This was no abandoned building, slowly decaying into the river from years of disuse. The sigils on the door suggested it was, instead, property of the crown, of Her Majesty. Why had it been left unguarded and unlocked? Arune again found no sign of magic, not the least iota.

What was Vykers up to?

The girl was just ahead of her, running into the warehouse's vast storage space, now currently filled with sand. When she hit the sand, Vykers' girl struggled to make progress, her feet sinking and stumbling with every step. Arune closed the gap with ease and stepped onto the sand just seconds behind her quarry.

Only it wasn't sand. It was salt. The instant she set foot upon it, she knew, as any Shaper would. Well, she didn't need her magic to catch the girl and question her. Arune sprinted at her target, reveling at the strength in Vykers' legs. In no time, she was within two strides of the girl.

And then disaster struck. She heard an odd whooshing noise and looked up to see an avalanche of salt bearing down on her. She had just enough time to cover her eyes and close her mouth, and then she was buried. Unable to use her magic to escape, Arune tried to fight through the still falling salt. She was blind and couldn't breathe, but at last she managed to push her head free of the pile and was promptly struck unconscious by a monstrous blow to the head.

Kittins & Rem, On the Road

Rem had gone downstairs and fetched a hot meal for both men.

Kittins nodded his thanks. He wasn't one for big, showy expressions of gratitude, and he'd come to mistrust just about everyone and everything, so the nod was the best he could do. Truth was, he was glad Rem had come along, spy or not. The captain had been ugly enough with half a face, but once the Shaper had burned the lot, Kittins had a hard time getting service, information or even eye contact from anyone. Having a traveling companion would grease the skids, as the saying went, as long as the actor didn't talk too much. Kittins hated that.

After both men had finished eating, Kittins said, "It's gonna work like this: you'll be in front, like you're on my trail, and I'll be in back. If the Shaper shows up, detain 'im long enough for me to catch up."

"You don't really think you can kill the Queen's Shaper, do you?"

"I nearly did."

"And you nearly died."

"Dyin's nothing. Living's the bitch." Kittins stood, packed his few extra items into his bed roll. "What'd Cindor tell you about my trip north?"

"Something about rumors of the Reaper up there. The hell of it is, I was already up north when he magicked me down to Lunessfor for this errand."

Kittins threw his bundle over his shoulder. "What were you doing up there?"

"Looking for the captain's...for Long Pete's kid."

"One child in the whole north?" said Kittins incredulously. "They'll never find her."

"Maybe they won't, and maybe they will," Rem replied angrily.

"I'll see you outside," Kittins said as he left the room.

Rem didn't like thinking of his friends endlessly wandering the frozen north. He would have given anything to rejoin them. If there was any bright side to his current fix, it was the prospect, however slim, of exacting some measure of vengeance upon Cindor. With that almost happy thought in mind, Rem lurched to his feet and worked his way out the door and downstairs to the common room, where he discovered, to his surprise, that Kittins had already settled his account.

Outside in the snowy street, Kittins stood holding the reins of his own horse and Rem's.

"Where'd you find her?" the embarrassed actor inquired.

"Other end of town. Wasn't hard to locate her, but I had to kill the man sittin' on her."

Rem was aghast. "You're kidding."

Kittins shot him a look with his death's head face that suggested the captain had never experienced a single moment of humor in his life.

"Okay," Rem gulped. "Is that, uh...is that going to be trouble for us?"

"I kill bastards like that every day; nobody ever misses 'em."

"Right," said Rem, mostly to himself.

"Now mount up," Kittins commanded, "and remember, you go well ahead of me."

There was something strangely liberating about being in the lead, not having to squint through the storm at a phantom's back, but instead being the first to ride through fresh snow. It felt like being the first man to plot a course in a new land. Of course, in the back of Rem's mind, he was aware that Cindor might appear at any moment and spoil his mood. He was also still smarting from the theft of his identity, career and theater company, but that was a worry for another day. He understood his old mates needed to work, and he could hardly blame them.

And this business about the Reaper? What was this nonsense? Sacking towns, cities and kingdoms was the Reaper's mission in life. Or so Rem had heard. As long as Vykers didn't come for Lunessfor or, say, Bysvaldia, it was no particular concern of Rem's. For all he knew, the Reaper would make a better ruler than half the lords in the land.

Out of nowhere, Rem was hit by a thought, a question so astounding, it nearly knocked him from his saddle and into the snow: what was the name of this land? He knew the names of the various kingdoms, baronies, city-states, et cetera. But what was the name of the greater whole? Had he forgotten it? Had he ever known it?

He pulled back on the reins, stopping his horse in its tracks. He needed to talk with Kittins, and Cindor be damned. Only Kittins was being entirely uncooperative. When Rem had stopped, Kittins did likewise. Rem tried walking towards the captain, and Kittins retreated. Finally, Rem jumped off his horse and began waving his arms.

It was a very unhappy Kittins who arrived at Rem's side some five minutes later.

"What?" Kittins asked, as sharply as possible.

"What is the name of this land?"

The captain grimaced (hard as it was to tell) and said, "I don't know. Aren't we in Serefordshire?"

"No," Rem answered, "I mean, the larger land, the whole land. What is the whole of it called?"

Now, even Kittins became alarmed. "It's, er...it's..."

"Can't think of it, can you?"

"'Course I can. I just wasn't expectin' the question. It'll come to me."

"I've got a Merchant says it won't."

It didn't.

"And what's that s'posed to signify?" Kittins demanded defensively.

"Signify?"

"I was teachin' myself to read before all o' this shit with the Great Eight," Kittins explained.

And shit it had been.

Whatever it was they'd been talking about, Rem couldn't regain the thread of it. Reluctantly, he remounted, flicked his mare's reins and continued in the direction he'd been heading. When he looked back, Kittins was already quite a ways behind him.

Rem couldn't shake the feeling he'd forgotten something.

The Giants & Nelby, the Forest

They followed the oursine tracks back to the spot where the beasts had run into Nelby. In the growing light of dawn, it was easy to see there were prints all over the place, but no sign of blood or bodies.

"Can you read this mess?" Karrakan asked.

"Can I? How long have you known me?" But as Karrakan opened his mouth to respond, Eoman said "Don't answer that." The king of the giants got down on one knee and scrutinized the various prints. "There!" he cried. "You see that?"

Karrakan followed his friend's outstretched finger until he saw it: a boot print.

"Oursine, unshod human feet, and that," Eoman declared. "I reckon one of those slavers took Mardine's child. Again. And you see these funny looking prints here?" he indicated a pair not far from the boot. "Those aren't human feet, and they're not rightly giant, either."

"That's all? But one man? It shouldn't be too difficult to rescue the girl then."

Eoman squinted at the snowy ground, color in his cheeks the only sign of his growing excitement. "I believe you're right, unless he meets up with more of his kind before we catch him. And more's always welcome to my axe."

Karrakan took a moment to readjust his hold on Nelby, since it looked like he and his king would soon be off again. "What do you say?"

"We follow the boots. If we stop to rest, we may lose him."

The sky continued to brighten, but Karrakan's mood did not, for he knew Eoman's thirst for vengeance would not be sated by the death of one man. Karrakan looked down at Nelby, still fast asleep despite the constant jostling, and pulled his coat flap more tightly around her. If he could just save this one human, he might not feel so terrible about what was coming. When he looked up again, Eoman was already several hundred strides away. Even from that distance, he could see his king put a finger to his lips: silence. That suggested that he thought the slaver was nearby.

By mid-morning, they found the cave-like place in which Innoman and the child had spent the night. They had to wake Nelby and ask her to crawl inside, because the opening was too small for either giant. She was hesitant, at first, but then realized that she was probably safer in the giants' company than she'd been in months. If they were unafraid of what they'd find in the cave, it stood to reason that Nelby had nothing to fear as well.

It was rough going, those first ten or fifteen feet. All of the strength and coordination seemed to have drained right out of Nelby's arms and legs, making her feel a thing of rags and string. The farther she crawled, however, the stronger and steadier she got. At the cave's center, the scent of Esmine almost brought Nelby to tears, and she cried out briefly, a short, sharp sob.

"What is it?"

"She was here," Nelby managed. "She was here."

But that man had also been here, that Innoman, and his scent was as powerful as Esmine's, though far less pleasant.

"How many others you reckon?"

"Just one."

"For now," she heard Eoman mutter to his friend.

Nelby crawled back out, blinking in the light.

Karrakan smiled at her. "You're looking better."

"Feeling it, too, thanks to you."

"I still can't let you walk," the giant said. "You'll be too slow. But you can ride on my back. That'll be a good deal easier on both of us. Unless..." he trailed off, looking towards his friend.

"Unless what?" Eoman growled.

"Unless you want to carry her a while."

Eoman stared at Nelby, his deep set eyes almost lost in shadow under his bushy brows. "Nah," said he. "I don't."

As Eoman set off in search of Innoman and Esmine, Karrakan leaned into Nelby before hoisting her on his back. "He doesn't like humans, but don't you worry: we'll change his mind yet."

Long & Company, Underground

The new chamber was filled with hundreds of mummified remains, all in a kneeling position, all facing the doorway in which Spirk, Long and Ron now stood, supporting Yendor between them.

"Those aren't children," Long said. "They look more like really small women."

"Women," Yendor breathed wistfully.

Spirk started into the room, but Long restrained him. "Let me," he said. "You just make sure nothin' jumps out and gets me."

The captain walked forward, still holding his glowing sword in front of him like some sort of religious talisman. By its light, he could see about half of the corpses. They had elongated heads with unusual braiding down the sides that came together in larger braids down their backs. Each wore a simple leather tunic, tied at the waist with more braids, though whether these were of hair or some other fiber, Long could not tell. The arms and legs of the supplicants, as Long thought of them, were ritualistically scarred in labyrinthine patterns that caught the captain's eyes and made him dizzy. Refocusing his thoughts, he saw that the fingers and toes of each body were far too long for humans, and the sunken eyes were much too big. The floor underneath each body was scratched and scrawled with symbols and runes Long had never before seen.

Well, of course, he thought sourly. With utmost caution, he inched his way back to his companions. "They may be female, but those ain't women," he said. Again, Spirk moved to investigate, and again Long held him back. "I don't think there's any reason to go poking this wasp's nest."

"But they don't feel dead," Spirk replied.

"All the more reason to leave 'em alone."

"But what if the way out's at the far end of this room?" Yendor cut in.

Long wanted to scream at him. "Don't you think you're hurt badly enough? The last thing we need is to tangle with some bizarre religious fanatics. If that's what they are." He took several deep breaths, thinking. "Here's the thing: they're all facin' the door, which was locked, no? They look like they're prayin'. Are they prayin' the door will hold against some outside threat? *We're outside*, which means…"

The two younger men turned towards the darkened plaza, leaving Long in sole support of Yendor.

"I think we better get outta here," Spirk suggested.

A deep, thunderous boom sounded in the distance, a noise that was more felt in the breastbone that heard with the ears.

"Oh, *do* you?" Long snapped.

"It's too bad we blew that door in, we coulda run inside and relocked it."

Long cast a last glance at the supplicants. "Another bad idea."

A second, more audible boom shook dust and cobwebs from the still invisible ceiling.

"Let's go!" said Ron.

"Which way?"

"To the right, to the right!" Long commanded.

Everyone took ahold of Yendor and carried him down to his litter, then the younger men commenced pulling it in direction Long had indicated. The captain strode into the lead, waving his sword back and forth. Now, along with the booming noises, there were other, even less comforting sounds: creaking, skittering, and moaning.

"Sounds like we've already kicked the wasp's nest to me," Yendor shared.

The other three men said nothing.

As the group scrambled into the unexplored areas of the plaza, shapes began to materialize out of the gloom. The giant mosquito-like creatures floated into view, apparently at the head of a steady stream of their kind. Behind the group, Yendor was unhappy to discover that some of the praying dead were now no longer praying nor dead, but staggering their way in his direction.

"The wasps are coming," he warned.

"Boys, we're gonna have to run for it. Follow as fast as you can, and if it comes down to you or Yendor, drop the litter," Long ordered.

Yendor wanted to object; he so dearly wanted to object, but he realized Long was right: you always cut the deadweight in a crisis.

The field of visibility bobbed up and down and wavered to and fro as the glowing objects in the hands of Long and Spirk were continually jostled in the sprint to safety, making the plaza look even more hellish than it had been in utter blackness. The peekaboo glimpses of flying creatures or mummified pursuers, added to the increasingly loud and frequent booming was almost more than any of the four could stand.

Long switched his sword to his left hand and kept his right on the wall, in case the group came to an intersection or dead-end without knowing it. It was the captain's plan to dodge into the first opening that presented itself, whether or not it was wide enough to accommodate Yendor's litter. Indeed, to Long's mind, the narrower the opening, the better, as narrower was easier to defend.

"Too close!" cried Spirk, as he unleashed a blast of light. Shrieks and squeals filled the air, along with the stink of ozone.

"What was that?" Long asked.

"Bugs!" Spirk answered.

"Run faster! Run faster!" Yendor pitched in. "Those weird women are almost in my lap!"

And they were. Whatever they'd been doing when the captain first inspected them, however long they'd been there, they were moving now and with unmasked animus and minimal difficulty. One of them dove for Yendor's litter and grabbed ahold of the old campaigner's foot. He would have lashed out with the other, but that leg was broken.

"Get off me, you Mahnus-cursed bitch!" Yendor screamed, waving his one good arm at the creature's head.

The break Long had been looking for appeared. Unfortunately, it was not to either side, but down, where an enormous crack split the floor. He could hurdle it. The younger men could hurdle it. But Yendor? Long risked a glance backwards and his heart practically leapt from his chest at the sheer number of supplicants in pursuit of him and his party. Worse than them, though, was the colossal shadow rapidly rising up behind them. Long made a decision.

"Jump, boys! Jump, if you want to keep living!"

The captain was not the specimen he'd once been—or imagined that he'd once been—but he cleared the gap with a couple of feet to spare, rolled onto his side, and hoped to watch Ron and Spirk follow his lead. When they hesitated, he jumped to his feet and yelled, "You've gotta jump and jump now!"

Spirk made as if to jump in unison with Ron, but just as Ron's feet left the floor, the young Shaper pulled back. He sent out another blast of light at the approaching enemy and then turned all his attention at Yendor, who fairly cowered on his litter, stunned by the still-smoking ruin of the thing that had been crawling on him. Suddenly, the whole litter took flight and shot across the gap so rapidly that it knocked both Long and Ron to either side before bouncing and skidding to a stop. With a mighty yell, Spirk jumped the gap himself, throwing a final salvo of arcane energies at his pursuers.

The mosquitoes had been banished, the supplicants had been cowed. Only the growing shadow continued to approach.

"No time to stop and stare, boys. Grab that litter and run!"

And run they did. Only, Yendor could not forget how Long had been willing to abandon him to those creatures, necessary or not. He could not forget how it had been Spirk, the much-maligned Spirk, who'd risked his own life to save Yendor. As the group continued its pell-mell dash into the darkness, Yendor wondered which of his friends had been right.

Arune, Vykers and Turley, In Lunessfor

She was aware; therefore, she was still alive. Of course she was. Vykers would hardly kill his own body. When Arune opened her eyes, salt crystals tumbled into them, making her tear up and squint in pain. She wanted to wipe the salt away, but her hands were pinioned to her sides. More than that, Arune realized, she was covered in salt, wrapped up in canvas or perhaps an old rug, and buried beneath even more salt. She couldn't move, and she couldn't shape. A weight suddenly landed on her chest, and, when her eyes finally cleared, she looked up into a pair of the most beautiful brown eyes she'd seen in ages—a beauty that was only slightly diminished by the hatred radiating from them.

"I am and ever will be the Reaper, and I thank you for that final lesson."

Arune wanted to speak, found there was salt in her mouth, as well—a small quantity, a few grains perhaps, but enough make her tongue feel dry and sluggish. The young woman raised a hand above her head, and Arune knew that although she could not see it, there was a weapon there. "How..." she coughed out.

"How?" the woman echoed. "How what?" The executioner's hand paused, dangling in the air like an accidental confession.

"How will you recover if you kill this body?"

Laughter. If Arune hadn't been watching her assailant's eyes, she might've taken the sound for joy.

"I can't believe you've forgotten that Her Majesty has four more copies of me."

"That is correct," another, more-familiar voice called from somewhere off to the right. "I do have four more, and I'm planning to keep them."

In an instant, the weight disappeared from Arune's chest as her captor rose and backed away.

"Salt," the Queen said. "Very clever. You're getting quite canny in your old age, Vykers."

The younger woman said nothing, and Arune held her tongue, too. The staccato racket of footsteps approaching was the only sound in the warehouse. A shadow crossed Arune's vision, and she turned her head slightly to see Her Majesty staring at the other woman.

"Oh, come off it!" she snapped. "I can bloody well see which of you is Vykers and which is the Shaper."

"But…" the young woman faltered.

"But nothing. I'm a goddess. Do you think this salt business applies to me?"

Even in the winter, with a draft running through the warehouse, Arune was becoming uncomfortably warm. She couldn't say anything, though, and risk reminding the Reaper of how helpless she was.

"What are you doing here?" Vykers asked.

Alheria leaned over Arune, regarding her the way one looks at something dead that's washed up on the beach. She took her time in answering Vykers' question, but eventually said, "You've been fairly screaming to get my attention—killing my warden, breaking into my warehouse, posting those bills all over town, and stealing my dagger. Did you really believe I wouldn't connect these events to you?"

Vykers glared at the Queen in sullen silence.

"And speaking of my dagger," Her Majesty gestured to the young woman's still-raised fist, "I'll take that back, if you don't mind."

"But I do mind," the Reaper responded. "The End shoved it in *my* guts, not yours. By rights, it's mine."

Alheria scoffed at this comment. "You'd make too dangerous a combination, you and that weapon, which is why I had it locked in a vault."

"Is that why you lied about my sword, too?"

This time, Vykers thought he saw the barest hint of surprise on the Queen's face. "Oh, you saw that, did you? Well, you're right again: that also is too powerful a weapon to be entrusted to you."

"Because you say so? I hope all the other gods aren't as arrogant as you."

Alheria flashed a quick, cryptic smile. "I'll make you a deal."

Vykers watched her, wondering how fast Igraine could throw the dagger at the goddess' chest and whether or not it would hit home.

"I'll trade you that dagger for your old body."

And that was when the Reaper understood the full extent of Her Majesty's machinations. "You did this!" he cried aloud in Igraine's voice. "You put me in here and Arune in *my* body!"

"And what if I did?" Alheria waved her hand dismissively. "I ordered you to leave Lunessfor, but I knew you would not. You're a stubborn lout, Tarmun Vykers, as bad as Mahnus and only half as charming. I took your sword to disarm you. I took your body to cripple you. But I did not take your life. I'll return your body for that dagger you're clutching."

The silence that followed had Arune half-convinced Vykers had left the warehouse. A black anxiety froze her bowels and twisted her stomach in knots. Surely, in his own body, Vykers would never respond in such a way.

Finally, the Reaper spoke. "What happens to her?"

"The Shaper? I'd put her in the body you're currently occupying, of course."

"I have a better idea," Vykers said, to Arune's terror. "Turley!" the Reaper called, "You can come out of the shadows now."

Aoife, the North

She should have known better. The End, or whatever he called himself now, would not be deterred by the loss of a few Svarren, or even a few hundred. He had his plans, as always, and one A'Shea—or *Umaena*—was not going to stop him. But...she *could* hector his army's flanks, forcing him to continually readjust, slow down, and plan for her next attack. Hopefully, that would delay his progress—if progress was the word for it—until help arrived to put him down forever.

She wondered why Vykers hadn't appeared. He was no people's champion, whatever his recent history said to the contrary; he was drawn to bloodshed like some savage beast—a wolf, a mountain lion, an oursa. He would come, if he wasn't already on his way.

Still, for added surety, she could lure him hither. She knew his feelings for her were stronger than her own for him. At least, that's what she told herself. The very act of thinking on him seemed an accusatory finger pointed at Aoife's breast. *Fool!* It seemed to say. *You want him.* "Nonsense!" she replied aloud. "He's a just a weapon, and I need every weapon I can find to stop my brother." But she was not convinced; her denials rang false.

Regardless of her motives, she was sure that the Reaper's presence, his help, was necessary.

"Where," she asked a snowy owl, "can the Reaper be found? Do any of your kin know?"

"I shall inquire," the bird responded, before taking flight.

"Is there any news of the Reaper?" Aoife asked of the rabbits and mice.

"None here," they told her, "But we shall search him out."

"You ancients!" she called to the trees, "What have you heard of the Reaper of late?"

"He is not in the forest," they said. "Of that we are certain."

Not in the forest? Then in the town. "Where are the rats and the ravens?" Aoife queried the wind, and in time the rats and ravens appeared.

"Your will?" they said.

"Send word to your brothers and sisters in Lunessfor: I seek the Reaper."

As the rats scurried off into their holes and crevices and the ravens took to the sky, the Umaena returned her attentions to her brother's host. She would spring up on its far side, kill as many Svarren as she could, and then disappear before the End got close to her. She did not imagine that he'd ever be foolish enough to encamp near the greenwood again, but if he did...

She sent out tendrils of thought, like the nascent roots of a seedling, and found a copse of fir trees not far from the enemy's left flank. There, she would build her next fort; there she would begin her next assault.

EIGHT

Vykers, Turley & Arune, In Lunessfor

"I don't know," Turley said hesitantly.

Igraine looked from Turley to Vykers and back. "Look," said she, "you'll be gettin' a stronger body. One that's not lame. You can't go back to your people, and if you have to spend the rest o' your life in the world of men, you might as well be comfortable."

"Yes. I understand that," the goblin hedged, "but..."

"It's bein' a woman, isn't it?"

Turley fidgeted, gazed at his feet in embarrassment. "Yes."

"It's not so bad. Not near as bad as I figured it'd be." Igraine paused, giving Turley a few moments to sit with the notion. Then, "So?"

The goblin closed his eyes as if in preparation for his own beheading and nodded.

Igraine smirked down at Vykers, turned to the Queen and said "Do it."

With Igraine's help, Vykers emerged from his salt cocoon, barely taking the time to dust himself off before leaping exultantly into the air and letting loose with a jubilant roar. He flexed his muscles, extended his claws, and bounced on the balls of his feet from left to right and back again, over and over, seemingly oblivious of the struggles of Turley in Igraine's body or Arune in her new goblin form. When Vykers had contented himself that he had, in fact, been returned to his proper state, he looked over at Arune with an expression of surprise.

"I thought you'd have tried to run off."

"To what purpose?" the goblin asked, in as miserable a voice as Vykers had ever heard from that body. "If there's any fate worse than death, you may well have found it for me."

Vykers was unmoved. "Good," he said. "Though I still might kill you one day."

"About my dagger..." Alheria interrupted.

Frightened to discover it was now on his person, Turley shrieked. Before the Queen could cross to the young woman and take it, Vykers vaulted the distance and ripped the invisible object from Igraine's belt.

"Not so fast," he chuckled. "I want my sword back, too."

The warehouse seemed to grow instantly darker, and the temperature dropped precipitously. "You tax my patience, Reaper."

Vykers removed the dagger from its sheath and held it out towards the Queen. And then he took a large step in her direction. "Is that a fact?" he sneered. "You've been fuckin' with me for years, and *I'm* taxing *your* patience?"

Incredibly, Alheria retreated from Vykers' unseen blade.

The Reaper squinted at her, suspicious. "There's a *reason* you're behavin' yourself, your Majesty. What is it?"

The Queen's eyebrows rose and her nostrils dilated ever so slightly. "Your game has improved, Reaper."

Turley and Arune watched this interchange with interest and more than a little trepidation.

"Well, of course, I've got another war for you to fight, haven't I?" the Queen said, "Or, rather, the same war."

"What do you mean, the same war?"

Now, Her Majesty turned away, wandered a bit out of Vykers' reach, as if she had all the time in the world. "Oh, it seems the End-of-All-Things isn't quite as dead as we all supposed. And now he's gallivanting around the north, butchering peasants left and right, and telling everyone he's you!"

"And they call *me* coldblooded."

"He's terrible, isn't he?"

"I was talkin' about *you*," Vykers growled. "And you can fight this one without me."

The Queen stepped aside and watched the Reaper stalk right past her to the door of the warehouse. When he got there, he turned and called out to Igraine.

"Turley, you comin'?"

It took a moment for the goblin to realize the Reaper was talking to him. Lacking a better alternative, he wobbled and bounced across the space to Vykers' side. Clearly, this being human business was trickier than it seemed.

When Vykers and his companion had left the warehouse, the Queen turned her attention to the discarded Shaper. "The crown has need of Shapers, even those as ridiculous-looking as you. Come!" she demanded, extending a hand to the goblin.

Arune, having even fewer options than Vykers' goblin friend, did as she was bade, taking ahold of Her Majesty's fingers and immediately vanishing from the warehouse.

Innoman & Esmine, In the Forest

Innoman dragged, pushed and carried Esmine as best he could, but she was large for a child and unresponsive to his threats. That was to be expected, he supposed: she'd lost her home, her mother, and her nanny. Who or whatever her father had been, Innoman had no idea, and the girl never spoke of him. Truth be told, she rarely spoke. So, what *could* Innoman threaten her with that she hadn't already experienced? Well, there was one thing...but even *he* was not so base. His problem remained, then, how to motivate her.

For he knew his time was running out. The longer he was away from the slavers who'd employed him, the more likely they were to suspect him of having been involved in the girls' escape. And that was just one of his worries. Though still young, this winter had proven a bitch and gave no sign of easing up. More snow and colder temperatures would surely mean death if Innoman could not find shelter, assuming he and the girl weren't eaten first by animals or more sinister things of the wilderness. All in all, it was a right tits-up, the very kind of affair Innoman had always sworn he'd avoid, with countless ways to die and no clear option for survival.

Already, his toes had gone numb. Another hour or two of that and they'd go numb for good.

"Pee," the girl said, and Innoman slowed to a stop.

He looked around and found a small clump of bushes just off to his right. "Those bushes, there."

Esmine trudged over to the designated spot and waited for Innoman to turn his head.

And what if the girl chose that time to make a run for it? Would he be any the worse without her? Wouldn't he actually be better off? He could travel at his own pace, have access to a wider range of sheltering possibilities and have only himself to feed.

On the other hand, she'd been his insurance, the one thing he could offer in trade for his own life, if things went south. Best to—

He felt a moment of overwhelming pain in the back of his head, accompanied by the image of lightning across his vision, and then he fell, face-first, into the snow.

His ears were ringing. His skull throbbed and expanded with every beat of his heart. And he was nauseous. Without warning, he lurched onto his side and vomited into the snow, over and over, until nothing came up but bile. Somewhere in all of that, he came to understand that his hands and feet were tied and that his great coat was missing. In a rage, he thrashed about, struggling to catch sight of the girl or at least loosen his bonds. He thought of yelling her name, decided against it. The last thing he needed was to alert whoever or whatever might be listening that he was helpless. He rocked to his left and right, eventually generating enough momentum to hurl himself into a sitting position, which made the pounding in his head feel even worse. If it weren't for the lack of blood on the snow, he'd have sworn the little brat had broken his pate. Briefly, he entertained fantasies of killing her. First, he had to catch her—again—and before he could attempt that, he had to get free of his bonds.

The problem was, the girl had really done the job right. She'd taken the laces from Innoman's boots, britches and other clothing and tied and double-tied his wrists and ankles. She'd put so many knots in the leather, he despaired of ever escaping its grasp. There was no way to tell time, not with the sun so obscured by snow clouds, but Innoman figured he'd been trying for well over an hour when he felt a tear of frustration roll down his cheek. It was entirely possible that he was going to freeze to death.

In the next moment, he looked up into the faces of two very unfriendly looking giants, one of whom had the bitch, Nelby, upon his back.

Suddenly, freezing to death didn't seem so bad.

The False Reaper & Omeyo, In Camp

The boy was burning at a fantastic rate. In his efforts to stay awake, he was using so much arcane energy that his lips were fixed in the rictus grin of a wildside mushroom addict battling the urge to relapse. Despite the cold, a thin patina of sweat was ever-present on his brow, and his hands were clenched into fists more often than not. Only the prospect of violence seemed to alleviate his silent torment. "Omeyo!" he yelled.

"Here," the general replied instantly.

"Find me a new target, a village or hamlet suitable to exercise my Svarren."

Omeyo dreaded saying what must be said. "Reaper," he began, "a large number of local villages have emptied of their own accord, and their occupants fled south or west." Before the Pretender could strike out in anger, Omeyo continued. "Yet, there remains one village too proud to turn tail and run."

The Pretender's grin stretched into something approaching a legitimate smile. "Excellent," he declared. "I do so love humbling the proud."

And how you would hate being humbled yourself, Omeyo thought.

"Instruct my Svarren as you see fit, but we shall take that town, and woe to anyone who has remained behind!"

A strange thought came to Omeyo just then: *Is that all there is? Killing others in order to make ourselves feel better? What little men we are, how tiny, and I, the smallest of the small that I serve such ends.* He bowed and left his master's presence with haste. To the boy, that might have looked like zealous obedience, but the truth was something else: the False Reaper was changing somehow, becoming more lunatic by the day, and this business of not sleeping? Insanity.

Glad though he was to get away from his master, Omeyo's brief moment of satisfaction came to an end as soon as he laid eyes on the Svarren command. Out of the frying pan, into the fire, the old saying went. *That kind of wisdom only comes in hindsight,* Omeyo brooded. *Then again, if it were possible to predict what the morrow has in store, who'd bother to get out of bed?* The general marveled at himself. *When did I become so philosophical? Or is it maudlin?*

Lost in such thoughts, he was caught off-guard when he walked right into the chest of an enormous Svarra. He looked up into its hideous visage, only to have the creature shove him backwards onto the seat of his trousers in the snow. Raucous laughter erupted from the Svarren's companions. With as much dignity as he could muster, Omeyo climbed to his feet again. A hard shove from behind sent him sprawling onto his face, right in front of a second wave of laughter. Someone commented in the Svarren's guttural tongue, and Omeyo felt taloned fingers on his hips, pulling him up to his hands and knees. A dagger of panic pierced the general's chest. His breath came in short, staccato bursts. Before he could rise any further, more Svarren closed in and began to pull and tear at his coat and doublet.

"Get back!" Omeyo yelled, with a strength born of terror.

The Svarren pressed in closer still. Just when Omeyo was about to give up hope, the False Reaper's voice bellowed, "Enough!" And the crush subsided.

This time, Omeyo had greater difficulty getting to his feet. His legs shook more than those of a newborn colt, and he wasn't convinced the worst had passed. He wanted to search out his master's face in the crowd, but understood that would make him appear weak to the Svarren. Instead, though it took every bit of courage he had, he forced himself to look into the eyes of each and every savage who had abused him. He hoped they found his glare intimidating, though he rather doubted it.

The False Reaper appeared at his side, and Omeyo exhaled, shocked to discover he'd been holding his breath since he got up.

"I expect this stupidity to stop immediately!" the boy declared. "None of you is so valuable to my cause that I cannot afford to lose you." Flames burst from his hands, and he waved them at the surrounding Svarren. "And perhaps I should make an example of a few of you. Who wants to die?"

The Svarren fairly leapt backwards and lowered their eyes.

"Pathetic as he is, I have need of this man's services, as I will of all my human officers, when I recruit them." And just when Omeyo's confidence was beginning to return, the False Reaper added, "You are not to harm my servant unless and until I say so."

It came to Omeyo then that this would be his last tour of duty, that he would die in the Pretender's service—not on the field of battle, but somewhere in the day-to-day routines of camp life. It was a bitter thing to contemplate: no glory, no wealth, no power, only an ugly, anonymous death.

The boy's voice intruded on Omeyo's miserable ruminations. "Find a different group of Svarren. You'll not have much luck leading these."

A small mercy, but better than none at all. Why did Omeyo fear it was the last mercy he'd ever know in the False Reaper's service?

He made his way to the opposite side of camp and chose the pack of Svarren that seemed the least hostile to him. "The Reaper has commanded us to raid a village not half a day's run from this spot. Which of you will accompany me?"

They all would, of course. The savages were born for violence, and prolonged time without it was unthinkable.

In little more time than it takes to saddle a horse—the only horse on this raid, as it turned out—Omeyo led his throng of slavering Svarren out of camp and onto the road towards the doomed village. *Better them than me,* he thought.

Mureen, the Forest

Her name was not Mureen. Of that, the giantess was certain, if she knew nothing else. And 'Mureen' reminded her of that fiend, Tinalia, and her equally loathsome son, Baris. No, she wanted a name of her own, the name she'd been given at birth.

Now that her nerves had calmed, she wished she'd had the presence of mind to return to Tinalia's cottage, though. She had nowhere else to go, and the place would have been all hers. Eventually she might have grown weary of it, but at least she'd have had time to think things through, time to figure out who she was and what she needed. Alas, she'd run so far with such frantic energy, she doubted she could retrace her steps if her life depended on it.

But what *should* she do? Where *should* she go? She felt as if she'd only recently been born into the world. Everything was strange and threatening...and yet not unfamiliar.

More than anything else, she needed sleep. Absent other ideas, she crawled under the snow-laden, low-hanging bows of a fir tree, spread one of her blankets on the ground and sat upon it. She then wrapped herself in the remaining blanket and used her bundle of stolen goods for a pillow. She fell asleep the instant she rolled onto her side...

...and was somewhat surprised to awaken the next day. There were good things in the forest, she knew, but bad ones, as well. That she hadn't been attacked during the night seemed a small miracle. Maybe, just maybe, things were starting to go her way.

The questions of the previous night remained, however: where should she go, and what should she do? There were no easy answers, but the giantess had learned to distrust all things easy. If she were ever to discover who she was and where she belonged, she would have to continue to work at it. But how?

All she could come up with was that other people—humans or giants—must have heard or known of her. *Someone must know me*, she thought. *But where can I find this person?* After a moment, an answer came to her: *Not in the wilderness*. She laughed out loud. *Of course! If you want to find people, you go where the people are.* It was so self-evident, even a child could have thought of it.

A child.

The giant's mood suddenly soured. She remembered the crying child in the farmstead she'd attacked. Why should this bother her so? What was it about children?

She'd had one of her own.

The giant shot to her feet, smacking her head on the branches above and causing a small cascade of snow to tumble onto her head and down the back of her neck.

Where is my child?

Tears welled up in the giant's eyes, and she felt a tightness in her chest that presaged a full-blown bout of sobbing. She would not, could not let that happen. It was time to act, to move, to find her child. With renewed energy, the giant shook off her blankets, packed her things, and gobbled down a large wedge of cheese. It was not of the best quality, but, to her, it seemed the most delicious, most *important* thing she'd ever eaten.

With a sense of purpose she hadn't felt since she'd crawled out of the frozen ground, the giant set off to find other people and, she hoped, her baby.

Long & Company, Underground

The gap had been wide enough to halt the advance of the supplicants, but it was useless against the gigantic mosquito-things and would likely prove so against the still charging colossus, as well.

"Keep moving!" Long yelled. "Keep moving!"

He needn't have bothered. Spirk and Ron were like sled dogs, furiously dragging Yendor's litter away with more speed than caution.

On this side of the gap, the street sloped slightly downwards, vanishing, as all things did in this place, into the blackness beyond. As Long ran, he risked a look backwards and immediately wished he hadn't. The dark colossus strode across the chasm as if it were no more than a hairline fissure in the rock, and Long finally got a look at this latest menace.

The monstrosity was at least twice the size of a giant, but infinitely more ugly. From the waist down, it almost looked like a giant, despite freakish genitalia that dangled to knee-length, but from the waist upwards, it looked like an immense, festering tumor with multiple warty arms and a great, yawning maw of a mouth. Myriad jagged teeth jutted from that mouth in such profusion that there was no visible pattern to them—no rows, no clumps, and all chaos. The thing's eyes cast a sickening yellow-white light that instilled in Long a sudden and very real desire to vomit.

"To the right!" Long bellowed. "Find a hole, a crack or a crevice! Anything too small for this bastard!"

The boys didn't need telling twice. They veered sharply to the right and raced away, desperate for a wall, a building, anything.

In Long's peripheral vision, an ugly and massive arm swept into view, heading directly for his back. He put on an extra burst of speed and felt the thing whooshing past behind him. A crash sounded off to his right, and he saw that his friends had at last discovered a wall.

The boys quickly recovered, changed course, and charged off in a new direction, following the wall, still looking for any avenue of escape. In another second, they jogged sharply to the right and were gone.

They'd found a doorway.

With the monster's footsteps ringing in his ears and vibrating in his bones, with its fetid breath corrupting his own, Long dove after his comrades, heedless of any damage he might suffer, and somersaulted into a passage that was, as hoped, too small for the thing at his heels. To Long's astonishment, his fellows grabbed him by his arms and dragged him another ten paces into the passage.

The monster roared and snarled at the entrance, pounding its fists in frustration on the sides of the opening.

"More!" Long yelled. "More!"

And the boys dragged him still farther into the passage.

Long had a hard time reaching his feet and thought maybe he'd cracked a kneecap in his fall. *Just what we fucking need*, he brooded. *My shoulder, my knee...what's next?*

At the doorway, the monster had not given up and was now attempting to widen the hole, bashing and ripping at its edges with unabated fury.

The captain said, "Let's keep moving. He's not gonna give up, and neither should we." But he passed Yendor's litter without a word or any effort to help pull it.

The passage continued for some time, and other doorways began to appear on the right and left. The monster was now lost in darkness behind them, though they could still hear him struggling to bust through the entrance. They passed several additional doors, when Long finally said, "Try this one," indicating a door on his left. It was shut and locked, but Ron was able to force it. He offered a big smile of surprise at his own strength, but said nothing. Long thrust his still-glowing sword into the new space and declared, "It's a shop o' some kind. It'll do. If that big bastard breaks through, he'll have to search every one o' these doors."

Long entered first, on the lookout for anything that might spring from the shadows and threaten him and his team any further. Behind him, Spirk took the foot of Yendor's litter and Ron took the head, carrying the half-conscious older man into the shop. In here, the combined light of Long's sword and Spirk's arrow did a fair job of illuminating the whole place. A low counter ran across the back half of the room, and Long moved towards it. It rose only to Long's hips, which, he considered, made sense, given the size of the supplicants they'd seen earlier.

"Let's put Yendor up here. Might be nice to get him off the floor."

The younger men did as their captain suggested, while Long set about closing and reinforcing the door. He found a couple of sturdy wooden chairs, which he stacked in the entrance. There was also an ancient but surprisingly sturdy ladder that was used, Long surmised, for fetching items off shelves. He shoved that into place against the chairs.

"This won't hold that thing back, but maybe the noise'll frighten him away, or he'll think it too much work to clear out. And it'll give us a few extra seconds to contemplate our deaths..." Long joked grimly.

No one responded.

When Long looked over, he found the two younger men examining the crockery on the shelves. Amazingly, everything seemed intact and still sealed. Long watched as Ron took one of the earthenware pots off a shelf at random and carried it over to the counter upon which Yendor lay.

"Dunno as I'd open that," Long warned.

Ron nodded. "I was gonna have Spirk check it, first."

Hearing his name, Spirk crossed to the counter and faced his companions. "I can already tell ya it ain't poison," said he. "But there is some little bit o' magic. Nothin' bad. I just don't know what."

The captain and the archer exchanged glances, and Long shrugged. "Okay, then, might as well see what's what, then."

As carefully as he could, Ron pulled his dagger and began poking and scraping against the top of the pot. Soon, he'd found the seal and broken it. The lid came off with a faint whooshing sound, and a fruity odor wafted out.

"I smell liquor!" Yendor boomed, startling his companions who'd thought him asleep.

"Yes, but..." Long began.

"But nothing!" Yendor barked. "You ain't broken. Someone's gotta taste the stuff to see if it's safe, and I elect me!"

The captain would have liked to object. He knew too well what his old friend was like on spirits. But Yendor's argument made some sense, too. If the mysterious liquor turned out to be fatal, it was better to lose the weakest member of the crew. "Fine," said Long. "Suit yourself."

"Give me a hand, eh, Ron?" Yendor prompted.

Seeing the captain had agreed, Ron moved the pot to Yendor's lips, while Spirk supported the man's head. Ron held his breath as he slowly tipped the pot enough to spill a small stream of its contents into Yendor's waiting mouth. The older man gulped. And gulped. And gulped. When Ron tried to pull again, Yendor reached out with his good arm and pulled the pot closer. Several gulps later, Yendor lay back, smiled, and died.

At least, that's how it looked to everyone else.

"He's still alive," Spirk said reassuringly.

"Now what?" Ron asked.

The captain sat on the floor and answered, "We wait."

Long dreamt of Esmun Janks and was still dreaming of him when Spirk nudged the captain and woke him. "Sorry," Long said, disoriented. "I didn't realize I'd fallen asleep."

Spirk kneeled down next to him. "We all did. Guess that monster's not chasing us anymore, huh?"

That made sense. Long thought to ask how long they'd been asleep, but then remembered there was really no way to tell underground. He was, however, quite hungry and had to piss something awful. "Help me move this stuff from the door," he told Spirk. "I think I'll take a peek outside and see what's what."

There was no sound beyond the door, nothing but silence and darkness. Long craned his neck into the passageway, poking his sword just ahead of himself, and found no monsters waiting to eviscerate him and his friends. Emboldened, he stepped outside the shop and listened again: still nothing. A door across the way was slightly ajar, and Long moved towards it and gently eased it open with the point of his sword. He'd expected a loud creaking noise, but the door was as silent as everything else in this damnable place. The new room was the twin of the one he'd come from, except that most of the shelves were empty, and equally empty pots filled up an entire corner of the space.

Well, thought Long, *I've finally got a pot to piss in. Maybe I'll live it up and piss in all of 'em.*

When he returned to his companions, he found the younger men gathered around Yendor, who was sitting up and in better spirits than he'd any right to be.

"Greetings, your Lordship!"

Oh, he was drunk.

"Prithee," said Yendor, "vouchsafe to grant me an audience with your most exalted self."

Long nearly cracked a grin, but found he was just as annoyed as he was amused. "What?"

"I'm feeling much better."

"So I see. But now you're drunk."

"Oh, aye," Yendor agreed, "drunk and then some. This… stuff…" he said, indicating the contents of a nearby pot, "is a most wondrous elixir. My pain is greatly reduced, and my injuries feel almost mended."

Long snapped his attention to Spirk. "Is this true?"

Predictably, Spirk shrugged. Long silently admonished himself for expecting too much of the young man. Whatever the origin of Spirk's powers, he had no training through which to understand or channel them. The captain turned his focus back to Yendor.

"And your belly…no discomfort there?"

"If this be poison, 'tis the happiest poison that ere I tasted."

Ron stepped forward. "I volunteer to take a sip."

"Oh, you volunteer, do you?" Long smiled. "Be my guest."

Ron picked up Yendor's half-empty pot and sampled its contents. He was about to put the pot back down when he thought better of it and took a second taste. "Damn tasty," he declared, surprise evident in his voice. He lifted the pot again to take a third sip when Long stopped him.

"Let's wait a few minutes, eh? Give it a little time first."

A scowl of resentment flashed across Ron's face so quickly that Long thought perhaps he'd imagined it. He certainly hoped that was the case.

"As you say," the younger man relented.

To Yendor, Long said, "Does this mean you're strong enough to hobble along under your own power?"

Without answering, the other man slid off the countertop and stood on both legs. He had the cheerful expression of a carnival magician after performing a magic trick.

"Mahnus' balls," Long muttered in disbelief. Then, "Let's see if we can't make you a crutch or cane of some sort out o' that litter. Oughta be something there we can use."

Working together, Long, Ron and Spirk were able to fashion a serviceable crutch out of wood and strips of cloth from their various garments. Yendor tried it out and, though he reeled from the drink, he was able to cross the room several times without stopping or falling.

"How are you feeling?" Long asked Ron.

"Like I want another drink."

"Hear, hear!" Yendor trumpeted. "Merrier more. The more merrier. The more, the merrier!" he managed at last.

Ron and Spirk laughed heartily at this, to which Yendor affected an awkward bow. Only Long remained, skeptical.

"If anyone here needs a taste o' this marvelous nectar, it's old grim Johnny over there!" Yendor said, waving an arm at his captain.

Long flushed with anger. "I'm sorry," he snapped, "if my daughter's kidnapping has adversely impacted your buffoonery."

Before things could degenerate completely, Spirk rushed to Long's side, took him by the arm and gently led him aside.

"Cap'n," said he, "I know you been feelin' poorly about your daughter. We all feel for you. That's why we're here. Only..." he paused, searching for the words he wanted, "we can't be miserable all the time. We'll go mad."

Long couldn't make eye contact with the Shaper. A good part of the captain wanted to rage, to smash things, to hurt himself and others. Another part wanted to weep, and still a third wanted to fall face-first on the ground in embarrassment at his own behavior.

Yendor appeared at his other shoulder and spoke softly into his ear. "I know you meant to leave me back at that great crack in the ground. And it hurts, my friend, but I know you thought it needful. And I forgive you."

Long felt an enormous wave of emotions coming to a crest in his bosom, so he called out, "Give me a draught of that liquor, Ron, will ya?"

In no time, the four friends were all rip-roaring drunk, sitting on the floor, their backs to one another, and their legs splayed out in every direction.

I knew a young lady from Kalimasai,
Made pastries so fine, with one taste you would cry,
For her cakes and her biscuits, you'd willingly die,
But the best of her wares was her succulent pie...

They sang, they laughed, they belched, they farted and laughed some more. They boasted and bragged and confessed.

And then they tumbled, one by one, off to sleep.

Rem & Kittins, On the Road

The whole trek made no sense to Rem. If the Queen or her Shaper had truly wanted Kittins to investigate these rumors up north, they could easily have sent him there in an instant, in the same way Cindor had retrieved the actor from Long's company. By the time Kittins arrived on foot—or horseback, if he was lucky enough to keep his mount alive so long—the Reaper might have moved on. So, the reasons Kittins was given for his journey were probably lies.

Then, what was the truth? What was the real purpose for this trip?

According to the captain, he'd developed an abiding hatred for the Shaper, and the visual evidence suggested the feeling was mutual. Could Her Majesty have sent Kittins north merely to keep him away from Cindor? Why not just kill Kittins? Why not magically banish him to some distant land from which return was impossible?

Could it be that Her Majesty had some future use for the captain? Rem turned the idea over and over in his mind and, as far-fetched as it seemed, found he could not dismiss it.

And then he asked himself again, *Why am I following Kittins?* The Shaper had commanded Rem to trail the captain, to spy on him, but what could he really expect to learn by stumbling after the man's shadow in a snowstorm? Clearly, Cindor did not trust Kittins. Was it possible he did not trust Her Majesty, either? Rem sighed. The gamesmanship of the powerful was so convoluted, so byzantine, as to defy reason. And here he was, stuck in the middle of it all. What a great play *that* would make.

If only he were still Remuel Wratch.

Well, he thought, *as the Poet once wrote, 'What is done cannot be now amended.'* He decided to pay Kittins a visit after sundown. He and the captain had reasoned that Cindor was unlikely to drop in on Rem when he might be asleep, so they spent their days apart, but often reunited after dark to exchange thoughts and information. Tonight, Rem was especially anxious to share his thoughts with the other man.

What would happen, he wondered, if the captain and I refused to be anyone's puppets?

Rem had come to hate sundown. The world went from terribly cold to unbearably cold—teeth chattering, hysteria-inducing, soul-sucking cold. It was flat-out unnatural. But he had to wait a bit more. He had to allow time for the hypothetical setting up of camp, the building of a fire, eating of meal and more. In reality, he was planning to do most of that when he reached Kittins. The captain usually made an enormous fire, far larger than necessary. Whether that was for Rem's benefit or was meant to frighten off nighttime predators, Rem didn't know. It didn't appear that Kittins was worried or afraid of anything. Life, death, violence, peace—it was all one to the captain.

When Rem judged he and his pony were on the verge of frostbite, he headed backwards, searching the woods on either side of the road for telltale signs of Kittins' fire. It took longer than Rem had expected, but his diligence was eventually rewarded with the flicker of flames through the trees. Despite the cold and his hunger and fatigue, the actor approached cautiously, just in case this fire was tended by someone or something other than the captain. But his luck held out, as he saw the man's death's head of a face basking in the light of his fire.

"Thought you might be comin' by tonight," Kittins hissed. He wasn't angry; it was just the quality of his almost lipless speech.

"I've been thinking..."

"Then you're a damned fool."

"Aye," said Rem, "I'll not deny it. But this mission of yours makes no sense." The actor hobbled his horse next to Kittins' and unrolled a heavy blanket across its back. He then crossed over to the captain and sat near him by the fire.

"Do tell."

"Why do *you* think you're out here?" Rem asked, since it was clear that he, too, wasn't sold on Her Majesty's story.

Kittins grunted, "So I won't kill her little magician."

"But if that's all it is, why wouldn't the Queen throw you in a dungeon or take your head off?"

Kittins stared up into the cloudy night sky. A few tiny snowflakes wandered downward and got lost in the flames. "I been wrestlin' with that very question for days and days. Got nothing to show for it but a nasty headache."

Rem was surprised to hear this. "So, you do feel pain?"

The captain snorted. "What do you think?" After a brief silence he continued, "Whether you feel it or not ain't the issue. It's how you deal with it that matters."

Rem gestured to Kittins' face. "Does that hurt? Still?"

"Only thing hurts about it is the look on women's faces when they see me. I could give a fuck what other men think o' me."

"I wish I felt that way," Rem said, remembering how he'd once reveled in the opinions and regard of others.

A long silence settled in between the two men as Kittins fed the fire and stared into its embers, disinclined to say anything further and apparently incurious about the purpose behind Rem's visit. Rem pulled some dried meat from his pack and offered the captain the biggest piece. Kittins took it without a word of thanks or acknowledgement.

"It seems to me," Rem said after a while, "that Her Majesty has some future plans for you, is what I'm getting at."

"Oh, aye, that old bitch is full o' plans. 'S why I want her dead. None of us'll ever be free 'til she stops makin' plans for us."

"Well," Rem laughed uncomfortably, "talking of killing her Shaper is one thing, but killing the Virgin Queen? Are you mad?"

Kittins continued to stare into the fire, as if daring it to look away. "You'd be mad, too, if you'd seen what I've seen, done what I've done. And if I'm mad, my friend, it's her fuckin' fault."

What could Rem say to that? Nothing. And so he sat and chewed his jerky.

"Time was, I used to dream of having a son. Not a whole crew o' boys, mind you. I'da been happy with just one. I used to imagine I'd show him how to hunt, how to fight, hells, even how to drink. And if he wasn't no good with the sword, I'da been frustrated, sure. Angry even. But I'da loved my boy just the same. He'da been mine."

Rem was astounded. Kittins, the taciturn one, was sharing something sacred. The only appropriate response was the church-goer's awestruck silence.

"But," Kittins continued, "I can see that's not to be." He tore a big chunk off his dried beef and chewed a while. "When that thrall took the left side o' my face, I told myself, 'It's not all bad. Some women like a man with scars. Makes him look dangerous.' But now? What woman in her right mind would find this attractive?"

Rem gathered himself and took a risk. "A blind woman?"

To his great relief, Kittins rumbled with laughter and even slapped him on the back. So what if the blow hurt like the endless hells? The captain's laughter had been worth it. Rem could still lighten anyone's mood whenever he chose.

"Listen," Kittins said after he'd composed himself. "I reckon the Queen doesn't know about your little spying mission, which means she won't know about Cindor's plan to visit you. I think I can kill him, and she'll never be the wiser, 'cause she won't be expecting him to leave her precious castle."

His moment of levity over, Rem was as sober as the village beadle. "You're still planning to do this?"

Kittins grinned in response.

"He's the most powerful mage in the kingdom!"

"All the more reason to kill him."

There was no talking the captain out of this, Rem could see. "How will you do it?"

"I reckon he's gotta come soon, when you're supposed to be wakin' up for the day. That's the kind o' bastard he is. And while you're talking to 'im, I'll shoot 'im in the back with an arrow—a poisoned arrow."

"And, uh, where are you going to get poison?"

"You'd be surprised what you can find in books," Kittins quipped. "But because he's a smart son of a bitch, he might be prepared for such an attack. So, I'm gonna use multiple poisons, and…you're gonna knife him in the gut soon as he's focused on the arrow."

"I'm going to…?"

"You are," Kittins confirmed, leaving no room for discussion or doubt. "But cheer up; your knife'll be poisoned, too. Oh, Cindor might kill one or the other of us, but he'll die next. O' that, I'm certain."

"I hope you'll forgive me if I don't share your…enthusiasm."

"It ain't a party, friend. It's a murder."

"Yes," Rem agreed. "It's a murder alright."

Alheria, Arune & Cindor, the Castle

Her Majesty returned without the Reaper, accompanied instead by a small, pathetic-looking goblin. Cindor could literally taste the magic emanating from the creature on his lips and tongue. It had a familiar, bitter tang that all Shapers recognized at once.

"Majesty?"

"A gift," Alheria explained, "from Tarmun Vykers."

This puzzled the Shaper. "Then he'll fight for you?"

"No. Not for me. He was quite explicit about that."

Cindor was stunned. "He said no?"

The Queen settled into her accustomed chair at the foot of the dais that held her throne. "He did. But he'll come 'round. Vykers won't be able to live with the possibility that an old foe somehow survived his onslaught. And, you know, he's never been able to resist the prospect of carnage."

"I see," the Shaper said. "And this…creature?"

"I'd like a glass of wine!" Alheria announced. "And this creature," she continued, pointing to Arune, "is what's left of the Reaper's private Shaper. Arune, I believe her name is."

"Shall I eliminate her?" Cindor asked.

"Bite your tongue! That *creature*, as you call her, knows more about the Reaper than anyone alive. Give her a room and see she stays there 'til I've decided what to do with her."

"Begging your pardon, your Majesty…" Arune cut in, "is there any chance…I mean, would you consider…"

"Transferring you into a human body?"

"If it's not too much trouble…"

Alheria stood and approached the goblin until the two were practically face-to-face. "You're a brave one, aren't you? But you've misread the situation terribly, I'm afraid. You are not in my employ; you are my slave. Please me, and we may talk. Displease me, and your next incarnation will make this goblin seem like a paragon of grace and beauty."

Arune bowed her head and stood in silence.

"Find her a room," the Queen told Cindor, "and put someone capable on guard outside it. Make sure she's comfortable, but do not pamper her."

"As you say," the Shaper replied. In the blink of an eye, he and his new charge disappeared.

A page approached Her Majesty and held out a goblet of wine on a small silver tray. Taking the wine, the Queen said, "Summon my four boys, and tell them to bring the sword."

The page did a quick about-face and left with alacrity.

The boys appeared before Her Majesty had even finished her wine. They entered the throne room two- by- two and advanced to the Queen's chair.

"Your will?" the one with the sword said.

Instead of answering, Alheria studied them a while: four perfect reproductions of Tarmun Vykers. Well, they had better hygiene, less wear and tear, and kept their beards and hair neatly trimmed. And none possessed the strange, chimeric quality Vykers had acquired from his former body guard. But these four were as close to being the Reaper as anyone had ever been or would ever be.

"My will," said the Queen, "is that you keep a hand on that sword at all times. The Reaper has returned to Lunessfor and expressed a desire to reclaim his sword. That cannot happen. Do you understand me? It cannot happen."

"Yes, my Queen," said the Vykers who currently held the sword.

"I may be mistaken, but you four would be wise to expect an attack at any time."

"Yes, my Queen," they all answered in unison.

Vykers & Turley, In Lunessfor

Turley had begun weeping almost as soon as Vykers led him out of the warehouse. He started slowly and quietly at first, a single tear working its way down his now smooth, beautiful left cheek. By the time he returned to Igraine's rented room he was sobbing uncontrollably. For most of the journey, the Reaper had ignored his tears, but he was the Reaper, after all, and possessed only so much patience.

"What?" he demanded without preamble.

"I'm sorry," Turley said, although he'd done nothing wrong. "I never thought...I wasn't expecting..."

"You don't like your new body." It was a statement. Vykers could bloody well see the goblin was unhappy in his new human—and female—form.

"It was hard enough leaving my kinfolk, but I dared to believe somehow I'd come back...But now? I'm wearing the face of a murderer! This girl killed a score or more of my people."

"They ain't your kin anymore," Vykers reminded him. "They threw you out and were gonna kill you, remember?"

Igraine sat dejectedly on the edge of a bed. A human would have wiped the snot trailing from her nose and down her face, but Turley ignored it.

Vykers was not the sensitive sort and had no idea what to tell the goblin. The truth was that the Reaper had thought only of his revenge upon the Shaper and not at all about the goblin's needs or desires. Vykers had found a convenient solution to his problems, but it came at Turley's expense. Still, he had a hard time accepting that his companion couldn't see the gift he'd been given.

"I miss my own body," Turley mewled. "My own fingers, my crippled foot. I don't even have a prick anymore!" He threw his hands up in a plaintive gesture.

Vykers was fed up. "Well I do. For the first time in ages, I've got mine back, and I intend to use it!" He strode angrily to the door without looking back.

"Where are you going?" the goblin fretted.

"The nearest brothel. See you tomorrow."

The sound of the door slamming shut was the loneliest thing Turley had ever heard.

There was a loud bang and light blazed into the darkened room, temporarily blinding the still groggy goblin. Then, a shadow blotted out the light, and the door swung shut again. Vykers had returned, and early, it seemed. He trudged over to his own bed and threw himself heavily down on the mattress. The whole room seemed to vibrate in response.

"I thought you said…" Turley began.

"Save it. I'm drunk, and I'm tired. And I forgot how women love to talk afterwards. Not me. I only wanna…"

Turley waited to hear the end of this sentence, but was treated instead to the Reaper's snoring. The goblin took some comfort in knowing the Reaper's head would torment him in the morning.

Except that it didn't, to Turley's amazement and deep disappointment. Incredibly, the Reaper got up first, went out, and came back with breakfast. Turley should have been grateful, but couldn't help feeling cheated at Vykers' mercurial recovery.

The Reaper acted as if nothing was amiss. "Look," said he, "I'm gonna call you Igraine from now on. This is who you are right now, so you might as well learn to deal with it. Igraine."

Igraine frowned with as much gusto as Turley could muster. Vykers ignored the woman and continued to eat. When he'd finished, he changed the subject yet again.

"I ain't missed how much attention I get just walkin' down the streets. Pain in the ass, really. Just another reason to get out of this Mahnus-cursed city."

Against his better judgement, Turley inquired, "Where would you go?"

"*We*," Vykers said, "will go north and fight the End-of-All-Things, o' course. How's that sound?"

Terrible, thought Turley. "But didn't you tell Her Majesty…"

Vykers belched, stood and stretched. "I know what I told her. But she expects me to go fight, anyway."

"Then why do it?"

"'Cause I want her to *think* she can anticipate my every move. I want to reinforce that thinking. Time comes, I'll do something else and surprise her."

Maybe. "You said 'we'?"

"Yeah. You're comin'. Couple o' months, I'll see you get your old body back."

"And the Shaper?"

"We'll see."

Arune, the Castle

Tears were slower in coming for Arune on account of her having already died once, but come they did. In her wildest imaginings, her most far-fetched nightmares, she'd never foreseen or predicted the fate she now endured, trapped in a body like a prison, in a room like a prison, in a castle like a prison. Even as a ghost in the forest, she'd had some hope of possessing an animal or even a human and finding her way back to civilization and a body of her own. Now? If there was a fate worse than death, Vykers had found it for her. And what galled her most was that he'd outsmarted her. That was the one advantage she'd always believed she held over the Reaper; now, she knew otherwise. What a fool she'd been.

Compounding her despair, the Reaper's return meant that Arune had lost any chance at reconciliation with Aoife. When Vykers learned what Arune had done in his name, she'd almost certainly lose her life as well.

Some people have an endless capacity for self-pity; others eventually become bored, tired of it, and move on to more profitable endeavors. Although only a day had passed, Arune was rapidly reaching the end of her interest in self-punishment. It was time to move on, to devote her energies elsewhere.

She turned her attention to her new quarters. They'd been designed to imprison Shapers, she was sure. For one thing, there was no window. The door, too, was unnaturally solid and featureless. The handle had worked when she'd been shown in, but now it was frozen in place. The walls featured some mildly interesting paintings and tapestries, but concealed nothing but bare stone behind them—no cracks, no secret doors, nothing that even suggested possibilities. And, of course, they were impervious to Arune's magics. There were plenty of books on the room's various shelves and tables, but none were helpful, promising instead *Knights of Passion* or *Folklore of the Northern Peoples*. The Shaper's guardians had even seen fit to remove (or simply not provide) anything that might be remotely dangerous to herself or others. She could fashion something to hang herself with, she didn't doubt, but would have a much harder time attempting to subdue her guards with the same shirt, gown or whatever it was.

But Arune had learned patience in her time as a ghost. She could wait with the best of 'em. And while she waited, she would learn what she could of her room, her captors, and general events and routines of the castle. Eventually, someone would come for her. By then, she would have a plan and a destination.

Her only fear was that in her now-excessive amount of spare time, she'd think too much on Vykers and, most especially, Aoife. Even if she managed to get free of her current imprisonment, she would never be free of her fear of Vykers and her longing for the A'Shea.

With a sigh that seemed to come from the very soles of her feet, she reached for *Folklore of the Northern Peoples*.

Omeyo & the Svarren, On the Attack

When would these bumpkins learn? There was no point in standing in the False Reaper's path, and no chance of surviving it, either. Omeyo brought his Svarren to a stop an arrow's flight from the little hamlet's outermost homes. *It could be a trap*, he thought. *And I might be the Virgin Queen, too.* If there was an army waiting to ambush him, he didn't see where it might be hidden. *In the town well, perhaps?*

His Svarren fighters did not seem the least reluctant to attack.

Still, something bothered the general. Using hand gestures,

he sent two teams of two to the left and right and then forward past the initial cottages. The sun had set, but there was light enough to see that folks were in their homes, going about the business of stoking their fires, making their meals and putting their young ones to bed. It was odd and inexplicable, from Omeyo's perspective. His scouts returned unharmed but more than ready for violence, so he suppressed his last misgivings and launched the attack.

A wise man knows when to listen to his gut.

No sooner had the Svarren passed the outer homes than a vast hedge writhed out of the ground and trapped them inside the town proper. And because vines and branches wear no armor, nobody heard anything until the growth had become too large to leap over. Yet, it was only a hedge. As long as the Svarren didn't engage it, they should have more than enough time to steal fire from the townspeople and burn every house and the blasted hedge to the ground. Yes, Omeyo had seen what had happened the last time the Svarren had encountered such a hedge. This time they would avoid it. No hedge, no matter how magical, could stop them from killing every man, woman and child in this village.

If only it were just the hedge.

Uncanny balls of light zipped out of the gathering darkness and blinded or burned Svarren wherever they found them. Giant, staggering tree shapes grabbed the attackers and tore them in halves. Enormous toads spat poison or acid. Satyrs gored them with their horns or stabbed them with lightning.

The villagers barred their doors and shuttered their windows, kept their weapons and their dogs close, and in all ways prepared for the end.

And the Svarren? They panicked. They'd heard rumors of what had befallen their brethren just a few days earlier, and superstition reigned supreme in their minds. If they had offended the old gods somehow, they knew that no quarter would be offered. They stampeded and fought for their lives. The very air crackled with lights and energy reminiscent of a Midsummer's festival, but the absence of laughter and the presence of screams destroyed the illusion. Death had come to the hamlet, though not as Omeyo had planned or intended.

Dark, towering, leafy shapes strode past in the flickering light, dragging or carrying Svarren corpses off on errands the nature of which Omeyo dared not contemplate. His force had been routed, and he alone remained untouched—by design, he reckoned, and not happenstance. Someone wanted him to return to his master with news of this defeat.

The trouble was, returning with said news could well mean death, especially after losing another group days earlier. And yet, Omeyo could hardly run away and hide from the False Reaper, could he?

The village square grew deathly quiet. Turning his horse left and right, the general saw no further movement and nothing of the fey. Even the bodies of the dead Svarren had disappeared. Then, somewhere, a door opened. Omeyo spun round to identify the source of the noise and found himself facing a stalwart villager extending a nasty pitchfork in his direction. Resigned, the general turned his mount a final time and rode out of town, unimpeded by hedges, brambles or anything else.

Every yard of every mile between himself and the False Reaper's camp proved a challenge. No sane man would move another inch in that direction, but Omeyo did, over and over again. He expected to be killed for his failure. That made perfect sense. Unfortunately, he also expected that his death would not be easy or fair. The Pretender and the End-of-All-Things before him were sadists. It was not enough to vanquish an enemy or punish a servant; their greatest joy was in humiliating their targets.

Omeyo struggled to imagine what fate awaited him in the False Reaper's camp. Ultimately, he would be chagrined at how obvious it was.

"Ah," the Pretender said calmly, "But of course you failed." Without further discussion, he turned to his two body guards, Tooth and Nail, and said "Do with him as you wish."

It was the most terrifying sentence Omeyo had ever heard. The next few minutes of his life became an ever-deepening nightmare, as the two brutes dragged him off, screaming, into the midst of their slavering, bestial clan. They used and abused the general in every way possible, until his conscious mind shut down, and he lost all sense of time, place or being.

Somehow, he eventually regained his wits and found himself on the verge of freezing to death in a gelid pile of his own blood and filth. He vomited and continued to do so, until he produced nothing but bile. Soon, there was even too little of that to bring up. He collapsed back onto his side, hoping, praying, that death would take him.

What he felt, instead, was a powerful, taloned hand gripping the top of his head and jerking him to his feet. With swollen, bloody eyes, he made out the face of a Svarren woman. She was staring back at him like a farmer's wife, attempting to gauge the ripeness of a fruit for picking. Omeyo would have thanked her for a quick broken neck. Alas, it was not to be. The Svarra shifted her grip and dragged the general through the camp, through a gauntlet of hooting, shrieking Svarren men, laughing obscenely at the spectacle they'd made of Omeyo. The night grew darker as the woman pulled Omeyo into her hovel and tossed him unceremoniously onto a pile of stinking furs.

Then she began licking Omeyo clean.

NINE

Rem & Kittins, On the Road

Cindor did not appear the next morning, which only increased Rem's anxiety, for the Shaper surely would appear one day, and the actor would rather have had it over than live in constant expectation of it. The continuous, gnawing dread was giving him an ulcer, he was certain.

The other thing was that for every morning Cindor did not appear, Rem was forced to endure another day's slog through the increasingly treacherous weather for no better reason than to maintain the illusion of obedience to the mage. Rem wasn't *actually* spying on Kittins; the two were in cahoots. There was nothing to be gained from taking a single additional step to the north. Rem wished again that Cindor would just jump in already and be done with it. Kittins would kill the Shaper...or Cindor would kill Kittins...and Rem. But it had gotten to the point where Rem almost considered being incinerated by the Shaper a better option than more travel.

And he was sick and tired of the cold. Even sitting in front of a fire at night, his back was cold. At least when he'd been travelling with Long Pete and the boys, he'd shared a tent and a bit of body heat. Now, he shivered through each night despite the fine gear he'd purchased, and on those rare occasions when he slept, he dreamt of more sleep, and of warmth.

The morning came, however, when Rem rolled out of his blankets and discovered the Shapers' feet not three inches away. He craned his neck upwards to afford himself a better view of the man without actually getting out of his tent, when Cindor reached down, touched him on the shoulder…and jumped.

It was a good thing Rem had been on the ground when Cindor touched him, because it saved him from having to fall once they reached the Shaper's quarters.

So much for Kittins' brilliant plan.

"You smell like a jakes," Cindor complained.

"Yes, well, there aren't a lot of bathhouses along the route, are there?"

"Mmmm," Cindor mused. "And what have you to report?"

Rem sat up. "Report? What report? It's cold up north. It snows too much. And Captain Kittins is a Mahnus-be-damned phantom."

"Has he stopped anywhere?"

Rem worked his way to his feet, stretched. "A couple of times, I think. He spent the night in some little town no one's ever heard of."

"When was this?"

"A week ago?"

"Did you see him speak with anyone?"

"He might have talked to a stable boy."

The Shaper shot Rem a look of disgust. "Some spy you are."

"I never said I was a spy. And what is it you're expecting Kittins to do in the midst of all of those snow drifts?"

Cindor's fingers crackled with energy, a warning that Rem had best watch his tongue. "I don't trust that monster to do the Queen's bidding, and it is my job to protect Her Majesty's interests at all costs. You would do well to take a similar view of *my* interests."

Rem nodded. It had taken him a while, but he'd learned the Shaper was happiest when he thought himself in control. No sense in giving him any other impression. "Is there any chance of a hot bath while I'm here?" he asked as meekly as possible.

"No," came the curt response. "You tarry too long here, and you'll lose your quarry. We got back immed…"

He touched Rem's shoulder, and again they jumped back to the frozen north. Rem had barely an instant to register their arrival when an enormous red blade sprouted from Cindor's chest, spattering blood all over the actor's coat.

"Stab him!" Kittins grunted from the Shaper's far side.

Rem pulled his envenomed blade and made ready to stab the mage, or perhaps slash his throat—he hadn't decided—when he noticed that Cindor was staring directly at him and calmly mouthing something inaudible. The fear of something imminent spurred Rem to strike, and he drove his knife into the Shaper's right eye, whereupon the man's lips ceased moving.

"Step back!" Kittins yelled.

The blade in Cindor's chest disappeared, only to reappear in a lightning fast slash through his neck, sending his head tumbling off into the snow, accompanied by a cascade of hot crimson.

"Get the head!"

"What?" Rem asked stupidly, still shocked from the sudden violence of his and Kittins' actions.

"The head! Get the fuckin' head!"

But when Rem looked, it was gone.

"It's not there."

Rem thought he'd known fear before, but a ranting, rampaging Kittins waving a bloody sword and screaming at him just about stopped the actor's heart. The captain let loose with a torrent of profanity as he hacked, stabbed and pummeled the Shaper's body into a feeble jelly. By the time he was finished, it was hard to tell where the fabric ended and the flesh began, to say nothing of the blood drenched snow.

Kittins bent down, grabbed one of Cindor's ankles, and began to drag the mess off towards his own camp. *What's he going to do with that?* Rem wondered. *Eat it?*

"Gotta burn this. Find that head or you're next!" Kittins barked.

But there was no head to be found, and, anyway, what difference could the head make without its body? Still, Rem searched. After what he'd just witnessed, he didn't want to risk angering the captain any further. The day was clear and cold, not a trace of clouds in the sky. As the sun crept higher, Rem's mood darkened. He hadn't found anything, and became increasingly bothered by that fact. How, after all, did a head just disappear? Where had it gone? Where *could* it go? He thought for a while that it might have been taken by animals—a fox, for instance. But there were no animal prints in the vicinity, which meant the head had disappeared on its own...

...Which meant it was still alive at the time.

Rem shuddered, and, this time, the cold had nothing to do with it. He heard Kittins' voice nearby and fairly jumped out of his boots.

"You scared the shit out of me!"

"I take it you didn't find the head," Kittins replied, much calmer than he'd been the last time Rem saw him.

"No."

"Figures."

To say that Rem was taken aback is an understatement. "How does it figure?" he demanded, temporarily forgetting the awesome threat his companion posed.

"He's a Mahnus-cursed Shaper, isn't he? 'Less you reduce the brain to ash, he ain't dead."

"What?"

"I saw an alchemist do something similar once," Kittins shrugged, as if that explained everything.

"How could he not be dead? I shoved a poisoned dagger into his brain, and you chopped his head clean off before making mincemeat of his body."

"I expect he planned for that type 'o treatment. I expect he knew it was comin', and he made plans."

The bottom dropped out of Rem's stomach, and the color drained from his face. "But that means..."

"He'll be comin' for us, yes," Kittins offered. "On the bright side, it won't be soon. I imagine he'll be some time recoverin'."

Rem's legs gave out and he landed on his ass in the now-frozen blood.

"What's wrong with you?" Kittins asked.

Instead of answering, Rem began laughing hysterically. Kittins had no patience for that and turned away to stalk back to his own campsite.

Well, Rem thought, I've just made a mortal enemy of the most powerful Shaper in the land. I certainly know how to pick my battles...

The Giants & Nelby, the Forest

Eoman had been elated to find Nelby's former captor tied up on the ground, because it suggested that Mardine's girl couldn't be far off. After what felt like several hours of fruitless searching, however, his enthusiasm slowly turned to frustration. Irritated, he called a temporary halt to the chase and sat on a stump to enjoy his lunch, a prodigious slab of pemmican. As he chewed, he watched Karrakan attend to the human woman and wondered if maybe they ought to have killed the slaver. The shaman had convinced his king that the man would die of cold soon, anyway, and it was best to let nature do her work without interference. Still, Eoman would've enjoyed pounding the bastard through the ice and into the frozen ground. It would have felt like justice. Once in a while, though, a king has to compromise if he wants to *remain* a king. Karrakan got his way, and the slaver was allowed to freeze to death. Eoman smiled, thinking it was just possible that the blackguard had gotten his face gnawed off by a wolf before that happened.

"Not sure I like that smile of yours," Karrakan called over to his king, "knowing the way your mind works."

"It's nothing," Eoman insisted. "But about this girl, now. Where in the endless hells can she be? How does a wee girl on her own elude us for so long?"

"She's afraid," Nelby said, so softly the two giants almost missed it.

"Makes sense," Karrakan nodded.

"If we don't find her by nightfall..."

"We'll find her."

"I hope you're right, 'Kan. I hope you're right."

He was not right.

Sundown came and went, and they hadn't found the child.

"Let's make camp," Eoman said irritably. "I want a good fire and some rest."

Giants have no difficulty finding wood for their fires, being much taller and stronger than humans. Tearing an old stump into kindling is easier for them than milking a cow. In no time,

Eoman had a great fire blazing in the center of a small clearing, whilst Karrakan unpacked, unfurled and erected their separate tents. Before the king could refuse to shelter Nelby, Karrakan offered to share his own. If the king's manners had deserted him, the shaman's had not. And the thrall woman was not to blame for the child's predicament, after all.

Under normal circumstances, Eoman and Karrakan would have wiled away the evening in stories, song and boasting. Somehow, Nelby's presence made Eoman more reserved than usual. After an extended silence, he finally said, "Not feeling hopeful about finding the wee one."

"That's where we differ!" Karrakan countered brightly. "Ours is the only fire in who knows how many leagues, and a beauty it is, too. That might draw the moppet forth. And I'll send my will-o'-wisps out, too. Children always find them fascinating!"

Although Eoman remained unconvinced, he noted a gleam of hope in the thrall woman's eyes. "Send 'em, then," he said to his shaman.

Karrakan's laughter seemed to sparkle from his lips into the night air, and, sure enough, his wisps appeared and spiraled off in every direction.

As the night wore on, Eoman and Nelby nodded off, too exhausted to maintain the watch. Only Karrakan seemed unaffected by the day's slog. Hours into his solo vigil, a small face appeared at the edge of the light.

Esmine had arrived.

Karrakan made not a move, but smiled broadly. Bait the hook properly, and the fishies always come. The shaman whispered an order to his will-o'-wisps, and they began to swirl about the girl, leading her ever closer to the fire. Once Esmine was close enough to see Nelby, the child cast aside her fears and rushed to the thrall woman's side, embracing her in a powerful hug that woke the woman and reduced her, immediately, to tears of gratitude and relief. Eoman woke, too, and sat by in silent witness, his stony heart softened by the sweet spectacle. In time, Esmine turned her attention to the two giants, entranced by their enormity.

"Mama?" she said.

She was not asking if either of them was her mother; no, she was asking if they knew of her, had known of her.

Karrakan held both hands out to the girl and she tottered over to him, grasping his nearest hand with both of her smaller ones, whereupon she examined it as if it were some sort of holy relic.

"The girl's a half breed," Eoman breathed, in a tone that was equal parts disgust and wonder.

"The girl's a *child*, my king."

"But...how? How is she possible?"

Nelby had scarcely said two words since her rescue by the giants. Now, she spoke up. "Her mother loved her father," she answered quietly, so as not to break whatever spell it was that captivated Esmine's attention.

"And who was her father?" Eoman wanted to know.

"A good man," Nelby replied. "And a loving, and a brave."

Esmine had crawled up onto Karrakan's lap and was tugging at his beard experimentally. "That's good enough for me," he beamed.

"Hmph!" the king scoffed. "And where was this good, brave and kind man when..."

Karrakan cut him off with a glance. It was not his place to silence his king, of course, but he also did not want the girl to hear the details of her mother's death.

Grudgingly, Eoman silently acknowledged that his friend was correct. Having just recovered the child, it would do no one any good to disturb her.

Nelby, however, caught the drift of his comment and responded anyway. "Her da went on a mission for the Queen, as I been told."

"Queen? What Queen?"

"Why, the Virgin Queen," Nelby responded, as if the answer were self-evident.

Eoman tossed a chunk of wood into the flames and watched until it caught fire. "The kings and queens of men cannot be trusted," he rumbled softly to himself. When he looked over at his shaman, he saw that the girl had fallen asleep in his lap.

Now that they'd found the child, what were they to do with her?

Vykers & Turley, Lunessfor

Over the years, Vykers had learned that if he looked angry enough, folks went out of their ways to avoid him, despite his fame. Thus, he wore the mother of all scowls as he dragged Igraine through streets of Lunessfor, even though he was, in truth, in a fairly good mood. And why not? The snow had stopped falling, the sun was out, and there was an almost festive atmosphere amongst the townspeople. *Sure,* Vykers thought. *That's because they live on this side o' the walls.* Outside the city, there was less security, more uncertainty.

Vykers couldn't wait to get back out there.

First, though, he had to reequip himself and his companion, which necessitated a lengthy jaunt through the market and the city's various neighborhoods. Everything was proceeding as expected, until the Reaper heard a familiar voice.

"I vas right!"

He turned. Not twenty feet away stood the bedraggled red knight he'd once defeated across the great sea. At the man's side stood the tall Ntambi warrior Vykers had likewise beaten.

"What?" Vykers said abruptly.

"I knew she vas you...student."

Vykers looked at Igraine and then back to the knight. "How's that?"

"She move like you...aldough today, she move...funny."

Again, Vykers looked at Igraine. Well, before, he'd lived inside her. Now, she was home to the goblin, Turley. He reckoned that, yes, that'd make a difference.

"So, you speak the Queen's tongue now, eh?" he asked of the knight.

"I try. Little choice, no?"

"And your friend?" Vykers nodded to the Ntambi warrior.

"Iss too hard for him."

"Huh. Are you lookin' for work?"

The man's face lit up like a summer sunrise. "Yes!"

"Good. Come with me."

"And zee udders?"

"What others?" Then Vykers remembered his other prizes, the other slaves he'd won in combat. "You're all still together?"

The red knight shook his head. "Nah. Two iss dead, one is vee don't know. But five of us dere iss."

"Bring 'em." Vykers explained where his lodgings were and gave the red knight just enough coin to ensure his continued interest. "Meet us there at midday."

Once his two newest companions had departed, the Reaper returned to the business of resupplying himself and Igraine. He wanted new armor, something light and flexible with just enough protection should he be grazed by an arrow or spear. And while his dagger was weapon enough for anyone, he wanted to hold it in reserve, to keep it a secret until such time as his need was desperate. Besides, he didn't feel right without a good sword on his hip.

As he walked along, he considered Turley/Igraine. The goblin was still struggling to adapt to his new, longer, fully functional legs, but he'd get the trick of it in time. And he'd stopped crying, too, which Vykers was glad to see.

The only difficulty, from the Reaper's perspective, was that Igraine was damned attractive. This put thoughts in his head that made him rather uncomfortable, considering there was a goblin inside all of that beauty. At the same time, Vykers felt an affinity, almost an affection for Igraine, for all they'd been through together and how well she'd served him. Perhaps if he viewed her as a daughter...

The red knight, the Ntambi warrior, and the rest of Vykers' former slaves were waiting for him outside his lodgings, as ordered. Vykers tossed them two great bundles of food he'd purchased and led them inside, where they spread out on the floor, not daring to occupy either of the beds.

"Your vill?" the red knight inquired as everyone ate.

"My vill?" Vykers joked. Seeing nobody got the jape, he moved on. "I'm goin' north. They say there's a madman up there uses my name while he raids. I wanna see for myself."

"And vee go vith?"

"That's the idea, 'less o' course you all have something better to do…"

None did.

"Good. Now, I'm gonna give you some gold, and you're gonna get all the gear you need and seven fast horses—better make it nine. You're gonna be cold, wet and tired from here on out. Make sure you buy enough food so we ain't hungry, too."

The red knight and his friends bought ten horses—one for each rider, and the rest for gear. Or eating, if worst came to worst. He made a deal with an armorer and purchased eight identical military swords, four bows, and four spears. He bought enough food and spirits to last a month. And, of course, he bought the best tents, bedrolls and blankets he could find.

Vykers was impressed. "You got a name?"

"Hjuest, and it please you."

"Ah, that's right. You didn't buy any wooden sticks to touch our enemies with, I see."

Hjuest winced at the reminder. "I hev learned."

"Good. I'll make you my sergeant."

"Sank you."

"We'll leave at sunset," the Reaper explained. "Out the southern gate 'n across that bridge. Not much of a ruse, but better 'n simply headin' straight north."

"Vee must deceive some vun?"

Vykers grinned. "The Queen."

Surprise was plain on the red knight's face.

"We won't fool her, o' course, but I ain't concedin' anything."

Hjuest nodded, as if this made perfect sense. Whatever else he was, the red knight was well-trained.

Innoman, the Forest

The cold was killing him, and despite his ever-increasing difficulty in remaining alert and lucid, Innoman expected death within minutes. Gods, he was drowsy! *What's the harm*, he wondered, *in a little nap? When I wake up, I'll feel…*Yet, part of him recognized that if he dozed off now, he would never awaken. It was so frustrating.

He gave a listless tug at the cords binding his hands and feet, but had even less strength to deal with them than he'd had just a few breaths earlier.

With a sort of muted urgency, he tried to clear his mind. He shook his head, flexed his arms and legs and inhaled a massive lungful of viciously cold air. It seemed to slow him even more.

There must be somethin'...

He labored to take in the details of the darkened forest surrounding him, but sleep continued to beckon and tease. Then, out of the corner of his eye, he caught movement in the underbrush, an area of blackness that separated itself from the larger whole. It moved in an unsettling, disjointed manner that reminded Innoman of nothing so much as a drunken spider.

'S probably a badger or some such, Innoman strove to convince himself.

But it was not. It was nothing of warm blood or honest intentions. As it crept closer, it resolved itself into a tiny man-shaped creature that might have risen no higher than Innoman's waist, had he been standing, and the thing's posture been fully erect. But it crouched and dragged the backs of its hands along the forest floor. In a trice, it vaulted onto the slaver's chest and leered down at him. It studied his bonds and sniffed his garments.

"Help?" Innoman forced out through cold-numbed lips.

The creature chortled in response and fairly cavorted on his captive's belly.

"Look you," the slaver spat, "you fuck with me, and I'll kill ya. Help me, and I'll reward ya."

This sent his tormentor into paroxysms of laughter. Suddenly, its face was terribly close to Innoman's, and it stared into his eyes with palpable malevolence. "Hyreeeee!" it shrieked.

For a heartbeat or two, all was silent, and then the whole forest came alive with answering shrieks. Similar black shapes bounded from the underbrush, fell from branches and even seemed to rise straight out of the ground. They rushed as a single organism to Innoman's prostrate form and swarmed his body. The slaver felt a sharp tug on his nose and saw the original creature attempting to pull his nostrils wider. The imp gave a sinister wink and then ushered his brethren towards Innoman's face. One by one, the darklings forced their way into the slaver' nose, mouth and ears, melting and oozing into his head as if they were not things of flesh and blood but of shadow.

And the pain was excruciating. Innoman screamed for as long as he was able, dying in agony, alone in the frozen dark.

Long Pete & Company, Underground

Long Pete awoke in a good mood and well before any of his friends and took a lengthy moment to savor the strange, sadly unfamiliar feeling of well-being that pulsed through him. It had to have been the drink, but he'd not gainsay it. He hadn't experienced anything like happiness in such a long time that he'd nearly forgotten what it felt like. Oh, he knew too well that he had to get on with finding Esmine. For the nonce, though, he wallowed in the absence of panic, fear or anger.

Spirk was the first of his companions to wake, but unlike Long, the young man was still rip-roaring drunk. He got up to relieve himself and toppled right back over, landing atop his fellows in a giggling lump. Even those crushed by his fall laughed as they struggled towards consciousness. At first, Long figured he'd sobered up before the younger men because of his extensive drinking experience. But that didn't explain why Yendor was still drunk. Nobody had more drinking experience than Yendor. Could it be they'd imbibed more of the stuff than he? That hardly seemed possible. Long had downed so much that, even now, his stomach sloshed when he moved about.

So, his friends were still drunk. What difference did it make? They'd enjoyed precious little merriment in Long's company; let 'em have this.

As Spirk mounted another effort to stand, he hiccupped and blinked out of existence, only to appear on the other side of the room, where he bonked his head on the wall and guffawed like the injury was the most amusing jest he'd ever heard.

Long jumped to his own feet, amazed. "Spirk!" he called. "Can you do that again?"

Still laughing, the young man hiccupped again and disappeared altogether. Seconds later, there was a knock on the door. Long hurriedly cleared it away and found the Shaper standing in the outer passageway.

"That's it, boy!" the captain exclaimed happily. "That's the Shaper's jump, the thing that took Rem away from us!"

Spirk and Ron were a touch slow to grasp the significance of it, but Yendor was practically hopping up and down with excitement, bad leg and all. "That's how we get out of this hole!" he yelped in inebriated joy.

"Spirk," Long said, clapping his hands on each of the Shaper's shoulders, "can you go somewhere on purpose?"

"Across the room?"

Spirk shrugged and started walking across, until the captain reached out, snagged his arm and said, "Like you did a minute ago, with magic."

This time, Spirk blipped across the room and crashed into a shelf of crockery. He turned and looked apologetically at his leader.

"That's fine, Spirk. That's fine. Now, can you take someone with you? Me, for instance?"

For the next half hour, they tried short jumps with each member of the group and then with everyone. Finally, Long was ready to get to the point.

"Let's try to jump out of here," he told Spirk. "Maybe you and me first, and then you can come back..."

"Sod that!" said Yendor. "We all go or none of us goes."

Long looked at each of his companions and saw they were in agreement. "Very well," he replied. "We all go."

"But first, let's gather a few o' these pots o' liquid bliss!" Yendor urged.

"Take all you can carry," Long chuckled. "What do I care?"

When they were all ready, Long got very close to Spirk and said as carefully as possible, "I want you to picture the forest right before we fell down here. That's where we want to go. Everyone link arms and..."

They were falling through the snow-laden boughs of an enormous fir tree. Grunts and gasps of surprise and pain rang out from everyone in the group, and then they plunged, one by one, into a vast snowdrift. Long scrambled to dig everyone out before they all died of exposure. Miraculously, everyone survived without anything more serious than bumps and bruises. Yendor's pots were not so lucky, though the group still had four unbroken ones.

"If I weren't s' drunk," the man mused, "I'd call this the greatest tragedy to befall mankind in an age."

Long wasn't bothered in the least. He and his friends were free of the hole and its all-encompassing darkness. Here, it was daytime, cold, but bright. The group was still lost and without either food or shelter, but everyone was alive! And the best news of all for Long's soul: the hunt for Esmine could resume.

Mureen, In Gandy

The giantess passed some homesteads that looked abandoned or were too small, just as she passed towns that seemed too large. She hadn't found what she was looking for, but remained convinced she'd know it when she saw it. Many days she searched, and many nights, she slept in the most unlikely places, but her spirits remained high. She was free and alive, and though she possessed but a few tools and small items of comfort, her self-confidence grew with every sunrise.

A day came when she crested a hill and caught sight of a village that seemed the perfect size for her plans. Not wanting to startle the town's citizens or provoke a violent response, the giantess walked to within bowshot of the nearest buildings and simply stood, waiting for someone to notice her.

It didn't take long.

A number of heads poked around the edges of buildings and shutters creaked open just the tiniest bit. Eventually, a lone man emerged from a growing crowd of spectators and started walking in the giantess' direction. He, too, stopped when he'd reached what he judged to be a safe distance.

His bristly hair was cut short, though the crown of his head had gone completely bald, but he boasted a neatly trimmed mustache and beard the color of ashes. He wore a long woolen robe underneath a wolf skin that he'd wrapped around his shoulders. On his feet, he wore boots that looked older than memory.

"Greetings!" he called out. "To what do we owe the pleasure of your visit, friend giant?"

"I'm afraid I'm down on my luck and looking for work," the giantess answered.

"What of your own people?"

"Well, that's the problem. I've taken a nasty fall, hit my head, and can't remember much of anything." And it wasn't entirely untrue, the giantess mused. How could she tell him the truth when she didn't know what it was?

The stranger appraised her with the shrewd look of a man buying a second-hand milk cow. "Taken a fall, have you?" He stepped closer, saw the giant's many scars, and said, "That must've been some fall."

"I *did* say it was nasty."

"So you did, so you did. But tell me, what help can you offer? What tasks can you perform?"

"I'm a giant. I figured there might be things to lift, move, carry about. That sort of thing."

The man came closer still. "Oh, we've plenty of that needs doing. But can you be trusted?"

No need to lie now. "I'm desperate, friend. I'm cold, hungry, lost and confused. In Alheria's name, I ask for succor."

The stranger was clearly impressed. "Alheria's name, is it? That's a plea of mickle might. Very well, giant, you may come into our village. Fair warning, though: first sign of trouble, and I'll blind you."

Ah. He was a magician of some sort. That explained why he'd come to greet her on his own.

"Your name, giant?"

"My name? My name is...*Mardine*."

The little village was named Gandy, and Gandy, it turned out, had quite a lot of work for Mardine to do. The villagers had heard all kinds of rumors of trouble—*more* trouble—up north, and had decided once and for all to fortify their town against raiders or anyone else unwelcome. They couldn't afford to pay Mardine in coin, but they gave her the entire ground floor of a two story home, shared the best of their food and drink with her, and made sure she was warm enough both day and night. No one in Gandy had ever encountered a giant before, and Mardine quickly became the town's most popular inhabitant. After sundown each evening, one family or another invited Mardine to dinner, or sometimes they brought dinner to her, and from then 'til bedtime, everyone shared stories and songs and peppered the giantess with a million questions, few of which she could answer. The town's oldest woman gave Mardine a quilt so large, it was even too big for a giant, but Mardine didn't complain. She was glad to have it. One of the men carved a prodigious cudgel for the giantess out of a good piece of ash. It was all he could do to lug the thing to her door, but she picked it up with no difficulty, much to the fellow's amusement.

During the days, Mardine worked hard, indeed. The townsfolk had tasked her with dragging felled trees back from the local woods. The snowy ground made the job somewhat easier than it might have been, but it was grueling work, nonetheless. The townsfolk set upon the trees and stripped them of their branches, while other folk dug great holes into which Mardine would place the cleaned logs. Finally, one or two of the stronger men climbed ladders and hacked the logs' tops into deadly points. In this manner, Mardine helped Gandy build a stockade around the village. It was exhausting labor, but with ample food, rest and exercise, Mardine found herself getting stronger and more confident by the day.

One afternoon, it was snowing so hard no one could see to get any work done, so a number of Mardine's new friends gathered at her place for a meal. Without really understanding why, she asked those assembled, "What kind of people steal children from their parents?"

It was a shocking question, to be sure, but one older fellow answered straight out. "Slavers, most likely."

"Slavers?" Mardine asked. "What good's a child slave?"

"I s'pose the whoremasters'd find a use for 'em. Or, might be they get sent into the mines, where bigger folks can't git."

"Whoremasters? The mines?" Mardine's mind was reeling at the possibilities.

"Why d'you ask, Mardine? You know someone who's lost a child?" one of the women asked.

Mardine grew somber. "I...I think I did."

There was never such a flock of concerned hens as rushed to Mardine's side that night. She was coddled and consoled, comforted and caressed. How could they help her? They all asked. What could they do?

Mardine had no idea, but was profoundly reassured by her new friends' concern. Now, at least, she had some allies. The evening passed in a lambent haze of sympathy and good intentions, and when Mardine went to bed that night, she felt more hopeful than she had in ages.

The next morning, Mardine was just getting ready for the day's work when there was a knock on her door. Answering it, she discovered the town's magician on her doorstep.

"Ambie!" she said, "How can I help you?"

"I believe," said the man, "that it is I who can help *you*."

"Oh?"

"There are a series of minor spells whereby a person can become calm enough to remember almost anything, up to and including birth, in some cases." Ambie said nothing more for the moment, but contented himself with watching the impact of this statement upon the giantess.

"I see," she said dubiously.

"T'isn't painful, if that's what worries you."

Mardine let loose with a nervous giggle. "I don't know *what's* worrying me, truth to tell."

"Well," Ambie replied, patting Mardine on her forearm, "you think about it today. I'll come back by this evening with a few friends, and, if you're interested, we'll give it a go."

Mardine bobbed her head in the affirmative, not trusting herself to say the right thing...and not at all sure what the right thing was. She desperately wanted to remember whatever it was she'd forgotten, but she feared, too, that she might learn things best left in the darkness and the fog.

She worked at a feverish pace, not because she was in any hurry to finish the job, but because the activity kept anxiety at bay. When she finally thought to ask someone the time of day, the sun was already slipping towards the horizon, and, yes, more snow began to fall.

Best get it over with.

When Mardine reached her cottage, she saw that Ambie and three or four others were already awaiting her arrival.

"Let's find out what I'm missing," Mardine said by way of greetings.

It was a decision that would change everything.

The False Reaper & The End, In Camp

The False Reaper stalked through camp, his visage in a fixed grimace, completely oblivious to the tears of agony that rolled down his cheeks. His battle with the End-of-All-Things consumed so much of his energy, his life-force, that the constant effort to maintain control was literally burning him alive. In the relatively short time since the End had begun his assault on the Pretender's mind, the boy had lost half his body weight. His fat and much of his muscle was gone. So, too, were his hair and many of his teeth. Now, he looked like nothing so much as a walking corpse, but a corpse with a disturbingly penetrating glare.

If only he could find that imbecile, Omeyo. The False Reaper knew he'd sent the man somewhere, on some errand, but couldn't recall the details no matter how hard he tried. Worse, he couldn't remember what he wanted of the fellow, either.

The End's laughter echoed out of the darkness, startling him.

"Fuck off!" the boy snarled.

More laughter. "Is that the best you can do with the language we gave you?"

The boy ignored him. Or tried.

"You didn't think you'd learned to talk with only Omeyo for company, did you? How naïve."

The False Reaper stuck his head into one of the Svarren's crude shelters, hoping to find his general. No luck.

"You're burning up, aren't you, boy?"

"Huh!" the boy scoffed.

"Burn, boy, burn!" the End cackled. "Sooner or later, you will fall, and I will rise."

The boy tried another hut: still no sign of Omeyo.

"I can feel you whimpering inside, you know."

"That's yourself you're feeling," the False Reaper retorted.

"It will be, when I've taken over."

"Where are the others?"

"I've consumed them!" the End exulted. "As I will consume you!"

"Unless..." the boy taunted.

The End was clearly amused. "Unless?"

"I throw myself in a bonfire."

"You haven't the courage!" the End snapped.

"No?" But as the False Reaper attempted to steer himself towards the camp's biggest fire, his legs locked up and he found himself rooted to the spot. "You!" he called to one of his Svarren. "Carry me to..."

The End had stolen his power of speech—a trick he'd used once before on an equally annoying fool.

"You see?" the End crooned. "You've nothing left. Only minutes remain before I claim this body as my own."

*I will never...*the boy thought at his nemesis. And then his reserves ran out, and his resistance collapsed. He had nothing left, was nothing.

His body juddered in place for a moment as if experiencing a seizure, and then blazing light exploded from him in all directions, accompanied by a clamorous boom that terrified the nearby Svarren.

"Bring me food!" the End screamed lustily. "I have not eaten in too long!"

In the shadows of the Svarren witch's hovel, Omeyo saw the lights, heard the boom, and recognized the voice. The End-of-All-Things had returned. Omeyo supposed he ought to care, but he had endured too much and wanted only to sink back into the comforting blackness of sleep.

The witch held him close to her bosom as a child holds a plaything, a poppet. The creature's odor was unspeakable, and yet...there was something in it, something entrancing, enthralling, that offered solace in spite of the circumstances.

She suckled Omeyo at her dugs. He drew strength from her, and his many hurts abated. Impossibly, he grew aroused, and found the witch more than willing to accommodate his desires.

Omeyo forgot all about the End for a while.

Turley, In Lunessfor

Turley felt as if he were in the bottom of a well with no possibility of escape. He'd believed the Reaper was his friend, but as the man's entourage had grown, Turley—Igraine—became little more than an afterthought. And afterthoughts could not fare well in such company. The goblin's spirits sank, and although he no longer wept at his misfortune, his mood was every bit as black as it had been when the body switch occurred.

For one thing, there was too much light, too much space in the world of men. The sky, even on cloudy days, seemed to go on forever and ever, and Turley was often seized with the odd fear that he might fall upwards into eternity. Then, there was the issue of distance. The goblin's entire world had existed within the walls of Her Majesty's castle. He'd never travelled a straight mile in his life, and yet now he rode mile upon mile, so far from his home that he doubted he could find his way back had he the Queen's Shaper as a guide. And it wasn't just the big things that unsettled him. The food was alien to him. The sounds of nature were utterly unfamiliar. He'd heard of horses before, but to be spending so much time astride one was terrifying. What if the beast came to resent him, threw him to the ground and ate him? Could there be a more terrible death?

And there were Vykers' men. They seemed congenial enough, but every so often he caught them ogling him, as if he were the main course at a Midwinter's Feast. They didn't know he was actually male, and a goblin to boot! Turley hoped the Reaper could keep his men in line—that certainly was part of his reputation—but the little goblin didn't see how Vykers could be everywhere at once and always awake. Inevitably, he'd wander out of earshot, and then...Turley shook his head violently, trying to dislodge the thoughts that plagued him. It didn't work.

He pondered his chances of successfully running away. They didn't appear favorable. Had anyone ever escaped the Reaper? And even should he prove the first to do so, where would he go? Amongst whom would he ever find comfort? It seemed his only viable option was to remain where he was and trust Vykers' word that Turley would someday return to his own body...if the Shaper currently using it wasn't killed first.

Yes, he was wrapped in another's skin, but his misery was all his own.

Vykers & Company, On the Road

Once outside of Lunessfor—a feat accomplished with such ease that Vykers couldn't help thinking the Queen had arranged it somehow—the Reaper wasted no time in heading north. He commanded his crew to push the horses until they dropped, assuring his men that he'd buy more at the next opportunity. That strategy would work in the populated areas, he knew, but as soon as they arrived in the more-rural north, they'd have to take greater care of their mounts. He might have hired a Shaper to transport everyone, if he'd trusted the toad-sucking bastards. But Arune and Her Majesty had permanently soured Vykers on magic and those who practiced it.

Didn't that also include Aoife, then?

Vykers hadn't thought of her in a stoat's age. He wondered where she was, what she might be doing—not that he cared overmuch, mind you. Only...he wouldn't hate seeing her again, if things worked out that way.

He redirected his thoughts towards the End-of-All-Things. Surely, the End could not still be alive. Alheria had probably just dropped his name as bait, a means of enticing Vykers, once again, into doing her bidding. Whoever and whatever this northern fucker was, he was no End-of-All-Things. Vykers almost wished he was, though. He'd enjoy killing that monster again.

He allowed his horse to slow so that one of his men could take the lead for a while and give him a chance to study his crew. In their new armor, they didn't look half as hopeless as they had just days before. Hjuest, in particular, looked much more dangerous in ring mail and wearing an actual steel sword at his hip.

As Vykers pulled up alongside his new sergeant, the man asked, "Iss how var, diss nort?"

"Two weeks, maybe three if the weather stays bad."

"Iss soon enuv?"

"It'll have to be." Vykers liked doing things in his own time; to do otherwise was to cede an advantage to the enemy. If this new End wanted to meet the Reaper sooner, he could damn well come looking for him.

The horses were blown in three days of hard riding, but there's always a knackery willing to take what's left and resell it as something better to the credulous and the desperate. This didn't bring much coin, but enough to replace one of the crew's mounts, whilst Vykers paid for the rest. As for the poor horses, Vykers felt some remorse. He'd killed countless men with less compunction, and he generally viewed horses as better company. How many more horses would die up north if this madman went unchecked? These horses, then, were making a noble sacrifice for their brethren. At least, Vykers hoped that was the case.

The new mounts didn't complain when the Reaper and his crew rode them out of the only stables they'd ever known and into the winter's fury.

"You get snow like this where you're from?" Vykers shouted to Hjuest over the howling wind.

"Ya. Sometimes."

Vykers looked at the Ntambi warrior, whose expression suggested he could give Igraine lessons in misery. "I don't guess he's seen a lot o' this shit," he said to Hjuest.

"Nah. I tink not."

They rode together in silence a while and then Hjuest asked, "How many horse you buy?"

"One for each of us, three for gear."

"Nah. I mean, from here to north."

"Don't you worry about that. I got nothin' else to do with my gold."

That evening, when they'd made camp and settled in, Hjuest approached the Reaper. "Spar?"

Vykers bust into a wide grin. "You kiddin'? I'll kick your ass from here to Threshmettle."

"You keek my ass?" Hjuest echoed, perplexed.

"Figure 'o speech. Means I'm gonna beat you again," Vykers laughed. "And I hope you're not usin' a wooden sword again."

Hjuest returned the Reaper's smile. "No. Steel sword."

While everyone else watched, Hjuest and Vykers sparred for half an hour, until the smaller man threw up his hands in defeat. "You win."

"But you're gettin' better."

"Had to ven I deedn't spik langvage. Vas a lot of vighting."

"And there'll be a lot more," Vykers assured the knight. "But I kinda miss all that red you wore."

"I vill hev again. Ven money."

"You outlive this winter, you'll have the money."

Hjuest nodded, as if this made all the sense in the world.

"Now, about the others," Vykers said, looking in the direction of his former slaves. "How're they holding up?"

"Holding up?"

"How are they doing?"

"Not bad. Ngoro not happy, but he vight."

Vykers indicated the Ntambi warrior. "That Ngoro?"

"Yah."

"Make sure he gets extra food and blankets."

"Yah."

They continued to push, push, push their way north. Only Vykers never seemed to tire, which made his already inflated reputation grow in the men's eyes. To them, he was a god. He would have denied it, had he known their feelings. As it was, he cared only to make as much distance with each day's effort as possible. He knew there would be bloodshed at the end of this road, and he yearned to get on with it.

Aoife, In the Village

Although she and the fey folk had repelled the Svarren attack and saved the village, Aoife forced its residents to evacuate, anyway.

"But why?" they complained.

"Because the End doesn't take defeat lightly. He'll return with his full force to punish each and every one of you for daring to stand against him. Thank the gods you survived his Svarren and get out while you still can."

"Where can we go?"

"South. As far and as fast as possible."

For those stubborn few who insisted on remaining behind, Aoife resorted to spellcraft, filling them with sudden and unyielding dread. Soon, they overtook their fellows in abandoning the town.

Aoife waited until the last of them had disappeared from sight and then set about laying traps against the End's return.

Unfortunately, she forgot that her brother could fly.

Walking across the town square, she was blasted from her feet by a bolt of lightning. She pinwheeled through the air and landed, hard, on somebody's woodpile. For several heartbeats, she was utterly disoriented and in terrible pain; still, she had the presence of mind to throw up defenses. In seconds, she was wrapped in a living cocoon, the inside of which bathed her in restorative nectars, whilst the outside projected poisonous thorns. Beyond that, a thick wall of vines and brambles formed—a sort of outer shell to her cocoon.

The End laughed at these efforts and shot great gouts of flame over Aoife's protections. For a moment, there was quiet, and the sorcerer came closer to inspect the damage. At this point, a great branch sprang from Aoife's shell and impaled the overconfident tyrant through the belly. He screamed in fury and agony, reducing the branch to ashes while he retreated to a safer distance. How many times would he get away with underestimating the A'Shea before she got the better of him?

He determined that she would not do so this time. Summoning all of his energies and focus, he ripped Aoife's cocoon from the ground as if by a giant hand and flung it so far into the sky that it temporarily disappeared from view. He expected to witness his sister's death on her return trip. Instead, her shell sprouted enormous spider legs, which reached the ground well before her and prevented much more than a violent jostling. This vine-and-leaf spider then proceeded to race away from the village with impressive speed.

The End soared into the air again and gave chase. If she reached a forest, he knew he'd never catch her. He continued to lambaste the retreating cocoon with fire, lightning and cold. In return, it often sprayed acid and noxious poisons in his direction. He had never known A'Shea were so powerful...unless she was no longer an A'Shea. If she was not, though, what in the endless hells *was* she?

So, they battled, mile after mile. When the End spied trees on the horizon, he became almost frantic to halt his sister's escape. He hit her with a wall of force so powerful that it shattered her shell and drove her into the icy snow beneath. Before her protective roots and branches could sprout again, he drenched the area with a foul ichor that suppressed all growth. With feigned indifference, he drifted down beside Aoife's unconscious form and studied her intently. She gave off waves of energy, and the End understood that to touch her would mean death, despite his own arcane prowess. Instead, he encased her in a shell of his own design, one that would protect him from her and not the other way 'round. He then levitated her into the air and compelled her little prison to follow him all the way back to his camp.

Perhaps there was some way he could leach her power away and use it for his own purposes. If not, the A'Shea might still serve as bait. The End hadn't forgotten her collusion with Tarmun Vykers at their last encounter. Maybe there was something between his sister and the Reaper.

Wouldn't their reunion just be delicious?

The Giants, In the Forest

"What we do," Eoman said, "is fetch Beesmarch, like I suggested. Then the three of us take these two girls to Zillia for safekeeping."

Although he was not the king of the giants, Karrakan got along better with most of them than did Eoman. The only exceptions, as fate would have it, were Beesmarch and Zillia. Ironically enough, they liked each other even less than the shaman did. While Karrakan dreaded the prospect of making conversation with either Beesmarch or Zillia, he almost couldn't wait to hear them berating one another. "Well," he sighed. "If you truly believe that's the best course of action."

Eoman kicked the ice off his boots and re-cinched his belt. "It's pretty clear the Svarren are up to something nasty. I'm seeing more and more of their scat every morning. Unless you want our lands overrun by the bastards, we'd best find out what it is they're after, and that means leaving the girls in Zillia's care."

Karrakan wondered if his king didn't have feelings for the crazy old witch. What he said was, "You sure you know where to find Beesmarch?"

"Oh, aye. He's a creature of habit, is our old friend. He'll be up on his same hill."

"If you say so." That was as far as Karrakan would go in the way of agreement. Eoman was king, after all, which meant the rest of the giants had to follow his lead. Someday, when things were quieter, Karrakan hoped to discuss why this was so with his liege lord.

As the giants bundled the girls up for travel, Eoman leaned into his friend and muttered "I still can't figure why the wee one's not worse off."

"Haven't you guessed?" Karrakan asked, surprised. "She's got talent."

Eoman choked on his own saliva, subsequently launching

into a prolonged coughing fit. "Talent?" he rasped, when the coughing had passed. "You mean magic?"

"Of course I mean magic."

The king shook his head, though whether from disbelief or disapproval, he wouldn't elaborate. "Let's get moving," was all he said.

It was a two-and-a-half day journey to Beesmarch's domain. Eoman, Karrakan and the girls arrived around midday, and Karrakan wondered aloud, "D'you suppose we'll find him home?"

"Go away!" thundered a voice that would have made Mahnus quail in his boots. It was so loud, so resonant, that snow tumbled from trees and icicles crashed to the forest floor.

"By the gods!" Eoman breathed. "How does he do that?"

"I hope we'll have an opportunity to find out," Karrakan answered.

"Go away!" the godlike voice insisted.

Eoman noticed Nelby and Esmine cowering under the shaman's robes. "Come out here and make us!" he yelled back into the forest.

This made Karrakan laugh heartily, and the shaman added, "Come on down here and fight, you surly old bastard!"

"I said go!" the voice bellowed.

"Oh, we heard you!" Eoman guffawed. "We're just not in the mood!" By now, Nelby was looking at the king as if he were stark, raving mad, which only served to make him laugh harder still.

Suddenly, a loud boom sounded through the trees, the noise of an enormous door slamming, perhaps, and the two giants exchanged a look of mischievous glee. Beesmarch was coming.

In short order, a huge shadow appeared, stomping through the trees, and heading in the group's direction. As it moved closer, everyone was able to hear the figure muttering an unending stream of profanity, most of which was horribly outdated. Seconds passed, and the shape resolved into another giant. And this one was larger than either Eoman or Karrakan.

"Humph!" the new giant grunted. "If it ain't the caperin'

King an' his idiot sidekick, Carbuncle."

The shaman laughed again. "*Karrakan.* You know it's Karrakan, you crabby old crank!"

"And I'll thank you to address your king with more respect!" Eoman added.

"Bah! Where's your kingdom, Eoman? Where your subjects? Are you the king of snow?"

Beesmarch was a full third taller than Eoman, with a beard so long that it brushed the tops of his feet when he walked. His brows and nose were equally prodigious, which made his eyes hard to make out even in the best of light. His hands, though, were outlandishly huge, and it seemed possible that he could carry a full grown horse in each if he chose. He was draped in a variety of furs and wore the head of some huge, long dead animal as a hat. As intimidating as he appeared though, he smelled of wood smoke, beeswax and rosewater.

Little Esmine was clearly intrigued by this.

"And what is *that*?" Beesmarch demanded, spying the child for the first time.

Rather than scurrying behind Karrakan, Esmine stepped into the open, fully revealing herself to Beesmarch.

"That," said Eoman, "is a child. Has it been so long?"

"I bloody well know what a child is, but this one looks like a changeling. What's wrong with her?"

Esmine took another step, reached out to Beesmarch's beard and gave it a good yank.

"She's half human."

"That's impossible!"

"True, nonetheless."

"Humph!" said Beesmarch. "That explains it, then. Anyway, what are you two and this...*thing*...doing on my land?"

"Your land?" Eoman challenged, one eyebrow cocked in disbelief.

"Aye, mine."

Rather than get into a pissing match with the bigger giant, Karrakan came to the point. "We rescued the girl from slavers, and we mean to leave her with Zillia, if the mad wench is still alive."

"Ha!" Beesmarch barked, though he offered nothing else.

"Truth is, the land's being overrun by Svarren of late, and we can't have the wee one along as we seek out the cause."

The word 'Svarren' seemed to catch the grumpy giant's interest, as his face became more animated. "Long teeth, is it? The filth have been skirting my forest for weeks now, but even skirtin's too close for me. You mean to kill them?"

"As many as we can find," Eoman grinned.

"Humph!" Beesmarch pulled on his own beard and stamped in a circle, wrestling with some question he wasn't willing to share. Finally, he let out a long breath and said, "I'll show you the king's hospitality, and you'll take me along for the killing. Fella's got to keep in fighting trim."

"You've got enough food for the five of us?"

"Five?" Beesmarch echoed, suspiciously.

Karrakan opened his long coat and robes and revealed Nelby.

"Humph!" said Beesmarch. "I should've known. Follow me."

Beesmarch lived inside the burned out stump of what must have once been the largest tree in existence. Now, its shell served as the walls of a surprisingly genteel abode. Beesmarch had built the roof himself out of whole logs, though he scraped the bark off first to retard rotting. The speaking or blowing end of a tremendous horn protruded from one wall, whilst the blaring end presumably emerged outside the home. It was this device, then, that the giant used to frighten off trespassers. High in the other walls, small windows of real glass let natural light into the main room, where it danced and sparkled off countless mobiles of colored glass, gems, and bits of polished silver and gold. Whenever Beesmarch moved past any of these, they tinkled and clinked with the most delicate tones. All in all, it was the sort of home Eoman might have expected of a fairy queen. This was a side of his old companion the king had never guessed at.

The central table was made of a single slab of center-cut hardwood, sanded and varnished to a high shine that accented the wood's many whorls and knots. It was a table, Eoman acknowledged, worthy of royalty. Upon this masterpiece, Beesmarch heaped piles of smoked boar and dried fish, along with a great, hearty dark bread, generous slabs of honey-butter, and several steins of a most delicious ale.

"Kinda pleasant to have company once in a while," the host admitted sheepishly. "Gotta have guests in order to show off."

"It's a beautiful home, Bees," Karrakan admitted. "I've never seen a better."

"Humph!" Beesmarch replied, though it was clear he was pleased with the compliment.

"It occurs to me that if we giant folk weren't so solitary and chose to live in cities like the humans, we'd be a force in this world," Eoman mused.

"We *are* a force in this world," Beesmarch countered. "And the next."

"I meant that we could muster an army and wipe out slavers and Svarren once and for all."

"Makes you wonder why we spread ourselves so far and wide in the first place," Karrakan said.

"You don't remember?" Beesmarch asked, astonished.

"And you do?"

Beesmarch tugged his beard again, crossed his arms and leaned on the tabletop. A faraway look came to his eyes. "They say we fled the humans in the Great Awakening." He looked over at Nelby and continued. "The little bastards were runnin' mad, burning, smashing, destroying everything they encountered, including each other. The king at the time is said to have proclaimed, 'You can't reason with a mad dog,' and giantkind escaped to the hills and forests. But we had a city, once."

"Te Connac," Karrakan whispered.

"Aye," said Beesmarch. "Te Connac."

"I've often thought to look for it," Eoman confessed.

"You'd have to dig. That was—what?—three thousand years ago?"

"We could dig. The three of us," Eoman proposed.

Beesmarch held up a hand. "First things first. We've got some Svarren to kill."

"And before that, we've got to see these girls to safety."

"Humph! With Zillia? They'd be safer in a porcupine's den!"

Karrakan had a good laugh at that. "We'd best get moving, if we mean to go at all."

Arune, the Castle

They would be expecting an escape attempt the first few times they visited her chambers, and so Arune did nothing. And she continued doing nothing every time they came by—with food, reading materials or anything else. She hoped to lull the Queen's staff into complaisance, and then make her move when they'd forgotten how dangerous she was. Accordingly, she did her best to act hopeless and defeated whenever her door opened, and not only then, but also around any object that might be used for magical spying. She'd been given a mirror that made her especially suspicious, although it occurred to her that the Queen—Alheria—might also wish to torment Arune with her new goblin's body. Whenever the Shaper looked into that mirror, she didn't have to try hard to appear depressed.

One evening, she heard the telltale signs of her door being unlocked. Arune moved close by, in the event an escape seemed possible. But as the door swung open, a massive wave of energy pushed her backwards, and Her Majesty stepped over the threshold and into the room.

Arune stumbled over her goblin's feet trying to compose herself.

Her Majesty chose not to remark on the Shaper's acrobatics. "You've been rather quiescent, haven't you?" Without waiting for a response, the Queen continued. "I'd have expected something altogether different from Vykers' former Shaper."

"That was a marriage of necessity," Arune mumbled.

"Ah, but whose necessity?"

"It was mutual."

Alheria smiled. "And now?"

"Clearly, the Reaper does not need me."

"But I do, as it happens."

Arune made a quick study of the still-open door and the

corridor behind it: no guards. What was the Queen after?

"I understand you served as a battle mage under that old miscreant, King Orstoth."

"Fourth battle mage, yes."

"That seems a touch low to me..." Her Majesty opined.

"Well, I've learned a great deal since then. And, of course, I've been dead."

"Indeed." Alheria looked about, as if she would sit down, but found nothing worth sitting upon. Disappointed, she went on, "Fourth or First, I would like to employ you within my own cadre of Shapers. I have temporarily lost one of my better magicians, and I need someone to fill that vacancy. I will promote one of the others into his place, but I'll want you to take the last spot."

Arune could not believe her good fortune, which in itself gave her pause. "What are the terms of this employment?" she asked.

Her Majesty looked at her with obvious amusement. "You do what I say, or I kill you."

Arune bobbed her head as if this was perfectly reasonable. But she'd had no cause to expect anything else. "As you say, Your Majesty."

"It is always and ever so, Shaper."

TEN

Mardine, In Gandy

Mardine's magically-induced remembering was traumatic for everyone. The moment she recalled Esmine's abduction and her own apparent death, the giantess shook off the various enchantments laid upon her, leapt to her feet, and set about packing her things for imminent departure. Her many friends were shocked and devastated by this unexpected turn of events, and although they tried to convince Mardine to slow down, to think things through and at least wait until the morrow to leave, she'd have none of it.

"My baby is out there somewhere!" she exclaimed in a near-sob. "Alone, in a frozen wilderness. I've got to find her!"

Some of the other women were weeping, along with one or two of the men. Almost everyone was searching, frantically, for answers, a solution, anything that would calm their giant friend and delay her departure.

"I'll go with you, Mardine," one of the farmers proclaimed. "At least for a day or two's ride."

"Me, too!" someone else said.

"And me. I'll go along!"

Before another hour had passed, Mardine and her humble escort were on their way out of the little village.

"I'm sorry about the walls," Mardine said to the man on her right.

"Ah, we'll manage," said he. "It's mostly done now, anyway."

"How will you find your girl?" the baker's wife asked.

"I don't know. But find her I must."

It was already night time when they set out, and every last one of them suffered for the cold, despite their heavy coats and furry hats and thick gloves and boots. Mardine felt the cold, too, but worried more about its effect on Esmine than on herself.

The group was still pushing forward, valiantly, when the sun came up. The blacksmith convinced Mardine to call a halt so he could start a fire and summon up a hot meal.

"Can't recall a winter like this is years," he said.

And it was true. The cold seemed a thing with a will of its own, an entity that loathed humans, giants and other such warm-bodied beings. It was as if it took offense at their presence in its domain and wanted to punish them all to death—not instantly, of course, but by degrees: cold, colder, oblivion.

The fire pushed it back a ways, but could not subdue it forever.

"I figure I can go another day with you, Mardine, but then I gotta head home. And I'm hopin' I won't have to make the trip alone," said the man who first volunteered for the journey.

Mardine smiled at him. "Of course," said she. "We all have folks depending on us, don't we?"

Everyone allowed as that was so. Mardine could only hope it was still the case for her.

Because they'd started out at such an unlikely time of day, they were all ready for sleep by mid-afternoon. Mardine wanted to keep moving, but couldn't endanger her friends any further. Too, this might be her last day of company for some time. With mixed feelings, she helped them set up their meager shelters around the fire and watched as, one by one, they settled off to sleep.

Tired as she was, the giantess was restless, tormented by the memories of mistakes she'd made, people she'd wronged, and, as ever, her wonderful husband and miraculous child. It was probably this restlessness that saved the rest of the group when the wolves attacked.

First, Mardine thought she saw a glint of light in the distant underbrush. Looking more carefully, she noted another glint several feet to the left of the first. In time, she saw a number of flickers and knew them to be eyes. In her peripheral vision, she saw a shadow slink by on her right, some twenty paces out. Instinctively, she glanced in the other direction and, yes, saw two more shadows attempting to outflank the little camp. Wasting no time, Mardine yelled "We are beset!" and grabbed a brand from the fire as a weapon.

Her companions awoke with shrieks and shouts of defiance, emerging from their shelters with hostile intent.

Loud snarling and howls presaged the wolves' attack, whilst also revealing them to be merely wolves. There were many worse possibilities. A large gray bounded from the bushes and launched himself at Mardine. Rather than brain him with the flaming log, she reached out with her left hand and caught the beast around the throat. A strange familiarity came over the whole scene then, as if Mardine had fought this very battle before. The wolf in her grip thrashed its hind legs in a bid to shake free of the giant's grip, but Mardine was unyielding. She squeezed her hand as tightly as possible and gave the wolf and good shake. Before she could cast it away, another wolf went after her legs.

All around her, Mardine could hear the sounds of combat— the snarling of wolves and humans, the yelps of pain from either species. It was, Mardine knew, a fight to the death for one party or the other. Either the wolves would feast, or their prey would have new pelts with which to warm themselves. There would be no middle ground, no stale mate.

Mardine dropped the dead wolf in her left hand and began bashing upon the other at her legs with her still-burning branch. The wolf's fur was wet from melted snow, but his whiskers caught easily enough, eliciting a high-pitched yip of pain from the creature. Seeing the branch would never do sufficient damage, Mardine gave the wolf a tremendous kick, sending it backwards into the fire. Still, its fur would not ignite, though its paws, nose and ears suffered considerable damage. The pain-crazed beast rolled off the flames and limped rapidly away into the shadows. Mardine stole a glance about herself and saw that the baker's wife was down, pinned by a large beast that held her face in its slavering jaws. It was too late for the woman, so the giantess looked elsewhere and found the blacksmith holding two more wolves at sword's length. Mardine rushed up behind them, grabbed both by their tails, and jerked them as hard as she could towards the fire. One of the tails came off in her hand, with a woeful howl from its former owner. The other wolf turned and snapped at Mardine's hands, only to be impaled from the front by the blacksmith.

"Here!" the man said, thrusting the hilt of the sword in Mardine's fist. "I've got another in my tent!"

Mardine went berserk, hacking and slashing at the wolves until none that were still within the fire's light survived, and those outside were mortally injured. The blacksmith came to the giant's side and started pulling bits of wood from the fire, which he then tossed into the darkness, expanding the light's reach ever so slightly. Mardine added more wood the fire to offset what had been thrown away and then turned her attention to her companions, praying to Alheria with every breath that they hadn't lost anyone more than the baker's wife.

And they hadn't, although one or two of the men had sustained injuries that could prove worrisome if they didn't make it back to their village in the next day or two.

"That's it," Mardine declared. "You folks need to go back home now. You'll not take another step in my company, or lose another drop of blood on my behalf." She started to cry then, and only the blacksmith could get her to stop.

"You didn't force us to come, Mardine," the man said. "We came of our own choosin'. None of this here's on you."

"Still," the giantess answered, "I won't lose another one of you."

"She's right," said one of the others. "But let's get these pelts, first, and wrap Bidrea for proper burial."

"Wolves don't normally attack people like that," one of the women observed. "Why do you s'pose they did this time?"

"I've heard rumors 'o Svarren hereabouts," the blacksmith replied. "Might be, they're competin' for the same food."

Svarren. Just the thought of them was almost enough to make Mardine turn around and head back with the others. But that might leave Esmine alone with the foul things. Better to die in the jaws of a wolf than whatever it was that Svarren did to their kills.

It was several more hours' labor skinning the wolves, bandaging the injured and repacking the gear. Daylight was still a long ways off, but the villagers, reenergized by fear, could not wait to begin their return journey home.

"You're sure she's out there?" the blacksmith asked at parting.

"I...need her to be out there."

If that answer was unexpected, the blacksmith showed no sign of it. With a farewell pat on Mardine's arm, he gathered his friends and started heading back the way they'd come but a few hours earlier.

Mardine watched them go until they were completely gone from sight. She couldn't remember feeling more lonely, even when she'd first climbed out of the ground, nameless and lost. Loneliness was not putting her any closer to Esmine, however, so she pulled her own collection of pelts and blankets tighter about herself and took the first step in what she hoped would be a journey of rescue, reunion, and salvation.

Long & Company, On the Trail

The worrisome thing was that it had been days and the other lads were still drunk. Not falling down, soiling-themselves drunk, but noticeably impaired. Long was not, but he was too concerned about his friends to ponder this little discrepancy. After all, they had so many challenges still ahead of them, and it was doubtful they'd succeed in full possession of their faculties. But drunk? The captain couldn't envision any scenario in which they found and rescued Esmine in their current conditions.

To make matters worse, the boys were behaving like children! Spirk had wandered off into the dark to relieve himself and discovered, through some process Long dared not think on, that he could cause his prick to glow just as Long's sword and Ron's arrow had earlier. More, he could make his piss glow as well, in an array of festive colors. The sound of him hooting with laughter out of the fire's reach sent chills up and down Long's spine. It was as if he were a captive witness to his friends' descent into madness. Naturally, Spirk's giddiness attracted Ron, and even Yendor ambled over on his surprisingly functional legs.

There was something about that liquor, sure. But Long could not allow his men to drink any more until their current intoxication wore off—assuming it *did* wear off. And what were they to do if they came under attack by brigands or Svarren or something even more sinister?

With as much authority as he could muster, Long barked at his friends to return to the fire. They couldn't walk a straight line between them, but somehow they made it back. The captain wanted to scold his men for their carelessness, but he'd drunk the liquor, too, hadn't he? Were his men to blame that he was made of stouter stuff? Of course, that had never been the case with that devil's elixir, Skent, but to each his poison.

"Boys," he began, "I don't know why you're all takin' so long to sober up, but I need you to do it already! Mahnus knows what's stalkin' us in these woods, and that ain't countin' the task ahead of us."

In response to this plea, Yendor broke into song:

A man's got two eyes and two ears and two nostrils,
Two nipples, two balls and one wick!
If you heat the thing up it'll spout such a flame,
It'll scorch the old huswife but quick!

Predictably, Ron and Spirk cackled with laughter. Before Long could staunch the flow of nonsense, Ron, quiet old Ron, took his turn with a song.

Dee ba dim champers
Dee ba dim champers
Dee ba dim champers
All day long,
First with the Mayor's wife,
Then with the rag witch
Last with the draft horse
Good and strong!

"Foh!" Long exclaimed. "None o' that, now!"

No one was listening to the captain, though. When Spirk's turn came, he was so excited that he bounced up and down on his log near the fire.

Oh, Molly, my lady… "Naw, that ain't it," Spirk muttered. *Oh lady, my Molly…*"Not so, neither. Is it…" *Oh my lady Molly?* "Oh, dash it all! Perchance it ain't Molly a 'tall!"

The young Shaper continued to wrangle with his memory of the elusive lyrics until everyone else had fallen asleep. And that meant that he had first watch. First watch was better'n second, but not quite so nice as third. Usually, Long shared stretches of all three watches, because, he said, it was he who'd dragged the boys off on this misadventure, and the least he could do was look out for 'em.

The one thing Spirk especially disliked about being alone was the burning. It seemed to become stronger at such times, and the Shaper had taken up grinding his teeth in response. Oh, Yendor had warned him not to, had promised that life without teeth was said to be awful. The thing of it was, the burning was approaching awful in its own right. The mysterious wine they'd found helped ease the discomfort, but there was only so much of that left, and Long wouldn't let Spirk touch it for the time being.

Looking for some way to distract himself, Spirk let his mind wander out into the night, and, as he did so, he became aware of the creatures that shared it with him. Several hundred feet behind him, for instance, a raccoon sat in a tree, staring at the fire's glow and wondering at it. Elsewhere, a fox hunted a chipmunk, deer nestled in a deadfall and, farther out, Svarren travelled a path perpendicular to that intended by the captain. Spirk agonized over whether he ought to wake his friend, but decided to wait until and unless the Svarren changed course and drew nearer. At the very edge of Spirk's perceptions, something evil awakened at the Shaper's touch and thrilled at the possibility of bloodshed. Spirk had no idea what was more evil than Svarren, and he had no desire to find out. He woke his captain.

"Next watch, already?" Long mumbled.

"I dunno. But there's somethin' out there."

"What?"

"I dunno."

Long was beginning to feel he'd been woken for nothing. "Where?"

"A few miles, maybe."

The captain was flabbergasted. "You can sense something miles away?"

Spirk looked embarrassed. "I guess so," he confessed.

Long sat up, simultaneously irritated and excited. "How long has this been going on?"

Spirk tossed a branch on the fire. "I dunno."

"Why do I feel like I'm playing a children's guessing game? Is this far away thing a threat?"

The Shaper shook his head up and down vigorously.

"Now we're getting somewhere. Is this thing moving towards us?"

"No. Not yet."

Long reached for his sword, tested the edge. The little group didn't have much left in the way of weapons, but they had a Shaper, however peculiar he might be. "I keep discoverin' you've got skills that might prove useful, like that Shaper's jump. And now, you tell me you can see for miles or some such."

Spirk said nothing.

"What I want to know is, can you be lookin' all the time?"

"I s'pose so."

"Do it. You might find those slavers we're lookin' for. You might even find Esmine."

It was a rather sophisticated thought for Spirk, but he wanted to tell his friend not to get his hopes up. He wanted to tell him to protect himself, protect his heart. There were a lot of things in the night, and few of them were good or helpful to Long's cause. Then...

"It's comin'!"

Long scrambled to his feet and began shaking Ron and Yendor awake. "Something bad's comin' and we need to build this fire as big as possible."

Neither man asked for clarification, but jumped right in to the effort to stoke the fire.

"Anything else you can tell us about this thing, Spirk?" Long asked.

"Uh-uh. Wait, no! It's that thing from...below."

Nobody had to ask *which* thing from below.

"Son of a bitch!" Long shouted.

"Where's a good stone doorway when you need one?" asked Yendor.

"He's fast," said Spirk, the pitch of his voice rising steadily.

Soon, the men had thrown all of the night's wood on the fire and had nothing left to add.

Long tapped Spirk on the shoulder. "Direction?"

The Shaper pointed off into the night. Beyond the fire's light, everything was black and blacker. A distant thudding noise began to grow in intensity.

"Backs to the fire, boys!" Long commanded. "I'm hopin' this bastard doesn't care for flames."

Ron nocked one of his few remaining arrows, figuring, if they didn't survive the next few minutes, that saving one or two would have been pointless. Long held his sword up as well, and even Yendor extended a dagger in what he hoped looked like bold defiance. What it felt like was futility.

The monstrosity appeared and seemed to pause for a moment, as if relishing its certain victory.

"'S times like this, I wish I'd lost both my eyes," Yendor quipped.

"He's in my head, he's in my head, he's in my heeeaaad!" Spirk screamed, his voice cracking and dying off on the last note.

The thing staggered nearer, but Long wasn't sure where to focus his attention, on his suddenly overwhelmed Shaper or on the monster. Spirk let out a final shriek and sank to his knees, both hands over his ears. Ron let fly with his arrow, which landed with a satisfyingly fleshy thump, and reached for another without once taking his eyes off his mark. Long put a hand on his Shaper's shoulder, as reassurance, if nothing else. Suddenly, the fire extinguished itself and the men all gasped or cried out in alarm. With a groan, Spirk fell face-first into the snow, and it seemed to Long and the others that the end had come. Just then, something much larger and heavier than Spirk hit the ground as well, and Long held his breath, not daring to move, not daring to hope.

In the silence that followed, he knelt by his fallen friend and felt for a pulse: the boy was alive.

"Lads?" Long said softly.

"Here," Ron whispered.

"Me, too," Yendor added.

"Anybody hurt?"

"Besides the Shaper?"

Long ignored the comment. There was no point in speculating. Instead, he got down on his hands and knees and felt for the fire, hoping to find coals that could be rekindled. There were none.

"That's some trick," Long said, whistling quietly. "Killed our whole fire."

"Never mind about the fire; is that monster dead?" Yendor said.

"Are you volunteerin' to go find out?" Long snapped. When Yendor said nothing in response, the captain continued. "I'm going to see if I can't restart this fire. If the monsters don't get us, the cold will."

A quarter hour later, the group was once again nestled around a bright, roaring blaze. Long sat closest to the fallen creature, while Ron and Yendor tended to the still-unconscious Spirk.

Abruptly, Long stood up and let out a heavy sigh. "'S'pose I oughta go put a sword in that fucker."

"What?" Ron asked, shocked. "Why?"

"In case he's only injured, like our Shaper here."

Yendor pointed his lone eye at Ron and said "Captain's right, Ron. It's gotta be done."

And, apparently, it had to be done by Long. Such were the rewards of leadership. "How about one of you brings a torch along so I don't stab myself by accident?"

Wordlessly, Yendor pulled a thick branch from the fire and rose to follow his captain.

The creature was much larger than it had seemed from a distance, maybe as tall as three men. Long wasted no time in stabbing its tumorous head—and not just once, but over and over, until there was no possibility the thing lived. When he was satisfied, Long stepped back to admire his handiwork.

Yendor waved a hand in front of his nose. "Damned thing stinks more'n a leper's privy."

Long was silent. He'd noticed that his sword was now smoking, so he stepped over to the nearest snow drift and plunged it in, repeatedly.

As Yendor and he walked back to the fire, Yendor asked him, "What do you think that thing is?"

That very question had been bothering Long since the first moment he'd seen the thing down in that Mahnus-cursed hole they'd all fallen into. What was it? He thought he knew, but didn't dare give voice to the idea. How could he tell his friends they'd just killed a god?

Vykers & Company, On the Road

What most men called nightmares were simply dreams to Tarmun Vykers. Images of death didn't frighten him, because he'd seen so much and caused most of it. Fire? Fire was a weapon, and he liked weapons. Dreams of loss or falling or monsters amused him. In fact, the only aspect of his dreams that bothered him to any degree was the frequent appearance of places, people or things that seemed familiar, but which he felt certain he'd never seen before. In his life, the Reaper had suffered tremendous pain of every sort, but he'd survived. He prided himself on his self-control. How was it, then, that he could neither banish nor explain these mysterious images? Rather than acknowledge his frustration, he chose to shove the question aside, to ignore these riddles. He opened his eyes, and immediately spotted another persistent annoyance.

Her Majesty stood just outside his tent, like a robin at a worm's hole, waiting for him to appear.

"What?" he snapped.

"Good morning to you, too."

At least it had stopped snowing. "This ain't how I like to start my days."

"You'd prefer putting someone's head on a spit, would you?"

Vykers grinned in spite of himself. "Yeah. Something like that." He crawled out of his blankets, pulled on his boots and stepped into the morning air. "You never visit unless you want something. What is it?"

The Queen said nothing, at first, so Vykers stared back at her. She had not bothered to dress for the weather and, being a goddess, it probably didn't affect her as much or in the same ways as it did men. As he looked at her, though, he caught a glint in her eye, something, the tiniest hint there was mischief in the offing, and he had no patience for it.

"Well, if you won't talk, I'm going to get a drink of water and..."

Her Majesty stepped aside, and revealed Turley—or rather, Arune—crouching behind her in the snow.

With dizzying speed, Vykers blew past the Queen and kicked Arune so hard that she flew backwards and collapsed on the ground with her arms and legs splayed wide.

"Stop!" Alheria commanded.

Vykers rounded on her, furious. "You knew this would happen." Again, he flashed his invisible dagger to her throat.

Her Majesty did not bat an eye. "I'd like that back, by the way."

"Sure. Where should I stick it?"

This time, she rolled her eyes. "Must you always be so insufferably juvenile?"

"What are you doing here, and why did you bring that... thing with you?" Vykers said as slowly and clearly as possible, withdrawing the knife from her throat. He noticed that none of his companions had awakened during the commotion save Igraine, who gazed longingly at Arune.

"I came to congratulate you on your decision to investigate this villain in the north."

"Ha!" Vykers scoffed. "That's weak. And I'm not doing this for you or your kingdom."

"Oh, I am sure of that, Reaper." Alheria walked over to where Arune lay in the snow and waved a few fingers at her. Evidently, this achieved some desired effect, because the

Queen then turned around and approached Vykers again. "But I thought that your former Shaper and I could transport you lot up there faster than an endless succession of horses."

"Anything you offer comes at a cost."

"The same is true of you, is it not?"

"That's as may be," Vykers retorted, "But I'm not the one rousing you outta bed."

"What is the harm in jumping you up there?"

"It changes the amount of time I have to get to know my men before we're in the shit together. It changes how much time I have to think on things."

"I've never known you to be so deliberative."

"You've never known me."

The Queen pulled that secret smile of hers again, the one that made Vykers want to smash her face in. As he was contemplating that possibility, she said, "Do you have any aversion to me helping your horses, then?"

She'd confused him again, damn her.

"My horses?"

"I take it your plan is to ride them into the ground and replace them as often as necessary? That seems such a waste."

"They're my horses and my coin."

"Yes, but if I could...*improve*...your horses, make them stronger and faster...?

"In exchange for?"

"Call it a peace offering."

There were a lot of things he might have said in response to that, but he let it go. The truth was he was tired of the conversation. Sometimes, talking to the Queen made him feel thousands of years old, and he just wanted to be done with the chit chat and gamesmanship and go about his business.

Seeing he did not overtly object to her proposal, Alheria walked into the center of Vykers' little encampment, did a half turn, and then reversed herself and did a full turn in the opposite direction. The Reaper was pretty sure the gestures, movements and such were for show, and that all Her Majesty really needed to complete her magic was the will for it to be so. She was a goddess, after all.

But this begged a whole series of questions that Vykers preferred not to dwell upon in Alheria's presence.

Having finished her spellcasting—or whatever it was—the Queen crossed over to Arune, touched the goblin's hand, and said, "If this troublemaker up north does turn out to be the End-of-All-Things, you can count on my help in putting him back in the ground."

There was a faint *whump!* And then Her Majesty and the Shaper were gone.

Igraine was still at the opening of her tent, staring at the space where the goblin's body had been moments ago. When she caught Vykers' eye, she ducked back inside her tent and pulled the flap shut.

He didn't have time to worry about Igraine right now; Alheria had disappeared again, and Vykers needed to spend some time sorting through all of his misgivings about her while they were still fresh in his memory. He decided to walk the perimeter of the encampment, ostensibly to check for signs of visitors in the night. In reality, he needed the movement to clear his mind.

Her Majesty was a goddess. Or was she? He'd seen her do things with magic that not even Arune, the Historian, or Pellas together could have accomplished. But if she was a goddess, why could she not simply destroy her enemies with a snap of her fingers? Why muster an army to fight the End if she had the means to eliminate him on her own? And why did she rely so heavily on Vykers' abilities, especially when she knew how little he trusted her and how much he coveted her crown? Why did a goddess need a mortal crown in the first place?

It was no use. He hadn't the skill or the patience to sort through riddles.

But he knew someone who might.

"Igraine," he called outside her tent. When she did not respond, he spoke another name at a much quieter volume, "Turley."

There was a rustling inside the tent, and then Igraine emerged. Without looking at Vykers, she crawled out into the snow, stood up and at last turned his way.

"Let's take a walk."

Igraine fell into step beside Vykers, Turley's unhappiness and resentment evident with every step.

"I think I told you you'd get your old body back one day," the Reaper said.

Turley's response was barely audible. "Yes."

"Then what's the problem?"

"I don't believe it."

Vykers had killed men—scores of 'em—for less than that. He wheeled on Igraine, put his hand around her throat, and pulled her face closer to his.

Turley's response was not what he expected. "You...have...fangs."

"I do," the Reaper grinned menacingly.

"And claws. You are not human?"

"I don't know." Vykers dropped his grip and stepped backwards, suddenly pensive.

Igraine, by contrast, was more animated than he'd ever seen her. "You don't know? But how is that possible? Every story in your legend proclaims you the greatest of human warriors! Even my people tell of your exploits."

The Reaper glanced over at the collection of tents, worried that Igraine's voice might rouse everyone from sleep, and then disturbed that it hadn't. "Why's everyone sleepin' so late?" he said, more to himself than Igraine.

"I believe Her Majesty enspelled them. If they're not dead, they'll wake eventually."

Vykers looked at the horses, all hobbled together under a large fir. They, at least, seemed okay. "You understand Her Majesty is Alheria?"

"I've seen sufficient evidence."

"Sufficient evidence." Who in the infinite hells talked like that... besides Alheria? "Right," said Vykers. "So, there's a few things I don't understand."

Igraine stood by patiently, waiting to hear more.

"Such as, why does Her Majesty always call on me when there's a problem? If she's really a goddess, what does she need me for?"

Igraine's face lit up, the first sign of happiness he'd ever seen from her whilst she was occupied by the goblin. "An excellent question."

"And she knows I don't like or trust her. More, I want her throne. Why doesn't she just kill me?"

The young woman was practically dancing with excitement. "I don't have any answers for you yet, Master, but I will think on these questions. You can be sure of that!"

Exactly as Vykers had suspected and hoped, Turley needed something to distract himself from his misery, and nothing, it seemed, pleased him more than a puzzle. And since the Reaper needed answers to these questions as well, it proved a mutually beneficial situation. "Good," he said. "Good to hear it."

Whilst Igraine ambled back to her tent, Vykers walked over to the horses and made sure they were warm enough and safe. As he approached them, though, he saw them watching him with new vision, with eyes full of understanding and knowledge that no other horses had ever possessed.

Kittins & Rem, On the Road

They'd taken to travelling together. They both figured Cindor knew about them now, so there was no point in trying to maintain the illusion. Rem was consumed with the question of what they'd do when Cindor finally recovered, although he was still finding it difficult to believe that *anyone* could recover from what he and Kittins had done to the man.

Kittins, on the other hand, didn't seem overly concerned. "I expect he'll torture and kill one or both of us," he said, matter-of-factly. In the meantime, the captain just wanted to reach his destination in the north, to find this character calling himself the Reaper, and report back to Her Majesty.

"And how do you plan to report back?"

"The fuck should I know? I'm just doing what I was ordered to do."

"Does that include killing her Shaper?"

"Hey, he's the one who sent you spyin' on *me*. If anyone's gotta apologize to the Queen, it's *him*."

Rem had never before realized what an optimistic fellow the captain was. That, combined with his scintillating conversational skills and his astonishing good looks made, him an excellent companion for such a long journey.

In other words, Rem was lonely and bored.

He leaned forward in the saddle to dust some of the snow off his horse, but the long-suffering beast hardly noticed, and Rem guessed he probably had more in common with his mount than his captain.

"Why doesn't Her Majesty investigate this fake Reaper herself?"

In a single grunt, Kittins managed to convey several thoughts: he didn't know, he didn't care, and he wanted to be left alone for a while. Rem was impressed by how much meaning his companion had eked out of such a brief, seemingly inarticulate response.

Then: "Do you think you could defeat the real Reaper in combat?"

Now Kittins came to life. "Been wondering that myself, lately. They say he's impossible to hit, faster than fast, stronger than strong—all o' that nonsense."

"He did kill the End-of-All-Things."

"Aye, there's that. But he nearly got himself killed in the process, didn't he?"

"Because the End stabbed him with an enchanted dagger."

"How'd he stab him if Vykers can't be hit?"

A good point, Rem had to admit. "So, you think maybe you could hit him? You haven't got a magic sword, have you?"

Kittins shook his head. "What I got's a magic *body*."

"Some girl tell you that?" Rem cracked.

"Yep," the captain growled. "Her Majesty."

Just when the conversation was finally getting interesting, Kittins fell silent and stayed that way. Rem leaned forward in his saddle again, this time to get a better look at Kittins' expression, but the big man ignored him completely, as if he weren't even there.

Rem then tried to think his way through his current engagement to something like a logical conclusion, some point at which his work would be done and he could move on to other pursuits. He thought then of Long and his other friends. He would love to have known if they'd had any luck in finding Esmine, or whether...well, he hoped Long wasn't suffering, anyway. That poor son-of-a-bitch had been through it and then some.

Which thought brought Rem 'round to his own fortunes. He missed his theater company, but he realized he missed Long and the rest of the boys more. It was a great thrill to entertain a large crowd—he'd even once thought it his calling in life—but Rem had felt like he'd been doing something important under Long's direction, something that mattered to the kingdom. He yearned to do something of importance again. But what? And how?

He might've been a spy, but he recently murdered—or at least grievously injured—the one man who tried to employ him in that regard.

No, Rem thought, *I should go back to doing what I know. I should return to the theater.*

That was when he spied the first group of refugees.

"See them?" he asked Kittins.

"Refugees."

"If you're right, things are getting bad up north."

"Yup."

"Could be another war."

"Good."

At first, Rem was shocked by this response, but he gradually came to agree with it: time to kill something.

The False Reaper, In the Void

The boy was back in that dark space, that void, that place of nothingness which nevertheless had boundaries. On previous visits, he'd seen everyone else he'd ever been, including the End-of-All-Things. This time, he saw only tiny puffs of steam, wisps really, that moaned and sobbed in eternal torment, wandering aimlessly about the void. These, the boy realized, were all that was left of his other selves. The End had boasted of consuming them, and it appeared that he'd done just that.

But now, the boy still had shape and form. Why was that? And for how long? The End had overthrown him; that much was clear. But he had not completely finished the boy, and that fact alone gave the former False Reaper hope. There might be a way to reverse this defeat, or, at the very least, to undermine the End's victory.

First, though, he had to find a way to communicate with these wailing wisps—if they were still capable of communicating, that is.

The boy tried moving towards them, but they seemed oblivious of his presence. He listened to their wailing more closely, in case there were any words amongst the noise: nothing. He then tried wailing himself. Perhaps he could attract their interest in the same way one can sometimes attract a cat by meowing. As foolish as he felt, he was eventually rewarded by their approach. A small group of them coalesced about the boy, and he whispered to them in response, still fearful of being overheard by the End.

"Is there nothing we can do to thwart the bastard?"

He thought the wisps might resume their moaning; instead, they hissed and rumbled.

"There's still energy in you," the boy observed, "still substance. If we could pool whatever we have left, we might manage one final throw of the die."

"At the right time, the right time, the right time..." one or several of the little clouds responded.

"Yes," the boy chuckled softly, "the readiness is all."

He'd entombed the A'Shea in ice. When he'd been certain she was unconscious, he broke through her shell, tore off her clothing, and encased her in a frozen, crystalline egg. There she slept and would sleep until the stars winked out and the world blew away in ashes on the wind. Oh, someone or something would try to save her; of that, the End had no doubt. In fact, he was rather looking forward to finding out who or what this would-be savior turned out to be. It would not be an exaggeration to say he had his heart set on Tarmun Vykers, but there were any number of other potential heroes that the End would enjoy killing almost as much.

In time, he grew bored of staring at his prize, his bait, and turned his thoughts more specifically towards those enemies. The boy had been planning to lure Her Majesty north, where he'd hoped to ambush her with his horde of Svarren—not a bad idea in principle, if the End had to admit it. How had the boy been planning to lure the Queen? And what was the endgame? Clearly, he hadn't understood the significance of Aoife, or he'd have tried to capture her sooner, himself. The End could retreat into his mind and query the boy, but it might be more satisfying to approach him once the End had a plan of his own.

Lure the Queen North using Aoife as bait...ambush her with Svarren...and then? Suppose Aoife meant nothing to Her Majesty. Would she still come if it was Vykers who'd been called to save the A'Shea? The End's mind was still too chaotic from the trauma of returning to the flesh. He caught himself thinking the same thoughts over and over and making no progress.

He needed help, briefly, from someone loyal, someone who...

"Where is General Omeyo?" the End barked at some nearby Svarren. "Omeyo!" he yelled.

Something happened, and the next time the End was aware of himself and his surroundings, he was sitting on a stool near a burning brazier, inside his tent. He'd been scrutinizing his fingers and nails, when all of a sudden, he realized he'd lost a few minutes, or even several. He looked up in alarm and saw that his servants—both Svarren and human—behaved normally, without any sense of unease or disturbance.

A half-naked figure appeared at the opening to the End's tent and then shuffled forward, closer to the light.

It was Omeyo, but a much changed Omeyo. His face and body were covered in blue and black tattoos of primitive design and more primitive execution. His hair was matted, his eyes were wild and bloodshot, and his mouth hung open, trailing a long strand of drool onto the master's rug.

The End clapped his hands once and Omeyo's posture improved immediately, as did his overall affect. Now, he seemed truly alert and awake.

"What have they done to you?"

"Nothing the boy didn't encourage."

"Ah," the End sighed. "Whatever became of gratitude, eh? You raised that bastard out of the mud, and how did he repay you? Don't answer! I can see well enough: with suffering and humiliation."

Omeyo blinked: yes.

"We must help each other, General. Oh, don't look surprised. Like you, I am struggling to recover from injury. Like you, I am struggling to find...*equilibrium*. But we'll regain our strength, you and I," the End winked. "And then we'll smash all those who seek to do us harm!"

If the general had his doubts, he didn't share them, nor were they visible on his face.

ELEVEN

Long & Company, the Circus Family Barr

The lone wagon stood off the right-hand side of the road, facing north. It was a large and ridiculous-looking thing, suitable for the business it advertised: the Circus Family Barr. Its sides were painted in garish colors and even more ludicrous designs, promising tumblers, jooglers (whatever these were), singers and clowns. A team of six—six!—oxen stood under heavy blankets at the front of the wagon, and a small, ineffectual fence had been erected around them, intended, perhaps, to forestall the predations of savage deer. Luckily, savage deer were in short supply in this part of the north. A stovepipe sprouted from the wagon's roof, belching wood smoke into the evening air and beckoning to anyone or thing that recognized the odor of roast meat.

Yendor took in the scene with no little amount of incredulity. "How have they survived so long?"

Long held up his hands. "Don't ask me. I've never seen so plain an invitation for plunder and pillage."

"These folks magic?" Yendor asked Spirk.

The young Shaper thought a moment and then shook his head.

"Mayhap they've a mercenary or two in that wagon," Ron suggested.

"I'd bloody well hope!" said Yendor. "Otherwise, them oxen won't be long for this world. Speakin' o' which...I wouldn't mind a good slab o' beef."

"I wonder if they'd sell us one..." Long mused aloud.

Without being asked or directed, Spirk crossed the road and walked right up to the wagon. "I hear music!" he beamed. "They're playin' music!"

"That we are!" called a voice from the wagon's roof. "That a crime hereabouts?"

A tall, wiry fellow with wild blue eyes, bushy eyebrows, a crooked smile, and a slightly oversized head regarded the group from the happy end of a crossbow.

"Not a crime!" Long was quick to point out. "No crime at all, but a welcome diversion from this hard weather!"

"Gather yer party and stand 'em all there," the man pointed, "so's I can see the lot."

The captain complied, ushering everyone to the spot specified. "This is all of us."

Meanwhile, another, shorter fellow with the same features emerged onto the wagon's roof from an open hatch. He, too, held a crossbow.

"Is it, now?" the first man challenged. "What, the four of you just out for a stroll?"

"We're on our way north!" Spirk shouted enthusiastically.

Long shot him an irritated look, but chimed in to support his claim, nonetheless. "That's true."

"Headin' north in winter? That don't seem likely," the stranger said.

"And the sooner we see your buttocks, the better!" the smaller man added aggressively.

The first man rolled his eyes and turned to his companion, "Their buttocks, Keenan? Really? Their buttocks?"

Keenan shrugged. "Well, yeah. I meant their backsides, but it's all one, ain't it?"

"No," the taller one snapped. "It ain't. You're suggestin' some sort o' sordid need to see their naked ass-flesh. Which I don't wanna see now or ever!"

"That's not what I meant and you know it!" Keenan argued.

"Maybe I do and maybe I don't. But them?"

"I don't think you wanna see my naked ass-flesh!" Spirk called up helpfully.

Quick as a wink, the taller man wheeled on Spirk, his

crossbow pointed right at the Shaper's chest. "I din't ask you!"

At this point, a third, even smaller version of the first two men appeared. This new arrival had the same features as the first two, though his hair was lighter and he seemed a little rounder, overall.

"What's all the fuss about?" he inquired.

"Never you mind!" said the tallest of the three. "Git back to basting that roast!"

At the word 'roast,' Long's stomach rumbled something terrible. He was just about to speak up when Yendor beat him to it.

"How much for some o' your roast?"

"Ye cain't have none!" the second man yelled.

"Wait!" the tallest said. "How much what? What are you offerin'?"

"Coin," Long replied confidently.

"Coin! Bah! What good's coin out here?"

"Drink!" said Spirk, holding out one of the group's last pots of magic elixir.

"No!" Yendor complained. "That's too valuable!"

This caught the stranger's attention. "Drink, you say? What kind o' drink?"

"Wondrous, magical drink!" Long replied, over Yendor's continued protestations.

"I'll be the judge o' that!" the second man, Keenan, declared. "Gimme a swig!"

Long retrieved the pot from Spirk's outstretched hands and walked over to the wagon. Keenan lay down on his stomach, grasped the pot, and lifted it up onto the roof.

Yendor scowled in disgust. "Mahnus' balls. Now we'll never see food or drink!"

Keenan stood and took an experimental sip of his new prize. Apparently pleased with the taste, he drank more.

"I'll have some o' that!" the smallest of the three bellowed, ripping the pot from Keenan's hands.

The first man watched his brothers—for that is what they appeared to be—but kept his crossbow trained on the men below. When the pot was half gone, he shoved through his comrades and grabbed it for himself. "That's enough for you lot!"

"Don't see any beef, do you?" Yendor grumbled in Long's ear.

Long held up a finger: wait. "You remember how that stuff works."

Soon, the three brothers were sitting on the roof of their wagon, singing like idiots, their legs dangling down towards Long and his crew. Unexpectedly, a woman—a sister—popped her head out of the roof's trap door and sneered at the brothers.

"I mighta known!" she howled. "I'm down here doin' all the work, and you shiftless tosspots are up here drinkin'!"

This precipitated an outburst of raucous laughter from her brothers, accompanied by an astounding variety of foul noises from the middle one.

"Here now, Mads," the tallest one said, "'Ave a sip o' this, and it'll set you right."

Suddenly, Mads noticed the strangers waiting below. "And oo's them?"

"Friends!" Keenan declared. "Sworn and proven this very day!"

Mads was about to object when the tallest brother forced the pot to her lips and made her drink. She wanted to resist, but succumbed to the drink's magic as quickly as her brothers had. After another few gulps, she raced below, threw open a door in the back of the wagon, and invited Long and his friends to dinner.

The inside of the wagon was a miracle of engineering, fully three times as large as the exterior and so filled with odd trinkets, toys and gewgaws that Long felt as if he were in a different world.

"Food for one, food for all!" Mads giggled, whilst doling out still-smoking slabs of meat on skewers of varying size.

"Where'd you happen to come by such bounty?" Long asked.

"Did you see them oxen?" the youngest brother asked.

"Aye."

"Used to be twice as many. We've learned over time to make our meat carry itself."

Feeding that many beasts must have been a burden, though.
"In that case," said Long, "you want to sell or trade one of your
remaining oxen?"

The brothers all laughed.

Long joined them. "I had to try," he said.

The middle brother, Keenan, then stood on his hands and
ate his meat off the floor. The youngest brother, whose name had
yet to be uttered, pulled off his boots and ate with his feet. The
tallest brother juggled his meal and several other objects, and
Mads played a multi-necked instrument for accompaniment.
Not being drunk—or *as* drunk—as their hosts, Long and his
friends were still awake when the members of the Circus Family
Barr began nodding off to sleep, sometimes in the middle of an
activity or sentence. At last, the four guests found themselves
alone and unsupervised in their hosts' abode, wondering what
was proper in such circumstances.

"I say we rob 'em blind!" Yendor declared.

"No, no," Long said, "we're not that sort anymore, are we?"

"I wouldn't mind buyin' one o' these," Spirk announced as
he fiddled with one of the family's toys.

Long urged him to put the thing down. "We'd better not.
You never know what's part of their show and what ain't."

"Surely we can pay for some more food," said Ron.

"Aye," Yendor agreed. "At least some o' that beef and some
bread."

"Or…" Long interjected, "we could join them in sleep. We're
safe and warm in here, and we can negotiate for supplies on the
morrow. I don't much relish the idea of settin' up tents tonight,
anyhow."

Everyone agreed this was the best course, although Yendor
privately worried they'd be forced to part with more of his magic
drink. Still, a night in the warm-and-dry with the promise of a
hot breakfast was too hard to resist.

There was plenty of room for everyone and, aside from some
rather remarkable snoring, all eight of the wagon's inhabitants
got in an exceptional night's sleep. The only unusual occurrence
happened sometime after midnight, when the tallest brother
started talking in his sleep. Long wasn't able to make much

sense of it, but he did hear, "With up so floating many bells down," which could only have been the result of the alcohol, for it didn't sound like anything a sane or sober man would say.

When dawn came, Long was jostled awake by a foul-smelling foot in his face. The big toe, in fact, was mere seconds from exploring his left nostril when the captain's eyes opened and he escaped that fate. All around him, his friends and their hosts were rousing themselves and endeavoring to stand. The brothers and their sister were finding the process more challenging because they were still drunk and would be for days yet, if Long's experience meant anything. Yet, the drink continued to inspire generosity and goodwill amongst the Circus Family Barr, and they set about making breakfast for everyone without the slightest hesitation or misgiving.

Every member of Long's crew was delighted to be eating beef two meals in a row, to say nothing of continuing to enjoy the warmth of the wagon and its owners, for every member of Long's crew was also aware that leaving the wagon would mean a return to the insufferable cold, the tedious walking and the same old conversations.

A time came, though, when Long could eat and drink no more, and he itched to get back on the road, in search of his daughter. He had a hard time convincing his mates of the necessity of leaving, but in the end their loyalty to him won out. By midday, the captain and his friends had extricated themselves from the wagon and the Circus Family Barr and returned to the road. Looking back, Long thought he saw tears in the tallest brother's eyes, whilst the younger brothers commenced wrestling and thrashing about in the snow. Mads watched Long and his friends walk away, and then she went back inside the wagon.

An hour down the road, Spirk said "I miss those fellers."

"Aye," said Ron.

Long put his hands in his pockets and realized all his coin was gone. "Hey, Yendor," he whispered, "have you got any coin left?"

The other man rifled through his pockets and came up empty. "Those bastards!" he exclaimed. "Spirk, 'ave you still got them pots 'o drink."

The Shaper had magically safeguarded his pockets. "I do!" he smiled.

"We need to save one of those," said Yendor. "Might be a way to make more of that stuff if we can hire the right alchemist or A'Shea or whatnot."

If we make it through this ordeal alive...Long thought.

Mardine, In the Forest

Mardine rushed into the clearing, glad to be free of shadows at last and basking in sunlight, even if it was *cold* sunlight. The last few days had proven an emotional maelstrom that had left her by turns on edge, exhausted or weeping. *This must be what madness feels like,* she ruminated. To be rid of these feelings for as much as an hour seemed too much to ask, too much to hope. Still, she'd felt worse: she'd been dead, after all.

And how was it she'd managed to come back? By what agency? Alheria's? She was far more a human goddess than the giants'. But hadn't Mardine conceived against all reason and borne a half-human child? Was it possible that Alheria had taken a special interest in Mardine, Esmine and Long Pete from the beginning? And, if so, might she not be watching over the girl even now?

Strange, miraculous things had happened, yes, but Alheria's intervention seemed beyond reason.

Mardine stopped a moment and savored the sun on her cheeks. The days were short, and the nights grew longer and longer. She'd heard stories in her youth that claimed if a person went north far enough, the night stretched on for weeks, only to be replaced by an equally endless day. Mardine never believed those stories, but now they worried her. The thought of her little girl wandering an unending frozen wasteland in the dark was unbearable.

The giantess had to figure out how she'd find Esmine in all that area. Mardine knew well enough how to find north; any fool could do that. But to find a single person in the north? And this was assuming that Esmine was still...No. Mardine wouldn't allow herself to finish that thought.

I will find more people. I will ask them if they've seen slavers, a child, a skinny little thrall woman. I will ask everyone I meet anything I can think to ask. First, though, she had to find people, and that was proving harder than she'd imagined. There were cities up north, but somehow she kept missing them, walking past or around or between them without ever knowing their proximity. It was frustrating, really. All a person had to do was use her nose, and the location of human settlements usually became evident.

The unexpected appearance of blood on the snow caused Mardine's heart to skip a beat and then to race wildly. *Esmine!* She thought, and then, *No. Calm yourself!* Cautiously, she looked about for more blood and shortly found an ever-growing trail of it amidst a sea of Svarren tracks. *Not Esmine, then. Probably.* The Svarren had killed something, maybe even one of their own, and trailed its blood across the forest floor. But so much blood. The pinkish snow gave way to crimson slush, and the stink of death pervaded everything. At the base of a tree, Mardine spied a dead porcupine or beaver. As she drew closer, though, she recognized it as a head of hair...without the head. The Svarren had torn some luckless human's scalp off, or eaten their way through his head and cast his hair aside as garbage. Mardine felt a terrible shiver that had nothing to do with the cold. Now that she knew what to look for, she saw signs of a massacre everywhere she looked—rib bones, a bloodied boot, a drenched and ragged shirt, an arm bone. Through the trees, she saw a large, square shadow that looked like a small hut or a big wagon. The Svarren were long gone, Mardine knew, but one or two of their victims might have survived and could still be saved. Abandoning caution, the giantess raced through the trees towards the shadow.

It was a wagon, and a large one, too. It lay on its side in a small lake of blood, smoke trailing from one window and various other, cruder holes. On one end, the remains of what must have been oxen were strewn about. Mardine suspected she'd find the former owners of those oxen inside the wagon, if anywhere. She hoped their end had been as quick and painless as possible, but she doubted it.

She poked her head in the window and was bewildered by the sight of broken toys, puppets, marionettes and more. The wagon's stove was still burning, and, amazingly, its flames hadn't spread through the interior. The Svarren had been either so fixated on eating or in such a hurry to move on that they'd missed their chance at more mayhem in setting the whole wagon ablaze. Mardine wished they had, though. A funeral pyre had more dignity than this grisly abattoir. Sadly, the giantess gave up any hope of finding survivors. She stepped back and took in the scene a final time. Whoever the Circus Family Barr had been, they'd deserved better than they'd gotten.

An idea came to Mardine, then: the Svarren left little alive in their wake, so there would be nothing of interest in the direction from which they'd come. Where were they going in such haste, however? Stalking a mob of Svarren was a dangerous proposition, but it might just lead to more people.

Vykers & Company, On the Road

It was times like this that Vykers fully believed in Alheria's deity. She'd done more than strengthen his horses; she'd *improved* them, improved them to the point that they could no longer really be considered horses. They were something else, and their otherness became apparent almost as soon as Vykers and his men mounted up for the day's journey. In seconds, the world around became liquid, a swirling mass of colors that was both dizzying and terrifying. But because each of the men could see one another and especially their leader, they maintained their composure and gradually adjusted to this strange new experience. It helped, too, that the horses did not seem in the least perturbed. But how they moved! Their gallop was somewhere between that of a normal horse and a Shaper's jump, a slower here-there. There was something eternal in it, too, as if everything else was transient and only their movement, lasting. Staring at his horse's hooves, Vykers couldn't say whether they even touched the ground. Yet, they devoured it. When the Reaper called for a water break and slowed his mount to a stop, he discovered a landscape he'd not been expecting for another week or more. Was it possible these stronger, better horses had covered so much territory in but a few hours? The evidence was undeniable.

It was not even midday, but Vykers called for his men to make camp. When Hjuest greeted this request with overt curiosity, all that the Reaper said was "I need to think."

"Your pardon, Master," Igraine said when Vykers reached for the water skin on his saddle. "But that is exactly what I *have* been doing all this while."

"And?" Vykers asked, before taking a great gulp of water.

"I believe I have reached some relatively sound conclusions."

"Go on."

"Assume Her Majesty is the goddess Alheria."

"I got no trouble with that."

"So, she has the power, the ability to destroy you. You tell me she once took your hands and feet. Another time, she allowed you to languish for years from a wound she might have healed with a wave of her hand. Finally, she allowed your Shaper to steal your body."

Vykers grunted in the affirmative.

"But in every case, you were not killed. Her Majesty weakens you, limits your effectiveness, but she does not kill you. I ask myself why. Is it because she cannot? No, we agree that she can. Is it then because she must not? Why? Why must she keep you alive? Because..." Igraine continued, "you serve some purpose that only you can fulfill."

"Which is?"

"I do not know. But consider: she is a goddess, yet she sent you to deal with the End-of-All-Things. From the stories and songs of your battle, Her Majesty did not even lift a finger against the mad sorcerer. And now, she sends you, again, to investigate rumors of his return. Why does she not investigate herself? Why does she not, in fact, already know the truth of it?"

Vykers didn't know if he was supposed to answer, but as he could not, he simply waited for Igraine to say more.

"I believe she does know whether the End has returned or not and, again, she will not be involved in the coming conflict. And why is that? Why would she abstain?"

"I give up. Why?"

"Because they share a connection, the End and Alheria."

"Meaning?"

"They were lovers, once, or they're family."

"Family."

It made sense. And it also explained why the Queen felt entitled to steal the dagger the End had used to stab Vykers. Possibly, it was a family heirloom. Or it was the only weapon that could truly finish the End or Alheria. But if they were family—or had been lovers—was the End Alheria's brother or son? Or had he been her husband? Was the End really Mahnus, returned from the endless hells to exact revenge upon his killer?

"Damn spider's web," Vykers muttered. "Closer you get to the middle, the stickier it gets."

"An apt assessment," Igraine grinned.

"So, Alheria can't or won't kill the End because they're family. Instead, she uses me to do it. But if that's all I mean to her, why didn't she finish me off the last time I fought the End?"

"There are two possibilities: one, she knew you hadn't fully destroyed the End, or, two, there's something else you're meant to do as well."

"Such as?"

This time Igraine threw up her hands in surrender. "I don't know. Perhaps she has more family members she needs killed."

It was an unpleasant thought, but somehow it felt like the truth. Unable to voice gratitude, Vykers patted Igraine on the shoulder. "You're pretty good at this thinkin' business. You figure anything else out, you let me know."

And against his better judgement, Turley was mollified. He'd made a contribution to Vykers' cause; he'd made a difference. Despite his continued dissatisfaction with his physical state, he was no longer as miserable and hopeless as he'd been just the day before. With a new spring in his step—or Igraine's step— Turley returned to his own horse and saddle and continued to grapple with the many mysteries surrounding the Reaper.

Sometime after nightfall, the party was attacked by Svarren. With the exception of Igraine, everyone was a highly trained and experienced professional soldier—in a group led by the legendary Reaper. The Svarren didn't have a chance. In fact, the only moment of drama came from an argument about who should have the right to kill the last few savages. If Vykers was selfish in anything, it was in killing. Whilst his men squabbled about the pecking order and propriety, he pushed them aside and flew into the last knot of Svarren, cutting through them with his fell dagger like a forge-heated sword cuts through a snowbank. Ferocious he was, but also canny. He spared the last of the Svarren for questioning.

While his men pinioned its arms against a large stone, Vykers carved runes in the flesh of the creature's face and chest with a borrowed blade. For every moment the Svarra hesitated, the Reaper carved another character. Soon, the crazed monster was babbling almost incoherently. Almost. The words "gathering" and "great war" were quite clear. When Vykers had gotten everything useful out of his captive, he released him to Hjuest, saying, "Pour some wine down his gullet and set him loose. He makes it back to his people, they'll know I'm after 'em."

Hjuest did not argue.

The Circus Family Barr, In the Forest

"D'you reckon we can git down now?" Mads asked.

"I 'spect so. Rate those things were movin', they must be clear to Picksworth by now."

"Glad to hear it!" Keenan exclaimed. "I'm tired o' smellin' your gas."

"'Taint my fault you chose the branch right under me," the tall brother retorted.

"Well, let's git to gittin'!" said Mads impatiently.

One by one, the members of the Circus Family Barr unwrapped themselves from the pine's sturdy branches and commenced climbing, swinging and tumbling down to the forest floor.

When the tallest brother was safe on the ground, he stretched his arms and back, let out a groan of pleasure and said, "We'd best see what's left of our wagon and gear."

"Ain't nothin' left of our oxen, I'll wager," the youngest brother said.

"Oh, there might be some odd bits 'n pieces," the tallest brother replied. "Nothin' that'll pull our wagon, though."

The siblings emerged from a deadfall and saw that their wagon was still in one piece, albeit toppled over on one side. Even the stove continued to spout smoke.

"Papa always built 'em strong!" Mads declared upon seeing the wagon.

"Strong but stupid," the middle brother said as he smacked the youngest on the back of his head.

The tallest brother, having recognized the beginnings of a brawl from previous experience, jumped between his brothers and ordered peace between them. "Stop it, now!" He yelled. "You'd think we got nothin' better to do!"

"How are we gonna right the wagon?" Mads asked.

"Let's make a lever outta something, and then we'll pry 'er back onto 'er wheels."

It was a solid plan, except that it failed to take into account the many combustibles inside the wagon, which all came into contact as they rocked the big thing upright. Mads had just enough time to say, "Do you smell somethin' peculiar?" And then the wagon exploded with such force that it sent the Circus Family Barr turning somersaults through the air even as they were pelted and perforated with flying shrapnel.

Omeyo & The End, In Camp

Omeyo was slowly regaining his wits—just in time, he supposed, to be driven out of them again in the End's service. The two men sat across from each other at a small table the End's servants had set up in his tent. But they needed a bigger table. There was so much food heaped between Omeyo and the sorcerer that they could barely see each other, but the End would not allow it to be cleared away. Instead, he attacked it like some starving beast, some fierce animal that hadn't eaten in a season. Omeyo couldn't recall ever seeing the End so obsessed with food, but his body's previous occupant, the False Reaper, had burned so much energy attempting to stave off the mad sorcerer's return that the body had practically perished. Thus, the End was eating to replenish his reserves. And possibly to intimidate his general.

"I tell you, I'll not make the same mistake twice with Tarmun Vykers and Her Bitchery. I'll choose the battle field. I'll choose the timing. And I'll make sure the fey have no part in this contest."

Wanting something to say, Omeyo mumbled, "That sounds like an excellent plan, Master."

"Are you not hungry?" the End grinned back at him. "I am. Eat something, man! Rebuild your strength."

The general picked at something fishlike that had been set down by his elbow.

The End continued blithely on, "As I was saying, I'll have every advantage this time around. Truth to tell, I've seen no evidence the Queen has even mustered an army to face me. After everything we went through before, she still underestimates me. Well, let her, I say! It is my turn to destroy *her* minions and humiliate *her!*"

The End said more, but Omeyo found his attention drifting off. If the sorcerer wanted to kill him for that, so be it. Omeyo had other things to think about. Or he imagined he did. The only thing that really came to mind was the Svarren woman who'd taken him in and...the general was again aroused and disgusted merely thinking of the creature. What had she done to him? Whatever it was, it was in no wise as bad as what her fellows had done. Omeyo returned to the present and saw the End staring at him intently.

"You've been hexed. And sexed," the End laughed. "Hexed and sexed! But I believe I can help you...that is, assuming you *want* to be helped."

Somehow, the general nodded his head, though he couldn't have said if he'd done it of his own free will or by force. In the next instant, the End leaned across the mountain of food, placed his hands on Omeyo's shoulders and infused him with such pain that he rapidly came to wish for death. Just as quickly, the pain subsided, and in its absence, a terrible clarity took hold of the general's perceptions. The first thought that came to him in this newly enlightened state was: *What a terrible world this is, how fraught with pointless suffering.* The second thought was: *I have to kill this bastard.* But what Omeyo said was, "Thank you, Master. I feel much better."

The End leaned backwards, a smug look upon his face, and selected the next item in his meal. "These Svarren have their uses, of course," he smirked, "but it's best not to get too involved with them."

Omeyo wanted to grab the nearest goblet and smash the sorcerer's face in. "I couldn't agree more," he said.

Kittins & Rem, On the Road

Rem had spoken to a few of the refuges whilst Kittins rode a good ways off, pretending to scout the path ahead. In reality, he didn't want to attract any more attention to or with his hideous face than necessary. For that, Rem was more than grateful. The refugees were frightened enough as it was.

Svarren were overrunning everything, everywhere, and although most villages had defenses adequate to repel a hundred or so, none were equipped to handle thousands of Svarren, and it seemed likely there might even be *tens* of thousands gathering, with more arriving every hour.

Some said the savages were being led by the Reaper, others said the End-of-All-Things had returned. Whatever the reason, folks were smart enough to know when the odds were against them, and heading to the more-populated south seemed the only viable response. Also, the Virgin Queen was the most powerful ruler in the land. If anyone was prepared to crush the assembling Svarren, it was she. Or so the refugees hoped.

Rem rejoined his companion and reported what he'd learned.

"The Reaper leadin' an army of Svarren? I doubt it," Kittins said.

"I doesn't make sense, does it?"

"There's more men would fight for him than Her Majesty."

"Which means it isn't the Reaper. But that doesn't make sense, either."

"Why?"

"Because," said Rem, "running about, killing folks in the Reaper's name is sure to attract the *real* Reaper."

"Maybe that's the point. Maybe whoever-this-is wants a reckoning."

Rem shook his head. "That's madness, suicide."

Kittins leaned his head to one side as if he didn't agree. "Maybe. Maybe not."

Both men rode in silence for several minutes, and then Rem said, "I imagine Her Majesty has thought all of this through."

"You imagine," Kittins scoffed.

"Then what's the purpose of your going north?"

"Keeping me away from her Shaper. Didn't work too well, did it?"

Rem reached over and grasped the reins of Kittins' horse, pulling the beast to a halt. "So why are you still going north? Surely, you don't want to run into this other Reaper."

The captain yanked his reins out of Rem's grip. "Why not? What else've I got to do?"

"I thought you wanted revenge on Her Majesty."

Kittins smiled his death's head smile. "Exactly." The captain then kicked his horse back into motion and opened a good lead on his companion.

The actor faced a moment of indecision: should he continue in Kittins' company and possibly get embroiled in a battle not his own, or should he attempt to find and rejoin Long Pete and the rest of his friends? *I'm probably safer in Kittins' company*, he thought, *especially if Cindor returns*. Resigned, he too spurred his horse onward, hoping to close the gap between himself and the captain.

Late afternoon, they crossed a stretch of Svarren tracks that seemed to run forever. Rem wanted to talk about it, but he could see Kittins wasn't similarly inclined. But what would they do if they ran into a large group of the creatures? Or thousands? Despite his apparent self-confidence, Kittins was no Tarmun Vykers. He and the actor stood no chance against anything more than a handful of Svarren. At least, that's the way Rem saw it. Should he counsel caution? *I'd have more luck urging a stone to sing sea shanties.*

Kittins held up a hand and gestured for Rem to stop moving and be quiet. Carefully, the big man slid down from his horse and walked to the fringe of the Svarren trail. Aware that the actor was still watching him, he pointed to something dark in the snow and quickly made his way back to the horses.

"What?" Rem whispered.

"Shit," Kittins answered. "And it's still steaming. Let's ride back the opposite way a while and then cut north."

So, the captain was not as foolhardy as he seemed.

The Circus Family Barr, the Forest

The Circus Family Barr was dragged back to consciousness, battered and bleeding, by the bizarre sound of groaning, creaking trees. Mads sat up first and realized that a sizable chunk had been blown from the trunk of a massive fir by the wagon's explosion. By the time the last Barr had reached a sitting position, it became evident the huge tree was falling on the performers.

"Aaaaaagh!" Keenan screamed.

The Giants & Company, Zillia's Cave

It was a long but mercifully uneventful trek to Zillia's cave, which was located far to the east and somewhat south of Beesmarch's tree.

"Wouldn't mind if she was even farther away," the biggest giant remarked.

Eoman didn't understand the bad blood between his friends, but he let it be. He had other, more pressing concerns. "I hope she's in," he said, looking at the mouth of Zillia's cave.

"Where else would she be, foul creature that she is?"

"Oh," Eoman laughed, "she's not so bad, Bees. I rather like her."

"We all know that!" Beesmarch responded. "What no one can figure is why!"

Karrakan glanced down at his two charges, Nelby and Esmine. "Don't you worry, girls. You'll like her plenty!"

The cave stood in the side of a massive hillside, with an entrance more than large enough to accommodate Eoman's entire party. Huge trees flanked the opening, and a fresh mantle of snow covered the hill from cave to crest. There were no footprints of any kind to be found in the area, which Eoman took to be a good sign that Zillia was still alive and at work. Otherwise, something less fastidious would have moved into the cave, leaving tracks and spoor everywhere.

"No sign of Svarren," said Karrakan. "That's a good sign."

"I was just thinking the same thing," Eoman said.

It was getting on towards evening, and the giants had been hoping to spend the night in Zillia's cave. If things went poorly, however, Eoman feared they might not have enough time to set up a decent camp before nightfall. *No point in puttin' this off,* the king thought.

With as much swagger as he could muster, he walked to the very mouth of the cave and called out, "It's Eoman, King of the Giants, who seeks entrance!"

An outburst of croaking came from within the cave.

"That's the old witch laughing at us!" Beesmarch insisted. "I warned you she'd respond this way."

A shape appeared in the gloom before Eoman could frame a response to Beesmarch's comment. In the next instant, the shape resolved into that of a female giant, dressed in rags, cobwebs and taffeta. Zillia was the last member of an offshoot branch of giantkind, almost as wide as she was tall, and a head shorter than Karrakan for all that. She looked a thing of dreams, not reality, but her smile was genuine enough.

"How long, how long has it been, my king?"

Eoman nearly choked up at her obeisance. "Too long," he admitted. "Far too long for a king to be gone from such a kind and loyal subject."

"Humph!" sniffed Beesmarch. "Pandering and sycophants!"

"Those are some big words, old friend."

"I read!" Beesmarch exclaimed. "You should try it."

Eoman laughed. "Too busy making the rounds."

By now, Zillia had caught sight of both Nelby and Esmine.

"And who's this, then?" she crooned merrily.

"Don't s'pose you ever met Mardine, did you?" Eoman asked by way of reply. "Big girl, red hair?"

"Mmmm…" Zillia said, as she scratched her chin. "Red hair's familiar."

"Well, the shorter one here's her daughter. And the human's her nanny."

Before anyone could warn her, Zillia asked, "And where's Mardine, then?" The spontaneous agony on the girls' faces was all the answer Zillia needed. "Ooh," she said softly, "I see."

"It's gettin' dark out here!" Beesmarch reminded everyone.

"Ah, yes. Come in, come in!" Zillia said.

If Beesmarch's tree was a revelation, Zillia's cave was no less astonishing. But a few strides inside, great veins of crystal glowed with light of different colors and intensities.

"Lovely!" Karrakan exclaimed.

"Humph!" said Beesmarch.

"I'd have bet my beard that'd be your reaction," Eoman chuckled.

"Keep yer beard. Yer ugly enough as 'tis."

The king would have laughed harder and longer, but he knew when to leave his old friend be. Instead, he merely rolled his eyes theatrically, to Zillia's delight.

Despite Beesmarch's persistent disapproval, the two girls shared Karrakan's enthusiasm for the crystals, and Esmine, in particular, was completely agog. As the group progressed farther inside, the air became warmer and an ethereal music seemed to emanate from the very walls and ceiling.

"Where is that coming from?" Karrakan wondered.

"Everywhere!" Zillia smiled. "But if you don't like it, I can stop it."

"Oh, I like it, I like it."

Beesmarch, of course, said, "I hate it."

"No you don't, you big liar!" Zillia teased.

"I think she's got the right of it, Bees," Eoman joined in jovially. "After all, it's not so much different from your wind chimes and mobiles." After a pause, he added, "And don't say 'humph'!"

Robbed of his favorite retort, Beesmarch could only chew his mustache and glower.

Zillia led them on, past a tunnel from which water could be heard burbling and gurgling. "Those are the baths," she said before hurrying on.

"Baths?" Eoman asked. "Hot or cold?"

"Both, truly! But there's time for that later."

The king sighed, "I'd love a hot bath."

"And I'd love for you to take one!" Beesmarch quipped.

The group passed into another, larger chamber, with a low table in the center. "Hungry?" Zillia inquired, her musical voice adding a note of welcome that her guests hadn't heard anywhere else in ages.

"Need you ask?"

"How can we fit 'round such a short table?" Beesmarch complained.

"We sit on cushions on the floor!" Zillia chirped.

"Witches..." the tallest giant muttered.

In no time, everyone had shoved in around the table. Even the two girls were comfortable enough to find themselves a spot between Zillia and Karrakan.

"Uh," Eoman said, "did you forget something?" he asked of his hostess.

"Have I?"

"Food!" said Beesmarch.

Zillia's eyes fairly twinkled with anticipation as she produced a small whistle from a string about her neck and blew upon it. An incredibly high-pitched but still audible whine sounded, and then the giantess let the whistle fall back into the folds of fabric at her throat.

Shortly, a small procession of wolverines entered the large chamber, walking on their hind legs, laden with platters of cheese, mushrooms, bread, jams, butter, dried fruit, and more. There was no meat—Zillia wouldn't eat or serve it—but there was plenty of every-and-anything else a person might wish to eat.

"Ale?" Beesmarch asked rather rudely.

"Wine," Zillia countered, seemingly oblivious of the fellow's temper. "Wine made of cranberries, blueberries, blackberries, thimbleberries and more."

Beesmarch clucked his tongue irritably. "I'd rather drink piss."

"That can be arranged," Zillia said, without surrendering an ounce of her good humor.

Karrakan was most interested in the wolverines. "Those animals..." he began.

"Friends," Zillia replied. "Family. I do for them, they do for me."

"They don't look like normal wolverines," Eoman opined.

"They're not. Your average wolverines are, well, common. These are their brighter, better cousins."

"Thank you, milady," one of the beasts croaked, causing Beesmarch to choke on his wine.

"They talk?" he gasped.

Zillia favored her guest with the biggest, most self-satisfied smile she could manage, but said nothing.

Karrakan, ever the peacemaker amongst his kin, said "I am amazed, Zillia."

From the looks on their faces, it was evident that the girls were equally amazed. Nelby and Esmine looked enthralled by the wolverines, the meal, the glowing crystals, even their hostess.

It is well, thought Eoman. "To the matter at hand," he said.

At this pronouncement, everyone fell silent, waiting to hear what the king had to say.

"Old friend," he said to his hostess, "I would beg a boon of you."

"The girls?"

"Your intuition remains as strong as ever!" Eoman said.

Zillia chortled at this and answered, "Not intuition, my king: common sense. But I'm curious as to why you'd leave them with me."

"They'd not be safe where Beesmarch, Karrakan and I must go."

"Svarren?"

"More common sense?"

"Intuition!" Zillia chortled again. "But, in truth, we've been overrun by them of late. It's high time someone investigated."

"We mean to do more than *investigate*," Beesmarch spat.

"What? Just you three? Why not take the brothers?"

Eoman was surprised. "The brothers? Last I heard, they were on the eastern coast."

"Ha!" Zillia laughed. "That was some time ago. They're north of me, now. Hunting, so they say."

Karrakan shot a meaningful glance at his king. "Hunting? Might be we share the same purpose."

Eoman nodded in agreement. The food and wine had gotten to him, and now he fancied a good night's sleep. But first he wanted that hot bath he'd heard tell of.

"Munch!" Zillia called to one of her wolverines. "Show our guests to the baths."

The Circus Family Barr, the Forest

The Circus Family Barr did not recover from their latest disaster so quickly. While none of its members had been crushed by the tree itself, all were struck and pinned by its various branches. The smallest was able to wiggle his way free, but he didn't possess the strength to free his siblings.

"I'm startin' ta think the gods hate clowns!" the tallest griped from beneath his branch.

"Everyone's a critic!" Mads responded. "Why should they be any different?"

"I think..." said Keenan, "I think I'm startin' to freeze to death."

"Well," the tallest brother sighed, "we've cheated death—what, now—three times in a row this day?"

"I s'pose there's worse ways to go than freezin'," the youngest brother offered.

The sudden and undeniable sound of a wolf's growl seemed to underscore the point.

Long & Company, On the Road

It was again snowing hard. If he ever got through this ordeal in one piece, Long vowed he'd move someplace where snow never fell, someplace sunny and warm all the time. He pictured himself with Esmine and lost himself in that daydream until, invariably, Mardine showed up, and he remembered he'd lost her for good. That part of the dream could never come true. And the reason for it would haunt Long forever.

It was snowing, yes, but the forest was thinning. It would be nice to get out of the trees for a while, whether it kept snowing or not. Hopefully, he and his mates could find a good place to shelter for the evening. Pine and fir trees could be added to the list of things of which he'd had his fill.

Once free of the forest, Long and his companions could see the outlines of a village in the distance. It was more than they'd hoped for, and they set off at a jog, so eager were they to reach it. Even Yendor, hopping along on his broken or mending or not-broken leg made good speed.

When they got within a hundred strides or so, Long held up a hand and pulled everyone to a stop.

"Something's wrong," he said.

"Yeah," said Spirk. "It's empty. Everyone's gone."

"Is that all?" Yendor demanded. "I was afraid there'd be magic or Svarren or some such."

Long lowered his hand. "Let's go."

The village was indeed deserted, and its most valuable items had been taken away by the villagers. Still, there was firewood, a few serviceable blankets, some crocks of preserved fruits and vegetables—not especially tasty under normal circumstance, but delicious to the captain and his friends.

As night fell, they holed up in a small cottage that Long felt had the most defensible position in town, but also the largest fireplace-to-room size relationship. It would be easy to heat and keep warm throughout the night. Fortuitously, the home's mattresses had been left behind, so Spirk and Ron dragged them near the fire. They were little more than great bags of straw, but to Long and company, they were the most comfortable bedding imaginable.

"Let's have one of those pots o' magic drink!" Yendor exclaimed, when everyone had finished eating.

"Let's not," Long answered.

"Now, Long," Yendor said, "I've put up with my share o' shit on this journey. I ain't asked for much, and," he added pointedly, "I been a loyal friend. I don't see how us havin' a little nip hurts you any."

The captain thought about this for several breaths. He didn't like it, but arguing against it would require more energy than he had and only serve to aggravate emotional wounds that were just beginning to heal. "Fine," he said. "You do as you list."

Long lay on his side, watching the fire and listening to his comrades get rip-roaring drunk. He abstained, though he knew it made him look rather a poor sport. But someone had to remain sober in case of emergency. Sober and alert, alas, were not one and the same thing, and it wasn't long before the captain drifted off to sleep.

His dreams were comforting, at first. There was the apple orchard. The trees were in bloom and yet somehow held apples, which Long picked whilst Esmine chased butterflies nearby. Mardine loomed just out of sight, making a pie. Outside? Sure. Why not. Slowly, though, these images of domestic bliss gave way to other, stranger visions. There was the giant thing Long and Spirk had killed in the forest. A god? There, too, was the huge face in the wall of the underground ruins. Who was she? Another god? Long felt he should recognize her. Her Majesty, the Virgin Queen, came into view then, and she looked angry. But angry at whom? Surely not Long. She'd rewarded him once for...something.

In the waking world, Yendor got up to piss and disturbed Long's sleep. Instead of apologizing, he said, "I wake you? Guess I wanted some company, then."

Long rolled onto his knees and stood. They'd found a ewer of water earlier that they'd all deemed safe to drink, and now the captain wanted some. "You don't look like a man who broke an arm, a leg and some ribs," he told Yendor.

Yendor giggled. Giggled! "It's this drink," he said. "It's got some strange healin' properties."

"Don't tell me your eye's grown back."

"No," Yendor confessed, "but..."

"But?"

Yendor hesitated. Even in his inebriated state, he didn't want to seem a fool.

"But?" Long asked again with greater emphasis.

"It ain't grown back, but I can see things with it all the same."

The captain crossed over to his friend, walked him back into the firelight, so he could read his expressions. "What do you mean, you can see things?"

Yendor lowered his head, ran a hand through his thinning hair and rubbed his scalp. "I can see in the dark."

It was a ridiculous claim, but Long had lived through so many unthinkable events, he half believed his friend. "You can see in the dark," he repeated.

"My eye's gone dark," Yendor said, lifting his eyepatch to reveal his ruined socket, "and now I can *see* in the dark."

"Show me." Long led Yendor outside the cabin and closed the door behind them. Absolutely nothing could be seen beyond three or four strides, so Long asked, "What can you see?"

"Fifteen, no, sixteen other buildings—cottages, a stable and such. Looks like there's a well across the road."

That wasn't good enough for the captain, who walked several steps away from his friend, held up two fingers and said, "How many fingers am I holding up?"

"Two, and stop scowlin' at me."

Long shot him an obscene gesture.

"One, now, and did you greet your ma with that finger?"

The captain returned to Yendor's side. "Okay. You can see in the dark. You just got yourself a new job: point-man whenever it's dark."

"Can we go back inside now? I'm freezin' my nuts off!"

Mardine, In the Village

On the other side of town, Mardine's eyes snapped open at the sound of laughter. Or what she thought was laughter.

She'd given up on the Svarren tracks earlier in the day when she thought she saw light through the trees. Following this new lead, she stumbled upon the village, elated at first, and then disappointed at its emptiness. She found a few things to eat in a root cellar and bundled herself into a storage closet in the middle of one of the homes, reasoning it would be easier to keep warm in such a tight space. She was cold, but she'd been colder. Much, much colder.

Long and his friends never checked this house when they came into town, and the noise of their search never roused the exhausted giantess. In the middle of the night, though, everything was so quiet that the slightest unexpected sound was like an alarm. Mardine sat in her makeshift den and listened, listened, listened for any further noise, but heard nothing. Perhaps she'd imagined it, or maybe it was something left over from a dream she'd been having. Try how she might to stay vigilant, sleep got the better of her again. The next time she woke up, the whole cottage was lighter.

It was morning, neither early nor late, but right in the heart of it. Mardine snacked on a handful of nuts she'd been given by her friends and decided to get on the road as quickly as possible. There was no one else in this village after all, and nothing of value to be gained by lingering. She despaired of finding anyone anywhere, in fact. It seemed the whole north had been evacuated, for reasons she'd yet to discover.

She gathered her many furs and blankets, threw them over her shoulders, and left the cottage. The day was overcast, but at least the snow had stopped falling. Mardine said a quick prayer to Alheria and set out in the direction that felt the most northern.

Once she'd gotten some ways from the village, she thought she heard more laughter coming from it, but it was too much effort to turn around and go back. There was no help to be found there, anyway.

The farther north she travelled, however, the more Svarren signs she came across, which might, she supposed, have accounted for the lack of people. The Svarren were—what?—migrating?

Massing for war? Raiding? Svarren were incapable of good, Mardine knew, thus, whatever they were doing had to be evil. The question was, was it any concern of hers? Mardine was desperate to find her daughter, her own. If the rest of the world burned while she searched, what did it matter? Hadn't Mardine given enough already?

Unfortunately, she didn't entirely believe such arguments. Like it or not, she was, had been, a citizen of the world. She, like anyone, had the power to tip the scales one way or the other. Sometimes, she felt such anger, she was afraid of her own potential for evil. There were days when all she wanted was to smash, crush, obliterate. There were other times when the memory of her daughter, new as it was, was like a beacon in a storm, drawing her ever closer to comfort and safety.

If only she could find her daughter. Everything, anything else was moot unless and until she found Esmine.

Find Esmine, she commanded herself. *Find Esmine, find Esmine, find Esmine*. It became her mantra, her only guiding principle.

The Circus Family Barr, the Forest

The wolves ate well, for three curtain calls is enough for anyone, even the Circus Family Barr.

The End & Omeyo, In Camp

"It is time to bait the trap," the End said to Omeyo. "My predecessor, the boy, did little to draw our enemies hence. I think perhaps he was a coward."

Omeyo blinked in plausible agreement. Nodding required too much energy, too much commitment.

"Butchering a bunch of peasants so far from the capital is hardly enough to attract Her Majesty's interest, to say nothing of the Reaper's. And I doubt either of them cares overmuch for the little people, anyway. No, I will see how Tarmun Vykers enjoys a glimpse of our frozen A'Shea. If he chooses to come after us, I'm certain the Queen will follow."

It was a strategy the general had heard over and over for days. He wondered if his master's mind was damaged in some way, that he kept repeating himself to no purpose. "And when will we begin, Master?" he asked, careful to include himself so that it would not appear he was demanding anything of the End.

"This evening, I think. The spell I'm thinking of works best in the dark."

Omeyo couldn't help himself. "And what of your old plans to destroy the world?"

The End regarded him as if he'd crossed a line, but then seemed to relax. "One cannot eat the whole cake before one has taken a first bite. Let us dispatch our enemies and then turn our attentions to everyone else."

When had the End become so rational?

As if he heard Omeyo's thoughts, the sorcerer continued, "I have learned a great deal during my brief exile. I have learned from the many mistakes—and some victories—of all my predecessors. I have acquired their memories and their skills. The next time the Reaper and I meet in battle, he will be facing a very different End-of-All-Things."

The End appraised his general's condition and then said, "Yes, I have changed. You have changed as well. I sense a growing apathy within you. I would not tread too far down that road, were I you."

But you are not me, Omeyo thought. "Your pardon, Master. How does this offend?"

"Those who no longer care make reckless decisions. You remember that cretin, General Shere?"

"Yes."

"Yes. Of course you do. I will not have a recurrence of that fiasco. I will have your loyalty, Omeyo, and I will compensate you generously for it."

"As you say."

"But I feel a test is warranted."

Here it comes.

"I want you to kill the Svarren witch who has ensnared you so."

Omeyo looked back at the End with dead eyes. "As you say."

It was nighttime at last, and the End dismissed all his slaves, servants and other handlers. He needed privacy, he needed focus. He sent out a series of Questing Eyes and Ears, far more than he'd ever been able to manage in his earlier existence. If the real Reaper was out there somewhere, the End would find him. Oh, Vykers would be stunned to discover his nemesis alive again and more than stunned to learn the End held the A'Shea captive! The sorcerer almost cackled in anticipation, but quickly suppressed the urge as something the old End would have done. Now, he was calm, rational, and in complete control.

Vykers & Company, On the Road

Every time he dismounted, Vykers was reminded of the fantastic nature of his horse and the other horses in his group. In little more than three days, they'd covered a month's journey. They'd almost gone too far, too quickly. The Reaper wanted more time to sit with whatever was coming, more time to formulate some sort of plan. If this idiot who'd been calling himself the Reaper was really the End as Alheria claimed, then the lunatic was probably setting a trap. Rushing into it could prove fatal.

The things that had worked so well against the End last time had been disruption and distraction. The End had believed himself to be facing a much smaller, single force that had dug itself in at the top of a hill; he hadn't expected or anticipated attacks from multiple directions by several different types of opponents. Ultimately, he'd been forced to confront the Reaper directly, and that, ironically, had been the end of the End. Or so everyone thought.

Would the same tactic work a second time? Doubtful. And anyway, the Queen had said nothing about sending her troops north to support Vykers. And the fey? The Reaper wasn't expecting to hear from them, either. Not after the way he and Aoife had parted company. That left the Svarren, and from everything Vykers had seen, they were on the End's side this time around. Well, fuck 'em. Vykers would find other allies, or he would fight his way through the End's hordes by himself.

He was in the middle of removing his horse's saddle when Igraine approached him. She looked left and right to ensure no one else was listening and then said, "Why does a goddess need a mortal throne? So that she is easier to find."

Vykers was amazed that he hadn't thought of this himself. But after further thought, he said "Easier for who?"

"Someone who knows her true identity, like a relative."

The Reaper threw a blanket over his mount and fed her a handful of oats, while he turned this new idea over in his head. "That fits what you said earlier, that Alheria and the End are related in some way."

"Doesn't it, though?" Igraine beamed.

"Not sure I find it as funny as you do..."

"Not funny, not remotely amusing. But I think we are untangling this knot."

Vykers patted Igraine on the shoulder. "*You* are untangling it. The real question is, what do we do with the rope once it's straight again?"

Although they hadn't been travelling with Vykers long, his men had established a precise routine for setting up camp and another for taking it down. By the time the Reaper was done caring for his horse, a healthy fire was burning in the center of a ring of fast-rising tents, and one of the men was beginning to boil something over the flames. Vykers thought to fetch firewood, but as he turned to go, he saw Ngoro approaching with a great armload.

"You stay. Get warm. I go," he told Vykers.

Normally, the Reaper didn't allow anyone to order him about, but he supposed the Ntambi meant it out of respect; he didn't want the Reaper to bother with such a lowly task, which only meant he didn't know the Reaper. No task was too low, and no throne was too high. If he had to kill Alheria at the end of all this shit, well, so be it.

He found a wood axe near the fire and again thought of helping procure firewood when Hjuest approached him.

"He told you to stay, yah?"

"He did. And I don't like being told what to do."

Hjuest shook his head. "He vas meaning to save you verk."

"Huh," Vykers grunted. "I need to do something besides sit in the saddle all day."

The red knight smiled. "I understand dat."

"Look," said Vykers, "I know Ngoro's not of your tribe…"

"Country."

"Right, country. But what about these others? How is it you can talk to them?"

"I just…learn. Is strange. Back home, I never knew I could speak like dis. So many langvages."

This peaked Vykers' interest. "How many?"

"Nine. With my own."

"You speak nine languages?" the Reaper repeated, stunned.

"Yah, but not very good."

"Good enough. You're a capable fighter. You are. But you shoulda been a herald, or an ambassador."

Hjuest looked well pleased with the comment, and Vykers resolved that if they all survived the next few days and weeks, he'd send the knight off to university. The Reaper had never had much use for bookish types before, but between the red knight and the erstwhile goblin, Vykers was discovering the value of talents that didn't involve bloodshed. He must have understood this before, surely, but relevant memories eluded him. As always.

Dinner was stew of a type Vykers had never tasted before. The ingredients were recognizable enough, but the company's self-appointed cook had used a combination of herbs and spices completely unfamiliar to the Reaper. The flavors were at once hotter and smokier than he was used to, and yet he found he could not stop eating the stuff. He was about to reach for a fifth bowl when the ground beneath him trembled and shook, causing him and everyone else to abandon their meals and brace for trouble.

Night had fallen, and shadows had grown to usurp the world around the camp, making it difficult to see the source of the tremors now growing in magnitude. Suddenly, the snow and ice surrounding the camp coalesced into something huge and manlike. In seconds, a face formed, and icy eyes swept Vykers' crew in search of the Reaper, himself.

"Ah!" said a booming voice that the Reaper recognized in an instant. "There you are, Reaper!"

Vykers gestured to his men to stand down, as he stood up. "Nice lookin' snowman you've got there."

The ice golem sneered at the comment. "As witty as ever, I see. I wonder, will you laugh when you see what I've got to show you?"

The End expected Vykers to follow his script, to ask "What have you got to show me?" But that was not Vykers' way. Instead, he sat back down and reached for his stew, as if the golem didn't even exist. Following his lead, Vykers' men did likewise.

"Fool!" the End screamed. "I've captured your A'Shea friend. How can you think to defeat me without her?"

Vykers remained seated, but turned at the waist and regarded the icy apparition. He casually dipped a hunk of hard bread into his bowl as if he were dining with a friend. "Caught the woman, did you? Good luck with her!" he quipped.

The End opened a window in the night air and an image appeared of a large boulder of ice with something dark trapped inside.

"Well, if it's really all the same to you, I think I shall have a little fun with her before I freeze her completely."

"Freeze her, don't freeze her. I'm still going to kill you again. And this time, I won't even leave enough of you for the worms to enjoy."

The golem roared and attacked. Its massive arms were like logs, smashing Vykers' men out of its way as it fought to close with the Reaper. For a moment, Vykers considered using the dagger, but decided against it. Better to leave that secret 'til needed. He grabbed the wood axe he'd almost taken earlier and bounded towards the ice monster. As he drew near, it blasted him with a gust of air so cold that he almost fell over from the shock of it. Fortunately, his men were seasoned, determined fighters. With Vykers occupying the golem's attentions, they spread out around the thing and attacked its legs. The golem's breath seemed to have a much greater impact on Vykers' companions, and several of them did fall to the ground, curled up like babies to conserve their waning warmth. The monster could not last, however, with so many men attacking it and Vykers in front. The Reaper dodged a sweeping blow from an arm and planted his axe halfway through the creature's shoulder with one mighty cleave. Soon, the attached arm would be lost to it. Vykers held onto the axe haft and kicked hard against the monster's torso in an effort to free his weapon. Because his men had been at work on the creature's flanks, its legs were weakened and it began to topple backwards. The Reaper jerked his axe free and delivered a second blow to the same spot, sheering right through the golem's shoulder. With a crack, it fell away, only to be replaced by the rapidly growing nub of a new arm. Again, the thing blasted Vykers with impossibly cold air, and he felt his skin burning under the assault. New arms—several of them—sprouted from the thing's torso, making the men's job that much harder. It made sense to Vykers, though: this monster wasn't human. Why restrict itself to human anatomy?

"Let's throw this fucker in the fire!" he yelled to his men.

The monster's legs fused into a central column that made it harder for the thing to move, but also harder to be moved. Vykers ran to the fire, placed the head of his axe in the coals, and took up a burning branch instead.

"Here!" he called to the nearest man. "If we can't pull him into the fire, we'll rebuild the fire around him!"

Soon, the other men had caught on to the Reaper's plan and numerous pieces of blazing firewood began to accumulate around the monster. Vykers retrieved his fire-heated axe and took great, sweeping swings at the thing's face, more to provide cover for his men than in any hope of doing real damage. There was a peculiar hissing of air, and a number of men yelled in surprise or pain as they were pelted with icicles shot from the golem's torso.

"Gods! The cold!" one of those stricken cried out.

"There'll be worse if we don't stop this bastard!" the Reaper said. With a great lunge, he planted his axe in the monster's neck. It did not howl, as he might've expected, but only grimaced in his direction and continued its assault on his crew. But Hjuest and the others were relentless in building and stoking a fire around their assailant and, as powerful as it was, it was only a matter of time before the combined might of the flames and Vykers' men proved too much for the golem. It did not die abruptly, but rather it slowly diminished until it was nothing more than a large pile of slush.

The End-of-All-Things' laughter rang out of the lowering sky. It was not a sound full of rage, but delight.

TWELVE

The Giants, In the Forest

It was a surprisingly difficult parting for the giants and Esmine, who put her little hands onto their faces and studied them in their smallest details, as if she would sculpt her dead mother's face from theirs. Karrakan, who'd come to care the most for the changeling girl, seemed utterly stricken to leave her behind, and even Beesmarch was more subdued in his habitual negativity. But it was Eoman who seemed to suffer most, which was odd, because he'd tried so hard to avoid becoming attached.

"I am king," he explained to his friends, "but I'll be king of nothing if we don't have more wee ones like this here!"

"Tush!" Zillia chuckled. "If we die out, it'll be because our men are so soft-hearted! Now go out and fight those damned Svarren. Clear the north of their stink once and for all! We'll still be here when you return."

They were standing just outside the mouth of Zillia's magical cave. There was an enchanting pinkness to the morning sky, the air really, as if it had been stained that way by the rising sun. It seemed auspicious, though no one was willing to say so aloud.

Eoman reached out a hand and stroked Esmine's cheek a final time with one large finger. "You be good to Zillia, now," he warned.

Her resultant smile put the morning sun to shame.

"Let's go," Beesmarch snapped, though no one believed his irritability in this instance.

With a final backward glance, Karrakan waved goodbye and followed his friends back into the forest. If the brothers were anywhere within a hundred miles, they'd be easily found.

And the principle reason for this was that their sibling rivalry knew no limits when it came to eating, wenching and killing. Eoman and his friends came upon an area that looked as if it had been hit by a tornado...except that tornadoes never occurred this far north.

"This devastation has a certain familiarity to it," Karrakan observed.

"My thoughts, too," said Eoman.

Beesmarch, as was his wont, simply grumbled.

They followed the wreckage of trees, bushes, and Svarren until they spotted the smoke from a campfire in the distance, and the sound of an argument reached their ears.

"That's them," Beesmarch frowned.

And he was correct. Huddled around a fire with their backs to their king's approach, the brothers—all three—were slapping and punching and poking at each other over a haunch of Mahnus-knew-what.

"Trandle," Eoman called.

All three giants turned in unison, ready to attack whoever it was that had interrupted their squabbling. Upon seeing their king and his friends, they relaxed considerably and broke into wide grins. The brothers, as they were known by anyone who spoke of them, were hirsute to the point of looking like oursine. Thick black manes graced their heads, and wiry black hair grew on their arms and even the backs of their fingers. They were younger than Eoman, Karrakan or Beesmarch, and possessed of a youthful enthusiasm that was almost infectious—almost, because Beesmarch at least was immune to enthusiasm.

"Are there any more of our folk hereabouts, do you think?" the king asked.

"Not that I've heard," Broadus responded.

It was not difficult to convince the brothers to join in Eoman's Svarren hunt, and though they were only six in number, they made a formidable force nonetheless.

"How do we start?" Trandle asked.

"The Long Teeth trails seem to be converging and heading in the same direction."

"North."

"Aye. North."

"Then we go north," said Calder, the third of the brothers.

"Brilliant," snapped Beesmarch, just loud enough so everyone heard.

Despite Beesmarch's superior size, Trandle shot him a look that promised violence if the jibes didn't cease forthwith. "Any idea what they're after?" he inquired of his king.

"Damned if I know," Eoman returned. "They've a habit of banding together once in a rare while. Planning something nasty, no doubt."

Broadus laughed—a big, rollicking sound. "Think I'll set me a record, then. Never killed more than fifty Svarren in one day. Might be, I'll get ten times that!"

This set off a boasting contest that lasted through the rest of the day, with Calder finally promising to exterminate every last Svarren in the world, to Eoman's great amusement.

"I'll hold you to it, friend!" he grinned affably.

"There's one thing bothers me," Beesmarch admitted. "Where's everyone else? We can't be the only ones in the north fed up with these filthy bastards."

Eoman combed his fingers through his beard and allowed that he'd wondered the same. "There's only two kinds of folk, when it comes to Svarren: those who stand and fight, and those who flee. You'd think we'd see one or the other soon enough, no?"

"I expect we will, any time now," Karrakan answered.

"Humph!" said Beesmarch.

Kittins & Rem, On the Road

Even in the bitter cold, they could smell the dead. Kittins gestured for Rem to slow his horse, and both men proceeded in silence. No other odors came to the ruin of Kittins' nose, but he pointed to it anyway and then to Rem's. *Do you smell anything?*

Rem shook his head. No smoke, no sweat, no horse dung.

There'd been a massacre up ahead, sure. But whoever had done it had moved on, leaving only the dead. As quietly as possible, Kittins drew his sword and indicated that Rem should do the same. They continued forward.

The snow was covered in blood so dark it was almost black, except in spots where thinner traces of it showed it to be red. Svarren and parts of Svarren were scattered everywhere, and amongst their remains, footprints.

Giant footprints.

Kittins dismounted and stooped to examine the prints, and it struck Rem that the captain looked like a predator, stalking his prey. But only a madman would stalk a giant.

"There's more than one o' these," Kittins breathed.

And only a madman with a death wish would stalk a group of giants.

"Any idea how many?"

Kittins stood and wandered through the maze of bloody offal. "Three or four, maybe. And it doesn't much matter if it's three or four, 'cause that's too many for us."

Rem pursed his lips, thinking. "Why assume they're hostile to us?"

"They're damned well hostile to Svarren."

"Which we aren't," Rem pointed out. "And anyway, anyone who hates Svarren can't be all bad."

Kittins coughed and Rem understood he was being laughed at. "You're too trusting. That'll get you killed one o' these days."

The actor wanted to ask, "And what has distrust done for you, but ruined your face and your life?" But the plain truth was, he was afraid of the captain, afraid that crossing him at the wrong time—and who could even guess when that might be?—would result in an instant beheading.

"Still," Kittins went on, "I've a mind to follow these giants. Never seen more than one at a time before; this might be interesting."

In days gone by, the formerly vainglorious actor would have chafed at the insinuation that his company wasn't interesting enough for his companion, but he had learned that in the captain's world, *interesting* was often synonymous with *life-threatening*, and, at present, Rem craved nothing so much as the *un*interesting. In an effort to remain on the captain's good side—assuming there was such a thing—Rem nodded in agreement.

The giants were not difficult to follow, as they made no effort to hide their tracks. On those rare occasions when Kittins and Rem lost the trail, they were able to pick it up again with just a few minutes' search. On each of these occasions, Rem secretly hoped the trail could not be rediscovered, only to be frustrated when it was. Heading north to sate Kittins' curiosity no longer made any sense to the actor. If Cindor was going to kill them both anyway, why endure a single moment's discomfort more than they had already? Why couldn't they run away to the southwest, or even the chain of islands off its shores? That part of the country was reputed to be warm all year 'round, with an abundance of exotic fruits and beautiful women. It was an impossibly long journey, certainly, but every step away from this hell would be a reward in and of itself. Well, Rem supposed, Kittins would hardly kill him merely for broaching the subject...

"Have you ever been to the far southwestern lands?"

"Once," Kittins grunted.

Rem brightened immediately at this news. "Are they as beautiful as they say?"

"Some parts."

Damn the man's laconic nature! "For instance?"

Kittins glanced irritably at his companion. "What's this, an exercise in self-abuse?"

Now he was talking.

"Whatever do you mean?"

"We're slogging through half the infinite hells, and you wanna talk paradise?"

"Why not? It lightens the load."

"I'll lighten *your* load," Kittins grumbled.

Later in the day and quite unexpectedly, Kittins said, "The ocean down there's warm enough to swim in."

"Is it?" Rem asked, not daring to say too much or too little.

"Almost as warm as bath water, with great, mighty waves the locals love to float around in. And blue? You never saw such a color."

So, the captain did have a lighter side. "I'd love to see that someday before I die," said Rem.

"Fat chance."

Sometimes, it's better to keep one's mouth shut.

About an hour shy of sunset, the tracks they'd been following merged with another set of giant tracks. It appeared this new, larger group had lingered a while, perhaps discussing something, before eventually deciding to move off together.

Kittins was almost gleeful. "I've never seen more than one giant, and I damned sure never thought I'd see a whole pack of 'em. There have to be six or seven in this group now. And they're headed the same way we are."

"Well, they're clearly not on the Svarren's side, so perhaps they're mustering against them," Rem offered.

"Of course they are."

Rem reached into his saddle bag to find something to eat, was dismayed by his dwindling supply.

Kittins noticed Rem's unease and tossed him a large chunk of jerked meat. "Number one rule o' campaigning: always carry more food than you think you'll ever need."

"Oh? And how much did you bring?"

"Enough to last 'til the end of the world."

Judging by the size of the man's various packs and bags, that wouldn't be long in coming. Again, Rem lapsed into silence.

Vykers & Company, On the Road

They'd emerged from the forest along a vast ridge, stretching directly northward. Other ridges ran parallel, like the fingers of some long-dead titan. Vykers reined his horse in and summoned Hjuest to his side.

"What do see on that other ridge?"

The red knight turned to his right and peered across the valley to the next ridge. "Looks like people."

"Those ain't people. Not like you mean it," Vykers said, directing his own attention towards the distant figures. "Those are giants."

Hjuest's eyes grew large at the pronouncement. "Tvari!" he called to one of the other men. Tvari pushed his horse through the throng and came to Hjuest's side, whereupon the red knight said something in a language unknown to Vykers. Tvari then gazed over at the alleged giants.

"Sen!" He said to Hjuest. Correct.

Hjuest smiled. "Yah, it is chiants."

"Chiants?" Vykers mocked.

The red knight looked flummoxed. "Ya? So? Chiants. As you said."

"Five?"

Hjuest said a few more words to Tvari, who responded with a single syllable, and then the red knight said, "Six!" aloud.

"Six giants," Vykers repeated to himself. "Six giants. Sure like to know what they're up to."

"Maybe the same as us?"

The Reaper flexed his shoulders, thinking, and put his hands atop his head. "Maybe," he said at last, though he did so with little conviction. "Only one way to find out."

"You propose a meeting?"

"Aye."

The ridge seemed to stretch onward forever, and, once it became clear they'd never get off it before sunset, Vykers began looking for a suitable camp. There wasn't much cover on the ridge, which meant they were all in for an especially cold night. On the positive side, however, the giants on the far ridge would be able to spot Vykers' campfire with ease. Better to let the big folk know he was there, rather than sneaking up on 'em. If they came to him, they'd feel like they were in control and, thus, would be more liable to be congenial. Of course, more liable didn't mean 'certain,' but it'd do in a pinch.

There was just the slightest hint of pink on the eastern horizon and most of the men weren't awake yet, when the giants came strolling up the ridge from the north and into Vykers' camp. It seemed they'd walked most of the night in order to identify the source and owners of the fire they'd seen. Vykers wasn't sure who or what they'd been expecting, but he clearly wasn't it.

"You're Tarmun Vykers," one of them said in a voice so deep it was practically unintelligible.

Vykers didn't stand, didn't budge an inch from his spot near the fire. "I am," said he calmly. "Who are you?"

The noise of conversation awakened the rest of Vykers' men, who quickly determined that continued silence and stillness were the order of the moment. The Reaper had things in hand. Or so they hoped.

"We're a bunch of giants, aren't we?" snapped the largest of them. One of his peers gave him a warning glare and he said no more.

"If you're here as friends, sit and enjoy the fire."

"Friends remains to be seen," said the giant who had spoken first. "I am Eoman Harkin Hainen, King of giant folk."

The biggest giant rolled his eyes and scowled, but kept his mouth shut.

"And we'd like to know," Eoman continued, "what your intentions are so far north of your human capital."

"Hjuest! Igraine!" Vykers called, "Let's get some food on the fire, eh? We've got guests." As the red knight and the young woman set about fixing a meal for everyone, the Reaper went on. "If you know who I am, then you know *what* I am. I go where I want and I do what I list."

The giants were not enjoying the Reaper's attitude much, but, in their exhaustion, could not resist his fire.

Vykers continued. "As it happens, I'm lookin' for a man carryin' out raids with Svarren and using my name to do it."

"And what is this man after, do you think?" Karrakan prompted.

"Have to ask him that before I kill him."

The massive quantity of food Vykers' companions prepared was little more than an appetizer to the giants, but it was hot, flavorful and always better than nothing. Five of the six giants seemed content with the offering. Beesmarch, however, seemed to grow more irritable than usual.

"You talk like a giant, Reaper," said he. "But all I see is a little man."

The comment had an instantaneous impact on everyone else, setting nerves on edge and igniting a fresh sense of alarm. Those who'd been eating, stopped; those who were not, stood and began to creep away from the fire.

The Reaper merely put his feet up on a large piece of firewood and gazed at Beesmarch in an almost bored manner. "You're the dumb one, then, are you?"

Eoman fought back a grin and said, "Let's have no hostilities. It's Svarren we're after."

"And supposin' I *want* hostilities?" Beesmarch rumbled.

Vykers tossed the bone he'd been gnawing into the fire and stood, languidly. "I'm ready."

Eoman stood as well, his temper flaring. "Bees, as your king, I command you to leave be!"

Around the fire, everyone had risen and assumed defensive stances at some distance from the two would-be combatants.

"Or what? You'll kill me? Isn't that what this wee one is intent on?" he asked, indicating Vykers.

To everyone's astonishment, Igraine stepped between Beesmarch and Vykers and said, "I suggest a bout without weapons. First to cry 'enough' loses."

Eoman and the other giants stared hopefully at their surly friend, whilst the humans did the same towards their leader.

Beesmarch seemed to chew on the suggestion for an eternity and then responded, "Good."

Vykers said nothing, but his silence was taken as tacit agreement.

"Rules?" Hjuest inquired.

"None o' your human bullshit—no pullin' my beard, nor bashin' me in the gonads."

Vykers walked five or so paces away from the fire into an open area and looked back at Beesmarch. "Agreed." This last was said to reassure the giant, but Vykers had found that those who insisted on stringent rules were usually the first to break them. This Beesmarch would cheat. Of that, Vykers was certain.

The giant flexed and reflexed his hands, tightened his belt a notch and moved to face the Reaper.

"First to cry "Enough!" Karrakan reminded the opponents.

Beesmarch actually laughed. "Won't be me!" He took a step towards Vykers and readied himself for a massive swing at the Reaper's chest.

Vykers studied the giant. Even for his kind, he was immense, a mountain. And with that observation, he knew how to attack his foe.

Beesmarch swung and, to his amazement, completely missed his target. The Reaper dodged and danced away, just out of reach. "So, it's to be like that, is it?" the giant taunted.

"That and worse," Vykers quipped.

The giant feinted at the Reaper's head and aimed a kick right at the man's privates.

The Reaper dodged aside, grinned. "Just like I figured."

Beesmarch unleashed a series of sweeping swings, attempting to overwhelm the Reaper with the speed and number of his attacks. None came close to the Reaper. "Stand still and fight, you little gnat!" Beesmarch roared.

Vykers did not stand still; he continued to appear where he wasn't expected and vanish before the giant could hit him, to Beesmarch's ever-growing frustration.

"This ain't a fight!" he complained. "It's a bleedin' cinque-pace! Stand still, you bastard!"

The harder Beesmarch tried to connect, the more fatigued he became, until, inevitably, he was gasping for air. In that moment, Vykers ran forward, bounded off the giant's thigh, leapt up his chest and jabbed two fingers in each of Beesmarch's eyes—not hard enough to blind him permanently, but firmly enough to disable him for the near future.

Beesmarch bellowed in pain, raising his left hand to his face and lashing out blindly with his right. The fight was over, but he could not acknowledge it. The Reaper closed in to deliver a blow of his own and the giant roared with such volume and ferocity that Vykers temporarily lost all sense of where he was and what he'd been doing. In that brief span, Beesmarch flailed blindly and just managed to clip Vykers on his right shoulder, sending him spinning through the air like a spent firework. The force of the hit and his subsequent landing in the snow cleared Vykers' mind, brought him back to the present.

"Well struck, giant!" he exclaimed.

But Beesmarch was not mollified. Compensating for his injury and lack of sight, he lowered himself into a crouch, whereupon Vykers again leapt up and slammed his palms over both of the giant's ears with a loud popping noise. Beesmarch fell over backwards, his hands on his ears, his eyes clenched shut, and his mouth in a tight line of agony. Because he either could not or would not say "Enough," his king said it for him.

"Enough, the Reaper wins."

Vykers didn't gloat, but walked calmly back to his spot by the fire and rummaged for more to eat. His shoulder throbbed, but he wouldn't give Beesmarch—or anyone else—the satisfaction of thinking he could be hurt.

The brothers helped Beesmarch to his feet and dragged him back to the fire as well.

"A drink!" Hjuest called out, hoping the proposal would smooth over any feelings of resentment.

It did. The five giants not involved in the fight were more than willing to drink all of the humans' liquor and even produced a small amount of their own from deep pockets. Even Beesmarch, his vision blurry and his hearing muffled, could not resist a taste of the humans' ale forever. It was half-gone before noon, but there was no one left awake to rue the fact. The combination of constant travel and strong spirits proved too much for everyone.

The following morning, Beesmarch's eyes were red with blood, giving him a demonic appearance, and his ears rung like a million funeral bells. Yet all that was nothing compared to the hangover he endured. "You'd've done better to kill me," he grumbled at the Reaper.

"You'll feel better once we find the Svarren," Vykers responded.

Beesmarch smiled. "Yes," he admitted, "I expect I will."

The End & Omeyo, In Camp

The End was in an uncommonly good mood, which made

Omeyo more wary than usual, if such a thing was possible. Both men toured the Svarren camps, inspecting their readiness for departure, action or whatever else the End might require. The sorcerer spoke in hushed tones to various Svarren throughout the tour, but Omeyo caught none of it. Not that he cared. He understood by the End's buoyancy that everything was going according to plan, which meant that Tarmun Vykers and perhaps even the Virgin Queen would be arriving in the vicinity shortly.

Omeyo considered the differences between the last time the End had engaged Vykers and the Queen and this time. Last time, the End had possessed a much larger host, but a host devoid of independent thought, a host without an innate appetite for carnage and destruction. Last time, the fey—impossible creatures of legend—had engaged the End's flanks from the forest. This time, there was no forest. Last time, the Queen's army had been waiting for the End. This time, the sorcerer had attempted to goad the Reaper and Her Majesty into rushing northward to confront him, sans army. Only time would tell if that strategy worked, but the general couldn't believe the famed Reaper would be foolhardy enough to attack without an army at his back. Last time, the End had possessed a magic sword; this time, he had no such weapon, but instead held a hostage in the form of the frozen A'Shea. Last time, the End had been a petulant, volatile lunatic. Now, he seemed more seasoned, more rational. Would any or all of these factors be enough to win the coming conflict? Omeyo had no way of knowing, but as he wanted nothing more than a swift death himself, he didn't suppose it much mattered either way.

Tooth and Nail appeared out of nowhere and watched Omeyo with hooded eyes as the End spoke to them. They were likely aware that their master had changed, that the End who'd given them permission to abuse the general had been supplanted, and now they stood upon uncertain ground. Did this new End still favor them over the general, or would he someday punish them for what they'd done? And what role did Omeyo himself play? If he gave the word, would his master kill his Svarren body guards?

In their primitive, savage faces, the general saw contempt,

resentment and even fear, which told him they would strike again if they could find a way to avoid the master's wrath. But the death they promised would not be swift, so Omeyo couldn't allow it. More, he supposed he'd have to find a way to kill the Svarren first. Again, the master came to mind. If only Omeyo could trick Tooth and Nail into doing something counter to the End's wishes...

"Time was, I was wont to pretend I could read your mind. Would that I truly could, general. Your face betrays a thousand private thoughts more interesting than anything I see on this frozen plain," the End said, interrupting Omeyo's scheming. "What are you thinking on?"

"I was remembering a battle in my youth," Omeyo lied.

"Be grateful you can recall your youth," the End said cryptically.

"I am, Master," Omeyo lied again. "But have you no instructions for me as regards the disposition of your forces?"

The End laughed. "It seems you've read *my* mind, general. I have found a mountain somewhat north and east of us that will serve our purposes. We'll set the host in that direction on the morrow, and there we'll lay our trap." Just when the general thought the conversation complete, the End said, "And have you killed that Svarren slut as I bid you?"

"Your pardon, Master," Omeyo sputtered. "I thought it best to catch her sleeping, which she hasn't done since you gave the order. It will be accomplished soon, though, according to your wishes."

The sorcerer nodded.

Omeyo waited patiently to hear more, but the End said nothing further, choosing instead to turn away and walk through the camp. Seeing that Tooth and Nail were still within ten strides or so, Omeyo quickly set off in pursuit of his master.

Aoife, Captive

She imagined herself standing naked on a glacier somewhere, the cruel wind raging between her legs, wrapping around her waist, whipping beneath her arms, and tearing through her hair. The cold was terrible, a malevolent, hungry thing whose appetite never abated and whose presence never faded.

On some level, Aoife understood that these thoughts, these sensations meant she was still alive. She remembered being struck by something and thrown onto a woodpile. There had followed a desperate struggle that seemed to last for ages. She was comfortable for a while, until she was not. Now, she was freezing and unable to rouse herself from her preternatural sleep. Something—everything—was wrong. Still, the Umaena would not allow herself to fade into oblivion without a fight.

Below her, far, far under the snow, she found seeds, frozen and sleeping just like her. But Aoife would wake them...if only she could maintain her concentration. She would...she would...

Something about seeds. Yes, *her* seeds. They were down there, in the dark, in the cold, awaiting her commands. She would conjure them from their dormancy and compel them to free her from...from...

They would embrace her, impart warmth, and carry her away.

Sprouts forced their way through the ice and snow inside the tent that held the Umaena. There were several Svarren guarding the tent on the outside, stationed so as to prevent entry, but none had imagined the most dangerous threat would come from within, and so the vines grew undetected. The block of ice that imprisoned Aoife had numerous fissures too small to be seen by mortal eyes, but not too small to be found by the creeping tendrils of the thing the Umaena had summoned. It worked its way inside the cracks and pushed, pulled, burgeoned into something large enough to burst the ice wide open.

The Svarren heard this noise and charged into the tent to investigate.

They never made it out again.

Mardine, On the Road

Mardine spotted a long train of refugees and made her way towards them as carefully, as openly as possible. The last thing she wanted was to frighten them into running away or, worse, attacking her.

They barely looked up at her approach, which told her something about their determination to keep moving.

"May I walk with you?" she asked the nearest man.

He looked at her from the corner of his eyes, but kept his focus on the trail in front of him. "A giant? Can't hurt to have you in our number."

"You're running from Svarren, aren't you?"

"And who ain't?"

"Have you seen a girl, might look a little like me?"

The fellow shook his head, kept plodding forward. "I seen some o' yer kinfolks' tracks, though."

This news just about dropped Mardine. "You what?"

"Said I seen some giant tracks a ways back. Not yourn. Too big, too many."

Suddenly, the giantess' heart was beating too rapidly and her breath was coming in great gulps. More giants? She'd never seen more than two at a time herself. Would she know any of them? Would they help her find Esmine or even rescue her if necessary?

"Which way?"

"North, o' course!" the man answered.

Mardine was gone before her "Thank you" reached the fellow's ears. She trotted along the refugees' back trail, wanted to race full speed towards the promised tracks, but fearing she'd run out of energy before she found them. She took a moment to glance backwards at the fleeing peasants, but they had already disappeared from sight. If Mardine had other questions, the opportunity to ask them was lost to her now. All she could do was press onwards and hope it didn't snow until she found what she was looking for.

Hope, however, had little impact on the weather, and Mardine hadn't travelled for more than fifteen minutes before tiny flakes began wafting down from above. *Well,* she hoped again, *maybe it won't get worse.* But of course it did. Soon, the snow was pelting her, burying the refugees' trail and everything else it encountered, including hope.

Mardine plunked herself down in the snow and wept in frustration. How many hardships had she endured? How many leagues had she walked, and how many meals had she missed? She would have done anything for Esmine, no question. But had all this sacrifice brought her any closer to finding her child? Briefly, the giantess considered lying down and letting the cold have her. Humans had a favorite curse, "Endless hells;" Mardine thought maybe she'd visited them all, and each was only a different type of pain. Endless pain. Fear, hunger, cold, fatigue, loneliness, regret, guilt—all of these and more too numerous to name made up Mardine's endless hells. Was this what men meant? What could possibly be worse than a mother's agony?

Tears froze on her cheeks, eliciting an hysterical laugh from the giantess. *Bad as it is for me, it must be worse for my little one.*

Mardine heaved herself onto her feet and resumed walking. After a time, she came upon a channel underneath the snow, crossing her path perpendicularly. On a hunch, she got down on hands and knees and scraped the snow away.

She'd found the tracks!

Joy flooded through her weary body so quickly, so entirely, that it temporarily overwhelmed her senses, and she sat back on her haunches, stupefied, like someone who'd just taken a great blow to the head. Her kinfolk! And not just two or three, but several! With frenzied speed, she scraped more snow off the footprints and tried to determine their makers' direction. West? Northwest? She couldn't be sure, but she did believe she could follow the channel they'd made well enough, snow storm or not.

For the longest time, Mardine had secretly worried that her daughter was dead—and Alheria knew she still might be—but worse still was the notion that Esmine was alive and Mardine simply could not find her in the vastness of the north. What could one giant do in all that space? But many giants? Many giants increased Mardine's chances of finding her child considerably.

The hope that had forsaken her earlier began to creep back into her bosom. Her inner cold, at last, began to thaw.

Omeyo & The End, In Camp

It was simple enough, really. Omeyo instructed one of the more credulous Svarren to deliver a large barrel of liquor to some of his brethren, who not so coincidentally lived within earshot of Tooth and Nail. Once the barrel was breached and the debauchery began, Tooth and Nail couldn't fail to notice and wander by to determine the reason for the revelry. Being Svarren—and especially nasty ones at that—they proceeded to lay claim to the liquor, even though it had not been delivered to them. This led, predictably, to a brawl that eventually ensnared every Long Tooth within two hundred paces. By the time Tooth and Nail and their supporters prevailed, a score of Svarren were wounded or dying, and someone had pissed into the barrel. Fortunately, the liquor in question was Skent, so a little more urine made no noticeable difference.

Having won the barrel, Tooth and Nail had it dragged back to their yurt, where they and their companions proceeded to drink it at an astounding rate. Soon, they were buggering everyone who came within arms' reach and killing those who resisted. Somehow the yurt caught on fire, but Tooth and Nail were so busy eating one of their former comrades that they failed to notice until it was too late. They then attacked the remainder of their supporters for allowing such a catastrophe to occur and, before long, the whole area erupted in bloodshed...

Which is exactly why the End had kept the entire host's alcohol under lock and key. Svarren are notoriously bad drunks, especially when the liquor in question is Skent. Sadly, the only witness to the barrel's provenance, the Svarren who'd carried it for Omeyo, had been killed in the first round of violence, so no one was able to enlighten a furious End-of-All-Things when he finally got wind of the disaster.

He came flaming out of the sky like a fallen star and thudded to a stop right in front of Tooth and Nail, who suddenly became terribly distracted by their own navels, their nails, or, in short, anything that took them away from the sorcerer's face.

"What," the End roared, "in the infinite hells is going on here? General Omeyo!"

The general rounded the nearest yurt at a trot, holding a map and a still-wet quill in his hand, as if he'd been working on war plans.

"Master?" he inquired, confused. When his eyes took in the devastation around him, the color drained from his visage.

"Explain this," the End demanded.

Omeyo looked around again, utterly bewildered. "It appears...the Svarren fought amongst themselves. There is a strong stink of alcohol. Perhaps..."

"Yes, yes, yes! I can bloody well see they fought over alcohol. But you witnessed none of this?"

"No, Master. I was working on the plans for decampment, so the army would be ready to march tomorrow as you commanded." Omeyo again held up the map and the ink quill.

The End rubbed his temples and heaved a sigh of exasperation. "Savages," he spat at Tooth and Nail. "You are aptly named. One of you must pay for this fiasco. Which of you will it be, however?"

The two Svarren immediately set upon one another, claws extended and teeth bared. So much for friendship. The End stepped backwards so as not to get any blood on his robes, whilst everyone else pressed forward to watch the spectacle, which was falling out exactly as Omeyo had planned.

In short order, both combatants were slathered in bloody filth, each fighting frantically to gain some advantage. One had lost an ear, but he'd bitten his rival's nose off. Omeyo nearly laughed aloud, but worried how that might look to his master. The loud snapping of bone heralded a decisive turn of events, and one Svarra staggered clear of his nemesis, his left arm hanging limply at his side. The more-whole of the Svarren sensed momentum was turning in his favor and leapt at his injured foe, focusing all his energies on the creature's only healthy arm. It was not a good strategy, because the one-armed fellow still had a mouth with plenty of jagged teeth, which he proceeded to sink into his tormentor's neck. The one bitten made the most natural and unfortunate choice of attempting to pull away, only to have a large chunk of his throat ripped out. Blood geysered from the wound, even as the Svarra held up a hand to stop it. Now, it was the one-armed combatant who pushed the attack, and his rapidly fading enemy who scrambled to defend himself. The wound to his neck was too great, however, and he finally collapsed into the slushy crimson snow. One-arm gave his body a thorough beating before turning back to the End for approval and was relieved to see the master smiling beatifically.

"Good show!" the End shouted. "Good show!"

And then he set the victor on fire with a snap of his fingers.

The Svarra shrieked and howled in torment and then joined his former companion on the ground.

"There will be discipline in my camp!" the End proclaimed, "Even if you are savages. Those we go to face will offer no quarter. They'll exploit every weakness. If any of you are as witless as these two," he nodded at the corpses of Tooth and Nail, "say so now, and you shall be free to go. If, on the other hand, you have the intelligence and the will to restrain yourselves until ordered to attack, unlimited plunder shall be yours!"

Those Svarren standing witness to the drama of the last few minutes roared their approval. Omeyo roared his, as well, though his reasons were different: he'd defeated his attackers with minimal effort and no trace of culpability.

He wondered if he might do the same to the End.

Alheria, Arune & Cindor, the Castle

The truth was that the Queen, Alheria, did not have the standard and expected contingent of Shapers, and the more Arune thought about it, the more sense it made. Her Majesty was a goddess, after all, the most powerful Shaper in existence. So Cindor had been—what?—cover? And why had Her Majesty bothered to take Arune under her wing? As gifted as she was, Arune was not the Shaper Cindor had been. What was Alheria playing at?

Even as she pondered this question, she was whisked from her chambers and dropped into Her Majesty's presence in the middle of an unfamiliar room.

"See," the Queen instructed without turning to acknowledge Arune's arrival, "the consequences of duplicity!"

Alheria stepped aside and revealed an odd shape resting on a table against the far wall. As Arune moved closer, she saw to her horror that it was Cindor's head. Sprouting from beneath his jawline was a great tumor—what Arune assumed to be the makings of his new body. The tumor, in turn, was nestled in a wide, shallow bowl with some sort of fabric at its bottom. The Queen's Shaper watched Arune's approach with his one remaining eye, his gaze full of embarrassment and contempt.

"*That's* my replacement?" he croaked in a voice that seemed to come from someone, some*where* else.

"Not a replacement," Her Majesty replied. "But perhaps a more obedient substitute. And no one alive knows more about Tarmun Vykers."

"Yes, yes. And Brouton's Bind?" Cindor spat.

"Has served us well, so far."

This was news to Arune, though its meaning was not immediately clear. Arune had suffered, *still* suffered from Brouton's Bind, and the Queen had made use of that fact? How? In what ways?

Cindor sneered. "And her current body?"

Alheria looked over at Arune, but continued to address Cindor, as if Arune weren't even present. "I very much doubt she will bind with *that*."

Reasoning she had nothing to lose, Arune cut in, "And what am I to make of this conversation, your Majesty?"

The Queen put her hands on Cindor's bald pate and he fell asleep. "Only that it is unwise to second-guess my orders and decisions. As it happens, Cindor is worth my trouble. *You* may not be. Do as I say, when I say, and you may come out of this in good shape."

"Yes, Highness."

"Now," the Queen said, "tell me everything you know about the Reaper."

Vykers & Alheria, In Camp

Vykers wandered away from the fire in order to relieve himself, and showed not the least surprise when Her Majesty materialized at his side.

"You got some special fascination with my privates?" the Reaper quipped, remembering a time when the Queen had commanded him to drop his breeches.

"You're the one waving them around all the time."

"Huh. What tidings? Shitty, I'm guessin'."

"I have verified that it is indeed the End-of-All-Things causing such trouble in the north."

Vykers shook out the last drops of piss. It wasn't pleasant when the stuff froze on the legs. "You'd know."

The Queen stiffened. "And what is that supposed to mean?"

"Bein' his mother and all."

Her Majesty's lips formed a hard, tight line. For several heartbeats, she appeared to stop breathing. "Is that what he told you?"

The Reaper snorted. "Ha! You think I'd believe anything he told me?" He was getting rather cold so far from the fire, so he crossed his arms over his chest and pretended to have all the patience in the world.

"Then where did you hear such a thing?"

"You don't deny it."

The Queen gestured, and a chair appeared at her back. Without looking at it, she sat and gathered her robes and furs about herself. The chair should have sunken into the snow, but did not. "I have made a few mistakes over the years. Who hasn't?"

"The End-of-All-Things is a big fuckin' mistake."

"Yes."

"Look, if you're not gonna provide a chair for me as well, can we at least have a little fire?"

Alheria waved her hand again and an area of warmth bloomed into being between her and the Reaper. "Campaigner's Fire," she said. "I would still like to know where you got this information."

Vykers cracked his neck nonchalantly. "And I'd still like to know why you didn't tell me this when I first faced that bastard."

"What difference would it have made? He posed a terrible threat and needed to be eliminated."

"And you, o' course, don't like killin' your own."

It was subtle, but Her Majesty winced at this comment. "Whereas you have no compunctions about whom or what you'll kill."

"I do not, no. So, how many other godlings you got runnin' around the countryside?"

"Let's talk about the End; he's the immediate problem."

"Until another one o' your bastards crawls out from under some rock and decides to fuck with us? Maybe I don't like cleanin' up after you."

Her Majesty produced a flask from the depths of her clothing, uncorked it, and took a healthy swig. "You are many things, Tarmun Vykers, but a good liar is not among them. You live to kill."

"I'm beginnin' to see that being a god has its limitations."

It was the Queen's turn to snort. "How little you know!"

"So, you interrupted a perfectly good piss to tell me the End is the End. Hardly seems worth leaving your castle for that."

"I came here to tell you that I plan to be present for his death this time."

Vykers smirked. "I'm sure he'll appreciate that."

"You're an insolent thing, Tarmun Vykers."

He bowed and began walking back to the campfire.

"And we'll have our own day of reckoning, you and I!" the Queen called after him.

"Lookin' forward to it!" he called back without turning around.

Kittins & Rem, On the Road

The north was unimaginably expansive, yes, and the part of it that Kittins and Rem had ridden into was naught but a great, snow-covered plain. When the weather was clear, a man could see for miles. At night, a fire could be spotted from an even greater distance. Kittins maintained that night-time fires were meant either as defensive measures or as traps; the only difficulty for those outside the fire's glow lay in determining which it was.

Rem stared at the far-off beacon, quite a ways to his right and somewhat behind him, and predicted the captain would insist on investigating.

"I say we go take a look."

Ha! That was all very well and good for Kittins, but Rem did not relish the idea.

"You can stay here if you like," the captain said, knowing Rem would do no such thing.

"And what is your plan if those tending that fire are hostile?"

"Kill 'em."

"Of course," Rem answered sarcastically.

"Well what the fuck else is there?" Kittins almost shouted, so fed up was he with Rem's resistance. "Kill or flee. And I ain't fleeing 'til killing's been tried and failed."

We could leave well enough alone, Rem thought. *Don't investigate in the first place.*

"Whoever it is might have food to share and liquor, might have news, or even a bleedin' map."

That, at least, made sense.

Rem put his hands up in a gesture of surrender. "As you wish."

"Smartest thing you've said in some time."

They rode slowly, carefully towards the fire, steeling themselves for whatever might eventuate. It was a much longer ride than either man had guessed, but when they were a few hundred yards out, Kittins pulled up and fixated on his saddle horn.

"What?" said Rem.

"See for yourself. Some o' those sitting 'round that fire are too big to be human."

Giants. And yet there were a number of humans as well.

"What are you thinking?"

"Giants and humans don't normally travel together," Kittins replied. "But they might do, if they were stalkin' a common enemy."

"Svarren?"

"Maybe. Or the Reaper."

"Or the End-of-All-Things."

"As we're none o' them, I don't see the harm in approaching."

What if they didn't like strangers coming at them out of the dark? Rem wondered. *Especially ones who looked like the captain.*

From the perspective of those around the fire, those approaching were more of a curiosity than a threat, although the bigger one looked like he'd been dead for ages.

Before Kittins could hail the camp, someone in the camp hailed him and his companion. "State yer business!"

"No business," Rem offered. "Just hoping to share your fire."

Three of the giants stood up, humongous silhouettes against the fire.

"Just the two o' you?"

"Just two," said Kittins.

"Dismount and come on, then."

Kittins and Rem did as instructed and led their horses the rest of the way. With every step, more details became apparent, and Rem's nervousness grew. Six giants? He'd never seen more than Mardine.

A lone man stood and turned towards them. "Mahnus' balls! Is that the Dead One I see?"

Rem was confused, but Kittins grinned and strode forward.

"So I've been called. And you are?" But as he drew nearer, he could clearly see who'd addressed him: the Reaper. "Apologies," said Kittins. "The light's not so good out here."

Those around the fire made way for the new arrivals, and one fellow in red even took care of the visitors' mounts.

Although he was a bit taller than Vykers, Kittins was still awestruck to find himself in the legend's presence. "Everyone knows who *you* are," he said, "but how is it you know about *me*?"

Vykers put a hand on the captain's shoulder. "You…did me a favor once."

"Did I?"

"Aye. But you'd never believe me if I told you about it. Point is, I owe you one. Welcome to our fire."

Rem was too stunned to talk. To meet both the Reaper and a half dozen giants in the same instant was almost too much to credit.

"Tarmun Vykers," the Reaper said, as he extended a hand to the actor.

"Remuel Wratch," Rem stammered.

Vykers laughed heartily at this. "The man who's been making his fortune playin' me? What's the money like?"

"Unimpressive, I'm afraid," said Rem. "Word is, I died a while back."

"You and me both!" Kittins added.

"I hear a good tale in the offing!" Karrakan said, not wanting to be left out of the discussion.

"And we'll have it!" Vykers declared, "Though we've no ale left to draw it out of you."

But the Reaper didn't hear most of it. He recognized the signs and felt himself again in the grip of something larger than himself, something directing and dictating his purpose. How else to explain his habit of finding an army just when he needed it most? He'd been alone, and then he'd found Turley. The two of them had run into Vykers' former slaves, still eager to serve. The group of them had happened upon six giants. And now, the Dead One himself had wandered into the Reaper's company. It remained to be seen whether or not the actor was worth anything in a fight; still and all, Vykers' army was growing. Would it be enough when they met up with the End-of-All-Things?

It would have to be.

The End & Omeyo, In Camp

The End had taken some pride in his newfound equanimity; it was, he thought, the secret to finally besting the Reaper and that old hag, the Virgin Queen. Little by little, however, he could feel it dissolving in the face of unforeseen setbacks. First, his bodyguard had taken it upon themselves to obliterate a good portion of their squad—or whatever it was Svarren called their stinking troops. Now, to the End's extreme aggravation, his captive had escaped! The A'Shea was loose in his camp and who knew what damage she was capable of wreaking upon the End's plans?

Without waiting another moment, the sorcerer shot into the air above his horde, set himself aflame and thundered commands to his Svarren.

"The human woman has escaped! Find her and kill her! Do not pause, do not speak with her, but kill her immediately!"

He repeated this message several times over until he was sure every last Svarra had seen or heard it, and then he descended gently to the ground and extinguished his flames. He'd suffered no damage, of course, but the urge to *inflict* damage still burned bright within him.

"Omeyo!" he yelled.

The general appeared almost instantaneously. It occurred to the End that he could make Omeyo appear whenever he wanted, magically rip him away from whatever he was doing and drop him right in front of his master, but the sorcerer had no desire to catch the man with his pants down. Besides, the End rather enjoyed watching the general scramble to please.

"Your will?"

"We shall have to delay our decampment until the A'Shea has been caught and killed. I should never have left her alive, but we will correct that oversight shortly. In the meantime, send out the scouts. Instruct them not to engage, but to return as soon as they see anyone or anything approaching our position. As soon as the A'Shea is dead, we march."

But no one could find the A'Shea, the Umaena, for she'd been taken back underground by the very plant she'd sprouted. There, the roots led her along pathways no mortal had ever seen, travelled or imagined, until she was again ensconced in the greenwood. Oh, there was snow and ice, without question. But what did the mightiest of trees care? Their new High Priestess had been delivered unto them, and they would nurture the Umaena back to full health as if she were all that mattered in the wide world.

Back in the End's camp, the sorcerer's calm façade continued to crumble and crack. His inability to find Aoife, much less determine how she'd escaped, was giving him fits, providing an unwelcome distraction when he most needed focus. He knew the Reaper was coming, and the Queen would not be far behind him. He wanted everything to fall out just as he'd planned, demanded, in fact. Aoife was not cooperating, however, and the End wondered, for the millionth time, why he hadn't killed her back in their family home, all those years ago. He clenched his teeth in irritation and called out to his general. It was embarrassing, but he'd have to reverse his earlier decision and move the army without finding Aoife. This made him look and feel weak, and he hated himself for it. Moving the Svarren and getting them ready for war might well erase the stench of this latest failure.

"Your will?" Omeyo asked as he stepped into view.

"We'll decamp according to our original plan. I'll not waste another moment on this cowardly A'Shea."

"As you wish." Omeyo nodded and bowed out of the End's presence.

Yes, the End thought. *As I wish.*

Cindor, the Castle

Cindor could do little but brood. There was no other way to pass the time. He'd tried reciting spells, but lacked his customary focus. He tried sleeping, but was too troubled by his feelings of helplessness. He'd made a mistake, a terrible, inexplicable mistake, and now he was completely at Her Majesty's mercy. The blob beneath his jaw that was his still-developing torso as yet possessed no arms or legs and was too weak to be of any assistance in moving himself about, and so he was condemned, for the foreseeable future, into staring at the door through which the Queen sometimes entered and exited.

And all because Cindor had tried to spy on her pet freak. Gods, Cindor had been trying to protect Her Majesty, and what had been his reward?

The door creaked open just the tiniest bit. A mouse would have found entry difficult. But as Cindor watched, riveted, a strange dimness flowed through the crack and into the room.

Once it was fully in front of the Shaper, the door closed and locked.

The Shaper would have begun casting a spell, but he lacked the strength for anything helpful. Instead, he pursed his lips and waited, hoping that somehow, someone he knew would arrive at the door in time to stop whatever was unfolding.

The shadow, meanwhile, resolved into the familiar shape of the Alchemist.

"D'Marei," Cindor spat.

"Yes," the Alchemist cackled. "And isn't the irony of this moment delicious?"

Before Cindor could speak another word, the Alchemist threw a handful of dust at him, instantly befuddling the Shaper.

"Hag's breath," D'Marei said. "It's wonderfully underappreciated stuff."

Cindor squinted back at the other man, then tried throwing his eyes as wide as possible. It was no use: a strange, hallucinogenic lassitude fell over him, and he was hard-pressed to string two thoughts together.

The Alchemist paced, rubbing his chin. "Now," said he, "I could smash your head to bits here and now, which would end your sorry life once and for all. I must admit I find that option rather tempting. Then again, I could simply take you with me, enslave you, carve you up and study you at my leisure."

Cindor missed most of this, but he certainly caught "enslave you." He put up a hellacious fight for clarity and his own freedom, but ultimately it was for naught. He was terribly enfeebled, and the Alchemist was strong.

"Sleep now," D'Marei urged. "I can't promise you'll feel better in the morning, but at least you'll feel!"

A swirling black hole opened in the room, and, after covering Cindor's head with cloth and scooping it up, the Alchemist stepped through and away.

Vykers & Company, In Camp

It was fair to say that alcohol had decided the group's make-up and mission. And Vykers wasn't bothered by this in the slightest.

Alcohol made it hard for men and giants to dissemble, and under its influence, each and every member of Vykers' squad—human, giant and actor alike—had avowed a passionate desire to kill Svarren and eradicate the creatures' leader, whatsoever he might be.

That was good enough for the Reaper.

And, in truth, it seemed to him that this was how things were meant to be, that those around him had been drawn there to aid him in whatever way possible. He sensed, too, that still more were on the way. The challenge lay in waiting long enough to let these unknown others arrive, but no so long that the End seized some advantage.

Vykers hated waiting.

But when he thought about it, they were—what?—fifteen strong? Even if some of those fifteen were giants, they were hardly enough to take on tens of thousands of Svarren and a mad sorcerer.

There was always Alheria, though. She *was* a goddess, after all. How many men was *she* worth, if, as she'd promised, she decided to attend the coming battle? Inebriated as he was, Vykers tried to run the numbers: say Alheria and the End fought one another. That left Vykers, six giants, six warriors, the Dead One and the actor to deal with the horde of Svarren. A sane man would have dismissed the idea as lunacy, but Vykers found it appealing.

A thought came to the Reaper just then: what if these battles between the End-of-All-Things and Her Majesty were truly and only between them? What if everyone else was incidental and the deaths of those fighting on either side, unnecessary?

But wasn't that always the case in war?

Maybe, Vykers reasoned. But most of the time, it was men fighting other men for things men understood. Who really knew what Alheria and her demented offspring wanted?

Vykers stood, preparing to pack his gear for another day's travel. The notion that everything he'd done in his last encounter with the End and everything he might yet do was only to settle bad blood between two immortals irked him. No, it angered him.

"Change of plans!" he announced to his fellows.

Humans and giants alike eyed him with a mix of curiosity and concern. Change of plans?

"The one thing I don't like is being pushed around like a pawn in someone else's game," Vykers went on, as his companions gathered around him. "And I've got a nasty feelin' we're bein' sent to it in a dispute that's got nothin' to do with us."

"But the Svarren," Beesmarch objected.

"Oh, we'll get to them. But I wanna do it when it's right for *us*, not Her Majesty. And where it suits us, not the End. I wanna make it plain that we're beholden to no one."

The brothers scowled at this, but Eoman and Karrakan nodded approvingly.

"What, then?" asked Beesmarch.

"We walk 'til we sight those Svarren bastards, then we go East or West along their front until we find some forest. Those fuckers might overrun us on open ground, but we're the ones'll have the advantage in the woods."

A few of the giants and men remained skeptical, but Karrakan, for one, was elated. "Well bethought!" he called out. "I know my will-o-wisps prefer the greenwood!"

Hjuest sidled up to Vykers and said, "Valk 'til we find a vood? Might be a long valk."

"So?" the Reaper shrugged. "You got somewhere to be?"

The red knight bowed his head in concession and rejoined the rest of the men.

"Good," said Vykers, before returning his attention to his gear. He barely looked up when Igraine approached. "Yes?"

"I think you've made the right decision."

"I'm glad you approve."

"I believe the answers you seek will only be found in a direct confrontation between Alheria and her son."

"Then we have to make sure that happens."

"Just so."

Travelling with giants was surprisingly easy. They walked at a great pace, seldom talked whilst in movement, and could seemingly go forever without needing a rest. Those facts, combined with the mystical nature of Vykers' horses, made the journey to the Svarren front and along it much simpler than the Reaper would have expected. The Dead One and his actor friend had a little difficulty keeping up, but they never complained, so that the group spotted the Svarren in only a few hours, whereas it might have been days under normal circumstances. Vykers then consulted the king of the giants and his shaman as to whether they ought to proceed in a western or eastern direction. Karrakan assured him that he 'felt' the closest forest to the southwest, so southwest they all went. In time, they lost sight of the Svarren horde, though Karrakan, who'd never been wrong so far, claimed he could still see them. That was good enough for Vykers. When the sought-for forest appeared on the horizon, the men gave a sigh of relief. Giants might have no problem with endless travel, but the humans were getting sick of it. Establishing a more permanent camp and resting for a few days seemed the most wonderful goal anyone could imagine. Beesmarch and the brothers groused about it, but the feeling was that they were secretly as content with resting as any of their smaller brethren.

The sun set before the crew finished making camp, but that mattered little. Everyone had his own tasks and knew them well, such that a hearty fire, a warm meal and numerous tents were ready to be enjoyed in less time than it took a milkmaid to lose her innocence.

The only complaint came from the fact that the giants had finished the men's supply of ale. What had been meant to last for weeks had instead lasted only an evening and a half, and some of the men weren't pleased.

Vykers shut their grumbling up but quick. "There'll be more liquor one day, boys, provided you survive these next few."

Once everyone was settled in 'round the fire, Hjuest leaned in to Vykers and asked, "Vhat now?"

"Vee vait," the Reaper joked. As Hjuest didn't laugh, Vykers elaborated. "I think we're meant to walk into a trap, but when the front door's standin' wide open, I like to climb in the window."

"And zen?"

"If the End wants us, he'll have to change his plans. He doesn't handle that sorta thing too well."

"And ze Qveen?"

"I expect we'll be hearing from her soon enough."

Hjuest bobbed his head to suggest he understood and moved off to communicate with the rest of the men. Igraine, Vykers noted, had seated herself between Eoman and Karrakan, though she kept her eyes down the whole time.

What am I gonna do about that one? Vykers wondered.

Mardine, On the Road

It was easy to track the other giants, but it eventually dawned on Mardine that six giants had no need to be secretive. Who in his right mind would dare to attack them? Mardine, on the other hand, was a single giant, and nowhere near as large as the males she was following. If she'd had any luck in the past few weeks, it was in not being eaten by any of the wilderness' myriad beasts of prey. Was this cause enough for hope? Mardine wouldn't allow herself to think so...yet. She was thankful for every day she'd been given to search for her daughter, and doubly so for the ease with which she could follow her kinfolk.

To her surprise, it appeared the giants she'd been following joined up with a larger group of men, for amidst the prints she'd come to think of as old friends, she found those of men and horses. There was no evidence of bloodshed or battle, so Mardine could only conclude they were all travelling together. A cooperative effort between men and giants? What could it be? She couldn't recall ever hearing of such a thing and wondered if she wasn't witnessing something momentous.

A small wisp of smoke floated up into the chill winter air from a great pile of ash nearby, the remains of the group's campfire. Mardine rushed to the blackened heap and was elated to find herself in a small but undeniable pocket of warmer air. More than that, the end of a charred bone jutted out of the ruins, as if beckoning the giantess forward. Mardine's stomach rumbled, and she accepted the bone's invitation, plucking it from the still-warm coals and holding it up before her eyes. She almost cried when she saw meat clinging to one end. It wasn't much, but it was far more than she'd had any right to expect. She felt a moment's concern about the origin of this prize, but as she inspected it further, she was convinced it was nothing more or less than a beef shank. Tears came unbidden to her eyes as she took an experimental nibble. Had anything ever tasted better? And though there was little left of the sinew, there was still the marrow—precious, precious nourishment for the giantess' body and soul. And better perhaps than all of this, the fire pit's lingering warmth meant Mardine was not far behind her quarry. When her meal was finished, she set off with renewed vigor and—try as she might to avoid it—hope.

She picked up her pace and broke into a jog. *I'll run 'til I find 'em or drop*, she resolved.

What she found first, though, was the largest gathering of Svarren she'd ever seen. Fortunately, they were still some ways off, but she could certainly smell and hear them and was beyond thankful she'd noticed them before they'd seen her. Those she'd been following seemed to have been of the same mind, for their tracks bent westward, avoiding direct confrontation with the savages. Mardine maintained her pace, tiring as it was, knowing that every step brought her closer to finding her kin and farther away from the Svarren.

Her spirits began to flag when the sun went down and she still hadn't caught up with the group ahead of her. Now, she feared meeting those things in the dark that she'd thus far avoided. Wouldn't it just make sense, to be killed just short of her goal, just short of safety? Swallowing her doubts, she continued to push forward, even as a bitterly cold wind lashed at her face and snow dusted her path. Every step became a life and death decision, demanding she either summon resources she didn't know she had, or stumble, fall, and succumb to winter's ravenous appetite. With each successful step, Mardine felt new amazement at her own tenacity, although she felt no confidence in her next effort.

Then came the moment when she couldn't lift her leg again, when all the strength that remained to her was barely enough to keep her upright. A tear worked its way down her cheek and quickly froze.

A light flickered in the distance, through some trees Mardine could not yet see. Deep, raucous laughter defeated the wind and bolstered the giantess' spirits. Only another giant could laugh like that.

Somehow, Mardine trudged onward; somehow she staggered into the firelight of Vykers' camp. Somehow, she made her way to the inner circle.

And then fell over onto Eoman's lap.

THIRTEEN

Mardine, In Vykers' Camp

The other giants made her comfortable, built her, in fact, a large cot right next to the fire and proceeded to tend to Mardine's every need. The brothers erected a lean-to over her cot and ensured the snow stayed off her. Beesmarch gave her his great bearskin robe. Karrakan cast spells of health and fortitude. But it was Eoman who did the most to revive the suffering giantess, merely by opening his mouth.

"Mardine," he said gently. "I am astounded to find you alive, and the best is, your daughter lives, too."

Mardine exploded with tears, and it was all the other six giants could do to assuage her torrent of emotion. The weeks and weeks of grief, fear, fatigue, and endless desperation that had built up inside her gushed forth like discharge from a septic wound. Those watching understood this was a necessary part of the giantess' healing, and so the men outside the circle of giants said nothing, but simply sat in silent vigil.

Hours later, when the giantess seemed to be resting peacefully, Vykers and his men shuffled off to their tents. Eoman sent the brothers off to sleep as well, though he, Karrakan, and Beesmarch continued to watch over Mardine and would do until late the next morning.

When Mardine finally woke, she found herself alone save Beesmarch. "Where are the others?" she asked the big giant.

"You're awake!" Beesmarch replied, almost smiling. "This is our home for the nonce, and so our kinfolk and the men are at work making it more comfortable—hunting, gathering firewood, finding water and the like."

"The other giant said my daughter is alive?"

"That was Eoman. He is your king—*our* king. And yes, Esmine is alive."

At hearing her daughter's name, Mardine again began to cry, but this was a gentler, happier episode. "And may I see her?"

Beesmarch's trace of smile disappeared. "She is very, very safe and well cared-for. But, alas, she is not with us."

Mardine bolted upright. "I have to find her!"

"Easy, easy," Beesmarch implored. "Eoman will take care of everything." Beesmarch wasn't entirely sure this was true, but, for once, he wasn't the least bit uncomfortable acknowledging someone else might have the answers.

"Where is my daughter?"

Beesmarch did his best to look into Mardine's eyes and provide reassurance. It was a new experience for him, but not as unpleasant as he'd feared. "She abides with one of our kin in a magical cave to the south."

"Just one of our kin?"

"And a human woman, Melme or Delby or some such."

More tears from Mardine. "Nelby, too? Oh, I have wronged that poor woman."

"She did not seem...resentful...when I saw her last," Beesmarch offered. "She...loves your Esmine very much, it seems."

Mardine felt another presence behind her and turned to see the king approaching. "Your Highness..." she said awkwardly.

"Please," he responded, shaking his head slightly. "Eoman."

"Eoman, then."

"Feeling better?"

"Much."

Eoman's face grew solemn. He looked both left and right before going on, as if to ensure no one else was listening. "*How*, though? I don't mean to dredge up painful memories, Mardine, but I saw you dead. I buried your...what was left of you. The gods know I'm delighted to see you alive, but how is this possible? Do you recall anything?"

What could she say? "I remember the cold and crawlin' out o' the ground. The rest...? I'm as confused as you."

The king sat back, considering Mardine's reply. "I'll confess, this shakes me to my very core, but as it seems a good thing and not a bad, I see no cause for fear."

The three giants sat in silence, enjoying one another's presence and the warmth of the campfire, when the Reaper caught Mardine's eye.

"I know that man."

"So do we all. I reckon everyone, everywhere knows of Tarmun Vykers."

The name was like the ringing of a bell to Mardine, and she instantly became more alert. "And how is it you travel with the Reaper?"

"We go to war, to exterminate the Svarren and the madman driving them."

Mardine looked around, confused. "But...where's your army?"

Beesmarch smirked at Eoman, who offered a rueful chuckle. "I grant you, we look like a pack o' fools.

"But...?"

Eoman shrugged. "No 'but.' The Reaper's got an idea that the Virgin Queen will do battle with this madman, leaving us free to deal with the Svarren."

"I saw thousands of them," Mardine gaped.

"Aye."

"And how many are you?"

"Less than a score. Speakin' of which, there's someone I want you to meet."

If it wasn't her daughter—and Beesmarch had said as much—Mardine couldn't imagine who it might be. While the king went and fetched whoever it was, Beesmarch offered Mardine a bowl of stew, which she sampled slowly at first and then wolfed down like the starving soul she was.

"More?" she asked.

"Much as you like," the big giant answered, refilling her bowl.

A shadow fell over Beesmarch's extended hand, and Mardine looked up to see one face she knew and another she'd never forget.

"Remuel Wratch!" she cried, rising to embrace him in a hug.

"And Captain Kittins!" the actor laughed merrily.

If Kittins was expecting a look of disgust, the giantess surprised him instead with sorrow and compassion. "What 'ave they done to you, Captain?"

"It's nothing," he said.

Suddenly, Mardine's eyes flew wide and filled again with tears. "Long," she whispered. "Where's my husband?" Encountering Rem and Kittins shook loose the last of her recalcitrant memories. "Where's Long Pete, then?"

It was Rem who answered, the only one who *could* answer. "The last I saw of him, he was wandering about up here somewhere, looking for Esmine."

"And she's alive!" Mardine sobbed.

"Is she?" Rem gasped. "That is wonderful news, Mardine!"

Even Kittins tried to look happy about it, but it was difficult, given his hellish face and naturally grim demeanor.

"And how long ago did you part with Long?" the giantess pressed.

"A fortnight, or thereabouts."

"And he's up here, you say? Up north?"

"Or heading this way."

Mardine made a move as if to go, but quickly stopped, raised a hand to her face and covered her eyes. "I don't know what to do, where to go."

"I'd counsel staying here," Eoman said. "We can't spare anyone to lead you south to Zillia's cave, and your husband's more likely to find a group of folks than a single individual."

"But…"

"He's right, Em," said Rem.

At the mention of her old nickname, the giantess seemed to deflate a bit. "I know," she whispered. "I know."

The End & Vykers, In Camp

The End was done being calm and reasonable. What had it gotten him? Everything was going to shit again, just as it had before, and he could not, would not allow that to happen.

He'd sent out Questing Eyes and Ears and determined that, yes, Tarmun Vykers had responded to his taunting. To a point. The Reaper had come right to the edge of the End's forces and chosen not to engage. So, he was no idiot, give the man a prize! But what he'd done instead was even more aggravating: he'd stumbled upon the only forest for leagues and encamped there. In a forest! The End cursed himself for not burning it down as soon as he'd become aware of it.

It wasn't that the End feared the Fey, it was more that he felt the Reaper didn't need any more allies than he already had. The End didn't like the idea of Vykers whittling away at his advantage in numbers, and in a strange, petulant way, the End didn't think it was fair, either. Why couldn't the Reaper just fight him on his own terms? Why did he always have to be so... tactical...about things?

Impulsively, the sorcerer sent another of his floating faces to threaten the Reaper. If the man wouldn't cooperate, then the End would force him to fight. Yes, it was late morning, not the ideal time to maximize the frightening aspects of this spell, but the End was tired of waiting.

When the spell made contact, his first glimpse of Vykers' camp unsettled him. Giants? *Seven* giants? Since when had giants and men banded together in warfare? And who or what was that big, ugly fellow who radiated magic? The End didn't have long to contemplate these questions before the Reaper stepped into view. On impulse, the sorcerer tried to lure Vykers into a trap.

"Lookin' for something?" he asked.

"I was just wondering why you and I couldn't settle this man to man."

"Oh, you've found a man to fight for you?"

The End seethed at this comment, but knew better than to let Vykers sense it. "Charming. I meant of course you and me. There's not really any need to delay this any longer is there?"

"Well, I *did* promise your mother I'd wait for her..."

Those listening in Vykers' camp erupted either into gasps of surprise or gales of laughter, and the End became so furious that he sent a blast of deathly cold air through his avatar to silence them. He was gratified to see he had cowed the majority of them, but Vykers remained unfazed.

"What do *you* know of my mother?" the End shrieked. How was it the Reaper was aware of things that the End barely recalled?

"Alheria?" Vykers yawned. "Seems she never much cared for you. Reckon you were an accident, like most bastards."

This time, a blast of fire ripped through Vykers' camp. When the flames cleared, only the Reaper remained in view, vexingly unscathed.

"Anyway," he said, as if there'd been no interruption, "she'll be here any time now, and you two can fight it out on your own."

"But you won't be alive to see it!" the End retorted, ending the spell and falling back onto his bed in a black rage. He had no choice, now: he *had* to send the Svarren, *all* the Svarren, to annihilate the Reaper and his little band before Alheria arrived.

Vykers & Company, In Camp

Vykers' newfound disdain for Shapers apparently did not extend to shamans, for he showed not the least hesitation in seeking out Karrakan and asking his opinion on a wide range of topics only loosely related to fighting the Svarren. One thing, in particular, peaked his curiosity.

"What do you make o' these woods?"

Karrakan inhaled deeply, as if he would take all of the forest in through his nostrils. "They are...especially alive," he replied.

"And this underbrush, here," said Vykers, pointing at some nearby bushes, "Does it seem to have gotten thicker, since yesterday?"

The shaman's eyebrows shot up. "What are you asking me?"

"Just wanna see if you can confirm a suspicion."

"Perhaps I can," said a voice Vykers hadn't heard in some time, and out of the shadow of a massive pine stepped his one-time lover, Aoife.

A trace of a grin played across the Reaper's face; he'd been right about the foliage and right about the A'Shea. As he studied her, though, she was not entirely the woman he remembered.

It might have been the quality of light underneath the forest's ancient trees, but Aoife's skin appeared to have turned a pale, almost iridescent green. Her lustrous red hair remained as impressive as ever, although it now seemed to have sprouted its own creepers, leaves and flowers. Finally, there was a power to her, an authority that Vykers had never sensed before. Where before she'd seemed vulnerable, now she seemed both immeasurably strong and equally dangerous. Vykers' smile widened.

As for Aoife's impression of the Reaper, well, suffice it to say she was confused. The last time she'd seen him, he'd felt somehow smaller, less substantial to her. But here again was the Tarmun Vykers who'd first captured her attention—swaggering, audacious, and as virile as any man could be without transforming into something else completely.

"Can't stay away, huh?" Vykers cracked.

"I can't stay away from this particular battle, no."

"And why is that?"

"Does it matter? We fight the same enemy."

Vykers looked around, peered into the bushes and shadows. "Where are your friends?"

"They'll come if I need them. Where are yours?"

"Who? My monsters? They're all dead, I'm sorry to say. I've got a handful of men with me, and we've joined up with this good giant and his kin."

Aoife was shocked. "And you think you're enough to defeat the End and his Svarren?"

"Might be we are, might be we aren't."

"And your Shaper?"

Vykers scowled, actually spat into the snow. "Forget about her."

Of course, as soon as he said that, the fate of his Shaper was all Aoife could think about. As long as she'd known them, they'd been inseparable, and the Umaena couldn't imagine what might have occurred to change things. She was also aware that she could not simply ask Vykers, either. Not after the way she and he had left things.

What Vykers said next, though, threw her thoughts into turmoil.

"So, how long's it been, then? Since we returned from across the sea?"

Why was he offering a false date? Was he pretending that the time they'd spent together in the old cottage was meaningless? Or was he pretending to have forgotten? Or had he truly forgotten it? If he was trying to insult the Umaena, he was doing a damned fine job of it. There were any number of biting retorts she might have made; she chose instead to ignore the question and focus on Vykers' companion, the unquestionably patient giant.

"And you," she said to Karrakan, "how have you found yourself in this miscreant's company?" It came out worse than she'd intended, and she could see the blow landed.

"Well," said Vykers, patting Karrakan his forearm, "I'll leave you with the shrub here. I've a sword to sharpen."

Shrub? Gods, the man was infuriating! Not wanting to seem at all affected by Vykers' comment, Aoife turned to the giant and said, "I sense some magic in you. Shall we stroll the verdant alleys of this wood and search for common cause?"

Karrakan switched his staff into his other hand, extended his now-free hand and answered, "It would be my pleasure."

Back in camp, Vykers called his inner circle together, which was comprised of Hjuest, Ngoro (though he could scarcely follow most conversation), Igraine, Kittins, and Rem.

"I have this feeling now and again," he began, "that things are comin' together of their own accord, or that something—or someone—is pulling 'em together. This is one o' those times." He paused for effect, let his words sink in, and gathered his thoughts. "We're not many, it's true, but we're battle-tested. We've got the Dead One," he gestured to Kittins, "and a handful of soldiers from different lands across the sea. We've got giants. And now, we've got the most powerful, pain-in-the-ass A'Shea you're ever like to meet. And what I'm feelin' is, this ain't no accident."

"It *is* strange," Kittins hissed.

"Strange indeed. And I'm still expectin' Her Majesty to join us. Now, you won't believe what I'm about to tell you, but I've seen the proof with my own eyes, and so has Igraine here. The Queen? The Virgin Queen? She's Alheria, the goddess." Vykers let that sink in for a moment while Hjuest spoke with Ngoro in hushed tones and Kittins rumbled something to Rem. "I figure you'll see the proof yourself soon enough. In order to beat the End once and for all, she's got to quit playing coy and let that fucker have it, else, where's her army?"

"But if she's a goddess," Rem interjected, "why does she need any of us?"

Vykers laughed appreciatively. "I been askin' the same question for some time. Maybe this is the fight where we'll get our answers."

Or we'll die, Rem thought. *Still, what a story, what a play it would make!*

"If we've been drawn together for some purpose, why aren't we fighting already?" Kittins complained.

"Because we're still waiting for someone," Igraine said, to the surprise of everyone present.

"Besides the Queen?"

"Besides the Queen," said Igraine.

Vykers looked over at Igraine in frustration. "Who else is there?"

Long & Company, On the Road

About midday, Ron said he smelled smoke. Long thought the young man might be delirious. After all, they'd been walking forever, with less and less to eat. It was only a matter of time until they...Then Long smelled it, too. The sky was clear for a change, and the captain was able to scan the horizon much easier than at any time in recent memory. Just on the edge of his vision, the land's crisp, white edge melted into something darker and blurrier.

"There's a forest up ahead!" Long croaked.

And there was much rejoicing. A forest meant firewood, shelter from the incessant wind, and perhaps even game. Even Yendor offered up a prayer of thanks to Mahnus, Alheria and a dozen minor gods known only to him.

"Don't waste your energy talkin'!" Long instructed. "We'll need every bit to get to them trees."

Of course he was correct. As has often been observed, things seen in the distance out-o'-doors are always farther off than they seem. The sun was quite low in the sky by the time the men came within a bowshot of the forest. Long worried they wouldn't have time to find wood and make a fire before dark, but, as it turned out, they had a more immediate concern.

Just as they reached the wood's outer edge, a man appeared and challenged them. And not just any man, but the Reaper himself. Long and his boys nearly fell over backwards in shock and fatigue.

"Who are you and what's your business here?" Vykers demanded.

"Please don't kill us, Master Reaper," Yendor simpered.

"Good. You know who I am. Now who in the infinite hells are you?"

Long Pete bullied himself into his best posture, cleared his throat and said, "I'm in charge o' these men. I'm a captain in the Queen's army, but folks call me Long Pete."

"Or just Long," Yendor amended. "We fought in the battle against the End."

"On whose side?" Vykers snarled.

Yendor giggled awkwardly. "Well, that's the thing, ain't it? Can I say both?"

"So you fought for the End."

"Only for the first half o' the battle."

"Then you're all turncoats, is that it?"

"Not me!" Spirk declared. "I fought fer the Queen the whole time."

Vykers made a face like he'd just noticed Spirk and wasn't sure where he'd come from. "That so? Well, you're a mixed lot, ain't you? What are you doin' here?"

"Nothin' you don't want us to!" Yendor cried.

"Lookin' for my daughter, who was kidnapped by slavers."

This pronouncement seemed to stir something in the Reaper, for he responded, "I believe we've got your missus with us."

Long merely stood, slack-jawed, trying to decide if he'd

fallen asleep and was dreaming the conversation. "No, no," said he, "Can't be. She's dead, I'm sorry to say."

Vykers nodded. "That's what the other giant said, too. But she don't look dead to me."

"Her hair?" Long asked, his voice beginning to quaver.

"Red. Orange, really."

"And she's a giant?"

"Big, big gal. Yes."

This time, Long did collapse, falling onto his knees with his face in the snow, sobbing like a child. Several heartbeats later, strong hands grasped the captain under his arms and lifted him onto his feet as if he weighed nothing.

"Follow me, captain," the Reaper said. "And the rest o' you, too."

The whole camp came to a standstill the moment Mardine and Long set eyes on each other, and time ceased to exist. No one breathed, no one moved, and even the fire went curiously quiet as the long-separated husband and wife regarded each other. Afterwards, no one watching could have said how it happened, but Mardine somehow found herself across the camp, in Long's arms, where both souls wept and laughed and wept some more. How in Mahnus' name had she escaped death? Why did he smell so awful? Was there a new trace of gray in her hair? What was that terrible smell? She'd gotten too thin! And, really, why *did* he smell so awful? More laughter, more tears. Finally, Long worked up the courage to mention Esmine, and Mardine almost cracked his heart with joy over the news the child was safe and sound and well out of harm's way. Gradually, the other members of camp lost interest or gave in to more pressing business and went about their affairs, giving the reunited couple all the space and time they needed.

Later, around the fire, Long and his friends were treated to a hearty meal and an even heartier welcome.

These men, Igraine suggested to Vykers, were the ones they'd been waiting for.

"What, these?" the Reaper asked incredulously. "Look at 'em! I've seen things dead a fortnight looked better than these men."

"And yet, there's something canny about that man's reunion with his wife, isn't there? In all this vastness, they find each other? Surely that's not coincidence."

Vykers didn't know what to make of it, and, frankly, he'd become tired of all the portents and omens of late. He decided to change the subject. "Gettin' used to that body finally?"

Igraine frowned, said nothing for a while. "I understand that's what you'd like, Master."

The End, In Camp

The End flew into a rage as great as or surpassing any he'd experienced in the past, as himself or any of his earlier iterations. Once he'd identified his target to his Svarren, they balked and refused to attack. They refused! They refused *him*! Oh, they muttered some incoherent horseshit about the old gods—*he was an old god!* And it was his will they should assault the forest!

Obviously, he could not tolerate such effrontery from his slaves. He'd have to make an example of some of their leaders, punish them in such a way that the rest would never forget, he'd have to...

Oh, you are doing so much better than I would have! The boy taunted from inside the End's mind.

The sorcerer did not respond. He would not allow himself to be toyed with by an idiot child that he'd already bested.

Can't even control a pack of Svarren...

The End shut him out. When he was certain that he was alone and in control again, however, he did pause to ruminate on how the boy had managed to break into his thoughts. Was he, the End, not getting enough rest? Enough nourishment? Or was he simply too distracted? Well, one thing at a time.

He sauntered out of his tent—more a pavilion now—and slowly, casually, walked in amongst the Svarren. They watched him with eyes full of fear, of skepticism, and even contempt. The End saw no obedience and certainly no adoration. Hadn't some sage once observed that it was better to be feared than loved? So be it: he would be feared.

With a wave of his hand, the End sent a number of miniature storms swirling around the camp, spitting out black matter wherever they went. And wherever the stuff landed, screams of alarm and agony blossomed. The End had used this spell before, but not quite in this way, and he found he rather enjoyed it. All around him, Svarren flesh was dissolving in a mist of blood. The End could almost taste it on his tongue, and though he'd never been a blood drinker, he was surprised at how pleasant the flavor was.

As for the Svarren, they fell away from the End in waves, scrambling, tumbling, fighting to get as far from the little black clouds as possible. Here, a Svarra clawed its way through a family member in a desperate bid for escape. There, a female with child was trampled by a frenzied mob, caring only to put distance between itself and painful, bloody death.

It was an accident, really; he hadn't meant to do it, but the End laughed at the spectacle before him, and the Svarren saw and heard him laughing. *What of it?* The End asked himself. Am I not their leader?

The False Reaper echoed his laughed, but the boy's was much more cynical.

It was time to finish the child, once and for all.

The End fled to a hilltop far from camp, where the Svarren would never find him, and sank into himself. In the darkness, he found the boy waiting for him.

"What a wreck you are," the boy called out. "Powerful, but without vision."

The End grabbed the boy's spirit and began crushing him. "And you? Nothing more than a nuisance, a child who possessed neither the intelligence nor the skill to rule! I shall consume you as I have all the others."

"Now!" the boy shrieked.

The faint wisps of the End's previous selves coalesced into a larger shape and cast a spell.

The End could not move. It was not an elaborate or strong spell, but he hadn't been expecting it; he hadn't believed his victims had so much energy left. And what had they accomplished, really? Already, he was picking their spell apart and regaining control of his resources. In minutes, he fought his way free and consumed the last of his enemies' essences—no more False Reaper, no more Old Hag, no more Ageless Necromancer. He had eaten them all, become them all. He was, he exulted, an army unto himself.

With a thought, he returned to his camp...

Only to find the whole Svarren horde in rapid retreat.

That had been the False Reaper's gambit!

The End took to the skies and attempted to mollify his allies, but they would none of him. He grew angry and threatened them, to no avail. He shot fire and frost at them, but they only retreated faster. Stealing an idea from the recently vanquished False Reaper, the End summoned all his strength and paralyzed the entire Svarren force and then paused to admire his handiwork. Had any other magician ever accomplished such a feat? Was anyone in the world mightier than he?

Vykers & Company, In Camp

Vykers was taking an afternoon nap when Hjuest came by with the news.

"The Svarren have run away."

"The fuck?"

"Vhat?"

The Reaper rubbed his eyes. "They've run away, you say? That don't make sense. Did somebody say the kid's a Shaper? I wanna talk to 'im."

Hjuest did an abbreviated bow and went off to fetch Spirk.

In the meantime, Vykers stood up, stretched, and checked that his sword and the dagger were still where he'd stashed them. Next, he cast about for something to drink and found a wineskin full of fresh water. No sooner had he drained it than Hjuest reappeared with Spirk in tow.

The Reaper stared at the young man as if he were an unexpected rash on the skin. "I hear you're a Shaper," he said with an obvious note of contempt.

"Well," Spirk sputtered, "I know a few things. Sorta. Sometimes."

Vykers was unconvinced. "You an idiot, boy?"

"I guess so, yeah."

"I never heard of an idiot Shaper before."

"Me, neither," Spirk said, helpfully.

The Reaper was flummoxed, but he had no time to wallow in confusion. "Look," said he, "can you spy on those Svarren with your thoughts like other Shapers do?"

"Sure!" Spirk answered, clearly star-struck to be conversing with the legendary Reaper.

"Well, do it!" Vykers barked, losing patience.

Spirk stepped away from the Reaper a couple of feet and closed his eyes. "Whadda ya wanna know?" he asked.

"What's going on! Why they're running away!"

"There's some nasty feller flyin' after 'em, scarin' 'em. He reminds me o' the End."

"Does he *look* like the End?"

Spirk made a face. "Not on the outside."

"But on the inside?"

"That's him."

Vykers sneered, clenched his fists. "What's he doin'?"

"Just sorta flyin' over them Svarren…wait! Wait, they're not movin' anymore."

The Reaper exchanged glances with Hjuest and then turned back to Spirk. "They've stopped?"

"More 'n stopped," Spirk replied. "They can't move. They're stuck or somethin'."

"Did the End do this to 'em?"

Spirk screwed up his face even more and said nothing for several seconds. Then, "Uh-huh. Looks like he froze 'em kinda."

Vykers looked over at Hjuest and nodded conspiratorially. "So," he said, "the End's troops are abandoning him."

"It looks zat vay, ya."

"Round everyone up," the Reaper commanded. "We're going to war."

Long Pete, In Vykers' Camp

Long Pete had been through a lot, too much in truth. He was

elated to be reunited with his wife and doubly so to learn that his daughter was still alive. But he was also bone-tired, and the last thing he wanted to do was get ready for battle, even if the End-of-All-Things had returned. No, Long wanted nothing more than to take his wife, fetch their daughter, and retire to his apple orchard.

But the Reaper took for granted that everyone in his company was willing to do his bidding, and the Reaper was a hard man to defy. Or, more accurately, simply the *wrong* man to defy.

And the odds did seem to be in the Reaper's favor this time, if the Svarren truly had deserted. There were the seven giants, a handful of battle-tested warriors, and Long's crew, which included the unpredictable magics of one Spirk Nessno. Long had also heard tell of a powerful A'Shea lurking about somewhere, and there was even a rumor that the Queen herself might show up at any moment. Long wasn't sure what the old woman could add to the fight, but she must have had Shapers at her disposal.

For all that, Long wanted to grab Mardine and sneak away whilst everyone else was preoccupied. It would mean leaving his friends Yendor, Spirk and Ron, but, dammit, hadn't Long sacrificed enough? Wasn't he entitled to a little peace and happiness before he found his grave?

Like everyone else, he checked his weapons.

Kittins, In Vykers' Camp

It hadn't escaped Kittins' attention that Long Pete had arrived. The big man hadn't seen much of Rem since then, either. It figured. Kittins had always been the odd man out in Long's little army; why should this time be any different? He was not a man for tales of youthful whoring and drinking songs; he was not the 'hail-fellow-well-met' type. Truth be told, he probably had more in common with the Reaper. *There* was a man he might exchange stories with…or sword blows. He had to admit the idea appealed to him. If the Reaper finished him, well, it was nobody's loss; if *he* somehow managed to kill the *Reaper*, though…

Kittins sharpened his blade and checked his daggers. He inspected his armor and tightened his straps.

Whatever happened in the next few hours, there'd be a shitload of death.

And Kittins was looking forward to it.

Aoife & Vykers, In Camp

Aoife was gathering pinecones when Vykers found her in a thicket. She looked up immediately when he stepped into view, her face an unreadable mask.

"Don't tell me you're gonna throw those at the End."

Aoife ignored him.

"Look," Vykers said, "I'd rather you stayed here."

"You'd rather?" Aoife snapped. "And why should I care what you'd rather?"

Suddenly, Vykers remembered why he'd spent so much of his life alone. "Suit yourself," he said, turning to leave.

"I have more of a stake in this fight than you!" Aoife scolded at his back.

Vykers stopped, turned back to the Umaena. "I got no stake at all, 'cept I feel like finishin' what I started last time. But what's the bastard to you?"

Aoife bit back whatever it was she'd been planning to say and then muttered, "You don't know the first thing about me, Tarmun Vykers."

"What are you angry at me for? I ain't seen you in months!"

Aoife's expression reflected her mounting fury. "That's the second time you've said that today, and you and I both know it's a lie."

"What are you on about?"

"Do you deny coming to my cabin, apologizing for your past behavior, and sharing my bed with me?"

For a time, it seemed Vykers had turned to stone, a display of emotionlessness that frightened Aoife more than if he'd started screaming. "We have both been betrayed," he growled at last. "You bedded an imposter."

It was an outlandish suggestion, and yet, in her heart, Aoife had known it all along. This beast, this force of nature in front of her was the real Tarmun Vykers. That thing she'd entertained some weeks earlier was…what, exactly?

"Figures, you couldn't tell the difference," the Reaper spat as he walked away.

What could Aoife say in response? That she *could* tell the difference? That she'd been wrong but knew the real Reaper now? And what would it matter, since she was devoted to growth and he to destruction?

"I'll see you in battle!" she yelled at his retreating back.

And then he was gone.

Alheria & Vykers, In Camp

Her Majesty caught Vykers in his worst mood in ages, so black that even she was tempted to flee from him.

"What?" he demanded, as she appeared before him.

"I've been watching, and, as promised, I am here to help you fight the End."

"Where's Arune?"

"Normally, I wouldn't stop you killing her, but, as it happens, Cindor has suffered a setback, and I need her help. As do you."

"Where is she?"

"Where you'll never find her. Now, let us talk about the End, shall we?"

The Queen launched into a detailed explanation about how she planned to attack the End and what she expected of Vykers and his companions. He didn't hear a word of it, though, so busy was he in plotting her murder and that of Arune, the End, and anyone else who stood in his way.

I am done bein' fucked with, he brooded. It is time for the Reaper to start a'-reapin'!

Vykers & Company, On the March

To Vykers' surprise, there was a bitch of a blizzard outside the forest. That he and his company had been unaware of it was testament, he supposed, to Aoife's power. And maybe she was right: maybe he didn't know much about her. Nevertheless, he and his troops left the forest and began marching in the direction specified by Alheria. The weather being what it was, it was almost impossible to stay on course, but Long Pete's young Shaper did manage to offer some timely instructions that kept everyone more or less on target.

"This weather's sorcerous," Karrakan shouted above the howling wind.

No shit, thought Vykers. "Won't matter," is what he yelled back.

The End, In Camp

The End was almost taken aback to discover Vykers and his handful of friends approaching through the storm. Were they mad? How in the world could such a tiny force ever hope to compete with the sorcerer? The answer, of course, was that they could not. It had to be a ruse, then, a feint of some sort. Surely, there was a larger force coming at him from a different direction. No matter how hard or how far he looked, however, the End was unable to find anyone else on the plain except for his frozen and, by now, *literally frozen* Svarren.

The Reaper had said something about Alheria. Was it possible she was lurking out in the storm somewhere? Or was he merely being paranoid? The End had underestimated the Reaper and his allies before, and it had cost him dearly. Fleetingly, he wondered if he could rally the Svarren to his cause a final time. Given the events of the last few days, he doubted it. The End pondered running, too, and hiding. He'd promised himself over and over that he'd be fully prepared for battle this time around, and yet all his grand schemes had fallen apart. But when would he ever have another chance to destroy the Reaper once and for all?

No; he was resigned.

Reaching out with all his energies, he commanded to storm to redouble its fury. *Let winter have him, if that's what he wants!* The End smiled.

Vykers & Company, On the March

It got so cold that Vykers' troops huddled together even as they moved. Spirk and Karrakan created pockets of warmth that enveloped most of the group, but even then they were sore beset by the lashing, gale-force winds and snow.

It came to Vykers then that this was the End's element, his gift. He'd made it snow during their first battle, and he was doing it again and worse this time. If the Queen was a goddess, and the End, one of her offspring, might he not be the God of Winter?

"Igraine!" he bellowed over the storm, "Is there a god of winter?"

Her expression was hard to read through the wind and cold, but she finally said, "There once was."

"What was his name?" Igraine yelled something in response, but Vykers couldn't make it out. He steered his mount closer to her and tried again. "What?"

"Eyatu."

Eyatu. The fuck kinda name is that? As strange, as foreign as it was in Vykers' ears and mouth, it also felt powerful. Eyatu. *I wonder if the End'll recognize it.*

Long, On the March

Long passed the time on the back of a spare mount, alternately marveling at the creature's strength and speed and worrying about Mardine. And Esmun Janks. There were two people in his life who'd died and come back. Janks' return had seemed an insolvable mystery, but now that Mardine had returned as well, Long had to admit there was something intentional, something purposeful going on. But what? And how did it involve him? He looked over at his wife, marching along with her kinfolk surrounding her, as if to protect her from further ills.

She had died because Long hadn't been there to protect her himself, hadn't been there to protect Esmine. Because he'd gone off to pursue glory and riches, like a damned fool, telling himself it was for his family, but all the while using the mission to feel better about himself. Ultimately, he hadn't felt better and had lost his family to boot. Now that he had a chance—a *second* chance—to become a worthy husband and father, what was he doing? Riding along with the Mahnus-cursed Reaper, into a fight that would almost certainly leave Mardine dead again or himself just dead.

He shook his head in disgust at himself. *I am no more and no better than these snowflakes, blown along on the wind, to land wherever it pleases Mahnus.*

The End & Alheria, at War

He felt her before he saw her. Alheria towered behind him, a hundred feet tall if an inch.

"Dismiss your storm, boy!" the Queen roared.

The End looked around and up at her and laughter bubbled out of him. "Really! Such a spectacle!"

A wall of force hit him so hard that he shot backwards, tumbling head over heels for a hundred strides before landing hard in the snow.

"Dismiss your storm!"

He blasted the colossus with ice, instead.

"Very well!"

A circle of fire erupted from the Queen and spread outwards for some time before petering out. It was a spell the End had once favored himself, although he had to admit the Queen had a much better grasp of it. The air had gone still and clear for a quarter mile in every direction, and the End was scorched, but not fatally so.

Whilst his back was turned, he felt the Shaper's jump at his back and he rapidly repositioned himself so that he could see both Her Majesty and the arriving enemies. Impressively, the Queen had jumped Vykers' whole group to within a few feet of the sorcerer.

"What is it you all want?" the End demanded petulantly.

"Your end," said Aoife.

The End wheeled in her direction. "Ah, sister!" he crooned. "Old scores, eh?"

At the word 'sister,' Vykers about fell off his horse. Instead, he drew his dagger and slowly dismounted.

"What madness are you babbling?" he called over to the End.

The sorcerer's eyebrows went up in a comical arch. "You didn't know? Why yes, Aoife is my sister, the little forest nymph!"

"And Alheria's your mother," said Vykers, struggling to make sense of things.

The End capered with delight. If he'd ever been sane, he was far from it now. "She didn't tell you that, Reaper! How did you discover it?"

"Enough" the gigantic Queen declared. "You talk too much, boy!" With that, she reached down and attempted to grab the sorcerer like an adult grabs a wayward toy.

The End cast his own Shaper's jump, just beyond the reach of Her Majesty and the Reaper. "But I'm having such a delightful time!"

"Are you, Eyatu?" Vykers snarled.

The End's smile vanished from his face, and his arms fell limply to his sides. He cocked his head at an angle, the way a dog does when it's confused. "I remem…"

Alheria hit him with a blast of arcane energy so intense that all her allies were left blind for several seconds afterwards. When Vykers' vision returned, he noticed a small shadow trailing behind the Queen: Arune. Old scores, indeed.

The End disappeared briefly, only to reappear farther way. He swept his arms upward and an army of ice golems sprang into being. Before the Reaper could stop her, Aoife rushed forward and threw a handful of pinecones in the End's direction. It seemed such an absurd, such a futile gesture, that Vykers could barely contain his frustration with the woman. In the next breath, however, he saw the cones explode. Their seeds must have taken root, for a forest of pines surged through the snow's icy mantle and raced skyward. The golems, it seemed, were not meant to battle trees, so they stood, awaiting the enemy's advance. As Vykers' group watched in fascination, the small forest grew and spread at an astonishing rate.

The mad sorcerer continued to back away, whilst Alheria

maneuvered to outflank him. With her prodigious gate, she managed the feat with ease, and the End was hard-pressed to elude her by conventional means. Yet, he could not wander too far from his golems and still control them.

Eoman looked over at Vykers, awaiting the man's signal to attack. Vykers caught his eye, nodded, and rushed forward, roaring. Seeing this, the rest of the giants and Vykers' men followed suit. Even Long's team was caught up in the frenzy of battle, and they, likewise, eagerly joined the fray.

The End sent spell after spell in Alheria's direction, to little or no avail. But the gigantic Queen had equal difficulty penetrating her son's defenses. Meanwhile, the battle was joined between the giants and the golems. Eoman and his friends smashed into the ice creatures, obliterating two or three on impact. The remaining golems, though, proved to be made of stronger stuff and fought with a ferocity that even Beesmarch found daunting.

The fey emerged from Aoife's still-growing forest in all their diversity—ogres, toads, satyrs, sprites, nixies and too many things whose names were yet unknown. Each and every one attacked the ice golems, or pressed the advance upon the End.

Vykers had no interest in the golems or the fey. He made his way through the living maze of combatants and charged the End. The sorcerer was not prepared to engage the Reaper, though, and so flew into the air, just beyond Vykers' reach. He recalled that the Reaper had flown before, but also that his enemy was less agile off his feet, and the End hoped this was still the case.

Aoife, too, had somehow gotten past the golems and made her way towards the sorcerer. She summoned a noxious green cloud from her forest and sent it wafting at her brother's head. Let him breathe that!

As amusing as the whole encounter seemed to the End, he was beginning to panic. Most of the spells he conjured to deal with his mortal foes were negated by the Queen, and his golems were falling without having inflicted much damage themselves. Having had and seen enough, the sorcerer tried to jump away again...only to find himself magically rooted to the spot. Fear seized his gut as he made a visual assessment of enemies and their positions. To his horror, Vykers was nearly upon him.

Long, at War

The ice monsters, as Long thought of them, were impressive creatures—immune to fear, pain or fatigue—but they did not like fire, as Spirk had quickly discovered. The boy, too, had become impressive in his own right. When Long had first met him, Spirk was an absolute nothing, a nobody with no prospects, no talents, and no future. Now, he was a true Shaper, perhaps not as powerful or adept as the End, but a force to be reckoned with nonetheless. Long was proud to know him.

One of the monsters lashed out at the captain, and before he could react, Kittins reached over and parried the blow.

"Thanks!" Long yelled.

Kittins turned away and kept battling his own monster.

Don't know what I ever did to that fella, Long mused. *Might have to buy him a drink to find out.*

His eyes then sought out Mardine, to ensure she was still alive and in no peril. As before, she was surrounded by her fellow giants and seemed in no danger of injury. Long was ashamed to admit they could protect her better than he.

Kittins

He could have let Long die, and why he hadn't was beyond Kittins. He'd no love for the man. He'd no love for anyone, including himself. Why had he parried that monster's blow?

Fuck it.

He kept fighting, hacking large chunks from the limbs and torsos of the ice creatures, but never quite able to hit their heads.

It was strange, fighting something with no feelings. The better part of every fight was emotional, and Kittins struck terror into most of his foes. But these things...?

He continued to hack and chop away.

Spirk

He'd never admit it, o' course, but Spirk was having the time of his life. He'd wanted to spout flame at the giant ice things, and spout flame he had! In fact, magic was coming easier and easier to him, and he started to wonder what wasn't possible. Was there anything he couldn't do?

Well, *concentrate*, if he was honest. Here he was in the biggest battle since the last biggest battle, and he was daydreaming! He refocused himself and blazed like a blacksmith's forge. The monsters did not like that.

Arune

Arune found it hard to remain hidden behind Alheria's robes and still toss out the requested defensive spells. The Queen kept moving, and whenever Arune looked up, she felt Vykers' eyes upon her. She was probably just imagining it, she knew, but it made her job more difficult, nevertheless.

And then, too, there was Aoife, crackling with eldritch energies and a determination that made her all the more beautiful to the Shaper. Was there anyone like Aoife in all the world? No; there was not.

And Arune had lost her. Had her and lost her.

Or maybe she'd never had her, because it was Vykers, always Vykers, whom the A'Shea was attracted to. And Arune would never be Vykers. He, too, was unique in all the world.

The End attempted to send out one of his horrible black clouds, but Alheria had explained to Arune how to counter it, and counter it she did. She watched with no little satisfaction when the End's spell fizzled out, and he frowned in alarm.

Not this time, you bastard!

Mardine

Given all she'd been through, all she had lost and regained, it made no sense that Mardine should relish such a life-threatening event. But she did. She reveled in smashing the creatures the End threw in her way. She exulted in the look of bewilderment on the wretched sorcerer's face. They had failed to kill him last time, but this time his army had abandoned him, and Vykers and Her Majesty had caught him utterly unprepared.

The End

His mother was stronger than he, and his sister, the one-time A'Shea, had become almost too much for him as well. As the accursed Reaper soared at him, the End reconciled himself to defeat. He could not win. He could not stop time.

But he could slow it down, and did so, knowing it was, at best, a temporary reprieve.

Mid-leap, the Reaper's flight became torpid, but all the more graceful for that. His sword hand was empty, but the End recognized this to be an imposture. He knew well what was hidden there; he had wielded it himself, when time was, and he quailed at its presence. He knew why it had been created. So much knowledge and none of it helpful.

He craned his neck and studied his mother. His mother, *ha!* What heresy. In her selfish pursuit of victory, she had no regard for familial ties. Ask Mahnus!

Alheria, Mahnus, Eyatu...and? Where were the other bastards? How many had Eyatu himself killed? It was a question his former selves might have answered, if he had not consumed their essences to fuel his present power. And what good had that done? He was bound to die, and shortly.

With a world-weary sigh, he allowed time to resume its natural course and immediately felt an agonizing pain in his lower right abdomen. Vykers had stabbed him in the exact same area in which he'd wounded the Reaper.

But the dagger had been created to kill gods, and the End's torso began to dissolve into itself.

The Reaper head-butted him, to add to the indignity of his death. As the End was falling backwards, he spied Aoife. If he had to die, he would not go to it alone. He put everything he had and was into a final blast at the Umaena's heart.

He never saw the outcome of his attack.

The End's body continued to crumble and erode, until there was nothing left, not even dust. But the imprint of a dagger in the snow gave evidence the weapon that had finished Eyatu had survived.

"I'll take that!" Alheria proclaimed before Vykers could even register what had happened.

"Of course you will," he sneered. He turned his attention to Aoife, who lay on the ground, gasping, and rapidly losing all color. He ran to her side, gently scooped her into his lap and felt her throat for a pulse. A terrible, terrible cold greeted his touch.

"Can none of you magic folk do *anything*?" he yelled, a plaintive quality to his voice that none present had heard before.

Alheria returned to her normal size and came to stand over the stricken Umaena. Before she or anyone else could speak Arune stepped forward, a look of absolute torment on her face. Though he still wanted her dead, Vykers held his breath and waited to see what she'd do.

The little goblin reached out a hand and caressed Aoife's forehead. Tears streamed down the goblin's face as she turned to Vykers. "For you," she whispered.

For me? Vykers echoed. *How for me?*

Slowly, Arune began to expand, and a brilliant, familiar light bloomed within her. Spirk gasped, remembering all too well when he'd last seen such a thing. At last, the little Shaper exploded in a shower of white sparks, bathing all those present in a radiance both cleaner and brighter than the snow on which they all stood. Even after the light subsided, no one spoke for the longest time, and only Spirk made any sound, sobbing quietly to himself.

Vykers was contemplating how best to dispose of Aoife's remains when he saw her looking up at him, a hesitant smile on her lips. He was not one to weep, and he'd never been generous with his praise, but he understood at once what had transpired.

He gazed into the clouds as if he could see Arune's departing spirit.

"We're even," he said solemnly.

The ice golems had collapsed when the End perished, and, once it was clear that Aoife would be okay, the fey returned to the little grove she'd created and, from thence, to places unknown to men.

Vykers placed Aoife into Karrakan's care and then moved to confront Alheria. "You owe me," he challenged.

"Do I? And what, pray tell, is it this time?"

"I wanna know what all o' this is really about. The End was your bastard; you knew that the first time I fought him, but you didn't intervene. You killed Mahnus, but you wouldn't…"

"I *thought* I killed Mahnus, yes," Alheria responded, silencing Vykers.

Those who hadn't heard this bit of news were equally silent, watching and waiting for more.

"But it seems he found a new host, much like Eyatu was wont to do."

"And—what?—you just discovered this?" Vykers shot back.

"Mahnus was…*is* more clever than Eyatu. At the very moment I thought I'd delivered the killing stroke, he found a host that was still in the womb. He grew up as a normal child, having no memory or knowledge of his former self. And because he lacked that knowledge, he was invisible to me." Alheria paused to ensure she had everyone's attention. "But he is amongst us today."

Some, like Yendor, burst out laughing at the idea. Others, like Hjuest, were as sober as could be.

"You're sayin' that one of us is Mahnus?" Kittins asked gruffly.

"That is precisely what I am saying."

Vykers had always wondered why his memory was so unreliable. Now, it seemed obvious. He stepped forward, willing to accept his birthright, and Alheria snickered at him.

"Not you, you big idiot!"

If Vykers was embarrassed by his own presumption, he was

even more baffled. Who else could it be?

One by one, most of the group turned their attention to the Shaper, Spirk. It made perfect sense, and Long Pete actually chuckled with delight at the irony of it all.

Spirk, unused to the attention, flushed a bright red that made his port wine birthmark even more unattractive.

"Wrong again, you fools! Now perhaps you see why it was so difficult for me to identify Mahnus."

"But if it's neither of these men," Eoman interjected, "then who is it?"

Alheria extended a finger and slowly swept it past each of the giants, past Vykers and Kittins, past all of Vykers' men, past Spirk and Rem, until she finally stopped at Long Pete.

Suddenly, the captain felt hollow. There was nothing inside him but echoes, anxiety and fear. He wanted to deny the claim, to offer proof that Alheria was mistaken. But he was too stunned to form anything like a coherent thought. He looked over at his friends, whose expressions of shock and disbelief were surely the cousins of his own. He noted, apropos of nothing, that his toes were freezing.

"That don't change things between you and me!" Vykers prodded Alheria. "You've been pushin' me around and manipulating me for ages, and I wanna know why."

Again, Kittins found himself secretly cheering the Reaper.

"Talk to Mahnus," the Queen said dismissively. "All this fighting has worn me out." She disappeared on that last word, leaving everyone reeling in her wake.

Everyone except the Reaper, that is. "Mahnus, is it?" he said to Long. "Gotta say, I ain't impressed." Vykers then spoke with his men and the giants and determined the wisest immediate choice was to return to the group's forest encampment and get some rest.

Vykers & Company, In Camp

Back at camp, everyone avoided Long like the pox, even Spirk, and especially Mardine. At first, the captain was hurt, and then he became angry. He pushed his way into the circle of giants relaxing about their own fire and insisted on speaking with Mardine.

"Or what?" Beesmarch threatened.

"I'll speak with him," Mardine told the big giant gently. "I'll be okay."

Long led her out of the firelight and off near his tent. He took Mardine's hands and looked deeply into her eyes.

"I don't know why she said it," Long began, meaning Alheria, "but I don't see any evidence that it's true."

Mardine smiled sadly at him. "You don't? You don't see me?"

"What do you mean?" Long asked, but he knew: she'd been dead, and now she wasn't. Janks had been dead, and now he wasn't. The End—the original End—had shown an odd fascination for the captain. The End had also taken Long's voice, and yet he'd regained it. And Long and Mardine had managed to conceive a child, against all reason. Long and his crew had fallen hundreds of feet into the ground and no one had been killed. And who could say what other coincidences had been his doing?

Long hung his head, beaten.

"I don't think...I don't think it's safe to raise Esmine around you, sweet," Mardine said.

"But Em," Long protested, "you *know* me! I'd never hurt you two for the world!"

Tears drenched Mardine's face, but her jaw was set, and her eyes were clear. "Never on purpose, no. But I can't allow any more accidents, either."

Mahnus' mortal heart broke.

Things were quiet in camp that night—profoundly, soul-searchingly quiet. The group had fragmented back into its original components, more or less, with the men and giants around separate fires. Only Aoife seemed willing and able to cross between the two, and she still required assistance to move.

Vykers had almost made peace with everything that had happened that day when Hjuest brought him sad news: Igraine had hanged herself. They'd found her, half-seated, at the foot of a cedar, her belt wrapped around her neck on the lowest tree limb. Knowing he'd never be able to return to his own body, Turley had chosen to die. Vykers thought back to Arune's sacrifice and realized it had cost more than he initially imagined. Arune may have made her choice, but it was Vykers who'd killed Turley. This brought the Frog to mind—Tadpole. Even when violence wasn't his intent, the Reaper still managed to get people killed. And, when he thought about it, Arune, Igraine and Turley had all died twice, while he'd never died once. Maybe it would be best for everyone if Vykers went off somewhere alone. Maybe the world didn't really need a weapon that killed friends along with foes. After all, where was the victory in indiscriminate death?

Unexpectedly, Yendor approached him with a pot of liquor.

"Share a drink with an old man?" he asked.

Vykers drank.

Out in the snow, hidden by the Svarren witch's magic, Omeyo and his mate watched the death of the End with no little amount of satisfaction. The general had only ever suffered in the master's service, and while Omeyo had landed on a fate unwished for and unforeseen, he was neither dead, nor in service to anyone.

Upon the End's death, the rest of the Svarren—those who survived the cold—shook off their stupor and resumed their trek southward.

Omeyo and his witch would join them—not as followers, but as rulers. Finally, Omeyo felt, he was in charge of his own destiny.

EPILOGUE

The air was warmer when everyone awoke the following morning, and patches of blue sky peeped through the treetops as if to announce that winter had finally come to an end. This did little to buoy anyone's mood, however, in the aftermath of a conflict that most were still unable to comprehend.

The Queen was Alheria? The End had been her son? The other fellow was Mahnus? Madness! Even the evidence of one's own eyes seemed impossible to credit. Were it not for the Reaper's stoic acceptance of these revelations, the whole affair would have seemed a fever dream, the result of an illness none knew they had.

Folks gathered around the camp's various fires, but no one spoke, or, if they did, it was only briefly and in whispers. Reality itself felt fragile, and the whole company seemed to hold its collective breath for fear of shattering the world beyond repair or reclamation.

Only the Reaper seemed unaffected, but then, he was still drunk from Yendor's magic liquor. He attempted a conversation with Aoife, but she was still too weak to make sense of things, and Vykers found his thoughts drifting off towards Arune and Turley. Aoife was alive, and they were not. Vykers could neither celebrate nor mourn.

Around midday, both giants and men began assembling their gear. As everyone was packing to leave, a stranger appeared in camp. At least, he'd looked like a stranger when Vykers first saw him. He was so emaciated and badly scarred, he was almost unrecognizable. When he opened his mouth to speak, however, the Reaper knew him at once.

"Historian. How did you find me?"

"How else? Her Majesty told me where you could be found."

Vykers scowled. "She can't leave well enough alone, can't she?"

"Reaper," the Historian rasped, "War is coming."

"Coming? When has it ever stopped?"

The Historian fell over, and Kittins just caught him before he hit the ground. Still, the Ahklatian was conscious. "The Emperor whose men you defeated across the sea has come to eliminate you."

Vykers had several good quips in mind, but something in the Historian's demeanor dissuaded him from such things. "How many troops?"

"All of his legions. The largest army in the history of the world."

Coming from a historian, this was most dire news.

"Even now," the Historian wheezed, "there are tens of thousands of ships approaching our eastern shores."

"Any of 'em carrying those big steel monsters?"

"Many."

The Reaper discovered the eyes of everyone in camp upon him. "Who's up for a fight?" he grinned.

Appendix A

Cast of Characters

Tarmun Vykers, A.K.A, "the Reaper"—a legendary warrior
Arune—A spectral Burner, one-time friend of Vykers who has stolen his body
Captain Kittins, A.K.A. the "Dead 'Un"—An officer in Her Majesty's Army
General Omeyo—Eyatu's mortal general
Aoife—An A'Shea or "Mender"
Too-Mai-Ten-La, A.K.A. "Toomt'-La"—a satyr, born of Aoife
Long, A.K.A, Long Pete—a former captain in Her Majesty's Army
Mardine—His wife, a giantess
Esmine—their child
Nelby—Esmine's nanny, a former thrall
Innoman—a slaver
Eoman Harkin Hainen—King of the Giants
Karrakan—a giant shaman
Beesmarch—a giant
Zillia—a giantess
Tinalia a Svarra
Baris—her son
Gorivar—a half-Svarren mage
Yendor Plotz—A drunk and friend to Long
Spirk Nessno—A Shaper and friend to Long
Ron—an archer and friend to Long and Spirk
Remuel Wratch, A.K.A. "Rem,"—a famous actor
Her Majesty, Alheria, A.K. A. "the Virgin Queen"—Ruler of the

Central or Midlands Kingdoms, and Goddess of Earth, Nature and life

Cindor—Her First Shaper

D'Marei—An alchemist

Mahnus—God of Creation and War

Eyatu—the God of Winter

The Historian, A.K.A, "the Ahklatian"—An ancient sage and Shaper

Appendix B

A Guide to Character Name Pronunciation

Author's note:

If you've read this far, these are your characters as much as mine. You may imagine their names however you'd like. This list is really for the sticklers amongst us.

Tarmun Vykers = Tahr-muhn Vahy-kurz
Aoife = Ee-fuh
Arune = Uh-roon
Mardine = Mahr-deen
Omeyo = Oh-mey-oh
Mahnus = Mahn-us
Alheria = Uh-lair-ee-uh
Eoman = Ay-mun
Karrakan = Care-i-cun
Innoman = Inn-o-mun
Eyatu = Ay-ah-too
Ahklatian = Uh-kley-shuhn

ABOUT THE AUTHOR

Allan Batchelder is a professional actor, educator and former stand up comedian. He has written several plays and screenplays, dialogue for computer games, and online articles about theatre and/or education. *Steel, Blood & Fire* is his first novel, the opening act in a planned series. Allan lives in Washington State with his wife, son, and two cats. And his computer.

Dear Reader:

Thank you for reading *Steel, Blood & Fire*. If you enjoyed it, please consider writing a review on Amazon, Goodreads, or anywhere else books are reviewed. Vykers is one tough bastard, but he can't survive without your support!

For updates and news about sequels, go to:

www.immortaltreachery.com

https://www.facebook.com/SteelBloodFire

And on Twitter at: @TarmunVykers

Immortal Treachery is:

Steel, Blood & Fire

As Flies to Wanton Boys

Corpse Cold

The Abject God

And, coming in 2018, *The End of All Things*

And now, turn the page for a preview of *As Flies to Wanton Boys*…

Curious about other Crossroad Press books?
Stop by our site:
http://store.crossroadpress.com
We offer quality writing
in digital, audio, and print formats.